RED FLAGS

a novel

ALSO BY BRANDI L. BATES

POETRY

Lunar Eclipse: The Collection of Poetry Vol. I
Ruminations: The Collection of Poetry Vol. II
Mood Swings

FICTION

Amid the Cacophony of Cries
The Head Mistress
Quirk
SOLEDAD
Remains to Be Seen

RED FLAGS

a novel

Murder, Manipulation, Espionage...

Brandi L. Bates

Gallington Press

Los Angeles   Atlanta   New York   London

Copyright © 2014 by Brandi L. Bates
ISBN-13:
978-0-692-20242-5

ISBN-10:
069-2202420

Printed in the United States of America.
First Edition

For
Freda Nichole
at last...

ONE

A RAVENOUS STORM leapt from her chest and curdled the breath that crept from her lips. Deidre Priest had never been this afraid in her life. The night was sweltering hot.

Although the sun had melted behind the horizon four hours ago, the air felt hard-boiled. The sky seemed to glow lavender. Humidity and abysmal air quality made everything sticky. Her blouse stuck to her back and chest like second skin. She was in the throes of July. Her air conditioner went on the fritz at the worst possible time. Humidity strangled moisture from the air and sweated out her perm.

Some maniac had run her off the road. One minute she was driving home from Akil's house with the windows rolled down, enjoying the dark open-skies, clearing her head to the melodious sounds of Ledisi, and the next moment she was being railroaded off of I-20.

From the rearview mirror, the headlights blazed so bright that she had to squint to make her way over to the shoulder. She'd exited, driven past Popeye's Chicken and Taco Bell when those blinding headlights tailgated her to the point where she knew it was cause for concern.

She pressed the pedal to the metal. Sped through West End, careered through Pittsburg, and just as she crested the corner of McDaniel, headlights pounced onto her car.

As she drove, she thumbed around in her purse, which sat wide open on the passenger seat. Somehow her cellular had gotten away from her. She felt around, but found everything *except* for the damn phone. That was her fate when in search of something; it always seemed to play hide and seek with her. Like finding a million knives and forks when all she needed was a spoon.

Her first thought was of Akil. They'd had one hell of a knock-down-drag-out. There was so much acrimony between them when she slammed the door leaving his house that she had heartburn. She could still feel stomach acids racing up and down her throat like it was the Talladega Superspeedway.

But there was no way he could have caught up to her that fast, not unless his engine was on steroids. His house was in Lithonia. She noticed the blazing headlights somewhere near Panola Road. She'd stopped at the BP to top off and when she hopped back on I-20, those lights had trailed her ever since.

Now she was on a street where the lights were dim, but as late as it was, children were still outside. She could tell by the run down dilapidated old houses, children with skin the color of Cocoa Puffs, barefoot, slap-boxing in the street and the lack of curb appeal from dank storefronts that she was in the mouth of poverty.

If she pulled over to search for her phone, would this creep do anything rash? She slowed to stop at a light which heated from green to yellow to red. Suddenly, those headlights slammed into the back of her Mini Cooper. The impact was so sudden and intense that her seat belt lanced a gash into her chest.

Within mere seconds, a dark van with pictures of popsicles, fudge pops, and ice cream sandwiches plastered all over it pulled up next to her driver's side. Loud lyrics of "Small World" chimed softly into the dark balmy night. It was a cheery Disney ditty turned diabolical. Everything was happening so fast, but she knew that something was terribly wrong once those headlights intentionally rear-ended her car.

The driver who tailgated her bumper for the past umpteen miles hopped from his vehicle and was now standing directly in front of her window. A dark hooded figure.

The menacing ice cream van pulled up slightly, just enough to block her and prevent her from moving forward. She'd been stood up. Unable to drive forward, unable to back up, and unable to get out, she frantically struggled to find her cellular. It was useless. Futile. Fruitless.

A sharp metallic sound wrapped on her doorframe. She turned to see a hooded figure pointing the barrel of a .45 caliber pistol in her face.

TWO

EBONY COOPER HAD just left choir rehearsal at Mount Moriah Church International, a mega church in Baltimore. She'd promised her girlfriends Samantha Porter and Ethel Myers that she would meet up with them to listen to open mic spoken word poetry at Cantrell's Coffeehouse and Lounge.

She wheeled her orange Volkswagen Beetle out of the parking lot and headed due south on West Hamburg. Within minutes she noticed that she was being followed by a pair of bright headlights. First she sped up, raced past M&T Bank Stadium, where the Ravens played, surpassed the speed limit past Solo Gibbs Park, and hung a sharp left on South Hanover Street.

She grew concerned when the driver who was following too close for comfort failed to slow down. As she sped up, the driver with the bright headlights sped up. Initially, she faked as though she were pulling into a McDonald's parking lot.

She remembered seeing an exposé on television stating if you felt you were being followed, to never ever drive directly home, but to instead drive somewhere well-lit and populated.

She had the presence of mind to drive to the nearest police station. Nobody was crazy enough to do anything stupid in a police station parking lot.

The police department on East Fayette Street immediately came to mind. She cranked her gospel music up full blast and began saying silent prayers to herself, hoping that Kirk Franklin's hype would help to drown out the fear that had suddenly flooded her body.

"Dear Lord, protect me from dangers seen and unseen. Satan, get thee behind me, in the name of Jesus!" Ebony incanted and plead the blood of Christ out loud, as though Providence was in the passenger seat.

But still her heart pounded and beads of sweat puckered her temples. She squeezed her steering wheel and raced her Beetle as fast as she'd ever driven it. Just as she reached the police department, the headlights continued trailing her. She rolled her eyes.

Suddenly, the vehicle rammed into her back fender. "Now wait one damn minute!" she shouted. She had somehow mustered enough courage to face whoever it was that had followed her. Feeling safe enough to open her door and climb from her car, Ebony unlocked the door.

Two shots rang out.

THREE

DETECTIVE PATRICIA GARBUTT was in the great room of her family's two-story craftsman home in Sandy Springs. She had just brought out a huge platter of tacos and balanced several cans of Coca-Cola under an armpit.

Her husband Anthony Eugene Bowers stood up from his well worn beige La-Z-Boy and grabbed the sodas. She placed the platter down on a coffee table in the center of the room, just before Tyler, their eight year old son, reached out to horde the snacks to himself.

"Oh, we're not sharing tonight?" Patricia sneered before plopping down between Tyler and her thirteen year old daughter Maria.

"He's so stingy, I swear!" Maria rolled her eyes and sucked her teeth.

"Look who's talking, Miss-won't-let-anybody-get-in the bathroom. Shut up with your big Pokémon head!" Tyler retorted before snickering to himself.

"Hey, hey, hey hunker down! That's your sister. What have I told you about that?" Anthony chimed in.

Patricia said nothing. She sighed and began pulling her hair back into a ponytail. This was family night. She had cooked hudut, carne asada tamales, escabeche, relleno, chirmole, rice and beans with stewed chicken for dinner, traditional Belizean food. But that was much earlier.

Every Saturday night was family night. No matter how busy their lives were, they always managed to make time to spend with family. Consistency was difficult, but it was the magic glue that helped keep them together.

Either they stayed home and watched movies, cooked a huge traditional Belizean dinner, went to visit relatives, went bowling, played miniature golf, or simply took the kids out for pizza and video games at Dave and Busters, or went Go Kart racing at Andretti's.

For as long as Patricia could remember, she'd done things with and for her family. She came from a large family and was raised to always put God first, then family, and then career. She was born and raised in Belize City, Belize, the largest city in that Central American nation.

Shortly before her twentieth birthday, her mother moved her and her brothers and sisters to the south of North America after her father died of a massive heart attack. They stayed close to the Gulf coast because the weather was reminiscent of her native Mayan land.

Her family was a tight knit unit and remained close although they were spilled along the southeast. One brother lived in Alabama, another in Florida, a sister resided in Tennessee, and another in New Orleans. But her mother and another sister made Atlanta Georgia home.

Patricia stood up, walked into the kitchen, opened the fridge and grabbed a bottle of New Castle Ale. She cracked open the tall bottle and poured it into a glass, sliced a wedge of orange and peeled it into her beer.

It stressed her nerves when the kids argued and fought. She had grown impatient with them this night. They were on her last nerve. She had been standing over a hot stove all afternoon, cooking, and her feet were aching.

That old adage was true: a woman's work was never done. It had been a long week. As she was walking back into the family room, her phone rang.

"Garbutt speaking."

"Detective, we need you. Looks like we might have a homicide on our hands. The details are sketchy." It was Jake, her partner for the past three years.

"Talk to me," she took a long breath and exhaled. She took the call into the kitchen. As she wedged her cellular phone between her right shoulder, she silently began wrapping foil over several dishes, and piled food into storage containers.

"We have an abandoned yellow 2011 Mini Cooper in Mechanicsville. No body. No sign of foul play other than a dented backside. Looks like they were rear ended."

"Yeah, and…" Patricia put the food into the refrigerator.

"Well, the DMV has it registered to a Deidre Priest. Her family filed a missing person's report forty-eight hours ago. She has no priors. Record's so clean you could eat on it." Jake yawned.

"And?"

"Here's where shit gets real. There was an orange 2008 Volkswagen Beetle, also found abandoned, still running, same type of back fender damage, only this one was found in Baltimore, Maryland. The Beetle's registered to Ebony Cooper, thirty-six years old, immaculate record. Friends say she was last seen leaving church."

"The Lord giveth and the Lord taketh away, eh." Patricia said.

"If your humor weren't so dark, I'd actually laugh," Jake chuckled. "Both women are the same age. Both are African American. We think there might be something cooking. Brody wants us on this first thing in the morning."

"Tell me I'm sleep and this is a dream," Patricia took a long gulp of her beer.

"Yeah, REM dream state. The part just before you have a lingering orgasm," Jake said. "Meet you at seven at Krispy Kreme in West End," then he ended the call.

Looking down, Patricia felt Baba Ignacio winding around her legs. Baba Ignacio was the family's tuxedo cat. He purred and gave her his soft yellow-green eyes. She picked him up and headed into the family room.

"I'm turning in. Just got a call that requires me to be up and at 'em before the cocks crow. Good night, my love," she leaned over and kissed Tyler on his forehead. "Bonita," she kissed Maria on the top of her head.

Anthony looked over at her, "everything all right?"

Patricia walked over to her husband and held his face between her palms, leaned down and kissed him on his lips. "Yes, Jake just called. I have to meet him in the morning in West End. Possible homicide," she said under her breath.

This year was going to mark Detective Garbutt's twentieth year on the force. She was looking to possibly retire. Although she had managed to dodge danger, it never prevented her husband from worrying. She tried her best to shelter her kids from her career. She had a tendency to compartmentalize her life.

Anthony grabbed the cat from his wife's arms and stood up. "Well, I'm joining you. It's late. I'm tired."

Upstairs, Patricia and Anthony's bedroom had French doors that opened to a patio. Anthony pulled back the sky blue silk drapes and opened the doors—allowed the soft sweet Georgia draft to waft inside and douse the air with hyacinths and Dogwood blossoms. Birch pollen lightly dusted his face.

A platinum moon gazed down at gabled roofs and wooden balconies. Well manicured lawns shone celadon and the brick facades of neighboring edifices coughed crimson and ochre.

Patricia gingerly set her glass of beer down on the white marble fireplace mantle and walked across their distressed, stained brown, wide-plank wooden floor. It was warm against her bare feet.

Alone, the couple was silent. The sounds of a chirping Whippoorwill, cicadas, and tree frogs hiding in palm fronds reverberated against the escritoire. Barely-there seafoam green and powder blue painted walls and groaning bookshelves engulfed and encapsulated their love, like candy coating.

Patricia walked up behind her husband, wrapped her arms around his waist, and kissed him on the back of his neck. "I love you."

FOUR

EARLY THE NEXT morning, Detective Garbutt climbed from bed, showered, and sipped a cup of organic Bolivian dark roast coffee as she waited for her hair to air dry.

Her hair hung down her back: jet black, wet and wavy. The house was quiet. She sat at her kitchen table, reading the Sunday Atlanta Journal Constitution. Outside, the sun was growing over the eastern horizon, illuminating an aquamarine sky.

Baba Ignacio purred loud and softly as he circled her legs under the table. He was hungry. She opened a can of Friskies tuna delight, and spooned it into his bowl before filling his water basin with fresh clean water.

She gazed at her favorite coffee mug and smiled at the way steam streamed and snaked upwards, dissipating into ether.

She liked it this way, when the house was quiet and serene. Tranquility sloshing through the house like incense smoke.

Rays from the rising sun spilled warm golden amber light onto the walls and drapes — promising another beautiful sunny day.

Patricia was grateful for her life and family. She'd seen and experienced untold death and dysfunction while working on the force over the past twenty years. Her life was spent steeped in a dystopia filled with so much vulgar perversity that merely being home, enjoying a cup of black coffee was enough to put her mind in an amicable place.

It was the simple things in life, such as quiet mornings having coffee while her family slept peacefully upstairs, that made her appreciate all that she had worked hard for. She gathered and collected her thoughts. Stacked them neatly.

She fired up the griddle. Began cooking peach pancakes with homemade Chai syrup for the kids, honey-cured ham and eggs over easy for Anthony. She wanted to make sure that her family was well fed before she took off for the day.

She skipped breakfast, as usual. Patricia wasn't much of a breakfast person. In fact, she challenged the belief that it was the most important meal of the day.

Soon Patricia was well on her way to Krispy Kreme Dougnuts to meet with her partner Jake. She was getting too old for this shit. But the retirement pay that she was promised was just too good to pass up.

Detective Jake Billingsley was couched in a booth, stuffing glazed doughnuts into his mouth as he read from an iPad.

He snickered silently to himself. Several old black men were sitting around a table sharing two dozen mixed doughnuts as they talked about sports and what was going on in the news. They bickered and blabbed about President Barack Obama, Tiger Woods, and how expensive everything had become. Especially the highway robbery that was the rising cost of petroleum.

Patricia walked in and sat across from Jake. He looked up and smiled. "Good morning Sunshine!" he said, giving her stark glacial blue eyes. He exuded cool, like fog.

Patricia frowned. She gave a smug reply. "Cut the crap, Jake. You know I'm far from a morning person. Tell me again why this couldn't wait until a decent hour when the rest of civilization is awake."

Jake never told Patricia his age, but she was certain he was much younger than she was. He was assigned to be her partner three years ago, after her other partner Detective King was gunned down in a Fulton County courthouse murder.

Some nut job somehow got free from his handcuffs, pistol-whipped a Bailiff with her own gun, and went on a killing spree. He shot a judge, an attorney, three civilians, and Detective King.

That day was the most somber day Patricia had ever known. Of all the murders Garbutt witnessed, that one hit close to home and touched her in a tender place. Sitting at the funeral, she felt like she would come apart at the seams.

Detective King was survived by a wife and three kids. Three young babies. Every now and again she'd visit the King family because she felt she was obligated. She believed she owed it to him.

It made her realize how delicate life was, how one day you're here and the next day you could be checking out. Losing someone you love has an enigmatic way of demystifying death.

In spite of our deepest held beliefs, no matter who we are, we all come here with expiration dates. It made her embrace her mortality — made her see how powerless against death humanity was.

"Good morning to you too. Lovely day in the city," Jake mocked. "Can I get you anything? Glazed original? Bear claw? Jelly-filled?" Jake was a spry cross between Johnny Depp and Ashton Kutcher, with stark glacial blue eyes, Hungarian features and an addiction to women. But he was brilliant and good at what he did.

"I'll take a glazed original. So what's up?" Patricia kicked her feet up onto a nearby mint green chair.

Pulling a warm doughnut from a Krispy Kreme box Jake said, "So, Deidre Priest was reported missing as of forty-eight hours ago. She was last seen at work on Friday afternoon. We believe she may have spoken to a male friend on Saturday. I have her cell phone records." Jake said as he stood up.

"How did they find the vehicle?"

"The vehicle was found parked on McDaniel Street last night. Neighborhood kids claim they didn't see anything, but it was clearly cleaned out. I think they may have swept out the cds or whatever. So we dusted and found several prints. A uniform, Officer Ruiz, saw it parked and still running while doing a routine traffic run."

"A Mini Cooper with the keys left inside, ignition going, in West End and no one saw anything? No one hopped in to take it for a spin? What happens when we call her cell phone number?" Patricia asked.

"Nothing. Goes straight to voicemail. I'm assuming it's either turned off or got tossed somewhere."

"And the Beetle, why is this significant...or even relevant for that matter? Could it be any more out of our jurisdiction?"

"The Beetle owner has also been reported missing. She was supposedly on her way to meet with friends and never showed up. They grew concerned when she never called back even into the early morning next day. They claim that's not in her character." Jake paused to take a gulp of milk.

Patricia looked through the report. She scanned the important headlines and highlighted things based on what she found to be significant.

"What stands out to me is the fact that the Beetle was actually left in the parking lot at a precinct. The music was still playing, engine still running, back fender dented like hell, and in the parking lot of a precinct," Jake stuffed a whole glazed doughnut into his mouth.

"Wow! That's pretty bold or stupid, depending on the perp. Do we know if these two women know each other or not? Yes, no, maybe so?" Patricia said, still leafing through the report.

"I'm willing to bet no, but stranger things have been known to occur. No way to tell yet," came a gluttonous reply.

After leaving Krispy Kreme, Jake and Patricia hopped into her black Crown Vic and drove over to the scene on McDaniel Street where Deidre Priest had last been seen. They found two spent shell casings that seemed to have been neglected by the CSI the night before. "Let's get these to Ballistics immediately, see if we can find some trace prints on them," Patricia said with satisfaction.

It was early in the morning. People wandered around like blown trash. The street was littered with empty Church's Chicken drink cups and broken bottles. There was a soiled pissy twin sized mattress teetering over the curb. Gnats and horseflies buzzed around it. What looked like a full track of hair weave danced in the breeze and broken fragments of glass covered the asphalt. Poverty fumed in silence.

FIVE

A CURSORY PREVIEW of the scene only made it painfully obvious that there were too many prints, too many factors unrelated to the missing person, and from what Detective Garbutt could gather from the report, the evidence had clearly been tampered with.

The car had been impounded, but Jake wanted to see what everything looked like in the daylight. He'd come down to the scene to bag and tag, and he'd also snapped pictures.

The skid marks where the Mini Cooper had been parked indicated that the vehicle had been rear-ended on the scene. There were actually two sets of skid marks.

Aside from strewn garbage that was already on the scene long before the Mini Cooper ended up there, there weren't many other clues. No one came forward to snitch. No one wanted to comply with the law, with Caesar, or with *one time*.

Patricia wondered if the missing person fled the scene after the accident or if there was foul play. She leaned toward foul play, but why was the car left running? What was the point of leaving a perfectly good running vehicle parked at the scene? This led her to believe that the missing person either knew who had rear-ended her or perhaps something happened to her when she left the vehicle.

"What was the gas level like when the uniforms took the Mini Cooper into custody? Was it empty?" Patricia asked Jake.

"On the contrary. Actually it was full," Jake replied.

Jake and Patricia decided to give Deidre Priest's male friend a visit. Being in homicide, they had both seen cases where the victim had been slain at the hand of someone they'd known and trusted.

"I think it's time we talk to the male friend," Patricia gazed out towards the Atlanta skyline. On the drive over to Akil's house Jake talked about the new woman he was dating.

"She's cute, sexy, and she has this funny little thing that she does with her lips. I tell you it drives me insane," Jake yammered on. "But I'm going to be totally transparent with you. You promise me this stays in this car, between you and me?"

Patricia bit down on her lip and nodded slowly. "Well...she's only nineteen. That's the issue." Jake slouched down in his seat in embarrassment.

"Nineteen, Jake? Are you kidding me? You can't be serious? What do you see in her?"

"It's complicated. When I met her I had no idea she was so young. We shot the breeze, went to a Brave's game together and before I knew it I was falling for her," Jake said. "But I wondered why she didn't have any beer."

"So I repeat, what do you see in her? That's damn near statutory, you know?"

"Everything. She's a breath of fresh air. She makes me feel new. She makes me feel alive. And the best part is that she's positive and optimistic. Unlike the average gal who blabbers on and on about nothing, this girl just exudes spunk. She still has that zest for life. Still hopeful about conquering the world and accomplishing her dreams. Whatever it is, she's got it. I figure I'll just keep her at bay for now, until she's at least twenty-one and then I'll make my move."

"Is that right?" Patricia said. "In my country girls get married as young as fourteen. So I guess I understand where you're coming from. Age is but a state of mind, no?"

"Exactly! See, you get it." Jake tilted his head in earnest agreement.

"I totally understand where you're coming from, Jake. But the fact of the matter is she's under age. You should cut your losses. I'm sure you won't have any problem meeting a woman closer to your age, who is mature enough and adult enough to make you happy."

"You're right Garbutt. I want that. I think I'm ready to settle down and get a wife. It's stressful being a bachelor. Not to mention expensive. Every time we go out, I have to pay and though it's not a problem, I get tired of shoveling out cash every time I want steak and a blowjob," Jake said sardonically.

"Who do you think you're kidding?" Patricia said. "You're most certainly not kidding me. *You*? Married? That's sitcom funny. That'd be the day that hell freezes over!"

"Well, don't be so quick to judge. I don't know if I ever told you, but you know my son Noah?"

"Yeah," Patricia said. Noah was the apple of Jake's eye. He always talked about his son. "Well, about four years ago on a rainy St. Patty's night, after I'd had a shitload of Irish ale, I collided with this stupendous piece of ass. I mean you should have seen the rack on her. She was bleach-blonde, wore red boots, a cowboy shirt, like she'd probably snagged it from a thrift store, and she was bathed with tattoos. She was a walking pin-up girl."

"Jake, please spare me the locker room jock details."

"Okay, okay. So anyway I'd had a shitload of beer and I was shitfaced. I met who would later become Noah's mom. Against my better judgment we didn't use rubbers and I failed to pull out. Let's just say that night was the beginning of my biggest nightmare and my biggest blessing."

"Why do you say your biggest nightmare?" Patricia asked as she merged onto I-20, due east.

"Well don't get me wrong, I mean I totally love Noah. He's freaking great; such a bright kid, so fearless and innocent, but his mom…that's another story. Heidi is a complete idiot. I doubt she ever passed a math test in her life. Had she been just a smidge smarter, I might have gone and got hitched with her. But my conscience wouldn't allow me."

"I never knew that Noah was the result of a one night stand. Your little gift from the Stork, huh?" Patricia chuckled.

"Heidi was the most expensive piece of ass I've ever had...and I'm still paying for it," Jake groaned.

"Everything happens for a reason, Jake!" Patricia smiled. "Even broken condoms, or in your case, a lack of better judgment."

"You don't understand. I was supposed to be like Maverick from *Top Gun*. I survived the Marines, served in Desert Storm, got out, joined the force, and who would've ever thought that a Bama brunette from Kennesaw would be the one to cool my jets?" Jake sighed.

SIX

AKIL ALLAH, A converted member of the Nation of Islam, was a forty-four year old reformed pothead. He lived in the basement of his mother's two-story brick Tudor.

Before he would allow Detectives Garbutt and Billingsley entrance into the home, he requested that they brandish a search warrant. From the outside, the home was immaculate.

A heavy chimney and decorative half-timbering gave the house a medieval feel. Hedges were neatly trimmed. Bermuda grass was lush green and manicured to perfection.

Passion fruit pink, coral, and white azalea bushes, redbuds, and oak leaf hydrangeas swiveled in the breeze. Late morning sun shone down on the home like stars over Alabama. Akil stood behind the front door, a pyknic physique, wearing a white mesh skull cap.

Patricia was still thinking about the conversation in the car, how Jake described his son as his biggest boon and his biggest disappointment.

Jake wondered why Akil was behaving like a fugitive. If he wanted to act suspect, they'd graciously do him the honor. Jake, who never left home without his department-issued firearm, stood back four to five feet away from the front door.

He was protecting both himself and his partner, and showing Akil that he was giving him space—a gesture born of respect. Even in war, there were rules of engagement.

"Sir, we just want to ask you a few questions. No big deal. You're not under arrest. We just have some questions. That's all," Jake said.

"I don't trust pigs!" Akil spoke in a low dulcet tone. His voice was a soft, creamy, buttery baritone, like he could do late night disc jockey work and be paid handsomely.

"Is that what you think we are? Pigs?" Patricia said, stepping in front of Jake.

A small child emerged from the side of the house. He looked to be no older than three years old. He was clean and well dressed in the latest pair of Nike Air Jordan basketball sneakers, and a bright orange Polo shirt, with a Polo player and horse splayed nearly across his chest.

"Rahmeek, get back in the house right now!" Akil yelled.

"Your boy?" Patricia asked. The young boy disappeared back into the house, obediently.

"Yes, he's my boy."

"I have one myself. They come here like miniature men, with ready-made opinions and personalities. In spite of what you may believe, we pigs have compassion. I give you my word that I wouldn't do anything to disrespect you in front of your son," Patricia said. "I'm Detective Garbutt, and this here is Detective Billingsley." They flashed their badges.

Akil hesitated momentarily before unlocking the door. "Come in. I was in the middle of fixing breakfast for my family," Akil said.

The home was decorated with a woman's soft touch and Southern charm. Turkey bacon and eggs danced in the air amid pungent scents of frankincense, myrrh, and black love incense. Kanye West brought up the background. He rapped about how one man could have all that power.

"You have to remove your shoes! No shoes indoors. Our home is our sanctuary." Akil reminded them of something his mother drummed into his mind with drill sergeant dexterity and effectiveness.

Patricia began removing her shoes. Jake thought better.

"I'll just stand here if you don't mind," he said.

The curious little boy returned. Silently, he gave them eyes of wonder. He stood no taller than a few feet in height, but he was fearless, acquisitive, and full of inquiry. His wiry frame bowed over with brand names—he was tony and caparisoned well.

"Almost time to eat. Go wash your hands and sit down at the table with your brother," Akil said. Akil was short and round, with a long beard and thick, bushy eyebrows. He sat down on a burgundy sofa and offered Detective Garbutt a seat across from him.

Suddenly a loud thunderous breaking sound emanated from the kitchen. Jake reached for his gun. Patricia braced herself.

SEVEN

A TOASTED CINNAMON-skinned boy poked his head out from the kitchen. He looked to be around five years old. He wore a white mesh skull cap, like his father. His resemblance to his father was a statement on the power of genetics.

"Daddy, I made a mistake," the boy said ruefully.

"I'll take care of it in a minute. Get ready to eat, Solomon. Get your brother and you two sit down quietly until I say so, okay?" Akil said as he gathered things around the front room; sprucing up for his uninvited guests.

"Yes daddy."

"Adorable children," Patricia said.

"We want to ask you some questions about Deidre Priest," she continued. Jake stood quietly eyeing hallways and windows. His eyes were whirling dervishes.

"What would you like to know? Has something happened to her? I've been trying to call her all weekend!" he said. A look of concern and worry washed over him. His muscles tensed.

"That's what we wanted to know. That's why we're here. We were hoping you could help us out with that. What was your relationship to Ms. Priest?" Detective Garbutt said.

"She's my Queen. We're supposed to get engaged in October. Been saving up for a ring for her, but it's been tough with me not working and all. This economy relentless."

Detective Garbutt took out a small notepad and began jotting something down. This prompted Jake to pull his iPad out. He had been carrying it.

She always teased him about his dependence on modern technology, while she chose to remain old school. Said she remembered things better that way. *What's to be done when you can't charge that thing?* She'd once said.

"So you two have been dating for how long exactly?" Detective Garbutt inquired. "Do you two share these boys?"

"Uh...approximately six and a half years in February." Akil replied. He began to fidget as though he was growing nervous. "No, I had my sons with another woman before I met Deidre."

"Daddy, he won't sit still!" one of the young boys called out from the kitchen.

"Excuse me but how long will this take?" Akil said.

"Not much longer," Jake said. "We appreciate your patience and cooperation."

"I know what this is about," Akil said. "Did she put a restraining order on me?"

Detective Garbutt glanced at Jake. "No, not to my knowledge. Did she have cause? Were you two physical or did you attack her? Stalk her?"

"No! I would never do anything like that. I would never harm Dee. She's my Queen. It was never anything like that. Me? Stalk? I have too many other important things to do with my time.

28

Besides the prophet Muhammad and the merciful and beneficent Most High Allah commands us to protect and cover our women. The reason why I asked about a restraining order is because we had a falling out a few days ago."

Both Jake and Patricia perked up upon hearing this. They grew more fascinated. Akil could incriminate himself. What he said next could very well determine what happened to Deidre Priest.

EIGHT

"WHAT TYPE OF falling out?" Detective Garbutt asked.

"Dee's a successful woman. She's educated. Graduated from CAU. She works for Coca-Cola as a marketing Accounts Director. She's been growing impatient with me not working and all," Akil's words were smothered in soft melancholia with a dash of nostalgia. He looked down at the carpet as he spoke.

"Can you explain further?" Detective Garbutt shifted her weight and crossed her right leg over her left knee. She jotted something down.

"I didn't see anything wrong with the way things were," he shrugged as though his intellect had become disjointed from his heart. "Since we've been dating I've just been having a hard time, that's all. It wasn't always like this. She knows this. She knows I'm no bum. She knows I'm out here trying to find work. I'm a man. I tried to explain to her that it's not as easy out here for black men as it is for black women. We don't get the same opportunities handed to us," he paused, looked up at Jake, sighed, then at Patricia, back at Jake.

"I don't expect either of you to understand, but black men don't have it as easy as other people," Akil paused for a moment, as though he was reflecting on what he had said.

Jake and Patricia remained silent. They lent him

an empathetic ear as best they could. The moment grew awkward.

"Dee would argue that was just my perspective. When we first started seeing each other she seemed to understand. But over the past year it's been like she simply cannot get past it. Maybe she stopped trying to understand me," he shrugged once more. "It always comes back to me and my lack of funds, or my inability to do the things for her that she'd like for me to do."

"And how did this lead to her possibly wanting to take out a protective order against you?" Jake interrupted. He had been listening intently and inputting data into his iPad. He adjusted his belt and tucked his white button-down shirt into his pants.

"She was frustrated with me. Said she was sick and tired of messing around without a promise of marriage. It sounded to me like she was hinting at seeing other people and just needed a convenient excuse. I got upset and punched a hole in the wall and upturned a table; my personal property, mind you. She got flustered and walked out. After that she refused my calls and started ignoring me," Akil said.

The moment of truth arrived like Hurricane Katrina and all her fury. The temperature in the room elevated a few notches. The toasted-cinnamon skinned boy came tumbling into the room. He had spilled orange juice down the front of his pants. Pulp was painted on his shirt.

"Listen, can we do this some other time? You all are interrupting my family time. I only get my sons on the weekends and y'all are really cutting into my personal space," Akil said, suddenly overcome with agitation. He grinded his teeth and took a long deep breath. Chest rose and fell.

"We understand. When would be a better time for us to come back?" Patricia said, as though it mattered. They would come back any time they damn well pleased.

NINE

A WEEK LATER, Patricia Garbutt sat on the edge of her seat in the bleachers at Milton High School. Her elbows rested on her knees. She had practically chewed her nails down to the nub. She was at Maria's Lacrosse tournament, in a state of nervosity, rubbing her hands together to dispel anxiety.

The Lady Eagles were down and the clock was ticking; moments seemed to fly off the clock like dandelion thistles floating away in the breeze.

Although Maria was merely a freshman, she had been hand-picked by the coach to play on this coveted Alpharetta team before she'd ever enrolled in the school. Maria was a perfectionist, like mom. She drove herself to exhaustion, practicing every day.

When it came to sports, specifically Lacrosse, she handled her Crosse like it was a wand. She wielded it with the same fierce passion that Ludwig Van Beethoven handled piano keys.

As she sat there utterly engulfed in the excitement of the game, Patricia's mind shifted gears. Drifted to a place she once called home. But if it were true that home is where the heart is, then this place was still home. This happened often.

One minute she was enjoying the anguish or joy of her life, caught in the every day, and the next moment she was floating away on an invisible time machine or mythical magic carpet ride to her childhood. Sometimes she found it disconcerting to separate daydreams from reality. They often were so perfectly interwoven that it all flooded together at the same time like a goulash.

This also occurred at night as she slept. Her dreams were so vividly realistic that it disappointed her when morning arrived. Her eyelids would fly open like shades, red with upset.

Those dreams were never the same, though they always took her back home. Always played host to wide swaths of lowland rainforest, and rich jungles replete with exotic flora and fauna, feathered and furry.

Her grandmother Papoose almost always occupied her dreams, with her leathery red carpal tunneled hands and long black braided ponytail, which looked and flowed like the Nile River.

Papoose always showed a certain fondness towards young Patricia. She reckoned she was Papoose's favorite. Papoose would direct young Patricia to sit on the back porch, between her legs, while she braided her hair and told stories of heroic Creoles, the return of the Jaguar King, and tales of the Mayans.

She'd talk of ancient giants who had arrived on the coast from that legendary magnificent coral reef and mysterious Blue Hole. Papoose believed that the original people of Maya came from the center of the Earth, to heal Creole land and help drive out the foreign Mestizos and Spanish invaders.

She always described them the same — towering twelve foot tall giants with skin so black and dazzling that they appeared to be made of coal and sparkled like onyx.

She claimed that after the Spanish invaders came, they drove many of the giants back home to that mysterious Blue Hole and their descendents erected hidden temples deep in the interior rainforests. Those Mayans resided beneath the forest floor and were ancient healers.

Patricia had floated away on the clouds of her colorful childhood. She was sitting on Papoose's rickety back porch, attempting to capture Clouded Sulphur butterflies and Praying Mantises with her bare cupped hands.

She heard Papoose speaking about the assault of the Mopan tribe of the north on the Yucatec tribe, who had brothers in Mexico. This was a time before the germinal Europeans arrived, spreading disease and warfare and plundering the villagers.

As always Papoose sat in her worn wicker makeshift chair, weaving baskets, which she'd go on to sale at the Marketplace for a wonderful profit, even in those days when a dollar stretched more than taffy. Papoose was telling a story to all of the grandchildren; Patricia and all of her brothers and sisters, cousins, and a few of the villager's children.

Papoose told of a time when the Jaguar Kings were forced to take cover in the rainforest, when the sword-wielding conquistadors arrived in Belize, aiming solely to plunder Mayan gold with claims of spreading the Gospel. The Mayan tribes that she spoke of were Papoose's ancestors. They were decimated by everything from Syphilis to what she affectionately called broken spirits.

"Lamanai, where the Gods were once welcomed and where drink offerings and animal sacrifices were made had become a breeding ground for the white man's God. For Catholicism. They destroyed our heritage — calling it pagan."

A gentle breeze caressed the children's brown faces, kicking up sumptuous and fragrant scents from the lush mangroves, and passion flowers. "Soon the humble beginnings of Belize were erected with woodchips and empty rum bottles," Papoose bemoaned. Thick patois raining from her lips.

She had sown bittersweet love-hate for Belize in the hearts of her grandchildren. They too yearned for the return of the black giants, the Mayan healers, and the Jaguar Kings of yore. But they also loved things as they had grown to become.

Papoose said that her people had lost everything once the white man set foot on their land. What disease hadn't wiped them out, taxes and brutal mistreatment did. Soon the Africans arrived, shackled cargo on large ships. Papoose couldn't read or write, but she cared for her entire family, surviving on basket weaving and her ability to heal neighboring villagers. Before her husband fell ill, he'd fish and sale conch, snapper, and Lobsters at the Marketplace.

Because Creoles were not allowed to own land, Papoose and her husband spent the bulk of their lives subsisting on meager wages. By twenty-first century American standards they were steeped sixty leagues below the poverty level. But they knew something that most people don't—they knew happiness. True happiness.

Papoose claimed that upon seeing the African slaves, they were afraid and astonished because those shackled men, women, and children looked exactly like the giants from the coral reef. Many of them looked like the native Mayan ancestors, with more stark robust features, sharp cheek bones, and wider, flatter noses. Only they carried a perpetual scowl—for they had survived unimaginable atrocities.

All of the children shuddered with delight and amazement as they listened to Papoose, amid chirping cicadas, summer insects making mating calls, sea birds hovering above the turquoise Caribbean Sea, crickets making whoopee, and the scent of black orchids floating into their nostrils.

They nibbled on bananas, mango, and limes they'd picked themselves. The children of their village had deemed themselves *Los niños del árbol de caoba* (Children of the Mahogany Tree). Like their national flag proclaimed, they flourished in the shade.

The shrill sound of the referee's whistle brought Patricia back to reality. The game was over. Maria's Lady Eagles had lost. *I really have to book a trip home to Belize City,* she thought to herself.

TEN

WHEN THEY GOT home, Maria trampled upstairs to her Bieber-postered bedroom to sulk in solitude.

She was in a sour truculent mood and the ride back to their house was drenched in silence. Her frustration was understandable, being the perfectionist that she was. The school year would commence in late August, and the Lady Eagle's pre-season upset demonstrated how much work was yet to be done.

"Be willing to lose. Can't win them all," Patricia said to Maria on the ride home as she focused on the road with both hands glued to the steering wheel. Maria took it with as much enthusiasm as she would take a gulp of castor oil. "You're being too hard on yourself. You all have to find your rhythm as a team. That's why Coach Tim has you all practicing diligently."

But it was of no consequence. Maria gave her a frosty shoulder and taciturn stare. As Patricia set down her purse on the family dining room table and began leafing through the day's mail, she noticed Anthony lying on the sofa drinking Diet Coke, watching a golf tournament.

"I thought you just *had* to stay home and cut the lawn. Maybe I'm crazy but the lawn looks the same as it looked when I left." Patricia looked out of the window, scratched her head, and sighed.

"Yeah I was getting around to it but Tiger's playing. I'll get to it after I'm finished watching this," he waved her off.

"Tony, I can't do this by myself!" she said, tossing the bills back down onto the table. Breathy with frustration.

It was a gorgeous, sunny, southern day. Margarine colored Monarch butterflies fluttered whimsically, spreading nectar and pollen from one shrub to another. The sun looked down on everything with radiance as all life forms in nature bowed in salutation at its warmth. The sky was perfectly pale periwinkle, without a cloud to be found.

"The only reason you got out of going to watch Maria is because you said you had so much work to do in the yard today, Tony!" Patricia's enmity bubbled over.

"I know, I know. You nagging me won't get it done any faster, Patricia!" he snapped back.

Patricia's eyes widened to the size of two plasma screen televisions. Her eyes grew red and belligerent and the hairs on her arms and neck bristled like boar's hair. Times like this Anthony could be a real killjoy—like a human hang nail. Thankfully, over the years, Patricia had grown a thick exterior to weather her husband's abrasive personality and snide snappy comebacks.

In the beginning, remarks such as these would hurt her feelings. She came to realize, like most people, she avoided truth. She criticized what she needed to see and hear most.

Anthony was right. Nagging wouldn't get him off the sofa any sooner than he made up his mind to do. Patricia paused momentarily, pulled up the strapless tube top she was wearing beneath her denim jacket, and began to saunter up the stairs.

Soon, she was stomping up each step as though she could take out her anger on the Berber carpet beneath her feet. She didn't want to argue. Arguing with Anthony was pointless. He didn't listen to her once he was angry, and she couldn't stand trying to reason with him.

She closed her eyes and bit down on her bottom lip. Imagined Anthony and the way he looked at her just before the bitch-ass remark he'd made. His face was livid with anger.

She slammed the door behind her. All she wanted him to do was mow the goddamned lawn, *was that too much to ask*? She wasn't stupid.

She knew her husband just wanted to stay home so he could watch porn and masturbate. Their son was at a neighbor's sleepover for the weekend, and with the house empty, she knew that's what prevented him from mowing the lawn.

He acted like she was trying to get a law passed through Congress the way he dragged his feet. Life could be so much simpler, but Anthony made everything more complicated. So fucking complicated.

Her mind went back to a time when she begged him to go to marriage counseling. This was about six or seven years ago, when the kids were much younger.

The pressures of having young children and a stubborn husband hindered Patricia's ability to move up in rank on the force. Every argument, every sarcastic comment was a heavy blow to her character.

Her hopes of making Lieutenant went down the drain that year. It was funny how much of an impact life at home had on her career. She was always angry—always in a funk or down in the dumps. Anthony reluctantly agreed to join her in marriage counseling. Reluctantly.

The past year had been rife with ups and downs. Someone once told her that you fall in and out of love in marriage, but sometimes she felt like Anthony was pushing her past the threshold of what she could and couldn't accept.

He was there physically, but emotionally he was absent. She was beginning to see a side of her husband that she disliked. They invested far too much into each other, their children, and their home, to consider divorce.

Separation wasn't a valid option because she couldn't pull the weight of things without him. Besides, he was Catholic and wouldn't hear of the thought.

She prayed for a ray of sunshine to illuminate the dark cloud that hung over their twenty year marriage. She couldn't imagine life without him. She knew he couldn't imagine life without his children and the children couldn't imagine life without the both of them. So she lived in a perpetual state of suspended unhappiness.

41

Being on the force and working homicide made her rough on the edges. In part, it desensitized her to things that average people had an aversion towards. She began undressing, as she walked into the restroom to turn on the shower.

She felt like things between she and Anthony were getting worse by the week and her life was becoming a rut. You know what they say about ruts? Soon they turn into graves.

After showering, Patricia was greeted by her husband. He was sitting on the bed holding a purring Baba Ignacio. He rubbed the cat's tummy slowly and looked up at his wife.

"You startled me, honey. I take it Tiger's finished swinging his golf club around? Is everything okay?" she asked, rolling her eyes and pursing her lips. She dabbed her face with a plush Egyptian cotton lavender towel and then proceeded to wrap it around her wet hair. She stood before her husband, fresh from the shower and dripping wet. She smelled like mint and vanilla. Like Easter Sunday.

"I was wondering the same thing myself," he said as he chewed the inside of his cheek. His wife was standing naked before him and all he could do was sit there rubbing the cat's belly as he chewed on the inside of his cheek.

Patricia placed her hands on her hips and sighed. She stretched slightly and then applied pressure to her shoulders, crossed her arms across her chest. She wondered when they'd have this conversation. It was long overdue.

"Just say what you mean," Patricia said.

"I think we should consider downsizing. You know, maybe looking for a smaller house or see what our options are. Perhaps put Tyler into a school where the tuition is a little cheaper. Money has really been tight lately," Anthony said, rubbing the bridge of his nose with his thumb and index finger.

"Why would money be tight, Tony? Are you doing something that I should be concerned about? Is there anything I should know?" Patricia replied and cocked her head to the side. She walked back into the bathroom and grabbed another towel. "You know I'd rather you be totally honest and truthful with me than to spare my feelings with a lie. You know me," she gave him that lingering pursed lip, tight-eyed smirk.

"Yeah I know, I know," he said, before taking a long exasperated sigh.

In those quiet moments, beneath a dusky sky, Patricia felt a lumpy disgust curdle in her throat. This disgust towards her husband was newfound, foreign. But somehow it was becoming increasingly familiar.

"What are you saying, Tony?" Patricia said, speaking with her hands. This time there was more bass in her voice. Her patience was growing thin and she was in no mood to go back and forth.

"I think I'm being perfectly clear here, Patricia. We need to reconsider some things. You know, since we used all the money from our home equity line and the interest rate on the mortgage is changing," he stopped rubbing the cat, covered his face with his two hands, and then let out another weary sigh. "I just feel like financially we're on borrowed time. And things down at the firm are really beginning to stress me."

She knew that he hated his job, but who didn't? Lately this was something that he spoke of increasingly. Anthony worked at an architectural firm. Over the past few months they'd faced budget cuts and had a few layoffs. This left a heavy load for the people who stayed on board.

Anthony was having long bouts of insomnia, sleepless nights where he tossed around the idea of leaving his family, or picking up that bottle, or pills. He even lost a few pounds due to stress and loss of appetite.

The layoffs and corporate restructuring at the firm aged Anthony at least ten years. His beard was sprinkled with flecks of gray. Shades of white began to take up residence on his temples and the front of a receding hairline. His shoulders began drooping, publishing his incumbent defeat.

Patricia had to act as though she didn't notice the tell-tell signs that stress was getting the best of her husband. "Borrowed time? Borrowed from whom? I don't understand. I'm not following you, Tony."

"Are you listening to anything I'm saying?" Anthony grew enraged. He stood to his feet. Baba Ignacio purred, hopped down onto the floor, and scurried out of the room, as though he understood this was his cue to leave the room.

Was their marriage perfect? No, but it was better than most. They loved each other. They'd withstood trying careers, two children, family, and the tests of time. They had the fortitude to get through this too. But they *both* had to want to get through it.

Something in Anthony's eyes said that he didn't have enough fight in him. He was leaking fortitude. "I'm sitting here telling you what the situation is. You act like you have no earthly clue what I'm saying; like I'm speaking Aramaic or something. Just...just forget I ever said shit!" he said before huffing out of the bedroom, slamming the door behind him.

"Tony! Tony!" Patricia shouted. Her voice hammered the air. She sounded like her mother, just like her mother.

She ran after him, stopping at the foot of the staircase. She heard her husband slam the door leading out to the garage. She let out a loaded sigh as she gripped the banister.

Part of her was glad he ran, and the other part of her wanted to get to the bottom of things—to flesh out their issues; to sort them out one-by-one.

Maria opened her bedroom door, saw her mother standing in the middle of the hallway bare naked, rolled her eyes, and shut the door immediately. Her attitude lingered in the hallway.

ELEVEN

LATER THAT NIGHT, she got a call from Brody. Brody was her overbearing slightly schizophrenic control freak boss.

There had been a murder. It was 2 A.M. and there had been a hit and run in Union City. Patricia hopped inside her Crown Vic, and was on I-285 heading to the Southside.

When she arrived at the scene, she saw Jake talking to a Union City uniform and GBI. The night was balmy as she approached the yellow taped off area where the body was laying in the middle of Jonesboro Road. There wasn't a star in the sky. Blackness cloaked the night.

The hit and run happened within the past hour and it was a grisly sight. Blood was everywhere, including a dark ink-like trail where the body had been dragged for at least one hundred feet.

It looked like a trail of tar under the moonlight. The body lay in state, in a mangled pile.

A black man with a thin wiry frame. Beneath the moon's eerie iridescent glow, his torn skin looked sinuous, like the leathery skin of a bat's wing.

Whatever happened to him left his ribcage cracked open, and his femur bone protruded through his leg, straight up, like a stake. Pieces of his skin and flesh puckered the trail of blood.

He was contorted like a gymnast—his head turned in a 180 degree angle. One of his shoes was across the street. If you didn't know any better, you would think he was road kill, a deer caught in the wrong place at the wrong time.

GBI blocked off the area. There were several neighborhood onlookers trying to sneak a peek of the crime scene.

Once Jake saw her, he interrupted his conversation and began walking over to her. Although this was a gory hit and run accident, Patricia had seen worse. Over the years she had grown desensitized to this type of murder scene.

If you saw one dead body, you'd seen them all. The only homicides that gave her pause were the ones involving small children.

"You good?" Patricia asked Jake, nonchalantly.

He bit down on his bottom lip and nodded his head. "Local uniform says they *think* it's a hit and run, but looking at this neighborhood, I can't imagine anyone taking a stroll around here. The couple in the car over there admits to running over the body, but they claim that the body was already there. They happened to stumble upon it on their way home from the Waffle House. The girl is pretty shaken up." Jake pointed across the street at a banged-up Toyota Tercel. The front bumper was sitting on the opposite side of the street. A human speed bump would give most anyone pause.

Patricia agreed with Jake. It was a non-descript neighborhood, saturated with newly built subdivisions, a couple of small country churches, and a few rickety old houses struggling to not be torn down amid the scourge of suburban sprawl.

This was an ancient town that developers came in and attempted to revitalize. Suburban sprawl in reverse. History lived here. There was an archaic set of train tracks that still played host to industrial trains every now and then and a handful of rocking chair wrap-around front porches. Old white men in bib overalls stared out of their windows.

A white Channel 2 van was parked catty-corner from where the body lay. Patricia jotted down a few notes on her notepad and stuffed it back into her back pocket. "The victim, did he have any identification on him?" she asked Jake.

"I just got here, probably five minutes before you. But from what GBI says, this guy was somehow just laying in the middle of the road when that couple ran over him," Jake said, cracking his knuckles.

She looked around, and judging from the predominance of hick town rednecks, there would be no real investigation into the details of this case. This was just another dead black man. They could not care less.

"Put out an all-points bulletin. If we don't have any I.D. then we'll just have to wait for the autopsy results. For now we'll report it as vehicular homicide. We don't know what vehicle we're looking for or what, but someone has to be taken into custody for this," Patricia said.

Just then Patricia received an urgent emergency text message from her younger sister Lisa. It said to call her ASAP, 9-11. *Fuck me!* Patricia thought.

She looked up into the black night sky and sighed. She was the rock for her family living in Atlanta. Every time they needed something done it was her that they called. She was growing tired of running to her family's rescue.

It was overwhelming—almost as if she had to constantly juggle two families and keep her sanity. She could barely conduct her life without having to run to their rescue and help clean up their messes. It had been this way all her life. When it was their turn to help her, they all seemed to stand by and watch her as she sank.

She walked back over to her car, opened the door, and gave Lisa a call. Jake walked back over to the lifeless body, and then he walked over to a few uniformed police officers as GBI stood talking. Lisa answered on the first ring. She sounded out of breath, as if she just completed a marathon.

TWELVE

LISA WAS THE youngest of Patricia's siblings. She was raised different from any of the rest of the children, largely because her childhood took place completely in the states.

Lisa's upbringing was the most liberal and because their mother was getting up in age she didn't spend as much time with Lisa as she did with Patricia or any of the older children.

Patricia heard rumors that her baby sister indulged in alternative lifestyles, but in her line of work everyone was innocent until proven guilty. Or at least that was the idea.

Mamí mentioned that Lisa was binging again. Patricia believed her sister was clinically anorexic and bulimic, but Belizeans didn't believe in such things so Lisa was never properly diagnosed.

"Lisa, where are you? What's going on? Do you realize what time it is?"

"I know, but can you please come pick me up…I came to this party with…a friend, but," she trailed off.

She stumbled over her words as though holding something back; something she didn't want her older sister to know about.

"What do you mean pick you up, Lisa? Why don't you call mamí? I'm busy working. Where are you?" Patricia grew frustrated. She didn't have the time or the inclination for any bullshit.

"Patty I really need you to do me this favor. Okay, I got jumped by a bunch of girls up here, and my friend left me stranded," she said before breaking into tears.

That gesture tugged at Patricia's heartstrings. If there was one thing she would always do was go to bat for her baby sister. She stood in front of her car, motioned for Jake. She told him she had to attend to family business, mentioned that it involved her sister.

"No problem Garbutt. I'll take care of things here. Not much more left to do anyhow. We put out an A.P.B. and we'll wait and see what the autopsy results reveal," he winked.

Lisa mentioned she was somewhere in East Atlanta. The area was a rough and tumble part of town. Sure enough when Patricia rounded the corner, she saw a few winos and homeless men and women loitering around like walking gnats.

When she saw the building where Lisa said she'd be, no one was standing there. Patricia whipped her cell phone from its holder on her waist, just to make sure she wasn't mistaking. Sure enough, Lisa said that she would meet her sister in front of Bank of America, across the street from Wendy's. It was just a stone's throw away from the freeway exit on Moreland.

Patricia leaned back in her seat and let out a heavy sigh. A cloying sound rumbled in her stomach. Something in her gut told her that something wasn't quite right. She had a strong psychic ability to sense when things were going wrong. She always felt it dead center in her gut first. If that didn't give her a kick in the pants then she would grow increasingly nauseous.

They say you're not supposed to have favorites among children, but her son was her obvious favorite. Everyone knew it. When something was wrong with her youngest child, she knew it. She sensed it. She felt it. She felt it in her bone marrow.

Patricia Garbutt and her husband sent their son to the Paideia School. He was fluent in three languages: English, Spanish, and French and already he had won several National Spelling Bee Tournaments. He was Patricia's absolute pride and joy.

So when Patricia got the text message from her husband saying that there had been an accident, she felt a bowling ball form in the pit of her stomach. First he called her, and then he sent her an urgent text message because she couldn't pick up the call due to the fact that she was pre-occupied trying to save her baby sister Lisa. *Jesus Christ, was there a full moon looming above the Earth tonight?*

As she text messaged her husband back, she suddenly heard a loud thud on the passenger side window. It sounded like a horse's kick, like horse shoe covered hoof against glass. There was pain in this sound. It was Lisa, wearing a frightful scowl.

THIRTEEN

SUDDENLY THE SKY grew darker, menacing. "Open the door, Patty! Please hurry, open the door!" Lisa shrieked. Terror was emblazoned across her brow now as she rattled the door handle, nearly pulling it off the door of the Crown Vic.

Although the night was warm, a chill stirred the air in that moment. Like Goosebumps along the skin of the night air. Patricia dropped her phone onto the floor and instinct took over. She unlocked the passenger side door and simultaneously reached for her Beretta 2mm, which she kept locked, loaded, and beneath her seat.

She asked her sister, "What in the hell is going on?" Lisa scrambled into the car and quickly shut the door behind her.

She wore so much makeup that Patricia barely recognized her. Her usual bronzed skin looked shiny and pink with a frosty glaze of glitter coating its surface. She'd poured the perfume on thick, something cheap, sweet and targeted towards pop icon fans. Smeared mascara and eyeliner gave her raccoon eyes.

"Just drive...drive away Patty!" Lisa said, visibly bruised, beaten and bleeding. An angry, belligerent, swelling bump protruded from above her right eye.

Patricia was about to open her door to see what all the confusion was about but after looking into her rearview mirror, she saw a mob of six or seven girls carrying sticks, bricks, and bats. All were black and butch looking. All teenagers. Products of a warmongering generation. A generation born and raised on gratuitous violence, MTV, and a procession of war-time presidents.

She hopped back into her car. It would be a lot easier to do that than to try to fetch her badge and yell *freeze, I'm a cop*! Those girls were in no condition to reason or think clearly. No mob ever was.

They were out for Lisa's blood and the best thing for Patricia to have done was to get her out of there as fast as possible.

However, there was no way in hell she was going to allow those hooligans to bully her sister. She pulled her gun on them. It was like the running of the bulls had feasted their eyes on a slaughterhouse.

Half of them stopped right there in their tracks, while a few of them turned tail and ran in the opposite direction. It was amazing how much power you wielded when you had a cold piece of steel in your hands. The sight of that firearm stopped the mob in its tracks.

She had no intentions on pulling her gun out on any innocent young civilians that night, but they were monsters in girl's bodies. The night was heating up, and the smell of oily exhaust coupled with mounting fears made Patricia more and more nauseous.

Patricia climbed back into her Crown Vic, searching for the right words. She struggled to catch her breath. Her chest rose and fell with sonorous thunder and lightning, acting the part of her heartbeat.

She looked over at Lisa. Her sister was craning over, trying to see which direction her attackers had fled.

"I'm not going anywhere until you tell me what in the hell is going on!" Patricia demanded, bringing two closed fists down on the steering wheel. She had to keep herself from strangling her sister.

Lisa turned the water works up full tilt. "Thank you Patty. I swear I'll pay you back. You have no idea how much I appreciate you," she snorted.

Patricia bit down on her bottom lip. "I'm listening..." she could feel her leg begin to shake. She couldn't tell if it was her nerves or anxiety, anger, or all three.

"Well...well—" she trailed off.

"Lisa, Goddammit spare me the bullshit, okay. I am not mamí! Tell me the truth. You called me. I was extremely busy. You have pulled me away from serious police business to come get you. There is something wrong with Tyler and I have to attend to him. You're bleeding, and wait until mamí sees this bump on your head. I want answers and I want them now," Patricia said, reaching over her sister's knees to open the glove compartment.

There was a stack of napkins from various fast food restaurants inside. She handed her a napkin with the Starbucks logo on it. Lisa took it, bowed her head before blowing her nose. She pulled down the mirror and saw the horror inscribed all over her face. Her busted lip and swollen head.

As Patricia lent her key to the ignition, Lisa began to confess. "Well, okay...I haven't told anyone this, not even J.R., but I date girls," she said.

"What!" Patricia shouted. This was the last thing she expected to hear spill from her sister's lips. She was a beautiful girl, too beautiful to say such an outlandish thing.

"I didn't want anyone in the family to know, not yet at least. Not until I was sure that I was going to bring the right girl around to meet the family."

Patricia sat frozen in shock. She couldn't move her lips and sound left her body. Even if sound were there, she wouldn't be able to gather the words to say. Lisa looked like the scared little girl that she was...rancid thoughts cluttered her mind. She reached over and grabbed her sister's hand.

"Please promise me you won't tell mamí about this, okay?"

"I promise I won't say anything, but what exactly does that have to do with this melee of a bee's hive you've pulled me into?"

"Well, I copped a ride here with my friend Miranda to meet up with this girl who I met on Craigslist..."

"Her name?" Patricia asked.

"Huh?"

"What's the girl's name that you met on Craigslist? And why in the hell are you cruising the internet to meet people, Lisa? You're so much better than that!" she said.

"I know. You're right Patty. The girl's name is Kiara."

"Okay, so you came here with Miranda to meet up with this…this Kiara character and?"

"Apparently she failed to tell me that her girlfriend or ex-girlfriend would also be at the club. Everything was cool and shit—"

"Watch your mouth!" Patricia interjected.

"Oh, oops! Sorry," she frowned. "Well, like I said…everything was cool and shit until her girlfriend saw us minding our business, enjoying our Malibu rum and pineapples. That hussy was stalking Kiara. She got her minions to attack me. And would you believe that bitch…I mean that hussy, Kiara, just took off and left me. I guess Miranda left me hanging too." Lisa snorted, blew her nose, folded her napkin and dabbed at her eyes.

After a brief moment Patricia released the parking brake and steered the Crown Vic in the direction of home.

She had to get to her son and her family. As she drove back to her house with Lisa in tow, she continued to probe for answers. She wanted Lisa to trust her enough to divulge secrets that she wouldn't otherwise divulge to mamí.

She could see her sister's life unraveling one strand at a time. It was like that first stray strand you see on a sweater. You know if you pull on it you'll only aggravate the integrity of the fabric and destroy the entire garment. Lisa was lost.

She was in desperate need of guidance and direction. Patricia didn't have the type of time and energy to invest into helping her. She was going to have to do this on her own: good, bad, or ugly. Sometimes that's just the way life goes.

As they entered her neighborhood a sudden feeling of dread washed over Patricia like a fine mist. From the moment she rocketed the Crown Vic into the subdivision, she felt a dreadful and ominous energy rain down upon her.

A powerful rush came over her. Something otherworldly. She glanced over at her baby sister. She held her glance for a lingering moment. The light from Sirius, or maybe it was Venus, bounced off her raven hair, giving it a sleek wet shine.

FOURTEEN

THERE WERE AT least three black and whites, along with a fire truck, and a few ambulance vans parked on her street. They surrounded the driveway to the house like a fence of law enforcement. There was no police tape. Patricia released a sigh.

Flickering blue lights beaming from the department cars struck her first—their indigo incandescent glow pierced her like a metaphysical revelation. Each vehicle was strategically wrapped around her home.

She didn't get a chance to park the car. She literally stopped in the middle of the street, reached for her hand bag, and hopped out of the car. She sprinted to her house, trampling the neighbor's manicured lawns and all. She trudged on Mary Margaret Oliver's pansies.

Her heart pounded. She couldn't think clearly. Thoughts raced around in her mind like the autobahn, forming a huge black Rorschach blot. She imagined the worse. In the dark, she ran across rocky ground. Portable radios and talkies chirped, buzzed, and squealed into the inky night.

Anthony saw her before she saw him. He dashed out from behind the ambulance van. "Oh, thank God you're here," his voice faltered in desperation. Fear was in his eyes.

"Where is Tyler?" Patricia screamed frantically.

"I need you to calm down, he's in the van. He's been shot."

"Omigod! Are you serious, Anthony? Fuck," she shouted. Her lungs felt like they would combust. Her throat tightened. "Where was he shot? When? With what gun?"

"While he was over Brendan's house, they got a hold of his father's Kimber .45 and Tyler accidently shot himself in the leg. He's going to be okay, but he lost a lot of blood. They have to get him to the hospital right away. I'm going to tailgate them. You can ride with me."

Patricia tried to respond but she couldn't stop shaking. She walked over and saw her baby covered in blood. He looked as though he wore clothes made of red velvet cake. She swallowed and her throat felt like sandpaper.

Patricia's eyes immediately went to the gaping hole in his leg. Blood was caked around the wound, clotting in the place where the bullet entered his flesh.

She touched his foot, but they told her that she couldn't climb inside the ambulance truck. They were getting ready to rush him to the ER. The medics started him on an I.V. drip and were administering oxygen.

Although they applied a bandage to the gunshot wound, she could see that her baby boy was in agony and shock. She imagined the bullet ricocheting through his little leg, doing its dastardly damage.

"Can you guys give him something for the pain? I am his mother, Detective Pat Garbutt...homicide," she said, brandishing her badge. "Is there a low dose morphine drip or something you can give him? Codeine perhaps?"

One of the medics nodded and said they would give him something for the pain. Tyler looked down at his mother. She could see agitation, terror and fear in his eyes. The uncertainty. She felt the ground quiver beneath her feet and the sky began to spin, kaleidoscope-like.

Tyler needed her, his mother, to be level-headed and calm. She was no good if she couldn't keep her composure. But this was heavy. This was freight ship heavy.

"Oh baby, mom is here. I'm not going to leave your side. Can you hear me sweetie? Tyler, I love you baby. Mom loves you. You are going to be just fine," she said, forcing herself to keep a stiff upper lip.

Tyler said nothing. A single tear trickled down the side of his face, but no words. He blinked his eyes a few times. Those swollen, red, puffy, raspberry lined windows. Blood was everywhere.

Lisa emerged from the car and looked on in shock. Maria was holding on to Anthony's arm as though she felt safe being in his warmth. She too was crying.

All three of them were huddled on the porch, beneath the orange-yellow gas lamp porch light. Several of their neighbors came outside to see what the commotion was about, the sirens, the flickering blue lights, and rotating red bulb atop the Fire engine.

From a few feet away, she could see pain in Anthony's eyes. He was trying his best to remain strong, but fear was let from his pores. He was an older frightened version of Tyler, standing there in a white polo shirt with the collar popped up like a preppy kid from the eighties.

Patricia sniffed and tried to stop her nose from running. She then wiped away a few errant tears. How could something like this happen? Her emotions were sparring with her intellect. She could not make sense of any of this.

She'd never felt so irresponsible or helpless in her life. She'd never felt so defenseless. She was in an unknown place. They all crowded into Anthony's filthy Navigator and followed the ambulance to Northside Hospital. They hadn't all been in his Navigator together since two Father's Day dinners ago, when the family treated him to Fogo De Chão.

She was ashamed that her husband's SUV looked like *Hoarders*…the automobile episode. She kicked manila folders full of files to the side. The girls had to push away compact discs, empty drink cups, books, and a few blueprints. The car smelled like Pierre Cardin, sweat, aftershave, and stale coffee. Patricia looked down to see an old cup of coffee from Dunkin Doughnuts. Only God knows how long *that* had been sitting there.

Her legs were shaking. Her hands were shaking. Patricia was kicking herself for allowing this to happen.

"Are you sure you're going to be okay?" Maria asked Lisa, breaking the silence which permeated Anthony's junky SUV.

Anthony looked at Lisa through the rearview mirror and squinted before placing his focus back on the road. Lisa remained silent and gazed out of the window nervously. The skies rattled as a few thunderclouds moved in from the south.

A few raindrops plopped down on the windshield as bolts of lightning flashed across the sky and down beneath the earth. Suddenly a deluge poured down—gave off sleek white dancing apparitions in the streets where oncoming cars and traffic lights flickered and flashed.

She wondered if anyone had taken a statement from Tyler's friend, Brendan. A part of her placed the blame on Anthony. She had to point blame at someone, anyone.

She chewed her bottom lip to prevent herself from starting an argument. Anthony turned on the disc player. The melodic tunes of Roy Ayers sauntered through the speakers.

She sank down in her seat and placed her palms to her eyes. She couldn't take it any longer. She felt like she was going to explode. The tears damming up behind her eyelids made her eyes burn. God knows she'd had it with being strong. This was her freaking son for crying out loud. She came face to face with her breaking point.

The weight of the world was on her shoulders. She needed to shrug. Needed to cuss. Wanted to fight, to break something. "Goddammit Tony, how could you let this happen?" she screamed before punching the dashboard.

FIFTEEN

ANTHONY HAULED OFF and backhanded her across the face. The impact shocked her more than the pain. She was stunned.

There was a sudden influx of stars. Radiant sparkly gnats shimmied across her field of vision. He had never laid a finger on her, not in over twenty years of them being together. Not even an accidental toe-scrape, as men tend to do, while getting cozy between the sheets. Several strands of hair were in her mouth. She looked at him as though he had lost his goddamned mind.

"I am getting so sick and tired of you and your shit, Patricia!" he yelled. Shortly after he said that, he swerved the car, nearly commandeering his SUV into oncoming traffic. The girls were silent like growing grass. Afraid for their lives. Afraid for Patricia's wellbeing. Trauma made men behave out of character.

"You must have lost your fucking mind, Tony! I know you didn't just hit me...in front of my daughter and sister," Patricia said as she rubbed the stinging spot on her face where his handprint lingered.

"No I haven't lost my mind. I need you to calm down. I am sick and tired of you and your shit. Earlier today you gave me lip. When I tried to be respectful and speak to you like an adult, you came at me like I was some sort of retard...and I'm tired of it. No wife of mine is going to disrespect me. You need to learn where the goddamn line of demarcation is between home and career."

"Excuse the fuck out of me, but don't you think this is taking things just a little bit too far?" she shouted. They were both trying to talk over each other.

A plum red sanguine shade of anger overshadowed them both. Patricia had to mentally remind herself that this was her husband. He was not a murder suspect. He was not the enemy. It took everything within her from kicking him in his salt and pepper stubbled chin.

"I'm just saying a man's home should be his sanctuary, not a battleground. And I've never hit you before because you've never been so out of control." There was more bass in his voice now.

Why did people feel they needed to raise their voice to get their point across?

"Tony, can we just...can we just stop right here and right now," she waved an imaginary white flag. "For Christ's sake, Maria's in the backseat."

The girls were silent. They both sat statue stiff. The sounds of windshield wiper blades dashing across wet glass was the only music to be heard. An aquatic staccato.

It was raining harder now. For a few moments, silence set like the sun over an azure Atlantic Ocean. She looked over her shoulder at Maria. Tears were welling up in her eyes. A few spilled. She dried them with the back of her hand and cried silently.

A FEW DAYS later Detective Patricia Garbutt and Detective Jake Billingsley were at Stone Mountain Park. There had been another murder. A woman's body was discovered by a pair of joggers. The decomposing corpse smelled like a smorgasbord of stink. It was the fetid, rotten, detestable odor of the woman's innards slowly cooking under stagnant sunrays.

The woman's left finger, her ring finger, was missing. There were signs of foul play, as though she had been sexually assaulted. Jake crouched down, and with a latex gloved finger, wiped away a creamy milk-like substance from the woman's inner thigh. He held that gloved finger up to his nose.

"Definitely smells of semen. I can sniff out the protein in it," he said to the medical examiner. She nodded and told him that the sexual assault had been performed post mortem.

"Sick fuck!" Patricia said.

The sun was at its height. Ninety seven degrees in the shade. Humidity was thick enough to slice with a butter knife. A golden haze glared down on Stone Mountain Park. Towering cedars, oaks, magnolias and several White fringe trees were in bloom.

Daisy flowers of rosy purple with knobby orange-brown centers, which resembled small beehives, were clustered around where the body lay. Butterflies fluttered and danced through the air, like flying Doritos. Almost too pretty a setting to be the scene of a crime.

The woman had something balled up in the other hand. Her whole hand. The medical examiner said that they'd read the contents. She was holding the Lotus Sutra, which was written in calligraphy on public school elementary grade paper.

The Lotus Sutra was one of the most important and influential sutras or sacred scriptures, of Buddhism. Of the countless scriptures of Mahayana Buddhism, few were more widely read or revered than the Lotus Sutra.

The body had been in the sun for a long time. At least seventy two hours. Her flesh was beginning to cook. The elements gave rise to bacteria, small critters, and decomposition had set in. Rigor Mortis.

She was a Caucasian woman, mid forties, with a meaty torso, sagging breasts, and doughy arms and legs. She had long, stringy, mousy hair streaked with brownish blood. Nude from head to toe, she was found lying on her back, which was still the color of mayonnaise, meanwhile her front parts had been tanned the color of a Georgia peach.

Jake investigated further. He pushed back the victim's hair to find an incision the size of a silver dollar. Maggots had begun to feast upon her flesh, but aside from that, the incision looked nearly perfect — as though done with laser precision.

It was apparent that her killer performed some type of surgical procedure on her. Jake looked up at the ME as he began pulling off the latex gloves he wore. "I need a copy of the autopsy report just as soon as you get it," Jake said.

Suddenly Patricia's phone jingled in her pocket. She pulled it out. An unfamiliar "PRIVATE CALLER" on the display stared back at her. She swallowed and took the call, walking away from the scene of the crime.

"Garbutt speaking."

"Glad to see you find cadaver I leave you," an impish male voice tinted with a Japanese accent said.

"Excuse me, who is this?" Detective Garbutt said, pulling the earpiece away to take another look at the display. She hoped that it was a prank call.

"You hear me correctly first time, Detective Patricia Garbutt. Tell boyfriend Jake I say hello. You guys should look out for ebony package soon. You find her car on McDaniel, few week back. Well, you might find her *hang* around Lake Allatoona, where the water is sweet," his broken English began to break up. The signal was fading.

The call ended. Detective Garbutt was flabbergasted. Who was this asshole who had her personal cell phone number? In all the years of being on the force, she never experienced a call from a suspect. It rattled her nerves. She immediately trotted back over to Jake and filled him in.

"It's probably just some kids. You don't think Maria or Tyler's little friends would do anything like that do you?" Jake said.

"Hell no! Not a chance in hell."

"Well just to call the creep's bluff, why don't we go by Lake Allatoona."

"I thought you'd never ask," Detective Garbutt said. "But he's admittedly taking credit for this Jane Doe. He knows that we're here. He's following us." A dark cloud began to move in from out of nowhere.

They wondered to themselves what the significance of the Lotus Sutra was. Neither of them had ever heard of such a thing until that day. It was a mystery within a mystery.

SIXTEEN

BY THE TIME Jake and Patricia drove to the other side of town from Stone Mountain Park to Northwestern Metro Atlanta, they intercepted over a dozen other fatalities on the police radio.

There was a vehicular homicide at the intersection of Cascade Road and Fairburn, in Southwest Atlanta. A police officer ran a red light and wrapped his APD squad car around an innocent civilian's sedan, killing a woman instantly.

There was a drowning in Lake Lanier. A kid who had been out floating on an inner tube had somehow collided with a Jet Ski motorist. Another kid had been found beaten to death by his step father, left in scolding hot bathwater. Floaters were the worst. Water did unimaginable damage to dead human bodies.

A poison victim on Georgia Tech's campus suffered an overdose of various designer drugs. Drove her into anaphylactic shock. A teen boxer died after a fatal blow to the head, and an Amber Alert body was found in a ravine near Windy Hill.

This was just another day, no different than any other, aside from the fact that some creep had gotten a hold of her personal phone number. Detective Garbutt had to admit that she was spooked.

When they arrived at Lake Allatoona they had no idea where to look first. The fact that the mysterious impish caller said something about "hanging" indicated that the body might be found near an area where there were lots of trees.

There was an abundance of trees everywhere. There were pines and acacia trees, oaks, magnolias, and dogwoods. Allatoona Lake itself was murky and green, the color of toad skin.

The lake was created and authorized for flood control, hydroelectric power generation, water supply, water quality, recreation, fish and wildlife management. But the outlook as to why they were there was grim. The drought had siphoned away a few feet of water.

There was 25,000 acres of public land around Lake Allatoona that was owned by the Army. The caller mentioned something about where the water was sweet. There was a park, just off of Lake Allatoona, called Sweetwater Park.

They climbed out of the Crown Vic and split off in two separate directions in search of this mysterious missing woman, Deidre Priest. Her boyfriend Akil mentioned something about her last seen wearing an orange dress and a silver necklace with wooden ringlets on it.

They searched for nearly two hours when Jake sent a text message to Detective Garbutt's phone. He'd found something. He was on the other side of the park, but she knew that he'd found something significant. Something groundbreaking. Something shocking. For some odd reason, she gathered that he had found the remains of Deidre Priest.

When she finally found Jake, Detective Garbutt wasn't expecting what met her eyes. Jake's back was to her. He wore faded denim jeans and a long sleeved Carolina blue shirt. In that light, he looked as though all of the color had left his face. Only a pale, ashen sun-ripened version of his complexion remained. Like weathered fabric left out in the sun too long.

Suddenly the potatoes and grits she'd had earlier that morning wanted to reemerge. Up they came for air, resurrected. Her breakfast forced itself up her throat with such vigor and fortitude that it wracked her body forward.

She puked into a marshy area near the mouth of the lake. The sky was ablaze in white hot sunshine and clouds were pompous and poised in the way they stood erect unmoving. Unstirred. Unchecked.

Detective Garbutt could feel a thin film of perspiration line the back of her neck, soaking the collar of her blouse. From where she stood, she could see the outline of a woman's body. There were raised engravings written across her breasts and down her torso. Like Braille. Someone had written the wisdom of the Lotus Sutra on the surface of her skin. Meaning and reason abandoned them both.

Silence sat between Detective Billingsley and Detective Garbutt. They were at a loss for words. They had never experienced anything quite like this, not in either of their careers, not even if they were to combine those careers. Crooked trees seemed to bow more from agony than from age. Detective Patricia Garbutt felt like a stanza at the end of a poem. The space at the end of a haiku.

SEVENTEEN

THE WOMAN'S REMAINS were completely desecrated, a tomb raider's canvas. Even a fool could see that she was a beautiful woman.

Her features were delicate and soft, tinged with innocent essence. Pain was the last emotion chiseled across her lips. She'd suffered before giving up the ghost. She had long thick hair. It was as limp and lifeless as the woman was. The elements had their way with her sinuous flesh and they'd won.

Jake turned to Patricia. He gave her a look as heavy as an anvil and suddenly she heard ringing in her ears. She turned away from him. He walked over to the body and crouched down. Pulling out a pair of latex gloves, he began to read the writing on the woman's lifeless body. Although it was legible, they couldn't ascertain the meaning.

Detective Garbutt's eyes were clouded with doubt and Georgia red dust, kicked up by a wind that came from the Gulf of Mexico. She took a deep breath, exhaled and bit down on her bottom lip. She whipped out her cell phone and called in the body.

Soon the scene would be crawling with GBI, medical examiners, and crime scene investigators. An eerie hummingbird fluttered between Detective Garbutt's eyes. It seemed to stare directly into her pupils, through her cornea. Past her iris.

For some strange reason she looked down at her hands. They were dirty. Filthy. How had her hands become so soiled? That kicked up Georgia red dust was getting in her eyes again. She rubbed them. She could feel that they were growing increasingly red. They tingled. Burned. She felt like she was underwater. She could swallow, but she reached out for a breath to catch.

Here was this woman who had lost her life at the hands of a mentally disturbed individual, no fault of her own, or was it? Detective Garbutt turned to see Jake looking at her scalp. He squinted up at her, "I see an incision. Just like the other Jane," he said as he began snapping pictures with a small digital camera.

Detective Garbutt sighed. Gave him a pensive look. They had a serial killer on their hands. And what frightened her more than anything else was the fact that he was smart. He was brilliant.

So far, they hadn't found a single print. But DNA was a tricky substance. It scrawled itself all over everything. It was inescapable. The only thing more brilliant than an intelligent serial killer was the DNA that he left behind. They had the best toxicologists in the country though. Their forensic scientists could get DNA from a mosquito's sneeze.

Jake said that Deidre Priest had been sexually assaulted post mortem. Not only did they have a serial killer on their hands, but they had a serial killer living with a serious case of necrophilia.

Detective Garbutt's face grew flushed and her heart rate sped. She thought of Anthony, how he'd slapped her in the car. She thought of Tyler. She felt like she was failing in the role of mother and wife. Her mouth was dry.

The fact that Jake found another incision let them both know that not only did they have a sadistic serial killer on their hands, but they also had a masochist who got his kicks by cutting into women's scalps and leading them on a goose chase. Failure and guilt were embossed on their hands. They'd have to return to the drawing board. Detective Garbutt was still thinking about Tyler.

She walked over and stood next to Jake. Jake wore a taciturn expression. She could tell by the look in his eye as he gazed off in the distance, that he wanted answers. He chewed on his inner cheek and squinted the sunshine out of his eyes. The fact that they'd found the body themselves meant that they had to wait until the county medical examiner arrived on the scene before they could go any further.

She glanced out over the swampy looking lake. In the distance, the sun beat down upon the water. Gave it a soft golden illumined sheen. The ripples of the lake took her to another place.

Suddenly she was shaken from her reverie, to her dismay. The remains of the woman Jake found were still fresh. The corpse hadn't grown cold yet. Even in the baking hot summer sun, lifeless bodies were still prone to hold a deathly chill. Once the spirit left the body, energy ceased to warm the skin.

EIGHTEEN

A LOOK OF shock was on her face. As if she saw something unbelievably duplicitous and terrifying as she gasped out her last breath. She wore a solemn gaze, as though whatever she saw the moment before she transitioned was final and hideous.

Jake took out a pack of Newports, stuck a cigarette in his mouth and lit it with a lighter he'd fetched from his pocket. They didn't know what to make of the scene. They had to wait for the county coroner and the medical examiner to bag and tag the remains. Detective Garbutt didn't know what was worse, waiting or the uncertainty. The mystery.

They couldn't tamper with any evidence. Weren't supposed to. Allatoona Lake was out of their jurisdiction. Contaminating the crime scene would destroy the investigation.

"Have you heard anything else from that weirdo who called you?" Jake said.

"No. Nothing."

"Gosh, I'd sure like to trace that call. I'm guessing there's something to this that I'm just not understanding," Jake added. "All the belletristic effort. I mean what's this guy trying to prove? Who in the hell does he think we are? I think this creep's been watching too much TV. Too many episodes of *Law and Order* or *First 48*," he chuckled.

"Have you heard anything back from the coroner on the missing person? Any leads whatsoever?"

Jake shook his head no.

Upon closer inspection, Detective Garbutt noticed the woman had a small tattoo behind her right ear. A pyramid with an eye hovering above it. Just like the image found on a one dollar bill. About the size of a quarter. Across the smalls of her back, another tattoo that read 'Do As Thou Wilt Shall Be the Whole of the law'. She had a hunch.

Reaching into her pocket, she found her phone. Scrolling through her new contacts, she located Akil Allah, Deidre Priest's boyfriend. Of course he didn't answer.

No one answered their phones anymore. Unfamiliar numbers were notoriously sent to voicemail, with a vengeance. If it was urgent the caller would leave a message.

"Whatcha thinkin'?"

"I'm thinking that if we can get the boyfriend to confirm any identifying tattoos then we have before us...Ms. Deidre Priest," Detective Garbutt said enthusiastically. The tattoos looked to be at least a year old. She knew for sure that they weren't placed under the skin post mortem. The lotus sutra script had been performed either just before the murder or soon after.

Later that evening Jake went home to his Spartan loft. He kept replaying Brody's words, "You know a person has the right to go missing."

He was pleasantly surprised to find his new friend waiting for him on his sofa. The television was on. The volume turned down low, almost to a faint hum. She'd draped his Atlanta Braves throw blanket over her shoulders, as Jake kept his loft cool.

NINETEEN

AURORA SUGGS WAS her name. Ever since they'd begun dating, Jake's self esteem surmounted levels he'd never known. She was the ultimate arm candy. Aurora Suggs was the girl every pimple-faced high school jock wanted and every four-eyed, brace-face girl wanted to be like.

She was like the gold coin you got when playing *Super Mario Brothers* — those coins that gave Mario the energy, stamina and endurance to leap higher, go further and faster through every stage of his journey.

Aurora looked up at Jake as he removed the key from the lock. She had a book in her hands. Chuck Palahniuk's *Diary*. It was actually a book Jake had picked up a few weeks ago that he hadn't had a chance to sink his teeth into yet. Aurora was a bookworm. She'd rather read than watch television.

One of the last times they'd seen each other, they chomped down on hotdogs and pop at the Varsity. They'd gotten into a heated debate over something trivial and meaningless. But Jake and his razor sharp wit lanced Aurora with his tongue. Said something biting and hurtful. Contrary to popular half truths, words can hurt. Words can break bones, hearts, marriages and much more.

Jake had mentioned something about her family. Called them poor white trash. It was true but how often does one need to have their nose smeared in their own pile of shit. None of us can help where we come from. Not one of us can reverse our lineage. If it were that easy, people would be switching out their families left and right.

Jake knew he could play the winning role as asshole when he chose. Aurora's presence was a subtle statement. It said that she had forgiven him. It said that she was willing to put it behind them if he was.

Aurora Suggs was nineteen years old. A blond runaway who was born and raised in Douglasville, Georgia. Her parents were from the trailer park, their parents were from the trailer park, and their parents before grew up in a trailer on a farm. Her mother's boyfriend Shadrach, was abusive. He tried to touch Aurora on a few separate occasions during her senior year in high school. At least that's what she told Jake.

Her mother was working long hours, a morning shift at the Wal-Mart on Thornton Road, and a third shift at the Waffle House. When ends became increasingly difficult to meet, Aurora was forced to pick up a job. The Family Dollar was the only place that would hire her, due to the fact that she was clinically bi-polar. Her highs were Mount Everest and her lows reached the depths of Dante's Inferno.

When she met Jake, while he stood in her line to pay for a pack of batteries, toilet paper, and a bag of pork skins, she saw something in him. She came on strong. She gave him those mesmerizing green eyes. She batted her lashes, flipped her curly blond hair, which she kept teased and packed with hairspray. It was like something out of the eighties.

Jake tossed his keys down and began unbuttoning his shirt. Sweat circles outlined his armpits. Bare chest, he walked over to the refrigerator and grabbed a Corona. After flicking the cap off the bottle, Jake plopped down onto the sofa next to Aurora. For a moment she stared at him blankly. There was vulnerability in her eyes. They didn't exchange words for a few moments.

Jake sipped his beer and reached for the remote control. Aurora stopped him. Placed a soft tanned hand with French tipped acrylic nails on top of his.

"You still mad at me?" Jake said nonchalantly.

Jake's loft featured exposed brick walls, glazed cement floors, and mismatched furniture he'd gotten from here, there and everywhere. He and Aurora sat on the vintage pear colored leather sofa that he snagged from a Salvation Army in West Cobb.

He kicked his feet up onto an ancient treasure chest made of aged maple. Aurora looked at him. She slid her arm around his waist, brought her lips near his, gazed into his eyes softly, and allowed Chuck Palahniuk to fall to the floor.

They kissed. Just a peck. Nothing hot or heavy. Jake pulled away slowly.

"What's wrong?" Aurora asked.

"Apparently you're not still mad at me," he said.

"Apparently not," she shrugged.

Aurora grabbed the remote control, turned the channel to the music station. A Steely Dan tune emerged from the speakers. Jake pulled Aurora on top of him, causing her to straddle him. They kissed. She moaned into his mouth. Reached her hands behind his neck and interlaced her fingers there.

Soon the Rolling Stones came on. They sang about a woman named *Angie*. Jake flung the Braves blanket across the room with his free hand. After taking another sip of his beer, he kissed Aurora again.

They spoke no words. Only the universal language of lust. Jake kissed Aurora's neck, all the way down to her navel. By the time Led Zeppelin came on, Jake was facilitating Aurora's orgasms.

Aurora made Jake feel like a rock star; like he lived a life of fast cars, beautiful women, big dreams, good music, and expensive taste. After they finished making love, they showered together. Soon they were heading out to dinner for a late night round of beers and a bite to eat.

The skies looked like piceous dark muddy waters, partly cloudy beneath a rain washed steamy evening. Meandering thunder storms and the remnants of Hurricane Isaac brought heavy rainfall and the threat of flash flooding. They drove to a popular eatery in the foothills of Northern Georgia, just outside of Alpharetta, called Woody's Steakhouse.

As soon as they entered the establishment, the scent of char grilled steak and mesquite salmon cooking over a cedar plank wafted into their noses. Jimi Hendrix and Lonnie Youngblood sang about

Georgia Blues in the background. The restaurant was relaxed and served abundant plates of sumptuous food.

Don't let the white tablecloths and fancy décor fool you. You could eat hearty and walk away fully satisfied at Woody's steakhouse. Jake ordered a Samuel Adams. "Perhaps you'd like a cocktail?"Jake offered.

"Jake, you know that I don't drink." Aurora replied, "How was your day anyway? I didn't ask earlier." Aurora ordered the sliders platter, which included four perfectly cooked, juicy patties with Bibb lettuce, a slice of tomato and sharp, nutty, melted cheese on a buttered brioche bun.

"*You* know I don't like to talk about work when I'm with you. This is my time to unwind and relax," Jake said, stretching his arms out wide along the worn leather seats of the booth. The lighting in the restaurant was dim, intimate, and warm. It gave off a soft amber bronze shine, reminiscent of aged Brandy. "But I will say this, today I saw one of the creepiest things I've ever experienced in my life. My partner and I believe we're dealing with a lunatic psychopath. Just what we need, someone who is a fan of Anthony Hopkins in *Silence of the Lambs*," Jake sighed heavily.

After finishing his beer, Jake ordered a Tanqueray Martini and a glass of California Cabernet Sauvignon for Aurora, although she'd explicitly stated that she didn't drink and had no desire for any spirits. He asked the waitress to bring a bottle of Sicily's *Nero d'Avola* to the table. The glass of wine sat poised in front of her like an acrylic painting.

"Bottoms up Princess," Jake said. Aurora stared at him quietly.

"So what do you mean by lunatic? What did you see if you don't mind my asking?" she said.

"Let's talk about you. Let's talk about us. Tell me why you refuse to touch that glass of wine. You look at it like it's the plague. I mean that's nothing more than a glass of fermented grape juice," Jake said, now feeling the full buzz of his beer and Martini, as the alcohol did a tango with his inhibitions. "You do like grape juice, don't you?"

"Are you trying to turn me into an alcoholic, Jake? Besides, all I've seen, all I've known is how alcohol turns people into zombies. It turns them into weak, ruthless criminals. I don't want to know what it will do to me if I start drinking it. I've never told you this, but my daddy was killed by a drunk driver. So no thank you," giving him those gregarious green eyes, full of pain and vulnerability.

For once in as long as Jake had known her, Aurora's words were brimming with an evocative and stirring Southern twang.

Just then the waitress brought Jake's culotte steak—a top sirloin cap, the most –prized cut of beef in Brazil. Culotte wasn't the tenderest bit of the cow, but it had an awful lot of flavor. The way they aged it and grilled it at Woody's brought out the citrus-tart essence of the meat, which is what you wanted in a steak instead of melted fat running down your chin.

After taking a bite, an ineffable look of pleasure surfaced across Jake's face. Another waiter walked by with a teeming plate of buttery steamed Lobster, caught fresh and shipped from Maine just that day. The large red crustacean caught Aurora off guard, broke her reverie.

"Alcohol doesn't turn people into ruthless criminals. C'mon…don't you think that's a bit much? It's like guns. Guns don't kill people. *People kill people*," Jake said sardonically. "Wine is the nectar of the gods. It's the people who abuse alcohol that allow it to make them do stupid things."

"Try telling that to the scumbag who killed my daddy," Aurora said, her eyes beginning to glaze over.

"I apologize," Jake replied. He had put his foot in his mouth once again. "I didn't know." *Gosh you did it again, idiot!* He thought to himself.

TWENTY

THE AUTOPSY RESULTS had come in on the corpses found at both Lake Allatoona and Stone Mountain Park. Blood levity levels determined that both women had been drugged. They found methamphetamines and Vicodin swimming in their veins.

Anthony Eugene Bowers was balancing himself over an unsteady ladder in an attempt to seal the attic vents. There was an infestation of bats in the attic of their Cobb County home—at least it wasn't termites. Detective Garbutt stood near the bottom of the ladder holding a glass of ice water in the turquoise plastic teal tumbler she'd gotten from Bed Bath and Beyond.

Her husband would no longer eschew home improvement projects after their altercation. It was her ace-in-the-hole. In the days immediately following the night he slapped her in the car, he went straight to attacking Patty's "Honey do" list.

They hadn't mentioned it ever since. It was like they were both attempting to avoid the mess they'd made. She thought it was ridiculous that he would attempt to seal their attic vents and the small cracks and crevices the bats were using as entrances into their abode, with his bare hands. Sometimes he didn't use his brain. Anthony's hands were covered with the polyurethane-scented sealant, soiled and tarry.

The sun was beginning to set, pulling a patchwork of celadon, cerise, and cerulean streaks down around the band of the horizon. Tyler had been released from the hospital and things had fizzled down to a simmer around the Garbutt house. Detective Garbutt received the text message from Brody about the autopsy results. She released a long pregnant sigh.

Soon detective Garbutt and Detective Billingsley were in her Crown Victoria, per usual. They were heading to Tybee Island for a few days of investigating. The perp sent another clue out into the atmosphere like a smoke signal, only he'd made a slight mistake.

A set of fingerprints were found on the corpse from Stone Mountain Park. Her dental records were checked and confirmed her identity as an Eileen Rosenthal of Savannah, Georgia.

Ironically, those same sets of prints matched another errant set of prints found on the corpse from Sweetwater at Allatoona Lake. Forensics confirmed that she was the missing Deidre Priest. But the kicker was that those prints matched a convicted murderer known as Rex Baldwin, also of Chatham County — otherwise known as Savannah, Georgia.

A team of cryptographers and code breakers were assigned to help tackle the Lotus Sutra chant, or what they assumed to be the Lotus Sutra. The same scholars who worked on decoding MS 408, the Voynich manuscript, were taking a look at the ancient script, which had been engraved on the women's bodies.

The remains of Deidra Priest had been gutted like a cow. There was no rhyme or reason to these killings. Still Brody sent them packing, on a mission to Georgia's coast. He said, "It's often the last key in the bunch that opens the lock." Brody always spoke in aphorisms. He thought it made him sound more cultured.

In actuality it made his subordinates despise him. They called him Alfred Hitchcock behind his back, with an emphasis on 'cock'.

Deidre Priest's uterus, cervix, heart, and brain had mysteriously been removed. There was no incision, other than the small one into the cranium. Initially they believed a type of laser was used to remove her organs, but there were no other points of entry. It was done by a professional with an eye for detail. Keen detail.

The drive to the coast reminded Jake of his hometown of Puget Sound, he said. Faint sea-salted air and hazy overcast skies that could only be found near the ocean. The perfect climate for growing coconuts, pineapples, lemons, and oranges.

It all brought him back to noonday paddling, in his canoe, the one he painted with orange, green, and blue stripes down the side, when he was fifteen years old. It brought him back to building boats with his dad and crabbing.

The last time he'd gone home to Washington, he and his brother Scott went whale watching. Scott snapped shots of humpbacks that he would later go on to sale to a magazine.

Tybee was a lot like Puget Sound; both offered the blood-pressure lowering pleasures of an unpretentious small town; easy like Sunday morning.

Tybee had a strong gravitational pull, plenty of pleasantly eclectic people, a twice-a-week farmer's market, and the atmosphere was low-key.

Before checking into their hotel rooms, Jake and Patricia grabbed crepes at Giuseppe's, a New Orleans styled bistro and café. Jake flirted openly with their waitress, a brunette with the confidence of a blond. Her name badge read 'Kay,' but she later told Jake to call her Laura. She was from Knoxville, Tennessee. She'd come to Georgia to get discovered.

The inlet connecting Tybee to the mainland was surrounded by a calm surf, made for kayaking and long boarding and stand up paddle-boarding, but the folks dwelling on Tybee Island didn't do those types of things. They left that type of tomfoolery to the teeny boppers.

Laura, from Giuseppe's, reminded him that sometimes an end is just a chance to start again. He wondered if she coined that phrase from a country western song.

Knoxville was the heart of country western, wasn't it?

"Sometimes it takes a while to find out who you really are; takes guts to not follow the blueprint of life handed to us by proponents of the cookie-cutter," Jake had told her nonchalantly. He eyed the brunette. Gave her his father's smile. Aurora was miles away in body and in mind.

He would consider himself beating his own record if he scored this weekend. Damn Brody. Damn this case. He needed a vacation. A real vacation. Not what Americans called *staycations*.

The detectives stayed in a raggedy piece of shit motel called the Sunset Inn, which resembled a barn, albeit one with patina-green, hand stained exterior and was apparently powered by solar energy.

The innkeeper sold eggplants, apples, and melons outside in the front of the motel. Plus, yams larger than your leg, lined the busy roadside lot. Tomatoes, peppers, and black-eyed peas also. "Welcome to Sunset Inn," said the innkeeper, in a pleasantly tannic tangy Bengali accent. Like his words gave him a peppery Calcutta kick in the throat every time his lips parted—leaving an almond after taste on the back of his tongue.

The website for the motel advertised breathtaking views overlooking the crystal blue ocean, calling it a dream escape, the ultimate island fantasy and describing the motel itself as having a unique and subtle aesthetic.

What it really was was something altogether different. The lobby smelled of cigar smoke and Indian food. Curry pumped from the air condition vents.

The owner and proprietor, Mr. Gupta, was the front desk concierge, the person who prepared the complementary Continental breakfast, and along with his wife, cleaned the motel rooms.

The walls of the lobby were painted a deep rich candy apple red matte and were studded with framed pictures of no particular theme. There were watercolors of marine scenes, several sailboats, seashells, lighthouses, starfish, and dolphins all in pastels.

There were also sepia and black and whites of the Island's civil war history, remnants of a time when the country was at war with itself. Archaic, bombed-out, beleaguered, and burned brick frames of buildings stood in defeat. The story of the Confederate beat down betrayed them.

There was virtually no view of the actual beach. The room was, however, overlooking a murky Poseidon green swimming pool. Several overweight folks from landlocked rural parts of Georgia were in the pool, badly in need of tans. Jethro, Bubba and Gump. So many doughy, pasty, white bodies dotted the pool that it looked like a Marshmallow man convention had come to Tybee Island, to soak in the scenery.

Leftover Continental Breakfast, store bought pancake and waffle mix droplets were stuck to the counters. Styrofoam cups half full of apple and orange juice made from concentrate were strewn around on the tables in the lobby. The motel guests had completely TKOed the mini doughnuts and Danishes.

While Jake screwed around in an attempt to pick up the brunette waitress from Giuseppe's,

Detective Garbutt did what the government paid her to do—investigated.

TWENTY-ONE

SHE BUSIED HERSELF with the details of the case almost immediately after settling into her motel room. It was a small space, cramped mainly by the California King-sized bed.

The bed took up the lion's share of the room. There was no coffeemaker. No refrigerator; just a gigantic bed, clad in a pale periwinkle blue blanket with Polynesian flowers. The walls were painted vomit mauve, with a wallpaper border near the ceiling, decorated with beach balls against a navy blue background.

Rex Baldwin, the suspect, worked as a short order cook at a local dive. According to records, he was also living on the island with his apparent girlfriend. He'd filed taxes in Chatham County for the past two years.

Later that night, just as the sun began to lean back on the horizon, the detectives went out to have a few words with Rex Baldwin. They were in communication with the local authorities. They let them know that they were doing an investigation and the local authorities of that sleepy beach town respectfully cooperated.

The streets of Tybee Island were laden with sand that had blown onto shore. The detectives, dressed low-key, in t-shirts and shorts, so as to blend in with the crowd, were heading to Spanky's beachside, where Rex Baldwin cooked chicken fingers and fries for a living.

Detective Garbutt thought it awfully odd that a man who was so smart as to make diametrically impossible incisions and craft murders better than Agatha Christie would find himself flipping frozen hamburger patties on the beach. You'd expect him to garner ransom money or at least try to live a little higher on the social totem pole. An underachiever was an underachiever.

By the water and under a fading sunset, beside long orange and yellow canoes, men drank bottles of Sierra Nevada's 2012 Estate Homegrown ale. A band provided live music out on the patio behind Spanky's.

In need of tuning, the strings of the violin seemed to quail at the touch of the bow. From where the restaurant was situated, the water looked green — greener than an olive orchard. Maybe it was the way the sun beat down upon the surface of the sea.

Red Snapper, Mahi-Mahi, and grouper was smoking on an open grill. A few crew from a yacht were having drinks and listening to the lead singer of the band. Her celestial form resembling Venus kept their rapt attention, not her voice, and certainly not the music.

"Went to Duke for education," Jake looked out at the churning waves, leaned close, his blue eyes camouflage with the sky, "got incredibly good grades, but nobody would hire him."

He was referring to Rex Baldwin. Things were beginning to make more sense now.

"So he moves in with the girl he's banging and gets this job on a wing and a prayer." Patricia said. Cool breezes blew through her hair.

"You can't outrun your shadow. The universe has an odd little way of seeing to it that killers are unemployable. Or underemployed, shall I say?" Jake added.

"Not Spanky!" Patricia said sardonically.

The air was wild and windy, like a tumbleweed town where nothing grows. Something in the air was sweet—sweeter than pineapple and guava chutney. There was something idyllic and charming about this town. Waves pounded the shore. The tide was high. There was an easy welcome at Tybee Island, and riotous beauty. Small palm trees and sand were constant companions.

A sense of calm and peace washed over the detectives, making it difficult to stay focused on the investigation.

The patio was lit via a string of lights that resembled luminous pearls on a string. The stuff that legendary Bokeh photography was made of. Patricia thought of that Bible verse, "Cast not your pearls before swine."

Diners were being served under an arbor, set aglow by intimate candles and torches in glass jars.

Tonight Spanky's was uncomplicated, unspoiled, and uncongested. The singer was now singing a cover of Bobby McFerrin's rendition of "Don't Worry, Be Happy".

Being there made you want to just embrace life without judgment. Live-and-let-live. So much of the experience of dining was about atmosphere and mood.

Patricia wouldn't dare eat anything from Spanky's. She was craving Korean barbecue. Pho to be exact. Pho and Chrysanthemum bread.

They asked to speak to the manager or whoever was responsible for hiring. An older woman with graying dirty blonde hair and sun baked leathery skin came to the front of the dive.

She had a smoker's cough, the lady who ran Spanky's. A smoker's cough and an alcoholic's slur. "What can I do you for?" she said, with a sweet home Alabama accent.

This is Detective Garbutt and I am Detective Billingsley, and we're here to see Mr. Rex Baldwin. We're doing an investigation and just want to ask him a few questions," Jake said.

"Who?" she said, before falling into a prolonged coughing fit. It was sad. "I don't know no Rex Baldwin. You sure you got the right place and the right person?"

Jake glanced over at Patricia.

"With all due respect ma'am, we'd appreciate if you'd cooperate with us. This is a federal investigation and you can get into a lot of trouble if you're lying to us. Are you familiar with the penalties of perjury or assisting a criminal?" Patricia said.

"We're looking for the man who works as a short order cook here. We believe he's been working here for the past two years," Jake chimed in.

A group of women in swimsuits and sarongs came in from River Street. A server walked by carrying a plate of blackened shrimp, Dungeness crab, fresh mollusks, fresh goat cheese and radicchio salad with figs, a bottle of Brother Thelonious Belgian style abbey ale, and margaritas. Another server walked by carrying a plate of grouper fingers and crab dip.

Suddenly smoker's cough seemed to have a change of heart. "Are you talking about Michael? I have several cooks. But none of 'em been here longer than eight or nine months, all but Michael...Michael Roth. He been here for about two years. But I don't have anyone working here by the name of no Rex Baldwin."

Detective Garbutt rolled her eyes. "Michael Roth," she said, pulling out her small notepad to jot down the name.

"Yes ma'am, Michael Roth. He been working here for about two years, but he's off tonight. Only cooks I have in the kitchen tonight are Alfredo Lopez and Tremaine Jackson. Would you like to speak to either one of them?" Smoker's cough said as she wrung her fingers. Beads of sweat began to break out on her temples.

"No thank you. That won't be necessary," Jake interjected. "Would you mind giving us Michael's address? This is a federal investigation."

Detective Garbutt eyed the woman from head to toe, trying to search for meaning for the sudden outbreak of nervous tension.

The woman coughed again. Phlegm rattled in her chest. "Sure, not a problem. If you'll follow me to my office, I can look it up for you."

Jake followed the woman, while Patricia remained in the front of Spanky's. She allowed her eyes to fan over the crowd of patrons.

She took note of all the entrances and exits, surveillance cameras. Surveillance cameras were everywhere. This was the brave new world we were living in.

Big Brother was everywhere, his roving red eye lurking from within every stop light, ATM, beltline, freeway and place of business. Hidden cameras were the rave of the twenty-first century. Hidden cameras and camera phones.

Everything was available to be tweeted and uploaded to Instagram or Youtube on any given day, no matter what season. Nothing was hidden from cameras, which were often hidden in plain sight.

After a few minutes Jake reemerged from the back of Spanky's with Michael Roth's address scribbled on a small post-it, in his hand.

The detective hopped into Patricia's Crown Victoria and rumbled a few miles down River Street. The address was fairly easy to find with the help of OnStar, but they had their doubts. If Rex Baldwin had filed taxes under one name, with W-2s stating that he was employed with Spanky's for the past twenty-four months, who was Michael Roth?

They parked a block away from the address they were given and started up the street. Several dogs were barking. A few people sat out on plastic chairs, soaking in the crisp beach air and fleeting sunlight. The sky was a luminous reddish-orange, almost piquant rustic color. The color of a rum cocktail.

Palm trees, hammocks, sand, shell shops, and a few tiki torches festooned the street. The smell of conch fritters and stone-crab scented the air. A man was sitting out on the porch of the white clapboard house, trimmed in pastel indigo. A small Pug was tied to the chair the man sat in.

He'd just finished mowing the lawn. The lawnmower was parked seven feet away from him. Grass shavings dusted the walkway. The yard was impeccably landscaped. Neatly trimmed camellia bushes, rhododendrons, and a dwarf Gingko biloba tree. A graceful butterfly bush.

He wiped sweat from his forehead with a balled up shirt that he used as a rag. Once he noticed that the detectives were walking in his direction, up the walkway leading up to where he was, the man stood to his feet.

He was a slight man, standing just a few inches above five feet. He looked to be no heavier than a hundred and fifty pounds. He had dark curly hair, with a puff of white in the front. He had small calloused hands. Chunky knuckles. Beady eyes that darted left to right, like the eyes of a crab. They didn't gaze. They ogled.

He wore a pair of dirty, faded, ripped Wrangler jeans. No shirt. "Excuse me sir, can you tell me where we can find Michael Roth?" Jake said.

"Who wants to know?" he said.

"How about Rex Baldwin?" Patricia said.

At the sound of those names coming from these radically unfamiliar people, the man took off running into the house. He slammed the door shut.

Jake pulled out his gun and banged on the door. "Open up, police!"

Patricia whipped out her cell phone and called for back-up. At the same time, she too pulled out her pistol and began to quickly walk around to the back of the bungalow.

She saw the man exit from a back door and run into the direction of the main drag. He had put on a black hoodie and ran with a dark duffle bag in his hands.

"Freeze, don't move! Stop running," she yelled at the top of her lungs. "Jake, he's back here! Help me catch him!"

TWENTY-TWO

QUICKER THAN THE speed of a lightning bolt, Jake had caught up to Patricia, passing her by even. That was a perk of having him as her partner. He was in good shape. Although he smoked cigarettes and was an avid beer connoisseur, he also worked out in the gym regularly. Balance was everything.

The man who they believed to be Rex Baldwin ran as though his life depended on it. He ran in the way that only a guilty man could. The distance between Jake and Rex Baldwin began to decrease as Jake took long strides, swiping up meters with each thrust of his knees. He hadn't even broken a sweat.

Patricia was winded by the time she reached the corner and so she stopped and began to run back towards the white bungalow. The sounds of police sirens filled the air. Back up was on the way.

Patricia rested for a few seconds before entering the darkened house. They didn't have a warrant, nor would they have time to obtain one in the few hours remaining before midnight. She struggled for a breath, while resting her hands on the tops of her knees.

She breathed through her nose between gulps of air through her mouth. Her chest was set ablaze as her heart rate surged. A sharp, biting pain skewered her side—she'd pulled a muscle. And she needed a drink of water. A tall cold glass of water hovered above her in an invisible thought bubble. She struggled to get enough oxygen.

Lights were still on inside the bungalow and the faint sound of a television. Patricia, with one hand grasping her pistol, banged on the door. "Is anyone inside? This is the police! Open up!"

There was no response, but she saw a light flicker and then go off from the window on the far right of the house. Someone was inside. The house was dark but someone was inside.

Patricia banged on the door once again before attempting to use the weight of her body to heave the door open. At first nothing happened.

A proliferation of pain shot down her arm. She wasn't strong enough to kick the door open. She looked around to see if any uniformed officers were nearby.

Several onlookers bloomed from their porches and began walking out into the middle of the street to catch a glimpse of the commotion. Even the porch of that white bungalow with its indigo trim was rich with crickets, tree frogs, grasshoppers, and a few praying mantises, all alive with copious chirps and guttural grunts.

Detective Garbutt honestly couldn't kick the door open because she wore canvas boat shoes with rubber soles. No *bueno*. Locating a tortoise sized stone which sat underneath a nearby blue wisteria, Patricia used it to smash one of the front windows open—the window nearest the front door. Shards of glass flew left and right.

After carefully climbing inside the small dark house, she made a swift sweeping motion with her pistol, ready to pump hot lead into anything moving. She pointed her pistol to the left. She pointed her pistol to the right. The inside of the house had the feel of a Danish cottage—modern aesthetic, mixed with a traditional, ethnic style. She could see this from the slight glimmer of glistening lamplight that shone from the back of the house.

There were books on a mahogany coffee table—Yohji Yamamoto's and Steve Martin's autobios. Pulitzer Prize-winning author Michael Chabon's *Telegraph Avenue* beckoned to have its spine cracked open to be devoured.

A few vinyl records were stacked against a wall and on the floor. Pink Floyd and the White Stripes. The walls were adorned with photographs of great blue herons, snowy egrets, and pelicans against a backdrop of impossibly blue sea.

Tables were festooned with potted succulents, air plants, even a Venus flytrap. More pictures, but of trees with leaves the color of 24-karat gold, gold turning quaking aspens and cottonwoods that blazed amber.

The kitchen was a small space off to the right. If you sneezed, you might miss it. Patricia slowly walked into the kitchen, the heart of the home. This had been the part of the house where the light flickered off, just before she nearly threw her arm out trying to break down the door.

Someone had abandoned a gigantic wooden bowl of salad—purple bok choy and redbor kale mixed with red-streaked mizuna.

There were two candles resting in mercury-glass candleholders. The candle wax melted down in gobs onto the table. A pack of Gauloise cigarettes were sitting on the table next to a plate of house made pickles and a lonely Reuben on light rye, loaded with delicatessen-style shreds of pastrami.

That's when Patricia saw something stir in her periphery to the right. The rest of the house was dark. The movement forced her stomach to groan a grotesque sound. With a quick sweeping motion, she brought her pistol to the place where she saw the movement, the crumpled blur that could easily be mistaken as an optical illusion.

A pale bare leg moved rapidly from the corner into an adjoining back room. It was a woman's leg—almost too pale and soft for someone living on Tybee Island, a coastal sun drenched oasis where tans were the rule rather than the exception.

"Police! Show your face now! Come out with your hands up in the air or I'll start shooting." Patricia said with mournful intensity and aggression. She didn't want to, but she would've lit that little cottage up if she had to. If she felt her life was in danger, she had the right to make the walls look like they were covered in polka-dot bullet wallpaper.

A rakish waif with mousy wet hair emerged from a back bedroom. Her two arms were twigs waving helplessly. A look of pure terror and anguish lived in her eyes. Thoughtful eyes. As she walked closer a scent of lemongrass and cloves grew strong. Then there was a subtle accompaniment of Sicilian mandarin, grapefruit peel, juniper, green mango—the aroma of the eternal sun-washed Mediterranean wrapped in clean 21st-century form. She had obviously just emerged from the shower.

"You're under arrest!" Patricia said.

The rakish girl wept copiously. She had Scandinavian features and Germanic cheekbones. Sloping shoulders and a graceful collarbone. She wore ecru yoga pants and a matching ecru low-cut shirt.

Patricia quickly wrestled the woman down to the floor. She didn't have any cuffs, so she simply patted her down and kept her pistol trained on the woman until back-up arrived.

"I'm Detective Garbutt. Who are you? What's your name and what's your relationship with Michael Roth?"

"Ginger Engstrom is my name," she said with a gleam in her eye, "Mike is my boyfriend."

"Is there a particular reason why you felt the need to run from me? If you would've simply opened the door when I first knocked I wouldn't have had to break your window. Is this your place or his?" Patricia took the woman's words with a grain of salt, knowing that intimate relationships made people palter.

"It's our home together. We live here together," Ginger Engstrom said.

The strepitous pug outside began to bark furiously. Someone was either on or near the front porch. Several police lights flickered and flashed as dusk began to set in. More neighbors sauntered closer to get a better perspective of what was going on at the white clapboard bungalow with the indigo trim.

Meanwhile, Jake was still chasing the suspect. They ran through traffic, nearly getting themselves killed by not one, but two trucks sitting up at least eight feet high — good-ole boy trucks, with men wearing confederate flag trucker hats at the wheel.

The night was warm and the breeze coming off the Atlantic gave off a Zen-like hush. This caused a chill to stir the air.

Michael Roth knocked down a woman who resembled Dolly Parton before running into Oysters at the Boat, a popular seafood restaurant. The woman with teased blonde hair and zinfandel painted nails toppled to the pavement in all her *Dollywood* glory.

Jake continued to chase the man. Jake was sweating profusely. Suddenly they found themselves among day trippers, bikers, kayakers, out-of-towners from as far as Tennessee and Kentucky.

There was nothing like ending the day with fresh oysters and cold beer. A few men sat at the bar craning over chilled mugs of craft beer. Orangey golden ale, stouts the color of ink, Belgian darks, and mouth puckering stouts poured from taps.

It was more tavern than restaurant at Oysters at the Boat. KISS, Willie Nelson and Grateful Dead sang from an antique juke box which was situated next to a ratty old couch — kitsch.

"Police! Stop! Police!" Jake yelled out.

Rex Baldwin might have made it to the back door and gotten away had it not been for a tall burly trucker who managed to stop him with one punch to his Adam's apple. The blow stopped him dead in his tracks.

Michael Roth flew backward and blacked out for a few minutes. When he regained consciousness the tall burly trucker had a big black Doc Martin pressed down on his chest, pinning him to the floor. Also, Jake was able to catch his breath, regain his composure and rally the help of Tybee Island's finest. Thank goodness for concerned citizens.

TWENTY-THREE

THE MONSTROSITY CASE that revolved around Deidre Priest and Michael Roth, also known as Rex Baldwin, grew into something altogether different than anyone imagined.

They came to learn that Michael Roth was using Rex Baldwin as an alias. The real Rex Baldwin was deceased. He'd been sleeping in his grave for the past fifteen years. Rex Baldwin was a crime and sometimes Sci-fi writer who hailed from Jekyll Island for many years.

His father and grandfather were both Neo Nazi Communist scientists who specialized in underground biological and chemical warfare tactics and technology.

He mentioned many of the research experiments that were financed by high ranking officials in the German, Soviet, and United States governments — MI-6, International intelligence agencies, and wealthy financiers which were performed on blacks, Jews, Native Americans, Hispanics, society's unwanted castaways, and the poor — pogroms that included mass sterilization, extinction and brain washing.

With their technology, they were able to craft a virus so powerful that it schlepped through entire villages in Libya, Somalia, Uganda, and Brazil and wiped out every living being.

Rex Baldwin inherited the journals from his father and grandfather—all detailing a mass genocide plan to control the population.

He included much of this in his writings. Extremely low vibration radiation was also used to wipe out entire classes of people that they believed were useless eaters who were using up the world's precious, finite, natural resources.

They had developed man-made plagues in their labs, which decimated the cells of the human body, from the inside out.

They designed and created diseases that could be transmitted sexually, airborne, and through contaminated water supplies in impoverished districts.

They were able to do these things under the guise of vaccinations, immunizations, and free food and water that was laced with highly toxic and deadly chemicals.

Detectives believed that Roth was acting out the murders that Rex Baldwin had previously written about, down to the gory details. He had studied every piece of literature this man had written.

The only thing left to do was to actually get their hands on much of the out-of-print works that Baldwin had penned. They believed they would find many more bodies and reheat many cases which had previously gone cold.

Michael Roth actually acquired false documentation and a false ID. His girlfriend Ginger Engstrom had no idea who she was dealing with. She'd never known the real Michael Roth and had no idea about the existence of Rex Baldwin. It was apparent that Michael Roth was obsessed with Rex Baldwin.

Rex Baldwin had written about a character named Roman Zebrinsky. Zebrinsky was a serial killer who had been sentenced to a mental institution in Uzbekistan for murdering and cannibalizing somewhere between fifty and one hundred women internationally.

He even served a few portions to his unknowing friends and family. He claimed he wanted to swallow the souls of his victims, thereby immortalizing them.

With a twisted ideology, Zebrinsky believed that he could freeze the gray matter of his victims to extract the substance of their DNA. Using references from his father's journals and findings, Baldwin's main character would surgically remove his victim's brains; extract the lymph and marrow from their bodies, claiming that he was imbibing the essence of their entire filial background.

Zebrinsky traveled the world over, murdering victims who he believed were descendants of ancient royalty, Black nobility, and the lost tribe of Judah's posterity.

With the black women, those who were the descendents of ancient Dogon tribes and the Egyptian priesthood, he would keep their cervical cells alive in test tubes in a bizarre belief that he was able to consume the life force from their melanin and the biochemical benefits of living on their pineal gland byproducts. That's where the detectives believed Deidre Priest and Ebony Cooper may have come in.

A few months had gone by. There was nothing more beautiful than fall with all its trappings. There was nothing more illustrious than fall foliage, bright golden needles of the larch, the occasional pastel lupine, sapphire delphiniums, quaking aspen, a deciduous conifer towering over poppies and Indian paintbrush. Velvety harvest hues.

Although Patricia was now taking high doses of Lunesta to remain asleep throughout the night, she and the family stole away to Anthony's parents' home in Connecticut for the last week of the kid's summer vacation. Every year, no matter how busy things were, they planned out their family vacation at the Bowers family home.

Anthony's mother Judy Kay greeted her grandchildren in all of her sartorial splendor and elegance. Smoky aquamarine dominated the room. Looking at Patricia in her faded denim and pulled back ponytail, Judy Kay opined. "Oh Patricia you should really stop wearing Wal-Mart makeup. It's bad for your pores," she said, glancing down at her Breguet timepiece.

Patricia rolled her eyes. Anthony's brown-eyed brother Frank—the one with perfectly windblown hair, studied fashion design at New York's Fashion Institute of Technology, and who had apprenticed at Gucci, Carolina Herrera and Nina Ricci said, "I doubt Wal-Mart even carries cosmetics mother. Anyhow, did you hear that Edvard Munch's

'Scream' sold for $120 million? Some hedge funder, I'll bet. I would have loved to get my hands on that beauty." He wasn't talking to anyone in particular. Just whoever might be listening.

His face was tucked between the pages of Fortune magazine. His children Charlie and Grace attended Andover and Hershey, respectively. Most of the year he worked from a studio apartment in N.Y.C's Chelsea. His wife was a German Baroness who owned diamond jewelry by Cartier and Van Cleef & Arpels. She refused to lift a finger. She never had and never would.

Anthony's other brother Larry, whose iPhone was ever present, and its ring always puncturing the silence, had married an Israeli-American woman and they lived in New Hampshire.

In spite of Judy Kay, Patricia, Anthony and the kids enjoyed their summer vacations in Greenwich, Connecticut. Everything about the home was warm and inviting; from the smoky aqua walls and furnishings in pale hues, to the zinc-topped potting bench where Grandpa Bowers would sit and tell the small children stories of when he fought in the war.

The simple comfort. The scent of peace, jasmine, honeysuckle, and apricot that seemed to loom omnipresent like the sun radiating from the tangy green peel of an unripe mango on the coast of Honduras.

The marble-lined walls in the bathroom. The guest bath with its spa-like ambiance. Deftly merged pieces. An ever present cool summer breeze.

Evergreen clematis shaded the pool arbor out back. There were tieback curtains in cream and Korean boxwoods to border individual areas.

Calla lilies, hydrangeas, soaring palms, crape myrtles, with creeping fig and clematis defining the courtyard walls.

The home's red-tiled roof and a quartet of chaise lounges greeted guests poolside. The 18th-century Gustavian demilune, which was always tucked neatly between a pair of armchairs that were covered in a Lee Jofa linen paisley. The whimsical fiery hues that emanated from the kitchen. The unexpectedly elegant pieces, including the 19th-century chinouserie table and 1950s Venetian glass floor lamp.

The bulk of their home was light flooded, wrapped with Paladian — the epitome of restful and relaxing. An Oushak rug inspired the living room's sage green and orange scheme.

Venetian lamps covered in orange Romo velvet and a pair of 19th century French chairs provided a fresh pop of color in the living room. The queridon table was from Parc Monceau. The Bowers had invested their money well and often spent six months out of the year traveling.

They had a vacation villa in Mustique that was to die for. In fact, they'd just gotten back from a fifteen day cruise in the Grand Caymans. Grandpa Bowers passed out Turks and Caicos souvenirs to everyone — t-shirts, key chains, caps, bottles of rum, and special handmade pieces crafted by the hands of the natives.

"We went to the Carlos Museum to hear a lecture about ancient Roman architecture and I thought of you, dad." Anthony remarked. "I remember how you once said how much of an impact Rome and Greece had on you."

The kids spent the long warm days rafting, playing tennis, lounging at the pool, mountain biking, and playing Frisbee with their cousins.

Anthony spent the days playing bridge with his father, studying nature photography, and golfing.

Patricia , when she wasn't on her laptop or on conference calls with Brody, was shooting trap and skeet, learning to knit, horseback riding, and at the shooting range. She loved going to the shooting range. She found it released stress better than anything on earth.

One day Anthony had come in from fishing for tarpon, bonefish, snook, and permit. His dad had caught a marlin, which apparently was a big deal. Anthony mentioned how much he missed having time to think, being out in the boat fishing with his dad, and how he missed being in the woods, the smell of his mother's pancakes or the country brusque scent of orange cinnamon French toast.

Anthony's eyes were cranberry red. He looked as though he had been crying. He was a man who had been defeated — defeated by life, by a shitty job and a boss that he absolutely loathed. He grew silent.

"What is the matter?" Patricia asked as though his feelings were eggshells.

"Everything," Anthony choked on the fibers of his words.

"I've been having this conversation with myself for the past... oh I don't know what, maybe the past year. I don't know how else to say it...we are flat out broke, Patty!" he said defiantly. The words escaped his lips in slow motion.

"What do you mean flat out broke?" Patricia looked up at her husband with pain leaking from both her voice and her eyes.

It was as though he spoke a foreign language. Patricia looked at her husband with wounded eyes and a sharp sparkly pain in her chest. Something was ripping apart in the center of her chest. Something was ripping apart and curling up on the edges.

"I thought my parents would be willing to bail us out of this one, but it's just too much. They told me that they just can't afford to keep loaning us anything with their retirement funds not being what they used to be. Be honest with you I think they're giving me the old run-around, but it's there fucking cash."

Patricia could feel the temperature in the room elevate. She grew hot under the collar. Her world was beginning to cave in on her like a building under demolition.

"How come you didn't say anything sooner?" she said.

Anthony swallowed. Patricia watched her husband's Adam's apple slowly move up and down.

"I didn't know how. I honestly didn't know how to come to you as my wife, to tell you that I had stopped paying the mortgage for the past six months."

At that moment, Patricia knew this was what lay at the root of their breakdown in communication. All of this time her husband had been putting on the biggest front in the history of their marriage.

"Is it something I did or said?" Patricia said. A lump was forming in her throat. She could feel her face flush pink. She could feel her heartbeat pumping through her face.

"No."

"Are you gambling?"

"No."

"Well what is it Tony? Why won't you tell me what the problem is? What's been preventing you from paying the bills? Why are we flat out broke?"

TWENTY-FOUR

EACH OF HIS WORDS were carefully chosen.

"I don't want you to be angry or upset with me. And the last thing I want you to do is to judge me but I just got caught up. I'm not as strong as I thought I was. I'm not who you think I am. Shit, Patty, I don't even know who I am anymore," Anthony said.

The texture of their marriage had deteriorated so completely that Patricia no longer recognized the man who had been her husband for the past twenty years. Here he was admitting that he was just a shell of the person he once had been.

"I have an addiction."

Patricia released a sigh. It was a sigh of frustration. She was a woman who had been betrayed—betrayed by her husband, the man she considered to be her best friend.

"It started with my addiction."

"Addiction! What are you addicted to?" Patricia's breathing changed. Suddenly breathing was becoming a labor intensive thing.

"Huh?" he stammered.

"What substance are you addicted to?"

"Anti-depressants. Will you just hear me out Patricia, please?"

She sat down and took a deep breath. All oxygen escaped the room in that moment. She tried to empty and fill her lungs with clean air. She sat before her husband like a great quarry of concrete.

She was no longer a woman, but an edifice of broken hope. The magic carpet ride of her once perfect marriage had met with turbulence. They'd had their share of ups and downs, but nothing quite like this.

"Go on. I'm listening." Patricia was suddenly more stoic than ever.

"It started with the addiction and getting creative with finding more and more access to different pharmacies and prescriptions. That's been going on for the past two years. But things really became impossible when I started having an affair with Claire."

"Who is Claire?"

"Claire is a girl who came on board with the company last year. She and her husband were going through a nasty divorce so I offered to help her get back on her feet after he left her and their three small children."

Patricia's chest tightened. She imagined her husband out on cool nights, arm in arm with some faceless woman—them fluttering about town like butterflies. Of course she imagined the woman was pretty, not just pretty, but beautiful. For Christ's sake, she imagined this other woman to be Vogue centerfold beautiful.

She imagined this Claire to be younger, with a smaller waistline, and much, much softer on the edges—a young woman with no major responsibilities. A damsel in distress. A woman with a waiting watering hole between her legs.

"Are you fucking kidding me Tony? What are you saying to me right now?" Patricia's voice rose vehemently.

"Keep your voice down in my parent's house," Anthony said between clenched teeth. "Have some respect. Claire needed me. Her husband literally walked out on her and those babies. This girl didn't even have money to buy toilet paper to wipe her behind. I'd go over there and there was nothing in her refrigerator — not one single can. I'd never seen anything like it."

"That's not your freaking problem, Anthony!" Patricia suddenly felt light-headed. She felt like she was going to faint. "Did you sleep with her, Tony? Did you have sex with this woman?" Her voice quivered from her lips like it belonged to another woman altogether.

He looked down at his feet or the floor, she couldn't tell which. He then began rubbing his hands together, like he was massaging the perspiration from his sweaty palms. "Yes. But it didn't start out that way. It started out as me trying to do something good for someone who needed an extra hand."

Patricia cast him a look full of perdition. Tears welled up in her eyes, to the point of overflowing. She began to weep.

"Do you love her?"

"Patty, why would you ask me a question like that? This isn't about whether I love her or not. I'm sitting here trying to tell you that I have not paid the mortgage and we are losing our house. I've been hiding the past due final notices from you. I have been scrimping and getting by with my parents' help. They're the ones who have been helping me at least keep the lights on. And...well the company let me go a few weeks ago."

"Are you serious, Tony? Are you fucking kidding me?" Patricia stood up and thrashed towards her husband. She threw several punches which landed heavily on the side of his face and one clipped his lip.

He grabbed her arms and held her tightly as his bottom lip bled and began to swell. For a moment she tried to fight him, but he was much stronger than she was. He held her until her anger died down. She cried silently as she pantomimed warfare. She tried to hold back tears by swallowing them, but Anthony's confession stung like the bite of a Black Mamba.

"I'm sorry. I'm so sorry. I feel horrible for what it's worth. And I can't begin to explain how torn apart it has me inside. I just don't know how I went from trying to help someone else out to this point where I've basically failed to protect you and the kids. I never thought in a million years that my parents would tell me no. I guess when the company finally let me go; it was the final coup, the final nail in the coffin. They told me I would have to try to figure this all out on my own," Anthony said. He began to cry too.

"So where do we go from here?" Patricia said. She was searching for truth. She was searching for something to grasp onto, anything. She felt like she was lost at sea without a life vest.

"We have to leave the house — if the Sheriff hasn't already put our things out on the curb when we get back to Georgia."

Patricia let out an exasperated sigh. "How could you do this to us, Tony? After all this time, after twenty years? How could you be so fucking weak?" Patricia said.

All of the strength had left her body. She had been steamed, pressed, and left out to dry. Her words were flimsy.

"I wish I could answer that. God, I wish I knew. I don't know Patty. I just don't know," he shook his head.

"Why would you wait until it got to this point to say something to me? If you had said something earlier maybe I could have done something to divert this path of destruction. This could have been prevented. All of this could have been prevented," Patricia's anger was beginning to rise again. She balled her fists.

TWENTY-FIVE

BY THE TIME the family returned to Georgia from Connecticut, something had broken. Anthony and Patricia hadn't touched one another in months and now she knew why. Now she understood why he had been conveniently falling asleep in the family room — his man cave.

Now she knew why he'd been so short with her and why he dragged his feet more often when she pleaded for him to do things around the house. The quarrel in the car the night Tyler accidently shot himself was like the calm before the storm compared to this.

They'd put on their best act in front of his family. They held hands and they kissed in the presence of his parents, but the truth was they were fragmented.

True to Anthony Eugene Bowers' word, when they rounded the corner to their block, they saw their furniture sitting in the driveway. A cold block of ice took the place of Patricia Garbutt's heart. She had no words. When Maria asked why all of their things were sitting outside, Patricia just covered her eyes. Her mouth was dry and the explanation refused to come forth.

"We're going to have to move," Anthony said wryly.

"No! Why do we have to move? I don't want to move!" Tyler shot up in his seat. He had been half asleep, but the gravity and tension of the situation woke him.

"I don't want to move either. All of my friends are here in this neighborhood. Will I still be able to go to the same school?" Maria whined.

"You haven't even started your new middle school, Maria! How can you miss something you've never known? Give me a break," Anthony said.

Patricia remained silent, but inside she bubbled with rage. Someone once said deep waters run silent. Her waters ran deep, but she could explode at any moment, like lava cooking beneath Earth's surface. She was liable to erupt at any time.

Was this the end? Was this the beginning of the end? A hollow sinking feeling surfaced in the pit of her stomach.

"Okay, everyone just relax. There's no sense in getting hysterical right now. We'll just have to figure this out together," Patricia said in her best strong voice. "Everything will be fine. We'll get through this like we get through everything...as a family."

They saw their neighbor Mary Margaret Oliver standing outside sweeping her front walkway and then watering the plants and flowers on her porch.

"I. Don't. Want. To. Move! And you can't make me. I won't do it!" Maria said indignantly.

"Maria, I don't need you to be a Drama Queen right now. You will do exactly what you are told to do, and you know what...just shut up. Shut your mouth, sit back and don't utter a single peep." Patricia turned around in her seat and screamed.

"I hate you! I'm fucking sick and tired of you both!" Maria shouted. Then she proceeded to open the car door, and jumped out, as the car was still moving. She nearly broke her neck tumbling onto the asphalt. Skinning knees and elbows in the process.

Anthony brought the car to a screeching halt, hopped out, and checked on his daughter.

TWENTY-SIX

AUTUMN CAME EARLY. The creeping Ivy that lived on the tall birch tree on the side of the house began turning a beautiful shade of crimson. Several leaves on neighboring trees in the area also began to transition into honey reds, golden ambers, and spicy mustards. Everything changed.

The breeze of fall took on a new texture.

On a fog-whipped afternoon, under a clay slate-colored sky, the Garbutt-Bowers clan faced their lowest low as a family. Anthony Bowers wasn't the type of man who would just fall off the wagon. The kids were confused and hurt. Patricia had to think of something fast, but as smart as she was, she didn't know how to factor life without her husband in the equation.

The universe seemed to be conspiring against her. Felt like she was under attack. When good things didn't come easy, she appreciated them all the more. She enjoyed the fruits of her labor and believed in hard work as the answer to all things. When tough times became the norm, she grew thicker skin.

People never truly knew how good they had it until the security they once enjoyed was suddenly taken away from them. As a family, they learned that anything could be taken away; at any time.

For the first few nights Patricia and the kids crashed at Jake's place. It was awkward but more than anything it embarrassed Patricia. It embarrassed her to have to sleep on an air mattress along with Tyler and Maria.

Jake's son Noah was a necessary distraction for Tyler. He'd finally received the brother he always wanted. Anthony claimed he was staying in a co-worker's basement, but Patricia felt deep down that was his ploy and he was probably staying with Claire.

As November's brisk winds ushered in a shift in seasons Detective Garbutt fell into a depression of her own—a depression that was darker than the Mississippi river. They were able to salvage a few things of sentimental value like their beds, old family photo albums, vital copies of birth certificates and passports, a low-slung leather butterfly chair, and a French antique armoire.

Most of all it was the home with its storied past, and the neighborhood that was full of trees as old as the house which made Patricia dovetail into her dark place. After the sting wore off and they were able to put furniture into a storage facility, Patricia and the kids moved in with her mother Mrs. Ortiz.

It was a small two-bedroom apartment in a complex designed for retirees and the convalesced. Lisa stayed there too. Patricia, Maria and Tyler slept together on her trusty air mattress that she'd purchased from Big Lots. It was uncomfortable and impossibly difficult for everyone involved. The apartment was small, the rooms cramped, and they were packed tight like pickles in a jar.

Mrs. Ortiz was a fiery, feisty, Belizean woman. She woke up before the sun each morning. Along with the faint sound of a neighbor's pet rooster, on any given morning you could hear Mrs. Ortiz up cooking breakfast, wrapping banana leaves, and ironing clothes. "Grauma use to seh an empty crocus bag kant stan up. Now eat up my chile!" This meant you couldn't work if you were extremely hungry.

Tyler and Maria loved and respected their "Grauma," who loved and doted on them. When Maria asked her why her mother never took them to Belize so they could meet other relatives, Mrs. Ortiz simply said "Blood tika dan wata but wata tase betta," and chuckled her throaty heavy chuckle which always made her entire body shake.

Although the apartment was small and cramped, laughter was always floating up to the sky. Love was their constant companion.

Anthony's addiction to *Abilify* didn't subside. Soon he'd slipped into a methadone-induced stupor that turned him into a nodding mess. He continued seeing Claire until Claire finally put him out.

He would go for days without washing his body or his clothes. He removed his shoes one night and the odor and funk was so devastating and emetic that Claire vomited.

There were rumors that he was living on the streets. Those liquid cuffs prevented him from getting back to normalcy. Yet and still, Patricia couldn't bring herself to file divorce papers.

Tyler had to be withdrawn from the Paideia School and subsequently registered into the local public school. Maria was disgusted in her new school, a low class, inner city, urban Mecca.

She was forced to rub elbows with peasants. What's worse, she'd become a peasant. More and more, she was beginning to fall victim to Lisa's negative influence. Lisa was binging again. Maria's grades went into freefall.

Detective Garbutt and Detective Billingsley sat side by side in their office. They were going over the details of the Michael Roth case. He'd been released on bail and they were attempting to gather as much evidence as possible. There was twenty-four hour hidden surveillance around him and Detective Garbutt ordered a tap to be placed on his phone.

The good thing was they had the Deputy District Attorney and the Prosecutors on their side. Lee Chong was a bulldog and won over seventy-five percent of his cases, winning Fulton County countless prosecutions.

"After seeing how absolutely heartless this monster acted in court, I doubt he's incapable of anything. You should have seen him at his arraignment," Jake let out a sigh.

"Lee Chong said he was as stoic and heartless as Mount Rushmore." Patricia told.

"I've got to show you something. The CSI's results came back from the lab. Apparently they found one hundred and forty-four vials of human DNA and remains. But get this, just about all of them are people linked to various public figures." Jake admitted.

"I'm not following you?"

"They found DNA belonging to Kissinger, Rockefeller, Rothschild, Kennedy, and a few more heavyweights. Can you believe that? I'm still wondering how this guy got Kennedy DNA," Jake snorted.

"Either Roth is brilliant or he's a sadist." Patricia opined.

"Or both," Jake reiterated.

"Are you serious? Why one hundred forty-four?" Detective Garbutt raised an eyebrow.

"I don't know. Maybe in reference to the whole Bible prophecy about only one hundred and forty-four thousand souls being saved from judgment at the end of the world," Jake replied.

"Wow! That's right. I almost forgot that one hundred and forty-four thousand chosen people are supposed to continue humanity, according to the Mayan calendar as well as the Holy Bible. What a crock of bullshit? Geez, this guy doesn't play around, does he? He really knows his stuff, huh?" Patricia said sardonically. Sarcasm doused the air.

"Either that or he's one sick and crazy son-of-a-bitch!"

"He's definitely one sick son-of-a-bitch!" Detective Garbutt agreed.

"They found them mostly in a bunch of deep freezers located deep down in the basement of the house we visited in Tybee. They found pubic hair, skin cells, fingernail clippings, toes, tongues, pancreases, livers, a few spleens, brains, nipples, foreskins, eyeballs, ears, a significant number of hearts...I can't recall the exact number," Jake said, as he reached across his desk for a file folder.

"Yikes!" Detective Garbutt commented. "How did the girlfriend not know that all of these body parts were scattered around in their basement? Somebody is lying. This just isn't adding up. Impossible."

"Right! I said the same thing, but she still maintains her innocence and even claims that Roth lied to her as well."

Silence set in for a moment. Detective Billingsley grabbed the folder and opened it. After flipping through a few pages, he handed his partner a sheet with more facts from the case on it.

"They were renting the house from an old geezer. When we told him about what was happening in his house without his knowledge, he nearly suffered a stroke. This guy is a certified psychopath. He passed his polygraphs with flying colors!" Billingsley chewed the inside of his cheek.

"Twinkle toes, you're killing me!" Patricia said. "Flying colors?" she was taken aback.

This was the type of case that made Detective Billingsley feel he was at the top of his game. They had their prime suspect pinned against the ropes. They had a mountain of evidence, but they couldn't immediately convict him. They couldn't prove that he killed Deidre Priest or Ebony Cooper, for that matter. All they could prove, without a shadow of a doubt at the time, is that he was behind some seriously heinous and gruesome homicides.

The results had come in on Deidre Priest and she was definitely the Jane Doe that they'd found at Sweetwater. The jury was still out on Ebony Cooper. She was still missing. The detectives in Baltimore were dragging their feet and shrouded in Bureaucratic red tape.

TWENTY-SEVEN

THEY CONSULTED THE expertise of Forensic Anthropologists from the University of Georgia and Forensic Pathologists from Emory University.

They also solicited the advice and assistance of Dr. Paige Porter-Fischer, one of the elite. Dr. Paige Porter-Fischer was an Emory University Forensic Entomologist who studied insects relating to decomposition of a human body. She was able to help them connect more dots with Eileen Rosenthal's remains. Even still, they continued looking for leads.

It was more to working a homicide case than just finding out who did it—the detectives were also trying to sniff out motive. What made a man like Roth commit such mayhem? Why? It was the minute details that could make or break this case. Not only did the reports need to be precise and concise, but each lead needed to be exhausted whether it pointed to a dead end or not.

It was up to them to separate fact from fiction. And working with district attorneys to complete the chain in the justice system was another kettle of fish.

Each case was different. The details surrounding Deidre Priest were unique to the details surrounding Eileen Rosenthal. The ancient Lotus Sutra script threw them for a loop.

Over the years working homicide, Detective Patricia Garbutt found that each case took her down a different avenue. Each and every person involved knew someone who knew someone else, and so on.

Maintaining balance between her family life, the situation with Anthony's meteoric demise, and the job was beginning to take its toll. She was growing more stress hair by the day. Tyler once called gray hair stress hair, when he was younger. Out of the mouth of babes.

"Who bonded Roth out?" Brody poked his head in through the door of their shared office.

"His mother did," Patricia answered.

"Have you gotten the results of the polymerase chain reaction from either of the bodies that were discovered?"

Detective Garbutt stared blankly at Jake. As usual, he rose to the occasion and came to her rescue.

"We're waiting for the results of the more accurate restriction fragment length polymorphism method from the crime lab. We know for a fact that Roth used bleach on his hands—" Jake trailed off.

"Which destroyed any blood and DNA evidence," Patricia sounded off.

Brody grumbled. "And what about prints? Were any found on the car that was found in Mechanicsville?"

"Nothing. After several hours on the scene, it looked like we took baths in fingerprint powder," Patricia ruminated.

"So let me get this straight, why do you guys think its Roth behind the Priest murder? Didn't something in the report mention that she and the boyfriend had a quarrel of sorts? Why hasn't he been charged?" Brody squinted as though the sun was in the building. His already pink face began to grow a bureaucratic red-tape red.

Jake stood up and took the brunt of Brody's wrath. "Well sir, the boyfriend, Akil Allah, has been questioned extensively. To be quite honest, we don't have enough evidence against him to charge him."

"Plus he has an airtight alibi," Patricia opined.

"And even though her body was nearly wrecked with its badly swollen and misshapen face, waxy gray skin and hideous livor mortis and postmortem hypostasis, we still were able to find a few of Roth's hair fibers and semen on her," Jake said.

"The soft tissue around the carvings in her skin had been dissected carefully, layer by layer, to create a three-dimensional representation of the instrument used. The crime lab found that the exact same scalpel and henna used on Eileen Rosenthal was also used on Deidre Priest," Patricia blurted.

Brody said nothing after that. He shook his head that he understood and continued to his office. He had a subtle limp from where he'd caught a bullet in his left thigh many years ago. Donning a classic middle age salt and pepper comb-over, Brody had a plump belly from years and years of good meals. If you were listening closely when he spoke, you could hear the faint remnants of his Chechnyan heritage. His mind was quick and nimble though.

Jake and Patricia gave each other a knowing stare weighty with unspoken innuendo.

Just then, Eric Asimov, another detective, popped his head in the office.

"Hey Jake, you busy?" he said with a rough grainy raspy voice.

"What's up?"Jake said, as he plopped his folder down onto his desk.

"So listen to this. I just got back from some ghetto apartment complex. Wait for it…this young hood rat leaves her two kids alone in the place. Two years old and six years old. There was *zero* electricity and to add insult to injury, she leaves the oven door open for heat. The Fisher Price flashlight cop was doing his rounds and finds the back door open, where someone's Pit bull had wandered in through the back door and was doing his business in one of the rooms. So he goes in and finds the six year old and two year old looking bug-eyed and frightened. Apparently, the mother had gone to a friend's place to charge her cell phone. Needless to say, she's in custody and the kids are with DEFACS."

Jake threw his head back and roared laughter. Eric broke out into laughter. Patricia was accustomed to this type of locker room banter and shot them both a solemn eye roll. "You can't be serious, Asimov? What in the hell was she thinking!"

"Garbutt, I'd never tell a lie."

All three detectives broke into infectious laughter.

TWENTY-EIGHT

THE HOLIDAYS ARRIVED like a menstrual cycle on wedding night—without an evite, text message, announcement or warning. One moment everyone was wearing tank tops, cut-off jeans, and flip flops, and the next moment girls could be seen wrapped in fleece scarves and Ugg boots.

One day it was summer and the next day there were commercials for the latest Christmas gadgets and toys.

Apple released the iPad mini and an iPhone 5 that was more coveted than the Holy Grail. Amazon released a new and improved Kindle Fire. Starbucks was selling their seven dollar eggnog lattes and peppermint mochas in their signature red Christmas cups with reindeer antlers and Hanukkah Menorah outlines.

It was all shits and giggles until Hurricane Sandy came with all of her vengeance and malice. She left countless hundreds of thousands of people without electricity. Overnight, the subway system in pockets of New York City and her outer boroughs were flooded. Torrential rains and five-knot winds had downed the entire northeastern seaboard. They lost their electricity, but not their power.

It was phenomenon like this that brought Americans together. Calamity had a peculiar way of bringing people together who hated one another. The universe knew just what to do to get our attention. For the intolerant angry birds, it sometimes required chaos and no pity. However, even in the midst of bedlam and misfortune we find our greatest assets and an inner strength that often catapults us to greater heights.

President Barack Obama was re-elected for another term. Four more years of hard times for the American people. Four more years of drones killing innocent Pakistani civilians. Congress had driven itself to a fiscal cliff and the blind fervently lead the blind.

The day after the election, the stock market tripped and took a nasty fall down Wall Street. It would be a cold winter, and not because of the waltz of the snowflakes.

For the first time in American history, the government was unable to pay its bills. The treasury was courting bankruptcy and the debt ceiling had a gun in its side. That was the American reality, according to CNN and Fox News.

When Wall Street sneezed, the world caught the flu. Mayhem befell many parts of the Western world. There were earthquakes, massive mudslides, wars and rumors of wars.

The people of Greece had taken to the streets in civil unrest because like America the great, their government was broke too. They were sick and tired of their elected officials lying to them and mishandling their tax dollars.

People continued living their lives in quiet desperation. The population continued to expand. More infants were born. Globally, endless war marched on seamlessly into endless war. Syria continued to antagonize Turkey. Israel continued to terrorize Palestine along the Gaza strip.

The nation's five largest banks were collapsing under their weight. For once, the giants like Bank of America, Goldman Sachs, Citigroup, Morgan Stanley, and JP Morgan Chase were shaken at their foundations and were faced with a lawsuit that would have uncontested repercussions and consequences.

TWENTY-NINE

EACH DAY WAS pregnant with possibility. Wintry weekends led to Joshua trees turning black against the sky. Michael Roth was brought back into custody. One look at his handiwork and the way he fled on foot that day on Tybee Island and the judge knew why the prosecution called him a flight risk.

The first interview Jake and Patricia sat down together with the lunatic who assumed the identity of Rex Baldwin and baffled them for months.

He was reticent. It was like trying to squeeze blood out of a beet. He was a massive presence in a small frame. Refusing to sit in the chair provided for him, he sat in lotus position in a corner. Claimed that he was observing something called *Vipassana*—said that he saw things as they actually were, as opposed to the illusion that everyone else lived in.

Sergeant Joel Gilbert said that Roth had arranged his space to resemble a monastic setting and said that he would sit in meditation for hours on end, even abstaining from food. He would sit in the mess hall among the other inmates, in his own atmospherically distant dimension. With pursed lips, he merely sat quiet and serene, during the initial interview with Jake and Patricia. Noble Silence was what he called it.

The second interview though, he was an open book. Jake was on vacation and Patricia was itching to get some questions answered.

"What a pleasure it is to see you this morning, Detective Garbutt. To whom do I owe the pleasure," Roth said in a nimble watery voice. Even in his prison issued orange jumpsuit he was polished and manicured. Neatly trimmed polished fingernails and close edged haircut.

There was a glow about the man.

"Well, I'm not so sure about that. We'll see just how much of a pleasure it is seeing me after you're convicted of mutilating those women. Why did you do it anyway, huh? Tell me that."

It was cold outside. The hawk landed early this season in the Peach State. It brought with it a biting chill that permeated down to the bone marrow. It left freezer burn and numb fingertips and toes if you stayed out in it too long. It was big sweaters — flannel coats — whiskey in flasks — plaid wool blankets type of weather.

One morning when Patricia ventured out in the early morning hours to take the trash out to the community garbage bin, her hair froze before she made it back inside Mrs. Ortiz' apartment. Yet it was much more arctic in the interview room.

A chill stirred when the security clearance bell buzzed to lock her in the interview room with him. The table and the chair were both cold and sterile. "I'm just here to free the silver butterfly that sleeps in the golden cocoon," he implored. His eyes were as gray as winter sky and hard like carbon steel.

She shuddered. "What's that supposed to mean? Excuse me for not matriculating through Hogwarts School of Wizardry, Harry," Patricia exclaimed.

Michael Roth leaned forward, licked his lips and whispered, "You know many of the ascended masters are walking around as ordinary as dental assistants and housewives. This is the reaping season...a gathering of the masters. This is a time to throw off the outward realities."

Patricia leaned back and sighed. Rubbing the bridge of her nose with her thumb and forefinger, she said. "Okay Michael Roth, explain everything to me like I am a third grader. Go slow and start from the beginning." She was stuffed from one of Mrs. Ortiz' big country breakfasts.

Her mother cooked tomato soup, grilled cheese sandwiches, pancakes, warm buttered cornbread, and hot cocoa and she forced everyone in the house to eat until they felt they would spontaneously combust. Patricia felt her stomach bubble with gas.

"Every great revolution comes about slowly. And with every great revolution, there's a changing of the guards. There is bloodshed. There is gold. There is heightened emotion. There is death. There can be no rebirth or renewal without bloodshed."

"Okay."

"We all incarnate on this planet like undeveloped rolls of film—full of precious potential. Very few of us remember why we've arrived here. Along the way, some of us even forget our mission. But it's our job to fulfill our destiny and to develop from the negatives. It's our duty to develop in the dark rooms of our journeys. Only then can we transform and develop and ascend."

His eyes became warm pools of light. Patricia glanced down at the floor and gave Michael Roth her shiny forehead. "You know Rome was the first country to not cancel debts. It was the first country that stripped its own citizens in the name of Western democracy and progress. Progress says 'you'll never get back what we lend you.' That's when more wealth began to accumulate in the coffers of the rich, and in the hands of the few," he murmured.

"Are you working for someone? Is that what you're trying to tell me? You're speaking Greek right now," she retorted.

"Maybe, maybe not."

"If you cooperate with us we may be able to give you a sweetheart deal. That's if you cooperate with us."

Michael Roth giggled hysterically. It was garish and immature and it was the sign of an insane man. "Have you seen the carbon footprint of someone in America or Europe versus say someone in Bangladesh? In fifteen thousand years human evolution hasn't changed much. Every five to seven years there's economic calamity and every time History repeats itself we pay for it, prices go up, lives are lost and wars are waged. My people are destroyed for lack of knowledge, for repeating History—the History we choose to ignore," he ranted.

"Is that why you murdered them? Why mutilate them? Why did you dissect them like fetal pigs? Where's the humanity in that, Roth?"

"It's the debt pushers, the World Bank, IMF, the controllers, those who sit behind the veil pulling the puppet strings of every world leader. Enron. LIBOR. Madoff. Those who introduced usury to exclude the peasantry and the working class with their goddamned interest rates. Interest makes you pay nine times the amount you borrow. The working class poor man's interest is the debt pusher's capital gains. That's the name of the game," he laughed again.

"So what, you're Robin Hood now? Doing this for the common folk?" she felt her stomach roll and buckle beneath her navel. It felt like the lining of her stomach was separating from her upper and lower intestines.

"I'm saying collapse is inevitable when economics is disconnected from reality; when unlimited economic progress moves along in a world of finite natural resources."

The air in the room became blustery and billowy. She shifted in her seat. "Embrace my aesthetic. My childhood was spent living in the Louisiana Bayou. This is what becomes of a man who has spent time living in Singapore. Do you want to know who I really am Detective Garbutt? Would you like to psycho-analyze me? Eh, Patricia Garbutt?" he fumed, nearly growling.

"Yes, tell me who you are. And while you're at it, why don't you explain to me why you basically have imitated Rex Baldwin. Are you so obsessed with him that you want to be him? And why did you feel the need to call me personally on my cell phone with the voice changer? Why Eileen Rosenthal? What did she have to do with all of this? What did Deidre Priest have to do with money hungry debt pushers?"

"Not why, but who? It's who they were...whose they were. It has everything to do with their genetic code, their bloodline, their lineage. Everything from Pegasus to Prometheus is a telling of our story."

"Okay, there's a great place to start. How about you tell me more about you. Tell me more about your childhood," Patricia indulged Michael Roth. Tickled his fancy. Played the cards he dealt.

He smiled. Still sitting Indian style in the chair, he reached out his handcuffed hands, palms facing upward. "My mother, she was a woman with rough-hewn sophistication."

Undulating waves of nausea befell Patricia. Gas darted around in her stomach, almost as though she would have an explosive bowel movement any second, but she couldn't leave. Not now, just when she was beginning to pull back the layers of Michael Roth.

She wished she'd brought her own tape recorder. The room was bugged, so all of this was being recorded, but that was beside the point. She couldn't think clearly and absorb everything at the same time. The body language and subtle nuances.

"Pop was a working man. A gnomic figure with tousled white hair, he always smelled of old factories and grime. His family was from Bollnäs, about one hundred and fifty miles from Stockholm...before Sweden went to shit. He was the first one to tell me that the same hands that deal in rosaries deal in pornography and pedophilia; he explained how hypocrisy reigns supreme! I grew up in a world of Japanese style monthlies and Scandinavian architecture. I fought for this country. Reckon I never did shape up to be much of a military man. I've been stationed in Hong Kong, Seoul, Tokyo, Frankfurt, Moscow..." he trailed off.

Patricia thought about how the crime lab found the exact same scalpel and henna were used on Eileen Rosenthal and Deidre Priest. At that moment she wanted to ask him about the significance of the Lotus Sutra script that he'd engraved on both women — why all of the pomp and ancient script? She wondered.

Why the need for the extensive post mortem personalization? But she held back. She allowed him to continue on with his musings. Surely a morsel of truth would fall from the plate eventually.

What she could gather for certain was that Michael Roth was a constellation of unlike parts.

"I fell in love with the girl with the poppy tattoo," he said. "She always had bitchin weed that would take all my troubles away. She took away the pain. She made life bearable again," Roth continued.

"Is that the woman you share a home with?"

"No, she's just a cunt who pays the bills. The girl with the poppy tattoo taught me things," he looked like he thought of faraway lands. "She taught me about the planetary alignment and how the Earth periodically and systematically would recalibrate herself and her vibration. She showed me how several key earthquakes would shift the planet off its axis. She gave me prophesy," he paused and took a deep cleansing breath. His chest rose and fell slowly.

"She taught me about crystals, cures, healing and the moment when all that has been lost will be found. She gave me hope."

"Mmm hmm," Patricia nodded.

"She taught me about the three days of darkness, the significance of the black sun and Venus with the partial eclipse. She gave me my mission, gave meaning to my life. She told me who was who and what was what. From that moment forward my eyes were open. I could perceive and discern the truth from the lies. It wasn't easy unlearning all the bullshit they indoctrinate us with, all over the globe. But I'm a better man for it."

"Is this when you started killing?"

Michael Roth gave Patricia Garbutt a solemn gaze. "There are some serious Draconian forces loose in this world—a whole galaxy of evil. They are lodged in every system of the Western world. They control the banking and the media, education, entertainment, politics, you name it."

"Quit the bullshit, Roth! I don't have time for conspiracies. Are you going to give me answers or are you going to continue to blow smoke up my ass?" Patricia yelled in a fit of indignation and anger.

Roth sat back slowly and began to laugh. "Emotion. Good. How very cute. I was beginning to think you were one of their little androids. As I was saying before your outburst, there are forces of evil that are so malicious and they are fascinated with our genetics. And that is why I grew interested in their genetics. I was able to trace certain bloodlines back to the twelfth century and beyond."

"Okay, and—"

"And I found that their primary motive and goal is absolute power and control—and greed is what feeds them. If you study the dolphin, you'll learn that dolphins send out a type of signal that paralyzes its prey just before they eat. Well, these entities, these men have this same type of technology, and they're able to paralyze minds through remote controls and signals they send out in our cell phones, televisions, and by radio waves. So I found a way to access some of the programs they use," he bellowed.

"How did you go about that?" Patricia found that suddenly she was being sucked into his narrative. She was fascinated with what he had to say.

He looked deep into her eyes. He looked into her soul. "Pull yourself out of the old paradigm that

151

was erected by the architect of this universe, that old demiurge from the fall. By fall I don't mean the fall they sold you in the bible. I mean the fall of a downward spiral. Now we are in an upward spiral. There are universes outside of this universe, demiurges and matrices outside of this matrix. Time is moving faster than ever before. The planet is ascending to new dimensions. Those people whose souls I took have given me the power to see into entire new realities."

"What kind of realities?" Patricia said in a weak and flimsy voice. The gas in her stomach had finally subsided.

"I've known you before Detective Garbutt," he said in the same exact voice he used over the phone when he called to lead them to Deidre Priest's remains. He literally changed his voice mid-conversation. She didn't believe anything like that was possible. It shook her to her core.

She tried to remain calm. She tried to keep her composure, but she felt like either she was losing her mind, or he was working some sort of Voodoo on her.

THIRTY

THE LONGER DETECTIVE Garbutt sat with Michael Roth the more she understood how easily he was able to elude authorities.

Here was a man who was deceptive, maniacally brilliant, and insane all at the same time. Patricia tried to swim through the acres of his bullshit to get to some sort of semblance of truth. She listened and tried to glean answers and revelation. She needed a confession. But it was apparent Michael Roth was careful about every word that left his mouth.

The truth of the matter was he did have some valuable things to say about the economy, money and the transfer of wealth. She really had never looked at things from this vantage point.

That was the upside of dealing with some of the most brilliant criminals — sometimes you were able to catch a glimpse of their ideology.

"Are there any more bodies? Is there anything else you want to share with me, Michael Roth? I feel like you're wasting my time and I don't have much more to give," Patricia sighed.

Michael Roth was silent. His face turned granite. The gray of his eyes became two iron marbles that penetrated its prey. Suddenly Patricia felt paralyzed. She couldn't move her arms or legs. All she could move were her eyes.

She tried to lift her right hand, tried to get the attention of the guards who stood just outside the door, but that was to no avail.

"Humanity has been made into a food source, Detective Garbutt. You've come here to question my actions and you can't even keep your life in order."

Her breath caught in her throat. She shivered as a league of Goosebumps materialized on the outskirts of her flesh.

"That's right, Detective Garbutt, I know all about you." He leaned in closer and spoke just above a whisper. His breath was tart. Veins grew and contracted in his neck. "Your marriage is in the toilet. Your husband would rather touch junk than you. Your children hate and don't respect you. After twenty years, you're moving backwards— had to run home to momma! You don't know what direction your life is heading in because it's all over the place—"

Patricia's heart sped and her breathing grew shallow. "Shut up! Just shut up! Shut up! You don't know shit! You don't know a goddamned thing about me," she tried to stand her ground but it was too late.

He was already inside her head. He began laughing hysterically. The longer he laughed, the more she despised him, but she still couldn't move a muscle. How could he know those things? How could he read her life so simply like it was a Twitter trending topic or the front page story of the New York Times?

"Don't you understand that you're just another cog in the wheel; another screw in the machine? You don't even know that you're just micro chipped cheap labor. When you finally lose your mind completely and topple over from the weight of stress, Fibromyalgia, Lupus, or when cancer begins to chew away at your internal organs, they'll just replace you with a new well read, exotic-looking Belizean or Boricua beauty. Sure they'll toss you a gold watch and a puny pin or metal of honor for all of your hard work and dedication on the force, but ultimately, they will have robbed you of the best years of your life. They'll siphon every last shred of life from your veins just before your heart gives out, and what do you have to show for it? A failed marriage with a dim wit that never could amount to anything more than premature ejaculation and latent erectile dysfunction?" There was spit in the corners of his mouth.

In that moment, Patricia hated him, but she hated herself more. Everything he said was fact. Not only had he struck a chord, but he was playing it like a mandolin.

"Code Red! Code Red!" Roth said in a creepy voice. "Isn't that what you're thinking? Two to three billion people need to be exterminated, starting with those in the bush, towel heads and the niggers, spics, kikes, homosexuals, retards, welfare queens, leeches of the system, and the rest of the useless eaters. Anything that can be separated isn't real. If your CSI do their job properly, you'll see that beneath and within the Lotus Sutra, is the Secret Covenant. The hidden mysteries. The keys to the Akashic Records. The sacred, secret knowledge. Because those women held the answers to all that was, all that is, and all that will be right there in the cells of their bodies."

Was this a confession? Was Michael Roth confessing to murdering Deidre Priest and Eileen Rosenthal? What about Ebony Cooper? By now, Patricia felt as though her bladder would burst and her bowels would explode all over the room like silly string.

She knew he was right. She was carrying an incredible load, especially since she and Anthony had their falling out. In the past week alone, her stress levels had reached Code Red.

While she and the kids were staying with her mother, Mrs. Ortiz was not only charging her rent, but she was running her ragged with demand after demand. Now she understood what sent Papi to an early grave—it was Mamí and her demands and constant meddling. There was a distinct difference between giving up and being fed up.

If Mrs. Ortiz wasn't stuffing her with over-saturated cholesterol laden carbohydrates and fat, she was demanding her to drive Lisa here and there, to pick her up, and to go to the market.

"Is that why you murdered them in cold blood?" Patricia said between clenched teeth. "You listen and you listen good. I will not stop until I pin your ass with a murder in the first degree and personally see to it that you rot in this place, if I find out that you murdered those women," suddenly regaining her motor movement. All the while, she was repeating 'Secret Covenant, Secret Covenant; Akashic records, Akashic records,' so she'd remember to research them as soon as she got a chance.

"Oh, I wouldn't be too sure of that Detective Patricia Garbutt. You don't have much time left, *mija*!" Michael Roth said calmly. "We play these roles — so much social conditioning — and we believe it's who we really are. But life unfolds spontaneously with each moment. It's only when we believe this to be real that it becomes a problem. Material reality is an illusion, Detective Garbutt!"

"Oh yeah? Are those handcuffs an illusion too?" She smirked, stood to her feet, fixed her blouse and headed towards the door. One thing was for certain, she was a changed being. She wasn't the same coming out of that interview room, as she had been when she emerged.

THIRTY-ONE

JAKE WAS OUT on a date with Aurora Suggs. They were having dinner at a place in downtown Newnan, called the Cellar.

Jake had heard a bunch of hoopla about the Cellar and decided to see if it was worth the hype. It was a contemporary space with blond-oak floors. The air was rich with the smells of Moroccan-spiced duck breast, smoked pork pot-pie and grits with bacon jam and plenty of hangar steak. Then there was lobster, lamb, smoked salmon, and grilled vegetables.

The walls were hung with gray-brown planks of weathered wood. Plants dangled from nautical ropes. The floors were constructed of antiqued stone and there was a pristine shade of paint on cabinets leading into the dining area.

Tablecloths were as crisp as the wait staff's shirts. Upon entering the building, you were treated to the melodic sounds of a beautiful black baby grand piano. Coltrane's 'Lazy Bird'. The space provided ample glass: floor−to−ceiling windows that overlooked the downtown square. It gave patrons the sense of being in a miniature Manhattan or Seattle, maybe even Austin.

He and Aurora parked a few blocks down and walked across the street to where the restaurant sat staring at a shuttered service station and down the road from a tattoo shop with a prominent window display.

He'd worn his Baume & Mercier polished and satin-finished steel watch—a timepiece worth over four grand. He got his hands on it through illegal means, but who would notice?

Over the years, Jake got his hands dirty a few times by taking payola to keep his mouth shut on several key cases. Dirty money paid better than the city of Atlanta or Fulton County.

It broke his heart to hear about drug deals, where ATF seized millions of dollars worth of product, only to have to burn it or turn it over to the feds. Not him though. No sir. He would always keep a little for himself, for a rainy day. He learned from the best...Brody. The department was crawling with dirty cops and even dirtier detectives.

He glanced over at Aurora Suggs. She looked terrific that night. She wore a bohemian necklace and a seductive black number. She arrived at the Cellar like the ball in Times Square. She wore a fiery lipstick by the name of Zeus. Only a certain woman could get away with wearing lipstick named Zeus. But being functional was better than being fabulous—Jake was falling in love with the way Aurora Suggs' mouth felt and even more with the way she felt when he was inside of her.

Under the faintly dim warm dusky lights of the restaurant, her eyes looked chlorine blue against backdrops of chartreuse. She smelled of lavender, orange blossom honey, kumquat and pomegranate.

Ever the arbiter of the eccentric, Jake stirred a Negroni and just before that, he'd ordered a shot of Vodka. He looked around and took in the rich, layered, collected, warm and expensive ambiance of the diners. There was old money in downtown Newnan, Georgia. Who would have ever thought?

There were votive candles on each table, giving faces a soft glow. Some had a vase with dahlias and mums.

Aurora sneezed violently, then again. She shook the table and nearly extinguished the candle flame. She took a sip of the warm mulled cider she'd been babysitting—the same cup she took one sip from and said tasted like a cup of apple orchard.

That was the thing about people like her who were raised in poverty; they treated everything like it might be their last. She'd try to horde and save a glass of water if you let her. One time when Jake treated her to dinner at a high end fancy place in Buckhead, called Yebo, she asked for a to-go container for a remnant of her roasted chicken, which was no bigger than her thumb.

"*Gesundheit!*" Jake said.

"Thanks Hun."

Jake smiled. He thought to himself, on clear nights like these one could see the Andromeda Galaxy. After their convivial meal together they would race back to his place to rekindle the romance.

The waiter, Alex, brought out their dinner and sat it before them. Kangaroo burger, sushi grade Ahi dusted with blackening spices and seared, served rare with wasabi and house sesame and cilantro aioli for Jake. Linda's conch fritters with key lime mustard and Remoulade sauce for Aurora.

Before her second bite of food but after her first, Aurora gave Jake a solemn stare. "Jake hun, do you remember me asking you how you'd feel about us moving in together baby?"

Jake had in fact not recalled them ever having that conversation. He had not recalled them having anything remotely close to that conversation because if they had, he would have immediately vetoed the motion.

"No, I don't remember," he said in between bites the size of Liverpool. He was starving up to this point, but he could feel his appetite slowly diminishing now. Aurora had lodged herself into an awkward position.

Suddenly Jake felt a sharp burning sensation lancing the soft tissue lining his throat. He had bit into something impossibly painful. He stopped chewing for a moment.

The look on Aurora Suggs' face said it all. She squinted just before a hideous, horrific, ghastly pained look broke out across her face.

Jake coughed. Jake tried to dislodge the sharp bone-like object that was now stuck in either his esophagus or his windpipe, or both.

THIRTY-TWO

JAKE'S EYES WIDENED to the size of the Twin Lakes. He coughed and coughed and coughed. He made sounds that were neither humane, nor animal in scope, but something foreign and alien.

Aurora stood up and began to scream out for help. Jake's face turned a shade of plum. He stuck his index finger and thumb in his mouth, but was only met with frustration.

His hands were thick and his fingers were fat—too fat to get past his tongue. Too fat to pinch the piece of food clogging his throat, making it increasingly difficult to breathe or swallow. He felt he would die. His breathing grew shallow and labored and the dim room became even dimmer.

It became dislodged, whatever caused such momentary agony. Just like that it was over. Jake coughed up a small, sharp edged bone. It resembled an arrowhead, only it had an ivory gristle color.

The grimace on Aurora's face was terrifying. She was horrified. While Jake choked, she sat transfixed and in shock. "Omigod baby are you okay?" she attempted to calm him.

Jake struggled to get his composure, his face more placidly pale and awash of color than a ghost. He'd been pressure washed by violent involuntary muscle spasms as the bone dislodged itself from his windpipe.

He took several deep throaty breaths. Cough. He couldn't bring his eyes to meet her gaze. There was nothing charismatic, sexy or charming about choking on food. To say he was embarrassed would be an understatement.

He hadn't been that embarrassed since he'd got caught watching internet porn on the police station's computer. He thought he'd muted the sound and minimized the screen while he went to the bathroom to relieve himself.

When he returned to his desk, located in a shared open bullpen, several pop-ups occupied his desktop. A galaxy of them. Blondes who wanted to be banged. Muzzled M.I.L.F.s with sagging tiddies. All much to his chagrin.

Needless to say, many of the other diners stopped eating and were giving Jake their undivided attention. He hurriedly paid Alex, exclaiming he was fine when asked if he needed any medical attention. The manager of the restaurant offered to comp his meal, which Jake hastily turned down. All he wanted to do was get the hell out of the Cellar. Fast.

That was one lesson he learned from his father. Always pay for your meal. Never take a freebie because when you accepted freebies, people would always expect something in return. Always in a suspended state of expectation. Even when that expectation was vehemently denied or unspoken. Especially when that expectation was vehemently denied or unspoken.

Outside, the cold air was just what he needed to get himself together. He wore a fallow look as though he'd been deconstructed. Two things he couldn't deal with: being sick and being embarrassed. The episode in the Cellar exposed him to the two things he hated most.

Aurora reached for Jake's hand as they walked down the blustery street. The wind beat against their faces with vengeance. Jake pulled his collar up and stuffed his hands deep into his jacket pockets. He gave no thought to Aurora Suggs standing next to him. He'd erected a wall between them.

He even walked faster than normal. All he wanted was to get the hell out of Newnan. He needed to get back to the familiar. He wanted to get out of the cold too.

Frosty weather had a way of making people speed walk. Their eyes grew teary with water from the impact of the breeze.

"Dang it, I forgot my purse," Aurora murmured .

They both stopped. Jake turned slightly and said, "Hurry and go get it. Meet me at the car, I'll get the heat on and warm the engine."

The idea sounded noble. At least to him. He picked up his pace and even began a light sprint to his car. Jake made it to his car, cranked on the ignition, and rotated the heat dial to the highest it would go.

He rolled the dial to the far right, where a sliver of bright cherry red would cause an intense wave of heat to pour into the car. He shivered as the invisible film of cold melted away.

There was a gigantic orange moon looming in the sky. Like a cosmic grapefruit. It was eerie. The normal dark shading on the moon looked like a watermark. The sky was inky nebulous oil on canvas.

Most leaves had been blown from their branches. Trees swayed with the wind, as naked as newborns and the breeze gave off a low humming sound. It was as if the night wailed.

Jake sat in the car quietly allowing warmth from the heater to thaw him. Wind continued to stir up fallen leaves and other debris just outside his car window.

Aurora was in his field of vision. To his right Jake could see her making her way to the car. She wore a pained look as she strained to cut through a thick gust of combative wind. She leaned into her gait as though that would ameliorate the resistance. Walking down the street was like being in a featherweight bout against a heavyweight champion.

Just as she began to cross the street where the parking lot was, a white Prius with a bike rack attached to the back came darting around the corner. The compact car manifested out of thin air. Aurora, in her rush to get to the warmth of the heated car, wasn't paying attention. She never saw it coming.

THIRTY-THREE

THE WHITE PRIUS with the bike rack attached to the trunk collided into Aurora Suggs with fury.

Fate and timing made for odd bedfellows, but they came together in a hideous conclusion to the night. Aurora's light frame provided no protection against the velocity of the speeding car. The sound of squealing tires against cold hard asphalt could be heard within a fifteen mile radius.

Jake could not believe his eyes. He had never witnessed anyone being hit by a car. The contents of his stomach gave way and he was forced to heave his pricy dinner from the Cellar: what little he'd scarfed down. It was bad enough his body had been wracked so violently just moments before, and now this. How much more could he take?

Aurora Suggs, once hit by the speeding Prius, bounced onto the hood, tumbled up and over the moving vehicle, and flew twelve feet into the air. She landed with a disheartening thud—breaking several bones in her body. It would take an X-ray scan to know exactly how many bones to be exact. Her tibia poked from her leg. Blunt force trauma to her skull.

There was a shattering that left her body motionless and momentarily breathless. The silence was akin to being in a bubble or a tiny molecule in the stuffing that fills soundproof walls. Deafening silence. Silent like outer space. The definitive absence of sound. The driver stopped a few feet away from the actual point of collision.

Jake, with a newfound sense of urgency broke into a sprint where Aurora Suggs' body lay. His breathing was erratic and fast. His heart hammered his chest and in those moments he braved cold because he was guided by adrenaline and fight-or-flight hormones pulverizing his nerves.

"AURORA!" He yelled her name as loud as he could, as if that would help her jump to her feet. As if his words were sniffing salt. As if the pitch and timbre of his words would be heard in the world of the unconscious.

Color drained from her body as she lay unconscious. Was she in shock? Could she be resuscitated? The guy who hit Aurora Suggs climbed from his car.

He looked exactly like the type of man who would drive a Prius—frail, short and wimpy. He wore pants and a shirt made of hemp. He looked like one of those tree-hugging, new age light workers: the type to chain himself to a Sequoia tree in hopes some corporation would be halted from eminent domain laws allowing it to be chopped down. No *real* man would drive a Prius.

He wore disappointment, confusion, and a look of utter befuddlement, like he'd wear a pair of TOMS.

No matter how hard he chanted, meditated, or tried to align his chakras, and no matter how much DMT he consumed or how many cannabis brownies he ate, he would never be able to wipe this from his psyche. For the rest of his days, he would be rehashing the tail of two scars. The day he killed a woman and the day he would never forgive himself.

Hitting someone with your car leaves an indelible gash on your memory—it fucks up everything. The thought that he may have taken this woman's life with his car embedded fear within his veins. Fear of the litigation that awaited him in the same way taxes and death awaited him.

Jake fell to his knees and craned over Aurora. "Oh God, please open your eyes baby. Breathe for me. You breathe, Goddammit!" he pleaded. His pleading was heightened by a heavy draft of cold air.

Constellations in the skies formed an asymmetrical formation and clusters of stars gave Jake a melancholic bow as Aurora Suggs' spirit slowly left her body.

"Bro! I am so sorry. I didn't see anyone. Is she okay?" a scrawny Yankee voice came from the man who had been driving the white Prius.

Jake ignored him while pouring all of his energy and attention into getting Aurora Suggs to open her eyes. This night was shaping up to be one of the worst he'd ever known. Stygian blackness mounted the evening.

THIRTY-FOUR

PATRICIA ARRIVED HOME to her mother's apartment late. She parked her car in the covered parking deck like she did every night. A few tenants, local neighborhood folks and their grandchildren were outside in the front of the building.

There was a blue tow truck across the street. Eddy's Tow Service. The driver was securing an old beat up work van that he was preparing to tow. The work van driver stood on the curb smoking a cigarette. He leaned against a chain link fence, shivering against the cold night air, as he wore nothing more than a t-shirt and dingy jeans.

That was the odd thing about being in the city as opposed to the suburbs, there were always people outside. There were always passing cars, the occasional train, and a plethora of Marta buses.

Tonight felt different in a quixotic type of way. Patricia Garbutt was exceedingly exhausted. She felt like she hadn't slept in months—nothing that a long hot bath and a good night's rest couldn't remedy.

Since the dramatic change in living arrangements, she couldn't find peace. She couldn't get comfortable sleeping on that air mattress, nor could she get comfortable sharing such small living quarters with her mother, sister, and two children. It was all too much.

It was different when she was younger, when Mrs. Ortiz would stuff her and her siblings in the bathtub, sometimes three or four of them at one time.

They did everything together as a family. They ate dinner together at the large cherry wood dinner table that her father had found and refurbished. They went to town together and church together. The love was legendary.

But as an adult things were different. She lived in a different world as far as she was concerned.

Patricia climbed from her Crown Victoria, opened the back door to retrieve her laptop bag and bags of groceries she'd picked up from Kroger, when her cell phone began to jingle.

She paused momentarily, cogitating whether she would answer the call or not. It might be important. It could be an urgent call from Brody — maybe a break or revelation in the Roth case.

Just when she reached into the side of her laptop bag to fumble in search of her cell phone, someone, a tall dark figure, approached from the back of the vehicle.

She didn't have much time to react, so she swiftly dropped her laptop bag, where it fell between where she stood and the open back car door of her Crown Vic.

Adrenaline and fear flooded her bloodstream in waves. Her heart sunk to her knees before bouncing slowly down to her ankles. Her stomach took a free-fall to her toes.

Her world literally stopped. Who could possibly know that she lived here? Had she been followed? The thought that she may have been under the surveillance of a suspect she'd helped to prosecute gave rise to a lump in her throat.

It was a visceral experience that made every hair on the surface of her body stand at attention saluting the skies—hairs with perfect posture. It was only after she began reaching for her firearm that she noticed the familiar days-old unshaven face, shrouded by a 'Tahiti' baseball cap—a souvenir from one of her in-laws' escapades in French Polynesia.

It was her estranged husband Anthony. He looked like hard boiled tough times on acid. He was a walking bounced check—the shell of whom he once was.

He'd lost a terrible amount of weight and there was a gaping wound on his face near his nose. Dried blood encrusted around the sore. He reached out both hands in a gesture that indicated he came in peace.

"Hey, how's it going?" came a hoarse and raspy voice.

"Anthony, you scared the shit out of me! What do you want?" Patricia sighed.

"I miss you. I miss, miss, miss the kids," he stuttered.

"Oh yeah, well what do you need? I mean you were the one who decided to start banging the charity case at work," Patricia said.

"I'm sorry, Patty. Do you think you'll ever be able to find it in your heart to forgive me?"

"You're the one who wanted this. You're the one who drove our marriage into the gutter. You're the one who lost our home...our HOME for God's sake, Tony!"

He reached out and moved closer. Patricia placed her hand on her pearl handle .38 and pulled it out. She didn't point it at him. She just pulled it out and held it down by her leg.

"Oh, you're going to shoot me now, Patty?" Anthony's voice quivered.

"You're still full of shit, Tony. You never cared about us. Did you even begin to think about how this would devastate the children? Maria's grades have plummeted. Tyler's having nightmares and I can't handle the creditors. They've been on my back like stink on shit," she snapped.

Anthony Eugene Bowers stood stark still. Silent. He gathered his words and weighed his wife's words. He remained quiet and still. There wasn't much he could say to assuage the situation. Whatever he said to her while at the height of her anger would only be met with hostility. Malice marked the space between them.

"Well I fucked up, Patty. I miss you and I really just want to see the kids."

"How did you find me?" ignoring her husband's request. She wondered if he was high. He looked like he was stoned out of his mind.

"I promised Jake a round of brew and a few lap dances on me." Never mind the fact that he was homeless and broke.

Patricia rolled her eyes and sighed. Jake had betrayed her trust, but then again she had not been completely forthcoming about her separation. In an effort to not have Jake, Brody or anyone in the department think any less of her, she downplayed the situation—outright lied about the drug habit and omitted the affair.

All Jake knew was that she and the kids had moved in with her mother and that would be her living arrangement until they got a new place. But by now he probably knew the truth.

"Are they home?" Anthony said.

"Do you really want them to see you like this?"

"Like what," he said looking down at himself as though nothing was out of order.

"Disheveled. Downtrodden. You look terrible Anthony. You're a disgrace to the Bowers name," she said, as though he'd chosen this despicable twist of fate. No one wanted to grow up to become a junkie. No one imagined themselves becoming a person who would buy methadone in a Waffle House booth.

"Patty they are my kids too. You are still my wife. I'm still daddy." His voice thundered.

Across the street the tow truck driver was helping to assist the owner of the van by removing items from inside. The owner of the van was struggling with arms full of propane tanks.

As he was placing one of the propane tanks down onto the curb, the nozzle popped off, and the cigarette that dangled from the side of his mouth served as ignition for the leaking flammable gas.

The owner of the van went up in flames. A few tongues of fire licked at the tow truck driver, as he was standing only a few feet away. The force of the blast caused him to fly backward as he tossed the propane tank he'd been holding in the direction of the street.

The owner of the van struggled, dropped to the pavement, and wiggled around, attempting to extinguish the flames. They burned away his clothes and torched his skin. Panic, pain, and growing fear of death overcame him. Flames of fire swallowed the man.

His portly body thrashed violently and involuntary nerves kicked in. He kicked and jittered around like a life-sized urban earthworm. His hair burned to ashes before everyone's eyes. His entire body was engulfed in flames.

The kids who were outside ran towards the flames like nocturnal bugs to a porch light.

THIRTY-FIVE

MID CONVERSATION, PATRICIA went into Detective mode. She darted out into oncoming traffic, leaving Anthony standing there—a disheveled pile of rubbish. She left her car doors wide open too.

"Everyone stand back! Somebody call an ambulance. Dial 911, fire!" she shouted at the gathering crowd.

No one paid her any attention but continued to watch the real life horror movie unfold before them. Everyone's face was aglow as though they were watching the lighting of the tree at Rockefeller Center, just before Christmas.

"Detective Garbutt, homicide," she yelled, making sure her voice carried into the crowd.

Some of the crowd began to disperse, the ones with warrants or those who were out on parole.

One kid, who was on a bike and holding a bottle of soda, began flinging its contents at the burning man. Another tall lanky kid with tattoos all over his neck and arms came bravely running out in house shoes. He was holding a heavy blanket, which he used to drape over the van owner.

The blanket began to douse the flames successfully. Soon, the sweet sound of a fire truck siren came hovering through the air, like an audible Frisbee.

Patricia went over to check on the tow truck driver.

"Sir, are you okay?" He was in utter shock and sorely unstable.

He ogled her—his eyes beady and bloodshot with terror and pain. Words escaped him.

She quickly turned to the owner of the van, who lay on his back bathed in third and fourth degree burns. He literally looked like he had been set in grease and left to fry to death. The skin on his face was inflamed, and began to swell, causing his face to grow three times its size.

The only thing worse than the image of this doughy burned man, with skin oozing, sizzling, and charbroiled like he was a deep-fried butterball turkey, was the god-awful smell. It was an odor that would stay with Patricia for years. The smell of barbecued human flesh. There was no other smell on earth that could compare.

When the sirens came, all neighborhood kids scattered. Patricia noticed her daughter running away, hand-in-hand with a guy twice her age.

Patricia was torn three ways. She had been hit with a triple whammy in less than an hour. "Maria! Maria, you hear me calling you! Stay right there...don't you move a muscle!" Her daughter ignored her and continued to run away from the scene.

Although it was cold out, the external temperature was nothing compared to how she felt inside. That sick and sadistic bastard Michael Roth's words were echoing in the back of her mind, in surround sound. What hurt most was the fact that what he said was the gospel truth.

The van owner, Patricia came to learn, was also the owner of a small propane tank company. His van had broken down while he was on the way to deliver an order on the other side of town.

He would survive, but he would be in intensive care at Grady for the next six months. He would have to undergo skin grafts for the next five years, and yet, he would look like 'Thing' from *Fantastic Four* for the remainder of his life.

After assisting the medics and the uniforms and the City of Atlanta investigators who arrived, Patricia finally returned to her Crown Vic. Anthony had fled and the groceries, along with her laptop bag, had grown legs, and run away.

THIRTY-SIX

THAT SAME NIGHT, Detective Garbutt received a call from Brody. "Get your ass down here. We have a situation! It's Roth. He escaped."

How could this happen? He was under strict security measures, yet he managed to get past all of them.

"The authorities in Tybee also said the home where Roth was living was wiped completely clean with muriatic acid. We believe the girlfriend aided in his escape. Her body was found a few miles away from the Atlanta Federal prison camp where Roth was being held. She'd been strangled. The MEs say her blood levity reveals that her body had been moved. I'm requesting her blood toxicology results and have asked that they swab her for DNA. Answers can always be found lurking within the evidence." Brody said.

By the time Detective Jake Billingsley arrived at the department, both he and Detective Patricia Garbutt were two nervous wrecks. She sat gripping a cup of Joe across from Brody, who also nursed a mug of black coffee.

"You two look like shit!" Brody murmured.

"I just witnessed a man being set on fire from a freak propane accident," Patricia said as she pulled her hair into a neat ponytail. "I can still smell the guy's flesh cooking. I've been nauseous for an hour." Her voice was void of emotion, but her hands wouldn't stop shaking.

"I just saw my," he stopped short and thought better. "I just witnessed a possible hit and run. Saw the whole gruesome thing. Got here as fast as I could." Jake lamented. His eyes were russet red and took on that sunken appearance shared by most people deprived of sleep.

"You can always dodge responsibilities, but you can never dodge the consequences of dodging your responsibilities," Brody said. "Now we have got to get our hands on this crazy son of a bitch! Either out of our incompetence or bribery, he slipped between the cracks. We've got several units out on the streets in search of the vehicle we believe the girlfriend was using. But by now, he may have ditched that vehicle. This is one smart guy and to find him, we have to think like him. We have to think smart. Can you handle this?" He said, looking back and forth at them both.

"I have one question," Detective Garbutt inquired.

Brody glared at her, but gave no response.

"How did he do it?"

"From the looks of it he overpowered one of the guards and slipped on the guard's uniform. The old switch-a-roo."

What actually happened was Michael Roth, in his short time at the junction of Boulevard and McDonough, psychologically manipulated several other inmates being detained at the medium security penitentiary.

One by one, he indoctrinated them into his personal belief system. Starting with his bunk-mate Jerry Warren, he won him over first. Jerry Warren, inmate #456-029-71863, was a twenty-two year old African American who had been charged with Grand Theft Auto. After getting to know Roth a little better, he confided that he was only stealing cars to sell parts to a local chop shop.

It was the only way he knew to survive and feed his family. What else could a four-time convicted felon do to eat? He said he tried to do things on the straight and narrow and get a job like the rest of the squares, but no one would hire him. He was deemed unemployable, and what's worse, he couldn't vote, nor could he qualify for a federal student loan. He couldn't better himself by society's standards, so he said to hell with society.

"2012 marks the opening of thousands upon thousands of cosmic portals all over the world. The truth has been suppressed brother. Your beliefs are merely the product of your parents, teachers, and the environment you were raised in. With acceptance comes change brother. Acceptance is key. Your mind can be your greatest asset or your greatest downfall. You can change your energy by changing your thoughts." Roth preached to his bunk-mate day in and day out.

Soon, he had a small cult following. During breakfast, lunch, dinner, and time on the yard, a group of inmates would gather around him, giving him their undivided attention. He possessed an undeniable magnetism.

"They can chain your body brothers, but they can never chain your mind. They can never put your thoughts in a cage. Only you can do that. Once you've been brainwashed into believing any dogma, you can never be free. They try to judge you and me, brothers, but then their hands are dirtier than ours. They tell us to be like Christ. They tell us to be like Elohim, but page after page of *their* so-called Holy book is filled with the fire, brimstone, and wrath of an angry mass-murdering god! Do you see what it all means brothers?"

"What do you believe?" An inmate asked Michael Roth.

"I don't believe anything. There is no absolute truth because everything is ever-evolving. We're always changing and the cells of our bodies are always transforming, every minute of every hour of every day. Everything in the universe is in constant motion. So how can there be absolute truth with regards to anything? We all are made up of imprints and conditioning…this is what fashions our beliefs."

One older graying inmate stood up and asked, "So you're telling me that you don't believe in Jesus?"

"Metals corrode. Organisms are born, age, and transform. For thousands and possibly millions of years mankind has roamed this planet—and yet you get handed a book that was written only two thousand years ago by the hands of a rag tag group of so-called wise scribes, and I'm expected to believe this is the ultimate and absolute wisdom of the ages? Who is this man that you call the Christ? Where are his remains? Where is the record of his actual birth and life, scientifically?"

"The Bible tells us he was resurrected on the third day and he's in heaven," the man replied.

"Truisms come to us in the funniest ways." Michael Roth said. "There is no god, brother. You're on your own. Where was your god when you were committing the crime that put you here? Where was your god when you plead not guilty? Where is your god when millions of innocent children die of AIDS in Africa or starve in Ethiopia? Where is your god when thousands of innocent civilians are blown to smithereens along the Gaza strip? Is that not what some call the Holy land? Where then is your god?

"We get trapped in linguistic constructs, social constructs. They expect us to live quiet peaceful lives, but from cradle to the grave violence, war, and death is enmeshed in every aspect of our lives. How is that possible? If you want to live a life full of love and peace, think loving and peaceful thoughts." Roth said. He bombarded the inmate with more questions than he could answer.

The men were quiet, including the older inmate who dared to challenge him.

"You make your own highs and your own lows, brothers. Everything is a coincidence of contraries. Our genetic background imprints and learning is what determines how we judge every situation. We are creating the reality we are experiencing from moment to moment. The universe you're living in is the universe of your own making, brothers.

"Brothers, you have to read Plato and Socrates. You have to embrace Sophist philosophy. Nothingness is more than what meets the eye. There's so much more that we don't know; so much more than we've been led to believe."

"Yo, my dude. I hear what you saying and all, but how did you get on this shit that you be dropping gems about? Like, did you go to a special school or whateva?" An extremely dark-skinned inmate with a short nappy afro asked. Quincy Haughton was his name. Quincy Haughton was like an inquisitive five year old, always questioning Roth.

With the help of his cult following, Michael Roth devised an elaborate scheme to escape from the penitentiary.

THIRTY-SEVEN

JAKE DIDN'T KNOW who to call. He realized how little of Aurora Suggs' personal life she shared. He didn't know where her family actually lived, so he went into the department's database and he found her mother's address. She'd moved fourteen times in the course of three years.

He wanted to personally offer up the news that her daughter had been killed. After locating Aurora's mother, Maryann Mathers, he drove over to her trailer at 3211 Nogales Place in Rex, Georgia. Unannounced. He knocked at the door, with its tattered screen.

He heard dogs barking behind him. The neighbors across the way had a family of flea-infested mutts they were housing. He noticed a makeshift dog run and all the signs that a dog fighting operation was at play.

He knocked at the door for five minutes before giving up hope; he felt it was the least he could do for Aurora Suggs. A short pygmy of a man suddenly materialized. He had a short salt and pepper crew cut and he smelled like a pack of unfiltered camels. He wore a pair of Doc Martens with dirty white shoelaces in them. Judging from the burns on the tips of his fingers and the remaining rotting teeth in his mouth, he was addicted to meth.

The sky was a menacing shade of oxblood, a harbinger of things to come. The man was weighed down by a lifetime of burden, dashed hopes, and bad dope.

He stared at Jake for a long time, longer than was appropriate. Then he told Jake that Maryann had got into a fight with her old man and she was living and sleeping in her car. He chewed tobacco and spit after approximately every three words.

Maryann's new home was her 1982 Nissan Sentra. She'd converted it into a studio apartment. It was sitting on stacked bricks a few blocks away from Nogales Homes—the trailer park. The paint job had faded ten summers ago.

Looking into her eyes, Jake saw repressed pain and an active spirit of regret. Her eyes were yellow; high blood pressure betraying her. Being in Atlanta homicide, Jake Billingsley learned to look through people, not merely at them. People wore their autobiographies on their faces and shoulders, if you had the eyes to see them.

People were the architects of their circumstances and their own undoing, and it didn't take long to realize that fact once you observed them.

He wondered why fate had dealt Maryanne Mathers such misfortune. He recalled Aurora saying that her mother never defended her, nor had she ever validated her. She'd turned a blind eye to her daughter's molester.

Although Jake tried to be indifferent, to not judge, and to see this woman for her virtues, her vices thundered like lightning bolts. Why would a woman allow herself to fall to such depths? The need to judge her was more addictive than caffeine.

Why would a woman allow herself to be possessed by such depravity to let a man touch her daughter right beneath her eyes? The irony was not lost on him. Women were the dumbest creatures on the planet, he thought.

When Jake approached Maryann, she was apprehensive initially. "I'm Jake Billingsley...Detective Jake Billingsley," he was stone-faced but gave her a firm handshake with both hands.

"Yeah! I have a right to be here. I ain't breaking no laws," Maryann Mathers said. She was missing all her front teeth, causing her to gum her words. Years of cheap dope had taken its toll.

"No, I'm not here to charge you with anything, ma'am. Actually, I knew your daughter."

"Knew?"

"Yes, ma'am. We dated for a while. She told me about you." Jake said. This was more difficult than he'd thought it would be.

"Mrs. Mathers, ma'am," Jake paused and swallowed the lump in his throat. "It's Aurora."

"Well, don't just stand there looking like an idiot. Say something." Maryann said. She frowned; giving rise to crow's feet and a creased forehead.

"With all due respect, Mrs. Mathers, Aurora was in a fatal accident and she didn't survive," he licked his lips and swallowed hard.

Maryann appeared to be lost in thought, as if she was sorting out what she'd heard. She dwelled in a momentary state of disbelief. While Jake's face remained relatively stoic and placid on the exterior, inside he felt like an urchin. In part, he was to blame.

He had insisted that they dine at the Cellar. He had insisted that she run back to get her purse alone. Why hadn't he accompanied her back to the restaurant to retrieve her purse? If he had accompanied her back into the restaurant to retrieve her bag, might they both have lost their lives on that frosty night?

"Ma'am, let me express my profound gratitude for your daughter. She was amazing. You raised her well." Jake said. He found it odd that Maryann Mathers hadn't shed a single tear. He found it very odd indeed.

Mrs. Mathers waved off Jake's words dismissively. "How old are you?" Her southern drawl drizzled the space between them, dipped in despair.

"Is that important?" Jake felt guilt slowly begin to engulf him.

"Do you know how old my daughter is?" Mrs. Mathers looked Jake up and down from head to toe, for the umpteenth time.

"She was eighteen when I first met her," he cleared his throat.

"Dear Lord, bless your heart," Mrs. Mathers chuckled lightly. "If there's one thing my daughter was good at was lying. She must have inherited that from her father."

"I beg your pardon," Jake said.

"My daughter is fourteen years old."

The color drained from Jake's face. Aurora had lied to him and betrayed his trust. Without his knowledge, he had committed statutory rape.

THIRTY-EIGHT

PATRICIA WORE HER winter parka with the fur-lined hood and APD in big yellow letters across the back. Her arms and legs felt like old cold oatmeal as she clamored the steps leading into the apartment. She hadn't slept in two days and she was running on black coffee and Rockstar energy drinks.

The Roth case was kicking her butt. She drove home in a caffeine and sugar crash-induced blur. Seeing herself in the rearview mirror, she fancied Mr. Magoo—eyes tight with sleeplessness. Her back and shoulders were tight and lumpy with stress.

Two Rudolf-nosed zits had taken up residence on her face, harbingers of a stress-induced flu, complete with rousing bouts of vomiting, body ache, sore throat, fever, and the squirts. She was already beginning to have a hacking cough. This always happened when she was under tremendous duress; characteristic of this time of the year.

She was angry with herself for not going to get that flu shot like she promised herself. When she entered the apartment, she wanted nothing more than to dive head first onto the air mattress and get some Rip Van Winkle type sleep.

Tyler ran up to his mother and wrapped both arms around her waist. He embraced her like the wobble of the planet depended on it, like the sunrise depended on the integrity of his love for her.

She bent over and kissed her son on the top of his head before cupping his tender, young, innocent face in the palms of her hands. She stared at him for a lingering second and sighed. "I love you so much little boy, do you know that?"

"I love you too mommy," Tyler replied with cloying sweetness. He smelled clean like Irish Spring soap and his Batman thermal pajamas smelled fresh from the dryer.

"Where's grauma?" Judging from the lingering savory aroma, Mrs. Ortiz had cooked lamb stew for dinner. Her big orange crock pot was out and on the counter and a pan of buttermilk cornbread sat half eaten atop the stove.

"She's in bed. She said she wasn't feeling well. I think she said her legs were bothering her. You know how her legs always bother her when it rains," Tyler chanted.

"Her joints," they both said in unison.

Even before moving in with Mrs. Ortiz, they were accustomed to hearing her speak of how rain threw her out of joint and made her creak. She said it even made her dentures hurt. So whenever it rained, Mrs. Ortiz stayed in bed if she could help it. She refused to put on her bra or her dentures. She just lay in bed watching Judge Joe Brown, Wendy Williams, Telemundo, HGTV and General Hospital.

"Where is your sister?" Patricia said. Before she asked the question, she held her breath for the answer. Her daughter was falling down the same rabbit hole as her father. It had always been that way in their family: Tyler clinging to his mother and Maria quick on her daddy's heels.

"She's downstairs with Lisa at Marquita's," Tyler replied.

"Who is Marquita?"

Tyler shrugged both shoulders. "I don't know. Lisa's friend, I guess," he turned back to the notebook he had been sketching in. He was drawing abstract robots that resembled *Iron Man*.

"Do you know what apartment unit this Marquita lives in?"

"I think it's 107. Yeah, it's apartment 107."

Patricia carried her heavy exhausted body back downstairs and found apartment 107. A woman with pointy blue acrylic nails and weave down to her waist, looking to be in her mid twenties, swung the door open with roaring attitude. "What?"

"Excuse me, but I'm looking for my daughter and sister." She could see Lisa sitting on a sofa smoking a joint.

Once she heard Patricia's voice she jumped up and dashed into the bathroom, slamming the door behind her. Patricia pushed her way past the woman. Mother's instincts kicked in and she headed towards the back of the apartment.

"Um, excuse the hell out of me but this is my house! You can't just Bogart up in here like you're the police!"

"I *am* the police!" Patricia said as she pulled out her badge, which hung from her neck, but was under her blouse.

She began knocking on doors when a guy swung open one of the bedroom doors at the end of the hallway. It was the same guy who she'd seen Maria holding hands with the previous night. He stood there with an expression that said, yeah, and…the fuck are you going to do about it?

To make matters worse, he was shirtless and all he wore was a pair of navy blue Tommy Hilfiger boxers. He had far too much hair on his face and chest and far too much bass in his voice to be anyone Maria should be holding hands with.

"Is my daughter in there? Maria Esmeralda Bowers!" Patricia screamed.

"Now wait one damn minute, this is still my house! You have no right to just Bogart in here like this," Marquita yelled.

Patricia turned to the woman, her face ruddy with anger and hurt. "My daughter is in this goddamn shithold and if somebody doesn't start talking, I'm taking every last person in."

"I had no idea ma'am. I'm sorry. I had no idea."Marquita said. Suddenly her demeanor softened.

Maria suddenly materialized from behind the guy in the blue boxers. She was struggling to put her clothes on. She quickly slipped her Hollister t-shirt over her head and zipped up her jeans. Her hair was all over her head, messy from rolling around in the sack. Patricia could feel her blood pressure going up like a hot-air balloon.

As her daughter began walking in her direction, she reached out and grabbed her by her hair. "You were in there having sex with this goddamn douche bag? Are you fucking kidding me! I could kill you with my bare hands."

Maria struggled to free herself from her mother's grasp, but she had her by the hair. "Let me go! Let go of my hair. I'm calling my daddy!"

The guy ran to Maria's rescue and tried to help her get free from her mother's tight fist. Lisa, hearing the drama heating up in the hallway, opened the door, and pushed past Marquita.

"No! No, it's okay, it's all my fault," she tried to shout over the ensuing madness.

Patricia pushed her younger sister backward, causing her to slam her head against the wall. Suddenly, Maria had the temerity to ball her hands into fists and began to thrash her mother.

Patricia gripped her daughter up by her collar and slammed her against the hallway wall. The guy backed away and so did Marquita. Patricia then began choking the life from her daughter with both hands. Maria attempted to catch her breath because she was beginning to turn mauve.

THIRTY-NINE

IN ADDITION TO fifteen foot fences, each H-block of the prison camp where Roth had been housed was encompassed by an eighteen foot concrete wall topped with barbed wire.

All gates on the complex were made of solid steel and electronically operated. Roth was able to get seven fellow prisoners to help him in his elaborate scheme to escape from their unit. The seven convicts overpowered and restrained three correctional officers and four other uninvolved inmates at approximately 10:17a.m.

The escape occurred during the slowest period of the day, when surveillance was at a minimum. Once one of the unsuspecting victims was subdued, the offenders removed his clothing, tied him up and gagged him in a broom closet behind locked doors. Once bound and gagged, the attackers ransacked clothing, credit cards, and identification from the victims.

The group basically impersonated correctional officers via phone and manufactured stories to ward off suspicion from authorities. It was part ambush and part mutiny, but brilliant in scope. Even the duped authorities had to give this maniacally odd genius credit.

Some of the depravity, lasciviousness and explosions of anger that Michael Roth encountered while being incarcerated served as inspiration and malicious insight. There were rapists, thieves, liars, murderers, and grifters cut from various fabrics of society. He took notes from them all.

Prison helped sharpen his mind and hone his craft as a killer. Prison was its own extraordinary kind of university, doling out priceless lessons which couldn't be learned anywhere else. Michael Roth was the only criminal of his kind—like a unicorn in his uniqueness.

He witnessed the racial divides, the black power criminals who fought with the skinheads and white supremacists. He witnessed the men who had wives and girlfriends but once they entered the prison complex, became wives and girlfriends.

He witnessed men become shadows of themselves once they were locked behind bars. And he witnessed the influx of designer drugs of every make and model, being bartered for cartons of cigarettes here and specialty gourmet cookies there.

That place was no different than the jungle. Parasites had titanium resolve. Territory was everything, even within the gates of the complex. No different than in the wild, territory was marked, only not by urine but by brute force and violence.

There were lions, gazelles, zebras, orangutans, aardvarks, pelicans, hippos, rhinos, and flamingos. There were scavengers, bottom-feeders, predators and their prey—an impeccable caste system like you wouldn't believe. Some of the corrections officers were no better than the men they were paid to maintain control over.

Some of the prisoners were innocent men whose only crime was the inability to hire effective legal defense. That place was its own university, doling out lessons that you could learn nowhere else. Like so many prestigious institutions around the world, it was a system based on cliques and reputation— no different than religious institutions or institutions of higher learning. Everything men touched became corrupted.

The only difference between prison inmates and regular people on the outside living their ordinary, puny, mediocre lives of quiet desperation was that the prisoner's bars were visible.

Michael Roth's favorite pastime was watching the shank fights. It never ceased to amaze him how creative some men could be when confronted with life or death situations. Even lames, mutes, and the autistic tapped into their inner Einstein and became revolutionary in their thinking in order to stay alive to see another day and taste another shitty taxpayer provided meal.

Michael Roth would meditate and chant at all times when he wasn't out speaking to his followers. He even convinced a few of them to get their hands on some books for him—mainly Mao, Hitler's Speeches, Madame Blavatsky, Aleister Crowley, Stalin's writings, and a whole lot of theosophy.

It was in that environment of crime and pent up masculine aggression that he hatched a plan to take the lives of the law enforcement that had put him there. He would take the lives of those he believed sided with the law, if for no other reason than their ability to out-smart him.

Although he had been in constant communication with Ginger Engstrom, he no longer trusted her. He knew from talking with other inmates that all phone calls were monitored and recorded. So, when Ginger Engstrom met him a few miles away after the escape, he knew the only way to guarantee his freedom would be to end her existence.

Just before he snapped her neck, he called her Judas and he thanked her. He held her fragile frame in his arms one last time. He kissed her and ran his fingers through her hair and over the ridges and ravines of her body, softly stroking her collar bones, the valley where her breasts met, and the delicate skin on the back of her neck.

He wanted to dissect her heart. He wanted to put it in a jar of formaldehyde so that he would possess the most quintessential part of Ginger Engstrom forever.

FORTY

AFTER PATRICIA STOPPED choking her daughter Maria, she began to drag her by her hair down the hallway and out of the apartment. The moment they were outside of Marquita's apartment, Patricia regained her composure.

It was almost as if someone had doused her with a bucket of warm comfort. Suddenly she could see straight. Suddenly she could breathe.

Seeing her daughter sauntering out of the bedroom with a grown man with hair on his chest sent a deluge of worry raining down and it made her see her inability to fully protect and shelter her firstborn. Their newfound environment hadn't been friendly to her brand of parenting. She needed her husband. Life at home was crumbling fast. It was like they were in a sinking ship, and they were fiercely bailing out water as fast as they could.

Of all the criminals and cases she handled on a daily basis, nothing and no one ruffled her feathers quite like her pubescent daughter. There was no pain like the pain a child could inflict upon you. Motherhood taught her some cold, hard lessons.

A mother's intuition is not hindered by time zones or geography. Like a GPS satellite signal, it was always on alert. From the moment she stepped foot into the apartment that evening, she knew that things were not right with Maria. In fact, when she saw her running hand in hand with the guy the night that van exploded, she knew things were terribly wrong. But what was she to do?

If it wasn't the separation from her husband or the Roth case, surely the stress from Maria would be the death of Detective Patricia Garbutt.

Her sister Lisa, who was higher than a satellite, was in tow, nibbling her fingernails down to their nubs in trepidation. Normally a mercurial young woman, the marijuana she had smoked had her on paranoia's razor sharp edge. It couldn't have boded over well with her raging case of Bulimia Nervosa, or perhaps the Cannabis helped it a bit.

Since last seeing her mother, Maria had gotten a riot of piercings and tattoos. She'd pierced her nose, navel and wore chest micro dermal piercings beneath her collar bone. She had a tattoo of her zodiac sign on her right inner ankle, Libra scales in shades of cadmium, ultramarine, and celadon.

Once everyone walked back home to the apartment, Patricia decided to make herself a stiff drink. She was so furious that she felt she would snap her daughter's neck or break her back, in a fit of rage.

Her daughter's back-talking was going to get her killed. She had no idea that her mother would rip her a new asshole if she wasn't careful. Stress made *normal* people do crazy shit, but stress made feisty, Belizean, homicide Detective mothers with guns do the unthinkable.

She stirred gin and tonic together in a squat tumbler. After she'd taken a few sips and felt the light buzz calm her nerves gently, she decided to confront Maria. Maria was curled up on the sofa, crying crocodile tears. Her feelings were more hurt than the physical things her mother had done to her.

"So are you going to tell me who this young man is that you've taken a liking to?" Patricia asked Maria.

Cold silence filled the air. Lisa sat at the kitchen table, still nibbling her fingernails. Tyler was fast asleep on the air mattress lying on the floor.

Maria couldn't stand to meet her mother's cold monochrome eyes. Thus, no answers came forth. The silence was maddening.

"You don't hear me talking to you? What, am I not speaking clearly or are you just going to sit there and ignore me?" Patricia's words floated like dust particles in the stuffy apartment.

"His name is Troy," Lisa's voice came from across the room. Maria shot her aunt Lisa a look of utter disgust and disapproval.

Patricia nodded and thanked her sister before giving Maria a stern pursed lip stare. "How old is Troy and what is his relationship to you?" she questioned her daughter once again.

"Look, I really don't feel like talking about this with you. I'm tired. Can I go to sleep, please ma'am!" Maria's sarcastic attitude was self evident.

"I don't give a damn about you being tired and don't you dare sit there and tune me out, and don't take that tone with me. I want to know who this *maggot* is who thinks he can lay up with my daughter. How old is he anyway? And how did you two meet." Patricia began to grow irate all over again.

"It's my fault, Patty. Really, it's all my fault. If anyone should be catching heat, it's me. I'm friends with Marquita. Marquita and Troy are sister and brother. Troy is nineteen but he looks more mature than he actually is. I introduced them. I guess they took a liking to one another and one thing led to another. The next thing I know, I'm watching a relationship develop and Troy told me that he wanted to date Maria. I figure she's a big girl and she can take care of herself, right?" Lisa shrugged.

"Take care of herself? Are you f—?" Patricia took a deep exasperated sigh. "Are you serious right now? She's barely thirteen years old, Lisa. You're supposed to be the young adult. You're supposed to be better than that. What would possess you to just throw my daughter to the wolves like this, Lisa? Are you dating this Marquita woman?"

Lisa grew silent and her eyes immediately went to the floor. She didn't have to answer Patricia. Her silence was more than obvious.

"I want to go live with my daddy! I hate it here and I hate you!" Maria shrieked.

"Believe you me, if your damn father wasn't so destitute I would allow you to go with him. I can't deal with you anymore. I don't even know who you are anymore. One day, you're my sweet baby girl, and the next, you've become this. Are you having sex too?"

"Yes mother! I am having sex with Troy. Troy is my man and we're having sex."

Patricia leaned over and slapped her daughter across the face. "Watch your tone in your grauma's house!"

Tyler tossed and turned, made a sleepy groan and then fell back asleep. The tension in the compact apartment was enough to spark an electrical fire.

"You're too young to have sex, you've barely had your first period and you are still wearing fucking training bras for crying out loud!" Patricia let out a weary breath of frustration. "Are you using protection?"

"I gave her some of my birth control pills," Lisa said.

"Troy always uses a rubber. I'm not that stupid!" Maria snapped back defiantly.

Patricia gulped the entire glass of gin and tonic before standing, walking over to the kitchen table, grabbing her purse, and traipsing out of the apartment—slamming the door behind her. She could feel another conniption revving up. The truth stung like the sting of an adder.

This was the straw that broke the camel's back. Patricia lost her nerve and if she remained in the apartment, surely she would have done something irrational; something that she might live to regret. Maria had become reckless and uncontrollable overnight. She was at the age where her mother's opinions played second fiddle to her friends'.

Maria seemed to go out of her way to hurt her mother's feelings. She was like a female version of her father—rebellious, cold and heartless.

FORTY-ONE

DETECTIVE PATRICIA GARBUTT didn't know where she was headed, but she knew she needed to get as far away from that apartment as possible.

She was tired. Tired of running. Tired of fighting with family. Tired of losing the battle, and the war. She felt she couldn't catch a break. She *really* had no place to turn.

Hopping into her Crown Vic, she kept her eyes trained on the lights of the Equitable Building. The sputtering exhaust coming from the muffler was her soundtrack. Beneath the languid spotless big black sky lounging impassively above, Patricia felt night embrace her. It was as though the pain she felt had reached up and tore even the stars from the sky.

She drove for a few miles before stopping at a local Waffle House that sat behind the off ramp of 285. Before she knew it, she pulled into the parking lot, turned the engine off, and cried like a newborn. She cried tears for old and new: pent up emotions that wanted out. Pain from the separation cloyed at her.

The worst part about it was she really didn't know what to do. She didn't know where to turn, or where to find solace. Sitting in her Crown Vic, Patricia slammed the palms of her hands against the steering wheel.

Crisp winter air outside was so cold it made her frigid fingertips sting. She prayed because she felt she was losing her center of gravity. She struggled to rediscover what mattered.

"Dear Lord, please help me. I don't know what else to do. I don't know where else to turn. Please give me guidance and direction, dear God. Give me strength. In the name of the father, the son, and the Holy Spirit: please cover my daughter. Please keep her safe. Please bring our family back together. In the name of Jesus, please deliver Anthony from the streets and from drugs. Please fix this mess, dear God."

A priest once told her that prayer was like pushing the reset button on life. She sure hoped he was right. When she opened her eyes after praying, she noticed a few people sitting on plastic chairs behind low income housing units. In spite of their apparent poverty, they were happy and they had each other.

After sitting in the parking lot for nearly twenty minutes, Detective Patricia Garbutt called her partner Jake.

Sensing urgency, pain and frustration in her voice, Jake invited her over to his place. Patricia reluctantly accepted.

They both were in need of a sabbatical—someplace sunny and warm, someplace where they could sip frothy tropical drinks with miniature umbrellas; someplace with powdery sugar white sand and vast open pastures of Santa Fe turquoise skies. Both had witnessed unspeakable trauma in the past seventy-two hours.

By the time Patricia arrived at Jake's, the gin and tonic she'd drank on an empty stomach had given her a sense of euphoria. And thank goodness, because while she sat in the parking lot of the Waffle House, her stomach was in knots, as she thought about Maria losing her tender virginity, her eyes grew heavy with tears.

Jake opened the front door to his intimate yet sparse, high-ceilinged, unpretentious loft, and a sweet, savory Indian scent wafted through the door — Nag Champa incense. Jake was holding a bottle of Dos Equise when he answered the door and he was shirtless, why was he shirtless?

Patricia was apprehensive. She had never been to Jake's place before. They'd always discussed cases either over the phone or met up at mutual places in the city, or at headquarters, of course.

Her eyes did a quick panoramic view of the sofa, the chest-turned-coffee table, art that didn't match, and the huge flat screen television that was the end-all-be-all of flat screen televisions. Jake's television defied any description other than epic.

Jake offered Patricia a beer. She excused herself to the restroom. She needed to relieve herself and she needed to wash up. She felt dirty, cold, and hungry. After washing her hands and splashing warm soapy water onto her face, Patricia re-emerged from the bathroom. Closer to godliness.

Jake sat with his legs spread wide on the end of his sofa. He'd slipped on a clean white t-shirt and a pair of faded jeans that fell loosely around his hips. The Beatles brought up the background. He removed the cap from a bottle of Dos Equise and placed a frosted glass next to the bottle of beer.

"Thanks," Patricia sighed, as she gulped down the beer.

"What's eating you?" Jake asked. He could sense that his partner was weathered and plagued by stress.

The air in his condo was redolent with a sweet floral scent, heavy with sandalwood, cloves and cardamom—signature spices used to dip Nag Champa.

An explosion of Plumeria danced around the room in aromatic tendrils. She noticed several items from Anthropologie: a set of Ayaka mugs here, a Persian rug there; several coffee table cook books stacked neatly in a cubby in the kitchen.

"I notice you have cinnamon gift soap in the bathroom. You've been doing some traveling and didn't invite little old me?" Patricia intoned, attempting to make light of the sullen heaviness on her chest.

Jake laughed out loud, as though he'd heard the most hilarious joke ever told. "Nah, I got it from an investigation at the St. Regis Hotel. You may remember the old wealthy woman they found drowned in a penthouse suite bathtub? Widowed heiress of a prominent Tuxedo Park businessman?"

Patricia nodded then chuckled. Everyone borrowed hotel soap, towels, and robes if they could get away with it. She had to admit that

Jake's place with its signature coziness, simplicity, and warmth was super-groovy.

It hadn't occurred to Patricia that she sat amid a riot of literary giants. First edition Dickens, Hemingway, Samuel Beckett, and Steinbeck. She'd never peg Jake to be much of a reader.

"If you're hungry, I've got takeout from Planet Bombay: aloo gobi, pumpkin curry, a little flaky roti," Jake offered.

Under the bright glare of lighting, Jake's Hungarian heritage seemed more pronounced than ever. He took a long sip of his beer. Patricia followed the up and down bouncing motion of his Adam's apple as he swallowed that slightly amber ale. Tall, with a thicket of dark hair, Jake represented stability in that moment.

"Jake, I just don't...I just—" the words caught in her throat.

"Say it, no judgment. Just say it Garbutt," Jake said, scooting closer to his partner.

"My life at home is turning into material for one psychotic HBO special. I haven't been completely forthcoming about what's going on in my life."

"Sure, it's no biggie."

"Let me finish. Anthony and I are separated. We lost our house. Foreclosure. I'm staying with my mother because it all came as such a surprise and it knocked me on my ass. Anthony completely cleaned out our bank accounts. He's hooked on prescription drugs and now he's out on the streets," her voice cracked.

"Damn!"

"Tonight when I got home, I found my daughter in bed with some slime ball from the apartment. In bed, Jake! My baby!" she said before the waterworks started all over again.

Jake didn't respond. He allowed Patricia to vent her frustration. Lady Antebellum's "Need You Now" came over the speakers and it was like a movie. The two partners moved closer to one another. Jake draped his free arm around Patricia's shoulder and pulled her face to his chest. The gesture was kind and appreciated.

For a moment, Patricia cried silent tears. She was a fractured woman wallowing in vulnerability. Jake gave her a few more minutes to gather herself before he stood and walked over into the kitchen. He stirred up something more potent than the beer — a White Manhattan, made with Death Door's white whiskey. It was a libation that would take away the pain, or at least numb her long enough to get her re-focused.

FORTY-TWO

PATRICIA DIDN'T REFUSE Jake's peace offering. He handed her the drink. After taking one sip, she upended the glass within seconds. Then she finished off her beer in one fell swoop.

Before Jake could sit back down, Patricia clasped him by the back of his neck and brought her lips to his. They gazed into each other's eyes with longing. Forbidden fruit was the sweetest. This was a moment he'd fantasized about, but successfully suppressed for fear of possible repercussions from Jeremy Thomas, their conservative chief of police, and Lieutenant Brody Maxwell—the man with the power to lay him off and promote him.

Jake tried to coax it down. The bulging erection in his jeans. Patricia's liquor-tinged lips were warm against his. She slid her tongue into his mouth and gave him passion he'd never known.

He felt the heaviness of that Belizean soul—her Mayan spirit and all of its lifetimes and manifestations could be felt in that kiss. It made him think of his childhood eating sandpears, crabapples, and pomegranates; the cool shade from the sassafras tree on the side of his family's home.

Jake tugged at her ponytail holder and dug his hand into her long curly raven hair. His other hand gripped her waist, like he never wanted to let her go. She cupped his stubbly unshaved face in her palms and kissed him with ferocity. Her body was a raw paradise begging to be explored.

"Are you sure you want to do this?" Jake said.

She gave him no answer. Not verbally. She spoke another dialect. Her response was equally as charming as a symphony, the vibrato of the ocean at the end of the day; like an oak tree blooming poetic.

Patricia pulled Jake to her and they kissed more fervently. It was fluid and natural. They moved together as though the thought of this night had been permeating the fabric of their lives.

Perhaps it was Patricia's vulnerability and transparency that made that moment even sweeter. Perhaps fate choreographed this dance, much in the same way a composer would direct the sopranos, altos, and tenors in concentrated balance.

As the night wore on, the two detectives made passionate love to one another. Jake took Patricia from the back; took her against the wall and wrapped her thick canopy of hair around his fists. With each pelvic thrust, he went deeper and deeper. She moaned out his name in slow breathy syllables that sounded like she was speaking pure Belizean patois.

She hadn't been taken like this in years. She could feel him grow harder inside of her, just before he was about to explode. He turned her around and gave her wet, open-mouth kisses. She sucked his tongue and he began kissing her like he was giving her cunnilingus.

Suddenly he stopped and fell to his knees. He then proceeded to put his mouth on her. He licked and sucked; made his tongue do figure eights, kick flips and back flips. She tilted and arched her back.

The sensations drove her mad with lust. She craved his manhood. They were lost in each other. Patricia came over and over again. She couldn't control her body; couldn't control the lingering orgasm that synced itself to her rapid heartbeat.

FORTY-THREE

BY WISDOM A house is built, someone once said. One moment of weakness had the potential to jeopardize everything: the investigation, the balance of order, and the texture of their working relationship.

Detective Billingsley and Detective Garbutt tossed wisdom and caution to the wind. The next morning the two partners woke up in an emotional alcohol-induced fog.

Jake woke first. For a few silent seconds he stared at Patricia. He thought of the night before and the legions of passion that woman exuded. For the first time, he'd seen a side of her that he'd never known. He liked passion. Passion was good. Without passion, sex was like cold pizza. It was still pleasurable, but it could always be better.

He'd always found her beautiful. She was more beautiful as she slept. She looked innocent, like she needed protection. Her features were so soft, and the curve of her lips and legs was angelic. He could stare at her lying there like that for hours on end. A woman's curves were enchanting.

He watched her eyes flutter behind her eyelids, dancing within the dream world. He wondered what she was dreaming, imagined he inhabited that deeply personal place. He didn't wake her. She needed all the rest she could stand. Exhaustion had taken its toll on them both.

He climbed out of bed and reached for the eggplant-colored towel that was draped over a chair. Wrapping it around his waist, he then went over to the pull-up bar that he'd installed over his bedroom door and performed ten sets of eight reps, like he did every morning.

Then he got down on the floor and did one hundred and fifty push-ups, before blending a green protein smoothie chockfull of kale and spirulina. He would normally put on his Insanity workout DVD, but because his partner was lying in his bed, with bed-head, and still smelling like sex, he decided to relish in the moment.

After performing his morning workout ritual, he took a quick shower. It wasn't until he'd brushed shaving cream on his face and brought the razor to his neck that Patricia awoke. He heard her tossing around beneath the weight of the blanket like she was searching for evidence in her dreams.

Jake looked over his shoulder and then trained his eyes on Patricia through the bathroom mirror. He wondered how long they would ignore the hulking cotton candy pink elephant in the room.

"My head is pounding," Patricia said.

"Yeah?" Jake replied. "You need an aspirin or two, or seven?" he said, reaching into his medicine cabinet, which was situated just behind the mirror over the wash basin sink.

It was an awkward moment waking up next to your homicide detective partner. Awkward indeed. Patricia felt sordid inside, as if she'd soiled her reputation. Not to mention, she was still married.

She knew how Jake spoke of the women he'd had in the sack. He treated them like a hunk of pork belly; devoured them and then simply tossed the bones to the left.

Her headache was part hangover, part shame. "Thanks Jake," she said. She walked over to grab the bottle of aspirin from him. She pulled the blanket off the bed, using it as a robe.

Jake found *that* to be comical, considering how he'd just licked and caressed every inch of her naked chestnut colored body.

"No problem," Jake said.

"We got a new lead yesterday on the Roth case," Patricia added. Strictly business.

"Oh yeah?"

"Yes, the car that Ginger Engstrom picked him up in was seen at an Exxon off of Peachtree. They captured a glimpse of the license plate from a street light cam. Just got in yesterday," Patricia said.

"I'll get on that as soon as possible," Jake muttered.

"You know the funny thing about this," Patricia said, as she popped three aspirin into her mouth, "what is the motive? I mean this psychopath is impenetrable and impossibly diabolical. Just the thought of putting him behind bars for life without the possibility of parole practically makes me wet."

Jake laughed out loud. "I'll fix you some breakfast. You'll need something to absorb all that alcohol and those aspirin."

Patricia hopped in the shower while Jake could be heard schlepping around in the kitchen, dusting, plating, pouring, and tweezing with mellow precision.

As Patricia stepped out of the hot steamy shower, Jake handed her a plate of quivering soft egg and Douglas fir custard with matsutake mushrooms, pumpkin with walnut miso, and crispy kale."

"What's the special occasion?" Patricia said. "I had no idea you moonlight as Wolfgang Puck in your spare time."

Jake flashed an effervescent smile. He was flattered.

"Look, don't get all weird on me Jake. What we did last night was a mistake. We both know that it can go no further than this room," Patricia said.

"Sure, what we do here stays here," Jake replied cheerfully.

"That's not quite what I mean," she paused. "I'm saying what we did was wrong and can never happen again. I don't know; I guess you're thinking I'm crazy. I was weak. You were here. But we are colleagues and I'm still legally married. I have to go home and sort things out," Patricia said ruefully.

She was struggling with a serious case of remorse and a monstrous hangover.

"I understand. Trust me, I do. To be honest, I'm still feeling crazy about seeing Aurora flying twenty feet in the air before losing her life."

"Well maybe you should consider taking a sabbatical or at least talking to a head doctor."

It was common practice for investigators to seek professional help after witnessing the death of a loved one. State funded of course. Jake waved it off.

"Nonsense," Jake said.

"I'm just saying you should consider taking some time out for yourself. When Tyler accidently shot himself in his leg I had nightmares for a month straight, nightmares that he'd never walk again. Every time I was forced to clean his bloody, pus-stained gauze, or help him bathe, I blamed myself. I beat myself up. I think that had a lot to do with the breakdown in communication between me and Anthony. I didn't take a leave of absence because the Roth investigation had been so demanding.

"Although he healed brilliantly, it just did something to me on the inside. I probably should have gone to see a shrink myself. I think something happens when someone close to home is taken out of here. We experience so many different emotions and if we don't channel it in constructive ways it can wreck havoc on our lives in other ways." Patricia confessed, before shoving several forkfuls of food into her mouth.

"There isn't anything a shrink can do for me." Jake reiterated, scratching the back of his head.

He hadn't confided that Aurora's mother Mrs. Mathers told him that her daughter was a minor. He kept that to himself. Either out of embarrassment or the idea that he'd been fooled, he knew that if he disclosed that information, surely Patricia would flip out. He had the presence of mind to know his partner was highly judgmental.

FORTY-FOUR

IT WAS A long drive home to the apartment. Patricia felt numb as she coasted from one side of town to the other.

She was feeling better since breakfast and the aspirin. There was an algid texture to the air. A stale breeze sliced through the skies with a pendulum strut. The sun grew pale. It was odd that when she looked at her phone, she found no voicemail messages from her mother or Tyler. Not a single text message.

She took the long scenic route home. Scenic drives were like celery-root soup for the soul — cleansing and therapeutic all at once. She drove through Virginia Highlands, and got a kick out of the splash of color from lime green Adirondacks sitting out in front of boutiques and Little Five Points local sidewalk artists strumming their folksy new grass; hipsters huddled over freshly brewed salted caramel mochas.

A white Toyota Venza pulled up alongside her. There was a Dalmatian hanging out of the back window. He was the size of an elk. The dog looked like it was smiling at her. She turned up the volume on her speaker and let the rifts of Santana calm her racing mind.

When Detective Patricia Garbutt arrived at the apartment, she knew immediately that something was out of order. For one thing, the door was unlocked. When she stuck her key into the lock, the door simply spilled open. The apartment was quiet and serene. A painful thought woke her ulcer.

"Mamí? Tyler? Maria?" Her thoughts immediately went to Anthony.

The last time he'd shown his face was down in the parking deck. He took off with their groceries and her laptop. "Son of a bitch, piece of shit!" she'd snapped under her breath.

She removed her key from the lock and pushed the door wide open. The silence was eerie. The air stagnant. All things considered, it was normally abuzz with noise from the television and decadent, savory aromas wafting from Mrs. Ortiz's kitchen.

Not paying attention, she nearly tripped over something lumpy and heavy. She figured it might have been one of the kid's hoodies or possibly a pair of shoes that had been left by the door. When she turned on the light switch, her voice caught in her throat at the bloody sight.

FORTY-FIVE

THE BLOODY MASS was Baba Ignacio. His limp lifeless body lay in state in the small foyer area of the apartment. A cold chill ran down her spine and her mouth became as pillowy and dry as cotton.

She left her gun in her car, but she wished she hadn't. Something was afoot. As she crouched down to get a better look at Baba Ignacio, she saw that someone had shot the cat.

She looked around and saw a spent casing. A Glock 9 millimeter. Her heart rate increased. Something stirred deep down in her gut. That was her intuition and she loathed what it was saying.

Call it cop instinct or homicide hunch, but she had a strange way of being able to determine with astonishing accuracy when foul play was at hand. And foul play was definitely at hand. There had never been a time where she felt that gut-wrenching feeling—and not been right about it.

It was a quality that sharpened and grew stronger over the years. It was a quality that separated good detectives from great detectives. It wasn't a characteristic that one could learn in college or the marines, or the police academy.

It wasn't a characteristic one could learn from experience either, though that helped. It was something you had to be born with. It was innate and it only worked during dire times.

Tyler was lying on the couch, fast asleep. It looked like he might have fallen asleep while playing video games or doodling, but the TV was off and his sketchbook was across the room on the dining room table.

"Honey, wake up. Where is everyone? What happened to the cat?" Patricia said, as she walked over to her son. Her words were weak and fluid.

He didn't respond. He wasn't much of a heavy sleeper, except for the weeks he was taking low dose Percocet after the accident. Other than that, her baby normally stirred at the sound of his mother's voice. His body was cool, not cold, but cooler than normal, under the circumstances. The apartment was warm. After thinking about it, she realized she smelled gas. Yes, that was definitely gas.

Suddenly, Patricia Garbutt's worse fears came rushing at her in vivid life-sized three dimensional proportions. She attempted to wake Tyler once more. This time she shook him with fury.

She quickly brought her two fingers to his neck, to check for his pulse. There was none. She gulped air. Felt her heart drop down to her feet.

She ran to her mother's room and found Mrs. Ortiz and Maria both lying on the bed. They looked like they were sleeping peacefully. The antique metallic lamp-light on the nightstand was on, casting a grim light on the side of her mother's sleeping face.

Patricia went over to her and gently attempted to rouse Mrs. Ortiz. No luck. She checked her pulse. It had escaped her. Mrs. Ortiz' neck rolled like a newborn. Patricia felt herself begin to panic more and more by the second. What was happening? What happened to everyone while she was gone?

She moved to Maria. No pulse. Patricia's eyes filled with tears. For reasons she would never understand, she thought of the sickness she had when she carried Maria, how even the smells of Dial antibacterial soap made her nauseous. She felt that familiar morning sickness nausea. She felt uncontrollable vomit force its way out of her mouth.

She quickly ran into Lisa's room. The door was pulled shut. She opened the door and saw her younger sister slumped over her desk as though she had just crashed after a long exhausting evening. The malefic gaseous odor was stronger in that compact space. Her laptop was up, the screensaver flashing images of psychedelic hearts and stars; dancing unicorns.

Patricia realized the horror of horrors. Her entire family had been assassinated. This was a hit. This was a contract killing and this was very personal.

FORTY-SIX

DETECTIVE GARBUTT RAN to the kitchen, and sure enough, each of the burners of the gas stove were turned on and the gas from the oven had been ignited; the oven door splayed spread eagle. Mrs. Ortiz's pan of cornbread was still untouched.

She immediately rotated on her heels and headed for the front door. She nearly collapsed once she'd made it outside. The fresh air was so clean and crisp that she nearly suffocated—like exposing a frostbite victim to too much heat at once; it could cause more harm than help. Her lungs felt as though they had been lacerated; another five minutes exposed to the gaseous carbon monoxide fumes and she too would have taken her last nap.

She vomited again. This last episode brought up pure stomach acid and bile the color of ectoplasm. It burned coming up and burned leaving her wracking body. It left a ghastly and horrific taste in her mouth.

She ran to her car with tears streaming from her eyes and down her face. The tears burned and scorched her face as the painful realization that her entire family had been massacred.

It began to slowly set in. It slowly settled into a dark sludge at the pit of her stomach, leaving pure unadulterated vitriol for the monster that was responsible.

Sure, everything faded. We all have a date with death at the end of this thing called life, but who was this asshole to take the lives of her family, as if he was God? Her family had been prematurely taken away from her, and this meant war. It was at that moment that Patricia Garbutt realized that we were born into this world alone, we took on this world alone, and ultimately, we died alone.

Her entire family. Mrs. Ortiz. Maria. Tyler. Lisa. That bastard had murdered her entire family, including Baba Ignacio. Things had gone too far, way too far. How would she tell her brothers and sisters that mamí was dead? How could she go on without her precious children?

Once Detective Garbutt made it to her car, she noticed a post-it note stuck to her steering wheel.

"Conservation of one's own strength; Destruction of enemy strength. We must not attack an objective we are not certain of winning." –Mao Zedong

It was written in Michael Roth's impish fourth grade scribble. His handwriting was chicken scratch. She could see where he'd pressed down with the pen on the semicolon and periods.

Detective Garbutt reached into her glove compartment in search of her emergency pack of cigarettes. She grabbed the pack of Cools and shook a cigarette from the package. Her hands were shaking like crazy. She was a nervous tearful mess — a train wreck with a ponytail.

She dialed 911 and lit a cigarette, while waiting for the operator to address her emergency. Taking a drag from one of those cancer sticks, she attempted to calm her trembling hands.

A dreadful sense of despondency began to immediately descend upon Detective Garbutt. It is impossible to realize how important your family is, until they are gone. She bawled until her eyes stung, red hot with agony. Everyone and everything that she lived for was lying dead in that apartment and the only thing that would keep her afloat now was inertia.

Soon, several APD came zipping up the street, followed by a paramedic van. The county coroner, CSIs, medical examiners, and GBI arrived twenty minutes later, just before Channel 5 News. A CBS chopper *thwap-thwap-thwapped* above the apartment complex, in search of the suspect.

Detective Garbutt was broken, but she understood that there was still much work to do. She knew Michael Roth was behind this, but he hadn't left a single print or clue placing him in or near the apartment.

"Get this to the lab and get our finest handwriting specialist on it pronto. Time is of the essence," Garbutt barked out orders to Emilio Sanchez, a CSI.

She retained what little strength she had left until she caught a glimpse of them wheeling the corpses out one by one, in body bags. Up until that point, body bags were mere artifacts of the trade; props. Today, body bags were a bitter reminder of how fragile life was.

Who was left? She thought of one of the last family nights they'd celebrated as an official family, before Anthony slithered off into his own personal abyss of drugs and depravity. When they were comfortable financially. While they were still in their gorgeous two-story, Craftsman-style Sandy Springs home.

They played several spirited games of charades while Patricia cooked baked macaroni and cheese and roasted a garlic-crusted pork shoulder. Anthony was tipsy and she had a slight buzz from sipping one too many New Castles. They had rough sex that night, as they always had when it stormed, hoping the kids would mistake the sounds of the bed's headboard for thunder.

She remembered the night as clear and vividly as though it were yesterday. It was a rainy night in Georgia. Tyler had received a fresh haircut earlier that morning. Anthony had taken the cars to be washed, but typical of Atlanta, it always rained on the days you washed your car. Maria hadn't transformed into Lucifer yet. She was on the phone all day, but excitedly ended her ever-so-significant-conversation to participate in family night. It was everyone's favorite thing.

When they brought Tyler's body out, she needed to be restrained. Chelsea Hopkins and Adam Curtis, two forensic scientists and personal friends, held Patricia up. Her knees had gone cripple at the sight of the child-sized body bag. She knew it was her baby. With that, she started crying all over again.

Her head ached from hours of tear letting and emotional anguish. She knew instantly that she wouldn't be right in the head.

Who was left? There would be no more family nights. No more trips to Dave and Busters. No more bowling, miniature golf, Six Flags or arguing over what they'd have on the pizza. Anthony loved anchovies, mushrooms and sausage. Maria always picked everything off of her pizza, and dabbed the excess grease from each slice before putting it into her mouth. She claimed she had to be careful of every calorie. Tyler, like his mother, only liked pepperoni and nothing else on his pizza.

Who was left? Every Saturday night had been family night. That was now a relic in history, no different than the Reagan era or a time when *Who's the Boss* came on prime time. There would be hell to pay for this, Patricia thought. She would personally see to it that that rat bastard Roth never lived to see another day, let alone face trial. She would kill him herself, she promised.

FORTY-SEVEN

DETECTIVE PATRICIA GARBUTT began the arduous task of calling each of her siblings to tell them the horrible news. It was a daunting task, but someone had to do it and she was that someone.

She was still parked in the parking deck of the apartment; her Crown Vic crouched in the corner, brooded in the darkness. She had nowhere else to go, after all. Her eyes were swollen and puffy with angst and anxiety seeped from her pores.

The day dragged along lazily, lopping pungent biting winds through the air as clouds gathered overhead. The sky was the color of already been chewed juicy fruit gum. There was a permanent deep chill in the air — atmospheric melancholia and airborne madness.

Patricia was brimming over with doubt — stewing in her smallness. She doubted herself and her ability to cope with any more traumas. It was like someone had hacked into her heart and read her fears out loud to the demonic spirits that lurk in the dark corners of every serial killer's psyche.

Yes, someone had hacked into her heart and read the sentences written on her capillaries and arteries; read down into her bone marrow. Words couldn't describe how painful this ordeal had been for her.

She was raised to believe that no matter how busy your life was, you always were to find time to spend with family. Blood was thicker than water, your job, your problems, and anything else that life may have presented you with.

This was now her cross to bear. And Detective Garbutt felt she was completely to blame. It was her that psychopath wanted. She was the one responsible for putting him behind bars.

She had always been raised to put God first, then family, and then career. She hadn't kept God first. She'd put everything before God, namely, the city of Atlanta. She couldn't recall the last time she'd attended church services. It was so long that she was embarrassed at the thought of walking down the aisle—the judgment, the stares, the onlookers, and their pointing fingers; their holier-than-thou Judas kisses on the cheek and pats on the back and church hugs, of course.

Patricia rang her oldest brother first. Angel Garbutt was the firstborn of the children. Angel was forty-nine years old and Patricia couldn't stand his guts. He was *persona non grata*.

He was six feet of inconsistency and drama. Patricia considered her oldest brother to be one of the biggest Bible thumping, womanizing, selfish hypocrites to ever walk the planet. He was Mrs. Ortiz's major source of financial support. He lived in Helena, Alabama—a suburb of Birmingham. He'd been married for sixteen years to his wife Rebecca and worked for Mercedes Benz as a Project Director at their plant in Birmingham.

He called himself an assistant priest at Our Lady of The Valley Catholic Church. But, if Patricia knew her brother, she knew he was probably bedding a few women in the congregation. He had.

In fact, Angel was having an ongoing affair with a woman at the church for the past five and a half years. They had a son together. No one in the family except for Mrs. Ortiz had knowledge of Angel's love child. It would have crushed Rebecca, although she knew her husband had a roaming eye.

Angel and Patricia had a falling out years ago, over money. Patricia loaned her brother forty-five hundred dollars as a *loan*. Needless to say, ten years passed, and Angel had yet to pay Patricia the forty-five hundred dollars back. Since then, Patricia's relationship with her brother was a distant one, thinly veiled with contempt, resentment, and a seething animosity. Words can't describe how little Angel cared.

Be that what it may, Mrs. Ortiz named Angel the executor over her estate. Should anything happen to her, Angel was responsible for delegating what would happen with her estate, money, family heirlooms, as well as seeing to it that each and every one of Mrs. Ortiz's wishes were carried out to a tee, according to her last living will and testament. She'd been very explicit in seeing to it that her oldest child handled everything as she'd instructed.

All things considered, Patricia felt that she should have been executor of estate, because she was the one who tended to all of her mother's needs. Angel was all the way in Alabama, and he only came to visit mamí at Christmas and Thanksgiving.

Any other time, Patricia had to drive mamí to see Angel and his bitch of a wife, Rebecca. Rebecca was a blonde, blue-eyed bitch on wheels. Patricia knew her sister-in-law was a coke head. She just *knew* it. She exhibited all the classic signs of a coke head. Yet, she couldn't prove it. So she kept her distance.

She refused to fight with Angel, which she'd done all her childhood. Angel had a virulent temper and he'd physically and mentally abused each of their sisters and brothers when they were growing up. Angel was an Aquarius, and everyone knew they were the most selfish and self-centered people of the zodiac.

When Angel heard the news that his mother had been murdered, he dropped the phone. Patricia could hear his deep throaty sobbing in the background. He was at a loss for words. Rebecca grabbed the phone and told Patricia she'd have him call her back as soon as he'd gathered himself. Rebecca also asked Patricia to give her all the funeral information. They'd be on their way down to Atlanta as soon as possible.

It was strange for Patricia because the last time she'd driven Mrs. Ortiz and the kids down to Birmingham to spend a three-day weekend with Angel's family, it was like her brother had become his wife's yes man. Patricia thought it only fitting that her bossy self-centered brother be married to and dominated by an even bossier wife.

Then there was Maurice Garbutt, who was a year and a half younger than Patricia. He was a jetsetter, living in Palm Beach, Florida. Known around South Beach for his lensless red framed glasses, sprightly colored pastel Lacoste polo shirts, or festooned in black diamond earrings, he made quite a name for himself for his kooky couture.

He didn't have any children. Maurice Garbutt was a bachelor and made a living designing apps for Fortune 500 companies. He'd always been somewhat of a computer geek. After graduating from college, he started his own small dot com company. He spent a few years in Silicon Valley before buying a mini mansion in south Florida.

Maurice Garbutt was handsome and smart according to society's standards, and he had a frenetic way of getting money and women to virtually follow him wherever he went. Of all her siblings, Maurice Garbutt resembled her the most— like her doppelganger, only with a "Y" chromosome. He was out of pocket. Patricia left him an urgent message to call her as soon as possible.

Selena Garbutt, who lived in New Orleans with her boyfriend of forever and their two children, was so crushed and devastated by the bad news that she descended into a panic attack. She was asthmatic, and Patricia knew it would be chancing it to tell her younger sister the news over the phone. "No, Patty…nooooo!"

It was a sound that would linger in Patricia's mind for months on end. Selena said she would pack up the family and be on her way that same night to help plan the funeral and see to it Patricia wasn't alone. She would even bring fresh beignets and coffee from Café Du Monde. She frequently made the drive from the French Quarter to Atlanta several times a year. Selena was Patricia's favorite sibling. They understood each other.

Jenny lived in Memphis with her husband Kirk. They didn't have any children, just a huge blue-eyed husky they treated better than most people treated their children.

Jenny was a free spirit. She prided herself on being an artist—choosing to spend her days making handmade jewelry, sculpting ceramics, and getting drunk on red wine while dousing canvases with oils and acrylics.

Her husband Kirk was a writer and self-proclaimed poet. Kirk hadn't published a shred of literature, but he worked the hell out of the spoken word circuit. He was a tall robust black man with long flowing dread locks that grazed his waist.

One time when Patricia and the family spent a week visiting Jenny and Kirk, she had to shampoo her hair and bleach all of the kid's clothing just to get the heavy scent of incense and sage out. Jenny and Kirk were two free souls with quirky eccentricities. They were made for one another.

Jenny was the sister who pretended she was a mermaid. As a child, she would tell people that she wasn't human, but a mermaid from another planet; another dimension. She was New Age before New Age was popular on the world scene. She practically lived in the bathtub and devoured all types of pseudo-scientific magazines and peer review journals on Indigo and Crystal children. She was heavy into the occult and all things esoteric.

Mamí would dole out repeated spanking after spanking for Jenny's refusal to climb out of the bathtub after soaking until her fingertips puckered. Nothing worked. She loved the water and that was that.

The thing about being around Jenny was you knew that she was a special soul. An old soul. She knew things no young person should ever know. One always knew when they were around those special rare souls; it was like the excitement you got when you'd discovered a beautifully human blog or lent your ears to an amazing playlist.

When she answered the call, she already knew why Patricia was calling her. It was mercurial and fascinating at the same time. "How did you know?" Patricia asked.

There was a pregnant pause over the line. "When is the funeral? Do you need help planning the wake?" Jenny asked. She was peaceful. She had moxy, but that day her voice was a raspy calm placid lake.

Patricia had no idea how to answer such a question. She was so taken aback that she was at a loss for words.

"I felt in my spirit that something wasn't right. Mamí and Lisa and Tyler were murdered. I saw it in my mind's eye. Me and Kirk will be on the road as soon as possible Patty," she said.

There was no rhyme or reason. Jenny answered the phone and it was more like she was *making* the phone call. Jenny was comforting; she was a breath of fresh air to her sister. All she knew how to do was be consoling. She was a tall glass of lavender lemonade on a hot summer day.

She said Kirk was on his way home from yoga at the local ashram. As soon as he got home, they would get on the road. She didn't want her sister to shoulder this alone. That was the thing with Jenny; she was a protector. Every family needed one.

FORTY-EIGHT

FOR THE NEXT three weeks Patricia slept at Jake's place. They agreed to put the past behind them and to let bygones be bygones...temporarily. He gave her his bed, while he slept on the sofa in the front room.

Winter was brutal. The sexiness had worn off, or perhaps it was the sight of her flabby thighs in house shoes and his morning breath. Enough calamity to kill any semblance of an affair. There's nothing like living with a person—to bring out their true identity.

Jake had nightmares about Aurora. He was waking up in cold sweat, so he started taking Lunesta just to get through the night.

It was a time of dark skies and luminous constellations. Detective Patricia Garbutt pined for the days when she awoke to sunlight pouring into her Sandy Springs home, casting a radiant glow on her crown maple dark amber hardwoods, the merriment in Tyler's laugh, and Maria's brazen raging pubescent sneer.

Yes, she even missed the arguments and the fights. And mamí, God, she missed mamí and Lisa. She was beginning to miss her husband Anthony, more and more. It got to the point where she would've been more than willing to work things out.

Loneliness didn't discriminate. Even in a room full of people, loneliness stalked Patricia like a cold-blooded psychopath. Her blues ranged from the color of Bermuda skies to majestic blue-granite pillars and the waters of Yelapa, Mexico. The pain was larger than life.

Every night she choked her anxiety and angst in Maple-Bourbon Smash or a bottle of red wine, in hopes that the taste of the dancing of the grape and its minerality would be enough to ostracize depression from her body. Didn't she know that you can't exorcise spirits with spirits?

To her consternation, pain merely bred like the plagues of Egypt and drowned her in an armada of shades of depression she never knew existed.

The funeral was a dreamy repast, more like a huge Ortiz-Garbutt family reunion. Relatives from Belize City had made the trek to see one of their own off to heaven.

It was the first time that all of the brothers and sisters, sons, daughters, aunts, uncles, nieces, nephews, and in-laws had gathered together in one place—the coup dé grâce: the hall had harlot-lipstick red walls and curry-colored tablecloths. It was like an Amy Winehouse song—dark, bluesy, but soulful.

In a funny way, it was like mamí's special way of looking down on the event and adding her sense of cruel Mayan humor.

The young children had little to no idea as to the real reason why they were seeing *all* of the family under one roof. Some spoke pure patois, some were quadroon, all were sullen in a peculiar and woeful way that they couldn't possibly understand. They shared stories and swapped ideas amidst games of red-light-green-light, 'Mother may I," "Simon says," and 'duck, duck, goose'.

The Ortiz tribe was a spicy Afro-Latin, Caribbean goulash, a splash of Brooklyn, Spain, India, Bali, New Orleans, Miami, and Gulf Coast, saturated with Mayan soul. Raven haired little girls. Schoolboys with Moorish eyes. Mulatto skin. High Mestizo cheekbones. Kriol everywhere.

At the wake, they dined on rice and beans, stewed chicken, fish tacos, barbecue, deep-dish pizza, bagels and lox, key lime pie, lobster rolls, and po'boy sandwiches. As diverse and multi-ethnic as they had become as a tribe.

After the funeral there was everything from Cajun queso, cucumber sandwiches, coddled egg, Swiss Chard with sweet garlic, blue-crab mousse, fried pickle chips, succulent short rib stew, to kale chips floating around the banquet hall where the reception was held.

The air was redolent of a heady consommé. On account of Jenny, several glasses of chardonnay accompanied mamí's 'home going'. Decadent butter-pecan blondie sundaes and mango-raspberry smoothies for the kids. Aussie-styled flat whites for the elders.

Maurice rhapsodized about how many accounts he'd acquired over the past year. "You know it feels really good to be successful, but now I have my eyes on starting a nonprofit. I'd like to divest a little. Maybe I'll volunteer my services and start conducting free programming classes," he quipped. He was a first rate version of a philanthropist in training.

Selena guffawed. "Maybe you should spread a little of that success to your little sister. I'm proud of you and I know papa would have been even more proud."

Their father, a blue-black man the color of dark roast, with an obsequious demeanor, still lived on in their hearts. He had been a hardworking man. Witty and adventurous.

He'd instilled priceless values in his sons and daughters and was a pillar of strength for the restless and the hopeful alike.

He was the one everyone went to when they needed direction and rational truth. Although he passed when they were all young children, they understood everything he preached. Especially the ones who bore children. Once you become a parent, you understand your parents even more, and you come to appreciate solid parenting.

Jenny said she could sense his presence silhouetted against the backdrop of the funeral service for mamí. She also asked everyone to evacuate the church before the funeral service so she could perform a proper spiritual cleansing, in which she proceeded to sweep through the building feather-fanning sage smoke and chanting blessings.

"If y'all are too afraid to say something about that damn Voodoo Jenny's doing, I'll step up and say something," Angel rebuffed.

"It's not Voodoo! She's setting the stage for your mother's departure to the other side. If she says your father's spirit is here welcoming his bride, then that's exactly what it is. It's a gesture born of respect and dignity. You should be glad someone here is clouty and gutsy enough to communicate with the spirit world," Kirk retorted.

"Whatever man, all I'm saying is that maybe this isn't the best time to be doing it. She was our mother too," Angel whispered loudly. Angel was a man who overvalued argument for the sake of argument, mainly because he liked to hear himself talk.

The Garbutts and Ortiz family were a mélange of storytellers, artists, and innovators, passionate about their reputation, and ubër passionate about family. The men were philosophers, fishermen, and carpenters—men who worked with their hands and provided for their families. Patricia hadn't told anyone about her separation from her husband Anthony.

It was awkward having Jake accompany her to her mother's funeral. After financing that, the family would have to put their heads together to figure out how they'd bury Lisa, Tyler, and Maria. It was a nightmare, everyone agreed; a headache of epic proportion.

"I still can't get past the fact that she's no longer here, mamí or Lisa. It won't be the same," Angel opined.

He and Maurice were standing near the long table that was brimming over with food. "You know, I have to admit that I feel mortally wounded brother," Maurice said. "Ma was our backbone, our last remaining link home. If I could get my hands on the bastard maggot meat that did this, I'll kill him," his eyes began to well with tears as he spoke. His jaws tightened and contracted.

Angel placed his hand on his brother's shoulder. His idea of being comforting. "That's what the law is for, Mo. In due time, they'll find the killer. Mamí's somewhere resting in peace. So too is Lisa and our little nephew and niece. Her death wasn't in vain. Everything's gon' be okay. Just keep reminding yourself that she would have wanted us to be strong, little brother," he whispered to Maurice before looking over at his wife Rebecca.

One of the main things that kept resonating with Patricia was how Rebecca had had one of the worst cases of post-partum depression she'd ever seen. Now this! This was a whole 'nother ball of wax.

Angel Garbutt told his wife for years about the size of the inheritance they'd receive once his mother passed away. His and her eyes were both on the prize. They both were nothing if not greedy, self-centered, and money hungry.

Rebecca was bugged eyed and overly energetic during the funeral. Patricia assumed her sister in-law had probably snorted a few lines before and

during the services. She was as geeked up as ever —
plastered to capacity. It was obvious when addicts
were huffing or tooting coke. It always revealed
itself. They were too jumpy, too jittery, too nervous,
or simply overexcited in the midst of an
inappropriate occasion.

Now she buzzed around from table to table,
offering unsolicited hugs and condolences. It
appeared pretentious and too painted on a gesture
in Patricia's opinion.

FORTY-NINE

THE FUNERAL WAS heartbreaking. The casket bearers almost dropped the casket. The reception afterwards was worse. There was pain embedded in the fabric of the carpet and in the texture of the air. It was like being in an infected bladder.

Angel Garbutt played the role of comforter, or at least he assumed that was what he was supposed to be doing. That was typical Angel Garbutt, always getting things wrong. He kept his dark Ray Bans on throughout the service, only pulling them down every now and then, to wipe a stray tear.

Selena Garbutt was a mess. You could see the wheels in her mind racing frantically. The voices in her head were calling out to her.

She was already living a complicated life and this just added more fat to her plate. She'd shown up to the funeral wearing far too much make-up. Her hair was big. Dyed chestnut brown with lowlights. She smelled of lilacs from Albuquerque — an Eau de toilette and oil hybrid she'd picked up during her travels. She'd lost weight since Patricia last saw her. She never left Nathan's presence. Ever.

Nathaniel Hayes was her live-in boyfriend. He wore blue jeans and a faded blue button-down shirt to the funeral. No one in the family liked him. He was a bum. He claimed he was of Dutch-Irish stock, that he had *hard worker* in his veins. That's what he said with his mouth.

He refused to work. He lived off of Selena. He drank like he was Irish; that was for sure. They'd been together off and on for years and started having babies two years ago.

If her father was still alive, he wouldn't have allowed such a man to breathe in his daughter's direction. Papa: a man who shined his wingtips, worked with his hands, and loved the sounds of Thelonious Monk's piano, Celia Cruz and Tito Puente. Papa believed a man who lived off of a woman's hard work was not fit to be called a man. Such a man was self-castrated; emasculated.

Mamí never really liked Nathan, but she knew he made her daughter happy, and that was all that mattered. If he could, he would have kissed fear from Selena's mouth. If he could.

Patricia once told her that she would have been better off getting sperm from a homeless sperm donor — at least the odds would be in her favor.

Despite the fact that no one liked Nathaniel, he was loyal, caring, and he loved himself some Selena Garbutt. His presence at the funeral service and the reception was barbed wire.

Every time Selena brought up the topic of marriage, Nathan changed the subject, got all quiet and weird, or dodged the subject altogether. It was anyone's guess what his angle was.

All they knew was that he was into kickboxing and mixed martial arts, Capoeira, and he smoked reefer twenty-four seven. He dressed like he still existed in the eighties. Members Only jackets in all primary colors. Patricia once told mamí that she believed he was secretly married. But after two, three, then four years passed, he proved to everyone that he was there for the long haul. In it to win it.

Nathan was in the fat-burning zone, slow and steady, whereas Selena wanted to be in the muscle-burning zone, fast paced, hot and heavy. Their children Sarah and Thelonious, named after the jazz greats, had accompanied them to the funeral. Both the girl and the boy were their father's doppelgangers.

Sarah was an adorable raven-haired girl. Thelonious, unlike his father, was quite industrious. Although he was only eighteen months old, he was already walking, talking, and showing signs that he was good with numbers.

Selena was all tears: red and puffy eyed, snotty-nosed, and upset for the duration of the day. They all were. She was sensitive and emotional as a child. Although she was older than Jenny and Lisa, she could be mistaken as the youngest.

J.R., Lisa's one-time boyfriend had been at the funeral and was now at the reception, gathering food on his plastic plate, and balancing a Styrofoam cup of punch. Patricia hadn't recognized him at the funeral, but decided to speak to him during the reception. He said he was taking classes at Georgia Perimeter College and he'd gotten a job as a cashier at Rite Aid.

Angel could see his brother was visibly shaking. In front of the crowd he did what he does best, perform. But now that he was alone, one on one with his big brother, Maurice Garbutt could be his authentic self. While his head was down, he quickly flicked a tear from his eye, in hopes that no one saw it.

Maurice Garbutt was rough on the edges, but soft and sensitive behind the façade. Although the funeral was arguably melancholic, the reception afterwards was festive and refreshing. When Belizeans came together they made merry. There was music and food. The atmosphere was light, but with a hint of sadness.

"Here have a drink," Angel said. He handed his brother a glass of wine. "Something to take the edge off."

Maurice Garbutt sipped the wine his brother handed him. "I always thought mamí would be here to see me get married and have kids of my own."

"Oh man, that's incidental. I understand how you feel, but —"

"That's just it, Angel, you don't understand. You're happily married. You have a family. Mamí met your family. She knew Rebecca. She'll never be able to know my family or my wife."

"But you have no wife or children, yet. Listen Maurice, you're successful. Focus on your career. Focus on your new foundation. Pour your energy into something bigger than yourself, and in that way you can leave your own legacy...a legacy that will benefit the Garbutts and the Ortiz family name. A legacy that will out-live you. Mamí was very proud of you and your accomplishments. We all are. We all have done different things with our lives. Maybe we're not all meant to get married and have a big family. Perhaps God wanted you to be the one to focus solely on bettering your life and being financially successful. That's all I'm trying to say to you."

Maurice licked his lips. "I just feel like I don't have anything now. I don't expect you to understand. You have Rebecca. I'm tired of random women. Sure, they're fun for a little while, but I want something more. I need more. I don't know man. I'm angry. I'm angry at mamí for leaving us so soon, and I'm livid with the bastard who murdered her."

Angel stepped backward and took a deep breath. "Well, Lisa lost her life too. And let's not forget Tyler and Maria. All of them were taken from us too soon. We'll never know what Lisa's family would have been like. None of us, not one of us is in a position to judge the will of God. Don't think that just because I have Rebecca that everything is peaches and cream. We haven't been happy in years. In fact," Angel paused before looking around to see if anyone else was in earshot. Seeing that no one was, he resumed.

"I have a son out of wedlock. Yeah, me. I have an illegitimate son and I love his mother. I love her as much as I love my wife. Nothing is as it seems, Mo! Sometimes life doesn't make sense. Sometimes, we have to try to make sense of senseless pain and sometimes we have to try to make meaning out of the meaningless. That's just the way God works.

Mamí is in a better place now. She's with papa. They're both in heaven looking down on us. We have to learn to find comfort in that."

"I don't believe that for one minute. I wish I could believe that, but I just don't. They are gone, all of them are gone. I don't know anything about Heaven. All I know is they're gone." Maurice Garbutt swallowed the rest of his wine and traipsed away.

FIFTY

LATER THAT SAME evening, after most of the family returned to their hotels and things quieted down, the siblings sat around getting drunk on Belikin, the beer of Belize. They shared stories from their childhood. Like Dubliners, they had the "Gift of the Gab".

Selena was suffering from Lupus. She came right out and said it. It was like watching a train wreck in slow motion. Although they were still young, important decisions would have to be made regarding Sarah and Thelonious. Just in case. Selena claimed that telling them what she was going through gave her comfort. *False comfort*, Patricia thought.

Patricia was thinking about how spoiled the next generation of Garbutts were, compared to her generation. How they took everything for granted. How they were the posterity of a third world Central American country, yet cared about nothing more than their smart phones, tablets, and X-box games.

Patricia and her siblings were no different, vacuous in their capacity to care about anything besides their Brazilian cherry hardwoods, soapstone countertops, the latest asset they'd added to their stock portfolio. It was peculiar how death had an inexplicable way of bringing truth to the surface.

She was proud of her ability to do for her family and she knew mamí was proud of having the ability to do for herself as well as her other siblings. They were rich compared to traditional Belizean standards. They'd made it.

The air was cool, but not oppressive. Seemed to generate its own breeze. The room was silent. Angel Garbutt bit down on his bottom lip. Two folds of skin materialized on his forehead.

Maurice Garbutt, whose eyes were already umber and watery, welled up once more. He felt like an anonymous coward among men, able to do little for anyone other than himself. Jenny looked as though she'd been bitten by a shark. Her eyes widened and her mouth gaped.

In those moments, Patricia saw her family slowly unraveling, like some phantom was pulling them a part one thread at a time. Eventually the whole garment would be nothing more than rags. She felt a hollow void form in her chest cavity. How much more heartbreak could one woman stand?

She also knew that nothing before that moment mattered. The only thing that mattered was how they would all deal with their own personal sagas.

"I didn't know a better way to say it," Selena said.

Nate's hands gathered around Selena's shoulders. He rubbed burden down her back and gently coaxed away the mounting anxiety she'd been carrying. Their love for one another was a thing of beauty. It left no room for the superficial.

As always, Patricia felt like a messenger, like she should have said something inspirational. "When were you diagnosed?"

Selena faced her sister. "I was diagnosed a few months ago. Mamí knew. She was the first person I told, after Nate of course."

Silence befell the building. Everyone was devastated. None of them knew anything about the disease. Selena explained that she had been taking her medications faithfully. She claimed that as long as she kept her stress levels down and her attitude positive that there would be no flare ups.

Everything about the evening seemed ephemeral, like a dream. Patricia still couldn't believe that her babies were gone. She sat there attempting to hold herself together, knowing that she'd never be able to kiss her precious son on the forehead anymore or tangle with her pre-teen daughter. The pain was unbearable, yet Patricia felt dastardly for feeling it. Logic told her to be strong, but her feelings were stepped upon. Courage and bravery escaped her grasp.

Shortly after Selena's confession, just before everyone prepared to leave the banquet hall, Patricia pulled her brother Angel to the side. By then he'd had oceans of Chardonnay to drink. His words were slurred and his thoughts askew.

Rebecca had to help him walk because his inebriation caused him to walk like a zombie. "Listen Angel, I know this may sound crazy, but I was wondering if by chance you could pay me back the money I loaned to you. I really, *really* could use it. To be quite honest with you, I'm down and out. I've been going through it and Anthony and I are separated. It's been unbelievably difficult to just maintain. Well, anyway, I'm rambling. Are you going to help me or not?"

"Patty, we just buried mamí and now you're asking me for money? It's not like I have a few thousand dollars just sitting around to give you." He grew indignant. "Who do you think is footing the bill for all of this?" He made a sweeping motion with his hand.

"Know what? You are fucking incredible, and you have a lot of fucking nerve," Patricia started. "You act like it's your money. It's not *your* fucking money, Angel. It was my money and you gave me your word you would pay me back. To add insult to fucking injury, I happen to know that mamí left you a significant amount of money in her will. This is the way you treat your own sister, Angel?"

Angel Garbutt took a step back and almost tripped over his foot. He caught himself, just before losing his footing. "We all need money Patty! I have a lot of pressure on me. I'm sorry, but I don't have the money to give you."

Maurice and Jennie looked over at their sister and brother arguing. This was the first time they'd seen or heard anything like this in years. They had no idea that Patricia had loaned money to Angel and that he had not repaid the loan. Rebecca was putting her jacket on and listening haphazardly.

"Look Angel, I don't want anything from you. I am not trying to make your life difficult, but I am separated from my husband and I have damn near lost everything that matters in life. The only thing I have left is my sanity and I'm slowly losing grips with it. I have been sleeping on an air mattress and my children were murdered. Isn't there anything you can do? You're telling me you don't have anything? Not even fifteen hundred dollars? I am not asking for a handout. You look at me as if I were some beggar...some charity case. I am your sister and I am asking for you to simply repay what you owe."

Angel shook his head. "I wish I could, Patty. I'm so sorry to hear that. I didn't know." He placed his hand on her shoulder and put on a more serious face. "I wish I could do more, but I can't. Trust in God. Pray about it..."

Patricia looked down at her brother's hand with malevolence and disdain. "Take your dirty hands off of me. You selfish, greedy, hypocritical, lying son of a bitch! How dare you stand there proclaiming to be high and mighty, you fake wannabe man-of-God. How dare you stand there and look down on me like I'm some charity case. I helped your cheating ass when no one would help you, not even mamí!" Patricia reached back and punched him in his chest. She'd lost all control.

Angel Garbutt fell backwards slightly, but he was unscathed and unfazed. Maurice Garbutt dashed over and stood between the two. "What in the world is going on? Are you kidding? We are family, not enemies. What has gotten into you?" He said to his sister. He didn't understand that she had reached her lowest point in life and didn't care anymore.

What happens to a woman who has lost everything? What happens to a woman who hits her lowest low? She'd hit a wall. She felt herself spinning out of control. With her brothers and sisters all around her, she'd never felt lonelier in all her life. She could no longer suppress the agony. Anxiety eclipsed everything, like the moon on a sunny day.

FIFTY-ONE

THREE DEAD BODIES were found in a car left parked on an exit ramp of interstate-85. Triple homicide. No gunshot wounds, no obvious signs of blunt force trauma or stab wounds. Nothing.

Twenty miles south of the city, the air smelled of chimney smoke. Pine trees quaked in the wind. It was just before dawn. The sun was still in its invisible place; in bed, under a blanket of darkness. The sky was a portrait of unredeeming charcoal. When they spoke, the detectives saw their breath in tendrils.

Cars zoomed by on the freeway—the sound of their tires swooshing and slicing through the air. They waited for the chief medical examiner to arrive at the scene. Exhaust flowed in plumes, like bushy tails from late model vehicles. Detective Garbutt could taste dust and oil on her tongue. Several big rigs and eighteen wheelers whizzed by: metal monsters of the road.

Two of the bodies found in the backseat were of men in their late thirties, maybe early forties. Both were skinny. Both were Caucasian. The other body was that of a woman, also Caucasian, late twenties, honey blond with highlights. The two men were found in the back seat slumped against each other as though they were asleep. The woman had been stuffed in the trunk.

"Is this...no way. Impossible. This can't be possible," Detective Garbutt said.

"What? What is it? Spit it out," Jake said.

"This looks like Roth."

Jake rushed over and dipped his head in to get a better look at the backseat. Seeing the likeness of Michael Roth, he bit down on his bottom lip and gave a low gruff, "humph, the resemblance is striking."

One of the lifeless bodies had the height, weight, and stature of Michael Roth: the dark curly hair with the puff of white in the front, those small manicured hands, and chunky knuckles.

Now that the spirit had left the body, the only thing that remained was a pale, pallid, creamy tone of death.

Why would someone do this? The vehicle was a 2009 Dodge Charger. Black. Smoke gray interior that smelled of old cigars and body odor mixed with a tinge of Scotch and cheap package store vodka. Shiny chrome rims were an indication that perhaps the bodies had been placed there post mortem. Only time would tell; time and a detailed autopsy report.

A slim caffeinated reporter emerged from a Channel 2 Action News van sniffing around for answers. Yellow police tape blocked off the perimeter of the exit ramp.

"Move away from the tape please," Jake shouted above the sound of oncoming traffic.

"I'd just like to ask a few questions," the energetic young reporter said.

"I understand, but I'm *just* doing my job. You have to stay back."

"You think there are any prints on the bodies?" Patricia asked the ME. A GBI van slowly pulled up and parked. The sound of crackling pebbles being crushed splashed against the early morning.

"I don't know," Jake murmured. He glanced at the plates on the car. "Alabama plates."

"Call Alabama and run them. We need a positive identification. I believe that's Roth."

"I'm on it."

FIFTY-TWO

"I WANT YOU and Billingsley off the Roth case," Brody told Patricia when she got back to the station. It hit her like a wall of bricks. Understanding and reason escaped her. She and Jake had poured their blood, sweat, and tears into this case over the course of the year. Sure, the going was tough, but that was no reason to pull the plug.

This was unlike Brody to throw in the towel just when they reached the edge of the finish line. He was snatching them from the jaws of victory.

"But why?"

"You're not making any progress and besides his body was positively identified. It's been what, months, and you two can't get your thumbs out of your ass long enough to connect two dots," adding a sardonic, "No disrespect."

Sometimes Brody could be the equivalent of a boil on the ass. This was one of those times. She swallowed the hard lump in her throat and tried not to say anything acidic.

"You can't take us off the case. We're just getting to the bottom of things." Detective Garbutt sighed and pressed a few strands of hair behind her ear. She wondered why Brody was so adamant. If Michael Roth was dead, and he most certainly was, why the rush now? What would it matter?

"Results came back from the crime lab. Roth and the other man, Cliff Howell, died of asphyxiation."

The jury was still out on the woman. Her identity had not been discovered.

So much was still up in the air...such as motive. Who killed Michael Roth and why? How did this all tie into Deidre Priest, Eileen Rosenthal, and Ginger Engstrom? Why was Ebony Cooper murdered? Why were any of the women murdered? Now that Michael Roth had been killed, would the murders stop?

Would they ever have the answers? All of these questions and more swam around Detective Garbutt's head. She wouldn't be able to get adequate rest until she had some definite answers.

All the years of ass-kissing and brown-nosing, the sexism, racism, being overlooked and undoubtedly underpaid—none of it had prepared Detective Patricia Garbutt for this. She wondered if this had anything to do with what she'd stumbled upon a few days earlier at Jake's place.

While Jake showered and butchered his rendition of a John Mayer live concert, to a retinue of invisible lady fans, she noticed what looked like a surveillance camera in the corner, where the ceiling and the wall joined.

It struck her as odd because heretofore, she had not seen this. Was it new? Was Jake spying on her?

It was in his bedroom. Being the detective that she was, she located Jake's cell phone. She didn't know what triggered this sudden interest, but she wrenched the back off the phone.

Her intuition was on high alert. It was clearer than if someone was standing right next to her whispering into her ear, guiding her hand. Sure enough, she saw the faint blinking red eye of a tracker.

She then quickly yanked the back off her phone. The same ominous blinking red eye. They were being observed, perhaps investigated, but why? By whom?

Detective Garbutt found a Russian passport with Jake's picture in it. Jacob Stanislaw, not Jake Billingsley. Her voice caught in her throat. Jacob Stanislaw was born in 1962. He was older than she thought. Older than she was.

She also found another passport; this one issued by the United States. Jake Billingsley, with a Bethesda home address. There was also a keycard enabling access into Quantico. She questioned everything; replayed entire conversations they'd shared.

She tried to mend together truth with fiction. Was his story about Noah even real? Who was he really? Why did he have a Russian passport?

She saw paperwork from the United States Marines. Discharge paperwork from Quantico. She didn't have time to read them all. Jake was on his way out of the shower.

She'd heard his opus end, just before the water splashing against his body stopped abruptly. She eyed a few commodities-grade gold coins, ten million in bearer bonds, and what could be anywhere between three and five million dollars in cut diamonds. What she didn't see was the wire transfer confirmation from a bank in the Caymans.

FIFTY-THREE

IT HAD BEEN two weeks after the funeral when Anthony Eugene Bowers phoned his wife. It was a call from a Georgia State inmate asking if she would accept the collect call.

During the pause for the name of the inmate, she recalled an icy, dank, dreary, sinking feeling in the center of her chest. "Patty, it's me…pick up the phone. Emerg—" it was the tattered and broken voice of her husband. She didn't know what to do with those feelings she harbored.

In that moment she knew for a fact that there was no true security in the world. Security was an illusion, like smoke and mirrors. The greatest magic trick God ever performed for humanity was security: now you see it, now you don't.

Her husband was an educated man, with a Bachelor's degree from UCONN, and a fine résumé to his name, yet there he was calling her collect from jail. It was an enigma to her how this could happen; how things could crescendo into such a crumble of ruins.

It was like the fact that so many college grads worked for so many college dropouts—an incredulous enigma. There was a day that this man made her panties soggy—that was how much he drove her crazy. She had been enthralled by him.

Here was a man who had been groomed for greatness. Today it eluded him. They'd lived, laughed, and loved one another for all those years and this was the first time she'd seen this side of him. She didn't believe it were possible. She didn't believe a man could fall so completely from grace.

She remembered Papoose saying something to the effect that always we learn by doing. No amount of information injected into a woman by books would make her the master of anything, and that included the art of staying married. "A skill is its own teacher, and each of us who aspires to mastery must become an apprentice," she said. "We will become writers if we love writing. We will become mothers if we love children and their laughter."

Patricia wondered how those matriarchs, whose blood pumped elegantly through her veins, rich in Kriol, Arawak, Punta, Garifuna, and Spanish history, held themselves together in the face of such connubial deterioration.

How did they cope with infidelity, or the drunkard husband, or the father of their children who decided he no longer wanted to be a provider? How did they keep themselves fastened, buttoned together, and poised when in the presence of such wracking heartbreak? Surely she could somehow summons some of that soldier courage.

"I'll accept," she spoke into the phone reluctantly.

"How are you honey?" Anthony mumbled. He sounded distant, in more ways than one. She no longer knew this man. This wasn't the Anthony Eugene Bowers that she married. His vocal chords were so affected by the abuse of drugs that his voice was string cheese.

"I've been better, but I won't complain. What happened? Where are you?"

"That's what I'm calling about. I got caught up and I need you to come down here and get me out of this place. Honey I c-c-c-can't spend another waking minute in here." He stuttered.

"What do you mean caught up? Caught up how? What were you charged with?"

"Technically I was charged with armed robbery; breaking and entering, but I swear to God I'm innocent. Baby, you have to believe me."

Patricia sighed. Frustration sprinkled the air. "So how did you get arrested? Were you there?"

"Yeah, I mean I was there but it really didn't happen the way they're making it seem."

She knew he was lying. Whenever he beat around the bush and stalled like this it only meant he was front and center in the middle of a lie.

"Look Tony, I'm in no position to help anyone right now. I am flat out broke. Why don't you call Claire? That is who was helping you with your habit and all, isn't it? I don't know if you heard it through the grapevine or not but the children..." she felt her voice falter and catch in the middle of her throat.

The proper way to say it was more difficult than figuring out Rubik's cube. She couldn't find the words. No, she knew the words like one knows their favorite box of cereal, it just pained her to utter them.

Anthony was so down and out, and strung out on drugs that he didn't know that his family had been detonated. He had no knowledge that his son and daughter had been murdered. It tore Patricia into shreds to have to explain to him.

She swallowed her pride, sniffed and came right out and said it. It was awkward having to tell a man over the phone that his children had been murdered. That was just wrong. Sure, Anthony had fallen off the wagon and he'd become a fucking loser, but shit. Patricia was already splintered and barely held together by stitches of hope for a brighter day.

Times like this, she wished she could fake her own death and relocate to some remote corner of the globe. She dreamed of munching cocoa puffs on Cocoa Island, in the Maldives. Fuck everything, they could have the case and the house and the whole lot, she could start over from scratch.

She knew that for every major battle life waged, surely there was a promised land of cookies and cream. Logic and reason told her that hurt didn't last forever, but at this point the light at the end of the tunnel grew dimmer by the day. She strained to locate the light at the end of the proverbial tunnel. Strained to find the blessing in the lesson.

For every sweet there was a bitter aftertaste. She envisioned pain carved on her husband's face. He made a sound that was inhuman, ghastly and terror-laced. It was the sound of a man who truly had nothing left to lose. Whatever shred of stability and hope he'd been holding onto had now snapped. Whatever life raft he'd been clinging onto had now begun to sink; crumbled and began to disintegrate like bread crumbs tossed into a lake.

He cried out loud; his voice reverberated against the cinder block walls of the jail. She could hear the sounds of other inmates, awaiting their turn to use the pay phone. She could also hear the sounds of doors opening and locking shut: the sounds of incarceration. She knew them all too well.

Someone once said that fate is nothing but the deeds committed in a prior state of existence. She thought long and hard about this. She wondered what she'd done to deserve all of this. Surely she'd lived a wickedly diabolical Hitler-esque existence in a past life to deserve this. Things had become more unstable than Chernobyl.

He asked her how this could all happen. Then he asked her to get someone on the phone and bail him out. Just like that, in a fraction of a second.

They needed to be together at a time like this, he said. In her loneliness, she was fearful that she'd do whatever it took to get her husband out of jail. People did stupid shit out of loneliness and fear, especially women.

Before she was a homicide detective and beneath that badge, she was a woman. Before she was a wife or mother, she was a woman. Under the steel and Teflon exterior, she was a woman, with weaknesses and self loathing, doubts and bittersweet self recriminating thoughts.

With all that was going on in her life she had no foundation from which she could draw strength, at least she didn't think so. There was more that needed to be said during the course of the conversation with Anthon, but Patricia put her mouth on safety. So much was left in the dark cavernous void.

She ended the conversation by giving him her word that she would do the best she could. That evening, Jake brought her flowers. He had Noah with him. They had just come back from Longhorn's Steak House. Jake held a white Styrofoam to-go container in one hand and held onto Noah's hand with his other.

Noah handed Patricia the flowers, a bouquet of white roses interspersed with baby's breath. She drummed up a smile, though inside she was broken. She thanked Noah and Jake for the flowers. Since the death of her children, she'd taken a motherly liking of Noah. Some days she looked at him and saw Tyler, or she'd pick up his toys and video games and burst into tears, with thoughts of her son.

She knew that for every gain, something needed to be sacrificed, and for every sacrifice, something was gained. That was how life on Earth balanced itself out. Without balance, nothing in this world or the world after could ever be truly sustained. Balance brought about structure in a person's life, and it took on a life of its own, a life with beautiful infrastructure.

There was a cold odious feeling that shivered itself down her spine when she looked into Jake's eyes. "How are you?" He gave her a half-hearted smug smile, one that surely dammed up leagues of lies. She knew that wasn't the time or place to confront him about what she'd seen.

"Fine, and you?"

FIFTY-FOUR

MEANWHILE, THE RED light surveillance sensor still blinked its cantankerous one eye. The thought occurred to Detective Garbutt that whoever decided to investigate she and Jake must have had good reason. She struggled with finding the best way to address the issue.

People who fought fire with fire went the way of Pompeii. Ashes. Besides, she didn't have the energy or the willpower to embark on another battle. Sometimes it was wise to choose one's battles carefully. It wasn't prudent to fight this war.

In the last week, she'd been in stressful, emotionally draining conversations with Brody and Anthony; she didn't have anything more to give. She was in a bellicose mood.

She wanted to get to the bottom of things. She wanted to fight, but she knew intuitively and perhaps instinctively, that she needed to be smart. It was the mark of a great woman to remain poised and calm while in the grips of pressure.

After putting Noah in the bathtub, Jake came back out into the open space. "I got the call from Brody."

"Yeah, he wants us off the case. I can't believe after all this time and hard work, that he'd just boot us off the case so easily."

"It's more going on than he's letting on," Jake muttered demurely.

"What are you driving at, Jake?"

"I don't know," he started. He sat down, ran brawny hands down the front of his jeans, rested his elbows on his knees and steepled his hands. Then he stood back up.

He was obviously troubled by the situation. He couldn't sit down or sit still for longer than thirty seconds. Something was up. Something was wrong. Patricia didn't know what to think.

"What's your problem?" Patricia repeated.

He gave her those chilly arctic blue eyes. "Never mind. I don't want to talk about it; not right now anyway. I've had a long day." He wanted to fume in silence.

"You and I both. Noah's mother giving you the third degree again?"

"Yep."

"Sure you don't want to talk about it?"

"Not now, but I could use a beer," he said, before walking away. "Let me get the kid to bed."

Jake was being cold and withdrawn. Patricia knew there was infinitely more bothering him than Noah's mother and Brody making the decision to kick them off the Roth case. She knew he was lying to her and whatever he lied about was giving him the blues.

Patricia went to the fridge and grabbed two ice cold bottles of Guinness. She popped the cap off and took a long gulp of that dark-as-Columbian coffee-brew. It was a hoppy brown ale. Tasted like the old Antebellum South via Brooklyn. Her eyes panned over the hearty red-brown stained, clear

271

lacquered solid beech cabinets. The Moen stainless steel faucet. Hyper-artisanal influence everywhere her eyes rested.

Outside, clouds combed out like low smoke over the linden trees, the verdant hills like tired, mossy stones. The sky was getting as black and misty as vintage vinyl. To the south, the awe-inspiring gracious skyline spread out. Jake emerged from the back, exuding cool like fog. Noah was tucked in and chasing sleep.

Jake grabbed the other Guinness. It waited patiently for him on the counter. He gulped it slowly. "I never asked you this, but I've always wondered...why is it that you kept your maiden name?"

Patricia sucked her teeth and rolled her eyes. That was the subject of many arguments between her and Anthony in the past. It made him bitterer than two-day old coffee.

"Well, the real reason is because I wanted to stay true to my Papa. He was my favorite person before he passed away. My mother felt the same way about her ancestry, which is why she chose to hold onto her family name. No matter who I marry, I'm always a Garbutt. I'll die as a Garbutt."

"Oh, okay. I see. Never pegged you as a feminist, so I knew it wasn't that. I just always wondered."

"Speaking of the devil, I spoke to the hubby earlier today. He's in jail. Robbery. He claims he's innocent and begged me to bail him out. Between him and my screwed up family, I don't know what to do or think for that matter." Patricia grew exasperated.

Jake turned on some Kings of Leon and began making himself a cocktail, something stronger than the Guinness he'd guzzled down. He pined for something that would do more damage to his kidneys and liver.

Patricia turned to gaze at the Jackson Pollock painting situated on the wall, inhaled its rich reds, gold leaf details, and slate grays. She gave Jake her back and her sensual magnanimous gait.

She was wearing one of his white button down shirts, and nothing else. His eyes drizzled down the ravine of her back, over the small of her back where her feminine skin puddled, subtle swelling hills, to the valley of her coco bread waterfall legs.

He harbored naughty, smutty thoughts. Patricia was a beautiful ruin. Even in her state of brokenness, she was beautiful. Like the Sphinx, you couldn't help but be awed by the power and strength she conveyed.

He wanted her kiss; for he knew that her kiss was what a walk through the Garden of Eden would feel like. If only he could get past her brick front heart.

He offered her another beer. Conversations were best when copious amounts of alcohol were involved. If nothing else, it smoothed out the enmity. Unleashed inhibitions. He stirred himself a negroni.

After a few drinks, the inner chaos and noise subsided. Jake's eyes had become two dimensionless aquamarine oceans. Patricia looked like Cancun on a rainy day. Under the affect of the beer and cocktails, he bronzed his affections for her.

He vowed to himself to return to her annually, she was his Mecca, and his Pilgrimage. He lusted for her. He wanted to treasure seek her body. After all, for the past year they'd spent what felt like every waking hour with one another. How could he not begin to fall in love with her?

"So, what are you going to do? You gonna get Anthony out of jail?"

"With what money? I don't even have two nickels to rub together right now. I'm filing bankruptcy. With the foreclosure and debt on my back, I can't take another day of these creditors ringing my phone. It's driving me apeshit! I've got to do what I gotta do. Got to utilize everything within me. I can't afford to go backwards, and Anthony keeps dragging me backwards. He chose to fuck up his life; *chose* to fuck up the good life we built. He *chose* to walk away. He has to live with his decisions. He made his bed. He has to sleep in it. I told him to go and call Claire. Have Claire bail him out. She's the one who's been engendering the affair that pulled him away from me and enabling his dope habit. Why can't anyone seem to understand I can't fix everything? My goddamn family was murdered in cold blood! The last thing on my mind is bailing Anthony out of jail. What I'd really like to do is put a round of slugs in the sonofabitch who took my family away from me."

She was angrier than Weimar Republic-era Berlin. There was no denying the fact that her life had become a Spielbergian drama.

Jake nodded. He eyed Patricia. The alcohol in his veins made her body look like a work of art — Frank Lloyd Wright-inspired architecture, her breasts soaring cliffs, her backside, the southernmost tip of the Baja Peninsula. Her curves were like narrow ancient alleyways. Her laughter was symphonic music to his ears.

"Come closer to me," he said.

It wasn't subtle, but it wasn't demanding either. They were both sitting on the sofa, each on opposing ends. He pulled her by her arm with desire and sophisticated restraint. Her touch, softer than silk, smoother than velvet, was a frolic through a botanical garden.

He wanted her lavender-scented body on top of his. He wondered how she always managed to smell as fresh as marigolds and daisies. Her natural body aroma was sweet and floral in the way that only the feminine could be.

He was growing hard under his pants. His brain was populous with quickened memories. He tried to touch her thoughts.

"Jake, I can't. Not tonight. I'm really not in the mood," her soft, warm, chocolaty eyes spoke.

"You know we can call the Deputy District Attorney. It's only a matter of a phone call. We can get Anthony out if it helps the situation. I'm just trying to help, that's all," he lied, although his heart was in the right place.

He looked at her as if to say, "I don't have to walk a mile in your shoes, I can see that you're a train wreck from across the room." He sympathized. She wasn't letting him in.

Everything in life had its price. That included lust. Jake rubbed Patricia's leg. She gave him a look. No words ushered forth, just that look. In his mind she was relenting. It was good that he was there for her. He'd been by her side through the most heinous time in her life: the shattering of her marriage and the death of her family. Their bond went beyond professional long ago.

Suddenly, with no rhyme or reason, Jake grabbed Patricia. Almost violently. There was an animalistic passion in his grasp. He kissed her with fury. He kissed her like a marooned man who had found the sensual touch of a woman. Their faces were so close that she could smell the liquor emanating from his pores. His eyes were closed, but hers were not. His skin was red and dewy with perspiration; partially out of frustration, partially out of lustful hunger.

Patricia didn't fight him. She went with the flow. There was a passionate resonance. The lust was thick and nougat sweet. They nibbled each other's lips and sucked one another's tongue. They embraced each other as they kissed. The alcohol in their systems swirled, swished, and made them weak.

Before long, Patricia began lifting Jake's shirt up and over his head. Tossed it onto the floor. He pulled her panties to the side. Drunken and lustful, both found a warm, welcoming oasis to meet them in their empty deserted places.

For Patricia, it was enough to fill the massive void that had formed in her life like a sudden sinkhole. Jake's hands felt warm and fleshy grazing her skin. The future was still unclear and the pain was still present, though muted.

FIFTY-FIVE

THEY TOOK SOMETHING away from each other, but they left something too. Only time would tell whether those things were good, bad, or indifferent.

Detective Jake Billingsley had been a womanizer once upon a time. Perhaps he still was. Perhaps that side of him had grown yellow on the edges. Some would say once a womanizer, always a womanizer, but somehow over the course of his knowing Detective Patricia Garbutt, comforting her through this nightmare, and watching Aurora Suggs be murdered, he'd abandoned his appetite for lying down with random women.

He was changing. Like any two beings that spent enough time with one another, they became a part of each other's ecology. She was like the moon, he like the ocean: being influenced and pulled by her waxing, waning, fullness.

He was growing into a more sensitive man. We all fuck around and become adults, eventually. The clock radio read 4:39AM. Jake and Patricia had fallen asleep nude in each other's arms. The only thing better than drunken sex was the deep sleep that an inebriated state provided. It was better than all the sleep aides developed and patented by all of the pharmaceutical companies combined.

A loud noise quickened the silence. The hairs on Jake's arms became antennae, grew erect, tasted and groped the darkness. His eyes flew open like shutters. Dilated pupils scanned the heavy blackness. There was a presence in the loft. This presence was menacing. He called out to his son, "Noah?"

Noah didn't respond. Patricia, who was fast asleep, snoring and drooling on his chest, stirred. He shook her gently and wiggled from beneath the weight of her sleepy body. They were both sticky from the fluids they'd shared. Those fluids dried and became glutinous glue fastening them together. Jake called out to his son again. "Noah?" Still no reply.

Something was terribly wrong. Noah, though only a child, wasn't that hard of a sleeper. If he'd fallen out of the bed or gotten out of bed to use the toilet, he would still respond to his father's voice.

The only sound that could be heard was a melodic cricket song sweetening the air outside. The wind rustled the trees, but other than that... silence.

A feeling of vulnerability surged through Jake's nerves like electricity. He felt it in his forearms, in the muscles of his thighs, and on his eyelids. He contracted his jaw and went in search of his Glock.

Patricia opened her eyes in the darkness. Sensing something was wrong, she quickly began groping around for her clothes. Another loud noise troubled the air. This time, the sound was angry and belligerent. It seemed to sip, savor and stay in the darkness, like a perfect stain.

That miserable feeling of vulnerability gnawed at Jake as he tripped over the mound of clothes at his feet. He couldn't remember where he'd put his gun. The darkness was inky and Stygian, the kind that houses monsters of all shapes and sizes.

Somewhere in the darkness, something floated around in the room where Patricia was. She too was groggy and hung-over, incapable of locating anything. Something, someone touched her arm. It didn't feel like fingers or skin, or even human for that matter, but something touched her arm. Silence and darkness drenched the room.

The sound of the toilet flushing provided a fleeting false sense of security. When Jake cut on the light of the bathroom, no one was there. But the toilet had been flushed. The water in the bowl was refilling itself, but Noah was not in the bathroom. Jake's face flushed pale and flaccid.

Patricia was still in the front of the loft, attempting to gather her thoughts. She sat up on the sofa, rubbing sleep from her eyes. Her hair was a jumbled hornet's nest. Jake was secretly afraid. Someone had flushed the toilet and left the bathroom in less than a fraction of a second. Logic told him this was impossible.

Naked and somber, he darted into the bedroom. Someone, something ran light trembling fingers across his left cheek; only it was less like fingers, more like hairs. When he reached out, nothing and no one was there. "Hey, Garbutt?"

"Yeah," Patricia said.

"You come in here? Use the bathroom?"

"No."

Turning on the lights, Jake was met by an empty bed, the bed sheets neatly tucked and in place as though Noah had never been there that night. He immediately hit the floor, pulling the covers aside, hoping Noah was playing hide and seek. Noah wasn't under the bed. He pulled open the closet doors frantically. The room was vacant. Abandoned. Where was Noah?

FIFTY-SIX

LOW CALORIE DESPAIR gripped Detective Jake Billingsley. The monster behind this had taken things too far. Somehow, he'd found a way into Jake's loft and kidnapped Noah like the true thief in the night that he was. To add insult to injury he made the bed behind him.

For the next few days the same hysterical madness that once gripped Patricia now took possession of Jake. His stomach churned with fear, trepidation, and the emptiness that a parent of a kidnapped child was forced to endure.

He'd lost his desire for food, his need for sleep, and for hours on end he searched all databases for the suspect. He dusted window sills and doorknobs, to no avail. He still felt lonelier than a dirty penny on the sidewalk. A contemporary vagabond.

Patricia mentioned the surveillance cameras matter-of-factly. Jake was sincerely shocked. He immediately snatched them from the walls and personally walked them into the crime lab.

He grew distant in those days. Patricia understood how he felt. She empathized in a way that no one else could.

The psycho behind this had a gift of knowing how to rally fears, and how to coach those fears to multiply; to crowd out rationale. He'd made both detectives' worse nightmares living, breathing, flesh and blood realities.

In those days, Jake went out at all hours of the night or early in the morning, during rush hour traffic-choked streets. He would peer into cars, assuming every crew cut having redneck was a possible suspect.

He even got into a nasty bar brawl at Murphy's Irish Pub with a few bikers. Earned himself a prized set of blackened eyes and a fractured wrist. Then he refused to wear the brace his doctor prescribed him to wear. He'd grown impossibly rebellious. Violence begat violence.

"What were you thinking," Patricia asked.

"Garbutt, do you know what I think? Huh?"

She was quiet. She could smell rivers of Michelob flowing from his breath and spilling from his pores. His speech slurred.

"I don't think nothing, yo! I think I'm sick and tired of standing by while criminals turn this great state into squalor, while the good guys are forced to sit down and behave themselves. Don't ask too many questions. Don't stir the pot too much. You wouldn't want to disrupt the boatloads of corruption out there. That's what I fucking think!" Jake said.

He was belligerent and drunk, but he spoke truth, and he spoke it indignantly. He had every right to do so. Patricia listened intently. Now, all the cards were on the table. She wanted to inquire about what she'd found that day: the passports, the diamonds. Surely that had something to do with Noah being kidnapped.

"Has anything materialized? A request for a ransom? Anything?" Patricia tread lightly. She was well aware of the fact that she was walking on eggshells.

Jake was a ticking time bomb. He was a swollen boil, capable of rupturing and oozing dehiscent poison at any moment. He needed to hammer his fists against something. Someone. Needed to kickbox someone. Something. A door, a wall. Anything. Perhaps this was that moment.

It was the nature of a man to fight when he had nothing left. Even if he didn't see an enemy in sight, he conjured up enemies.

Patricia wondered how Noah's mother was coping. The last time she saw her, Heidi was standing outside in front of her apartment, barefoot, wearing a UGA shirt that looked to be three sizes too small. Her nipples poked out and spoke to you.

Patricia guessed she was trying her luck at getting Jake to sleep with her again. She had bleached blonde hair that was dyed flamingo pink on the ends. Powerade blue eyes. Surely she could not work a real job; not with flamingo pink dye in her hair.

"Nope," he said. "You know...my dad was a retired Blue Angel, from Dothan Alabama. That's what brought me down south from the West. After my parents went splitsville, I wanted to know more about this place. I fell in love with all the trees and the way stone grey skies blend into those trees when you're out on the open road. I respected the slower pace and how men genuinely worked with their hands."

Patricia wondered where all this was going, but kept mum. She silently searched for the chink in his armor. She listened and squinted her eyes, nodded her head. She knew that friction drove change.

"I fell in love with all the verdant, lush bonsai-like scenery and violet wildflowers blushing sherry, like beautiful soldiers greeting you out on the open road. All the Tom Thumb stations, weeping willows, and roadside places to buy boiled peanuts and fresh seafood. And then I got into criminal justice. Before entering criminal justice, I actually believed in real justice. I believed in the American Judicial System. I believed in the law."

"Are you saying you no longer believe in those things?"

"Not saying that at all. It's just different now. Now I know the truth. I know the truth from the inside. Before I was on the outside, looking in. A man can never know the truth about a thing by looking at it from the outside. Things appear different, based on our perspective. Now I know that men have replaced worshipping God with worshipping money. With that comes corruption."

"Mmm-hmm," Patricia agreed.

"I learned that there was more corruption going on between so-called law enforcement than there was out on the streets. More dirt in the courts than being prosecuted *by* the courts," his voice faltered. "I guess what I'm trying to say is I think this shit is bigger than Michael Roth, Rex Baldwin or whoever in the hell he is."

"What exactly are you saying?"

Patricia knew that this was a turning point but Jake was so vague that she couldn't put her finger on anything. People changed for two reasons: either they'd been hurt enough that they had to or they learned enough that they wanted to. She and Jake had experienced enough pain and learned enough. Change was inevitable. But at what cost? What would have to be sacrificed?

FIFTY-SEVEN

THE MONSTER BEHIND these heinous crimes had not made a single phone call or demand for money. It was as though the detective's trail had grown cold. At least before they had phone calls. They had demands. They had...something.

A few weeks previous, Jake requested a No-knock warrant, which was now nearly as useless as the trace software that Patricia brought into the investigation just before Brody called them off the case. It was as creepy as being in a Tim Burton movie.

Patricia was hoping for a phone call from the sadistic fuck. Patricia could still recall the sound of that slightly Asiatic voice; perhaps it was voice-altering equipment being used.

Now, both Jake and Patricia were numb. It was as though God had poured scorn on them in deep immeasurable heaps. What they knew for sure was that Noah had been kidnapped and Michael Roth or Rex Baldwin was as dead as disco music, platforms and bell bottoms.

Where they had not been fragile, they were fragile now. They'd both lost their children at the hands of this sick murderer, and they didn't completely understand why he'd gone on such a vendetta. They were only doing their jobs, why had he made things so personal? They were each other's source of strength.

That night in Jake's loft he admitted to Patricia that he was CIA. She was shocked. She believed she would be able to determine the difference between a Federal agent and an ordinary Fulton County officer. She was wrong. There is more that we don't know we don't know than what we *know* we don't know.

Meanwhile, Noah was hogtied, gagged, and stowed in a Samsonite suitcase. His kidnapper fed him a double cheeseburger from Checkers and then stuffed him into a suitcase which was then placed in a storage unit.

The young child whined and cried out like an undiscovered operatic soprano.

"All they want us to do is keep killing each other anyhow. That's all they want. There ain't no damn war on crime or drugs or anything for that matter," the kidnapper said out loud.

He smoked a joint to calm his nerves. He didn't know that he would have to kidnap nobody's child as a part of the deal, but he did what he was told. Just like a good obedient nigga.

He remembered his golden days; the days when he rolled out with his boys, his entourage, his crew. He didn't just show up at the club. He arrived.

Back then, Atlanta was like Motown. He knew all the biggest names: Jermaine Dupri, Puff, Dallas Austin...you name them, he knew them on a personal, first-name basis. He would be personally invited to Andre Rison's house parties. Those were the days. Freaknik merely meant he could hand pick bitches like he was picking apples. The thicker, the better.

You knew when he arrived because a fleet of high end luxury vehicles were always in tow. He never traveled anywhere without his boys and he made certain that everyone in his crew ate good.

There were Lambos with custom shoes, shipped straight from Italy. Rare Rolls-Royces. Bentleys, H2s, and Porches. Benz trucks sitting on twenty-fours. They'd line up along the curb, looking prettier than anything at Fashion week. FaSho...million dollar motorcades were his MO.

He couldn't even lie, he missed those days. He missed the power. He missed the glory. He missed the stacks. Wasn't nothing fun about playing the square, being broke and living in his mother's fucking basement. It hurt his ego every time he opened his eyes and saw that shit. He was not about *that* life.

And the women...God, he missed all that pussy that got thrown at him by the hour. Red bones, Filipinos, Dominicans, blondes, bitches from East Africa, France, Brazil. His favorites were those exotic bitches down in South Beach. You damn right he wanted that life back. But he was a changed man, or so that's what he told himself.

FIFTY-EIGHT

BACK THEN HE was Gavin Jones; better known as O.G. Big Half Dead. He'd made a name for himself out in Atlanta, although he was from Long Beach. He started off small; selling coke and dro, but then he linked up with some Chicago cats, some Gangsta Disciple niggas. They put him up on the arms game.

Late nineties, early two thousand, he had three or four crash houses. These were the drop off and pick up spots. But don't get it twisted; these weren't your typical dope houses. No, these were upper echelon marble mansions; the type of shit you would see in a Sotheby's Portfolio.

Whatever was shipped in from Florida to New York inevitably found its way through Gavin's organization. What started out as slangin' marijuana and cocaine, ended up as a multi-million dollar gun running enterprise.

Gavin was even doing deals with the Arabs: diamonds and opium. In this way he learned how to stay ahead of the drug game. For a long time, he had the Atlanta Police Department on payroll. He had the deputy District Attorney in his back pocket, and he had a counsel of lawyers who woke up swinging.

He paid a legion of Gangsta Disciples every two weeks, no different than an ordinary nine to five.

But these cats were to provide him with constant protection, no matter what.

He also had a team of bad ass mules. They looked like housewives. They moved weight all over the country in beat down minivans and RVs, but no one would ever know because they looked like the women you would see on *Price Is Right* or *Wheel of Fortune*. Wisteria Lane housewives.

Around that time, he was dating a woman from Baltimore. Ebony Cooper. She was a good girl. She was born and raised in the church. It was funny how even back then he was attracted to goodie two shoes...the type of woman who never used profanity, smoked, drank alcohol, or even stayed out past midnight. The only thing he loved more than his toys, his jet skies, boats, Ducatis and German engineered sports cars, was Ebony.

They met in the gym. He didn't even have a membership or anything. He was just in there scoping out the scene, looking for something to take home and poke.

She caught his eye; her smooth cinnamon brown skin and eyes that glimmered in the sunshine. She wore a winning smile. She was on the treadmill, running. Ass was tight. Lips were right. Stomach was flat and the titties were popping up and down like popcorn. He had to holler.

They talked, exchanged phone numbers and before you knew it, were dating exclusively. Gavin still had his side pieces and a few regular honey dips that let him lay pipe, but Ebony was wife material.

Although she appreciated how he upgraded her life, she couldn't swallow the fact that it was being funded by illegal means. She was a cosmetologist.

She made a decent living doing hair, but she'd never seen the kind of money that Gavin lavished on her. That is until she found out the whole truth how exactly he earned a living. She wasn't with it. She was angry with herself for not seeing it early on.

He was able to hide it from her for awhile, but she was no spring chicken. She knew how to research like she was one of the CIA's finest agents.

You'd be surprised what you could find utilizing Google, Facebook, and good old fashioned woman's intuition. Adding insult to injury, she found out about his other woman, Deidre Priest.

It was the *way* she found out. Someone mailed her a DVD, and on that DVD was Gavin eating Deidre's pussy. It was over ninety minutes of footage. They left nothing to the imagination. Ninety minutes of sucking, fucking, slobbing, and gobbling.

When she approached him about it, he didn't even deny it because he knew he was caught. He knew that someone, who he later learned was an ole snitch-ass rat from his crew, who grew disgruntled with the fact that he wasn't making more money, found the sex tape and sent it to Ebony.

Gavin saw it coming. It was only a matter of time before one of the women found out about the other, but he loved them both.

Before long Ebony was rejecting his calls and ignoring his advances, but by then it was too late.

She was pregnant with his child. She wanted to abort the baby so bad, but after adamant vigilant prayer and some time went by she decided to have the baby. It was a little boy... Solomon.

Shortly after giving birth to their son Solomon, Ebony decided to up and move back to Baltimore. She did this partly to fuck with Gavin, knowing that Solomon was his first born it would hurt his ego to not have an active relationship with him.

He may have been a thug, a dope dealer, a rogue, a pariah in the face of his enemies — but he believed in fatherhood. He believed in being there for his firstborn. It was something he'd told Ebony. He'd told her how much he wanted her to bear his seed. Every time he came inside of her, he hoped that she would conceive.

She knew he wouldn't fight her in court because he had too much dirt under his fingernails to go anywhere near a court. But she also couldn't live with the fact that she was still in love with Gavin and she refused to share him with his other woman, Deidre. It was just too much drama for her to handle.

After a year and a half, Ebony agreed to start letting Gavin see his son. In appreciation, Gavin began showering Ebony with gifts. He bought her a new orange Beetle, a small house in the 'burbs, just on the outskirts of Baltimore, and even helped her invest in a beauty salon of her own.

It was like old times with them and they fell back into the swing of things. Although she was in Baltimore and he was in Atlanta, it was nothing for him to hop on the road and drive to pick up his baby boy. Before long, Gavin and Ebony were fucking again. It was explosive. There was nothing like makeup sex, or the sex you had with an old lover that you haven't had closure with.

Gavin would drive to Baltimore and stay for two weeks at a time. He'd always stay at the finest hotels he could find. Ebony and their son Solomon would stay with him. At night, once they put the baby to sleep, they would go at it like animals. Right there in the suite, they would be fucking like college freshmen.

Gavin missed those days too. Ebony and Deidre were the only two women that he went raw dog with; for everybody else, he strapped a jimmy on. Couldn't trust bitches these days. Bitches knew they could eat good off the child support alone — they could do better living off child support from his earnings than by finding decent employment, so he refused to enter into that game of Russian Roulette.

When it came to Ebony though, he would dick her down like he was angry with her. Always, he had to teach her a lesson. So he would grudge fuck her. She liked it rough.

One memorable balmy night he took her out on the balcony of the Four Seasons Penthouse suite. He even wore an Ozwald Boateng tailored suit he'd gotten on his last trip to London. They'd had dinner at Pabu, the Japanese spot downstairs in the hotel. After being immersed in the ambiance of those bamboo ceilings, sake bottles, ceramic sake flasks, and beautifully crafted solid wood tabletops, Ebony was horny.

The night was warm and her panties were moist. So, she casually led Gavin out onto the balcony which was overlooking the harbor. Out amid the Maryland crab-scented bay, she climbed atop her man, straddled him, and dared him to fuck her until he couldn't take anymore. Not being a man to resist a challenge, he obliged. That was the night their second child was conceived...Rahmeek.

Who were they fooling? They couldn't be together. Gavin refused to stop messing with his other woman Deidre and Deidre was the most down ass bitch a nigga could ever ask for. She knew about his organization and she kept her lips sealed.

She knew about Ebony, but she just told herself, *men will be men and let the chips fall where they may.* Her loyalty paid off, because Gavin ended up breaking things off with Ebony for once and for all. He still played an active regular role in his children's lives, but minus their mother. Instead of staying for weeks on end in Baltimore, he would pick up his babies and bring them back down to Atlanta.

FIFTY-NINE

SHORTLY AFTER RAHMEEK was born, Gavin met his meteoric downfall. It was the trial of the century. The Feds had used wire taps to track him down and set him up.

State of the art trap-and-catch equipment was used to record hours worth of damaging evidence that was later used against him in the court of law. They also got insider information from the same punk-ass nigga who sent his sex DVD to Ebony. That dude turned state witness and sang like Marvin Gaye performing the famous national anthem. Gavin "O.G. Big Half Dead" Jones died, and in his place Akil Allah was born.

When he was sentenced to do forty-five years to life at the Jesup Federal Correctional Institute, he thought his life was over. After all, he lost everything he'd ever worked for.

He lost the million dollar home off Paces Ferry, the mansion in Tuxedo Park, and the home in the Country Club of the South. He lost his fleet of foreign made automobiles, the yachts, the Harleys, and all his cash was seized by the Feds. No more Rolex watches or Oswald Boateng tailored suits.

Worst of all, he would never see his boys again. His seeds meant everything to him. He knew Deidre would hold him down no matter what. But for all the cats that he thought had his back, each one of them turned *their* backs on him. Several of them turned state witness and testified against him, in return for lighter sentences and other plea deals with the prosecution.

Just prior to his arrest, Deidre helped Gavin stash a few commodities-grade gold coins, ten million in bearer bonds, and what could be anywhere between three and five million dollars in cut diamonds. He gave her account information from his bank in the Caymans; told her about his fake shell of a corporation Solomon and Bro. Inc., and made her swear that she wouldn't say shit to the Feds.

After a few months in prison he'd given his life to Allah. He read the Koran, did five hundred pushups, and prayed five times daily. He vowed that he would clean up his life and be a positive role model to his two sons.

While in prison, he was approached by an officer with a Russian accent, who offered him a deal he simply couldn't resist. The man offered to get him out of prison legally, but he would have to drop some names of his allies. In exchange for freedom, for the opportunity to see his sons again, all he had to do was name the powerful men who he did business with.

These men were some of the most powerful and elite people on the planet. They called themselves *Moriah Conquering Wind* or the *Olympians*. They had cells in every branch of the government, in every major country of the globe: London, New York, Washington D.C., Vatican City, and all over the world.

They were a part of this weird secret society that got together in Bohemian Grove, California every year and sprinkled themselves among the banking industry and all of the major media outlets like film, television, and publishing. They were a strange bunch. They got together for peculiar masked costume orgies and performed mock Satanic rituals. All types of weird shit.

He knew that some of them were members of something called the Bilderberg Group, but hell if he knew what that was. Some of them were members of an ancient order of Chaldean Priests — some shit that went back to the days of Babylon. They were all about Islamic mysticism and Sufism.

They were Jesuits and called themselves Knights Templars. Some of them were members of what they called the Council on Foreign Relations.

Others were sprinkled in groups like the John Birch Society, Ford Foundation, International Monetary Fund, Committee of 300, Trilateral Commission, and the Rand Foundation — as in Ayn Rand.

They were heavy into their symbolism and chanting something called the Lotus Sutra. They were big on rituals, numerology, and the occult. They were everywhere: Japan, Britain, and even what they called Shambhala. Some of them were Freemasons; others were powerful politicians, Senators, and judges in the Federal Government. They ran Capitol Hill.

These people attended the Davos World Economic Forums, G8, and G20 meetings. They were presidents of Lucis Trust, The World Bank, Rosicrucians, Club of Rome, chairmen of the one hundred most powerful corporations in the world such as General Electric, Wal-Mart, DaimlerChrysler, Coca Cola, British Petroleum, Chase Manhattan Bank, American Express, Goldman Sachs, Microsoft; Vice Presidents of the United States, Directors of CIA and the FBI, General Secretaries of NATO, and members of Congress, European Prime ministers and leaders of opposition parties, Al Qaeda, the Royal Saudi Family, and CEOs of the leading newspapers in the world.

They controlled countless billions of dollars through hedge funds and also had their hands in arms trading, conflict diamonds, and the cocoa fields of Columbia, Venezuela, and Nicaragua. He, Gavin, Akil Allah, just wanted to stay paid, not get caught up in all that weird, mystic, spooky, faggot-ass shit them white boys were into.

Akil was faced with spending the rest of his life in a box, or being free, but he also knew that his life would be marked. He had something to gain, but he also had something to lose.

He gave it some thought, and figured he would drop names, because he remembered that he had a stash. He could get his sons and pick up and start over in another country. Fuck his old life. Gavin Jones was dead. Fuck America, he would never look back. So he snitched.

SIXTY

THE SNAG IN his plan came when he was released from prison. He learned that his mother was diagnosed with stage four breast cancer. She was terminal and she needed him. But she also needed to stay in the states where she could be treated. Otherwise, he would have dipped out to Dubai or Cuba—anywhere that had no extradition laws.

He moved into his mother's home with her and helped out where he could. It broke his heart to accompany his mother to her chemo sessions; to witness the woman who he thought was so strong be ravished by that debilitating disease. He learned that for every superhero, there was kryptonite. If it could happen to Clark Kent, it could happen to his mother, and it did.

She lost every bit of hair on her body, even her eyebrows. She lost so much weight that she could barely walk without a cane or a walker. She was so frail and so helpless. He couldn't just dip out on Ma Dukes—not like that. It was the hardest thing he'd ever experienced, watching cancer ravage his mother's body.

So Akil stayed and helped his mother out. He even worked out a deal with his sons' mother Ebony, where he would still get to see them in the summer and some weekends. He also found out that he had been set up.

The man who approached him, the man with the Russian accent, was an undercover Federal Agent. He'd sold out his connects to an agent. Fucking Federali.

A part of him felt free now that he had been released from prison and was able to be with his children and his mother in her last days, but he also slept with a perpetual dark cloud over his head. And because of that, he slept fully locked and loaded. He knew they would be out for his blood.

The day came when he began seeing the retribution. That day was the day his woman came up missing and some detectives came knocking at his door asking questions. He knew *they'd* got her — those crazy-ass demonic motherfuckers, and there was no telling how horribly they tortured her.

He also heard from a little bird that his sons' mother had come up missing too. Those motherfuckers went for the jugular. They were picking off the people who meant the most to him. So he kept his sons with him twenty-four seven. He wouldn't take his eyes off them.

One day recently, he got a call from the man with the Russian accent.

"Man, I don't have anything to say to you over the phone. I've learned my lesson. If you want to talk, then we have to talk in person," Akil said.

"Meet me in an hour at Atlantic Station. California Pizza Kitchen," the voice over the phone said.

"Bet!"

It took approximately one hour, and Akil was pulling into the parking garage of Atlantic Station. He had Solomon and Rahmeek with him. He gathered his sons, held their hands, and walked into California Pizza Kitchen.

Being there reminded him of his childhood in Long Beach, California. The bright colors, the lighting, and the open space were reminiscent of his home town, with the Pacific Ocean and the plethora of people from diverse ethnic backgrounds. The mood was light and calming like a sunset in the Bahamas.

He immediately noticed the slightly overweight man. He was sitting in a booth wearing a white button down short sleeved shirt with burgundy stripes. He had an unlit cigar in his mouth. Smug ass sonofabitch. He wore a Rolex; oyster perpetual submarine date in 18 karat white gold. He smelled of Aqua di Gió. Gucci loafers.

Akil took a deep breath and collected his thoughts. He knew the man meant business. "Mr. Allah, so glad to see you again. How do you do?" the man said.

"Hey, how's it going?" Akil said, directing his two young sons to climb into the booth directly across from the man. The two men shook hands.

"I didn't know you were bringing the family. You have such handsome sons…they look like you, my man."

Akil didn't respond. He gave the man a frozen stoic look that said: *Don't get fucked up in this restaurant!*

"Let's talk. What is it that you want from me? I gave you everything I have, told you everything I know. What else is there? What do you want from me man?"

"I have a proposition for you Mr. Allah. Now, as you know…Ms. Priest was taken care of, if you get my drift?"

Akil swallowed the hard-as-steel lump that formed in his throat. He still couldn't believe his baby was gone. He blamed himself. He knew that if she had never got caught up with him that she would probably still be alive today. He loved the shit out of that woman—Deidre Priest. He swallowed again and looked down at the menu in front of him to deflect the anger that was boiling up inside.

"And, well, Ms. Cooper has also been taken care of. But, I'm not here to deliver bad news. I'm here to offer you a ray of hope. If you can take care of this simple assignment then your remaining family will have the privilege of having their lives spared," the man said before taking a sip of the ice water that sat in front of him.

"Where is she?" Akil mustered the courage to ask. He was referring to his sons' mother, Ebony Cooper. He'd had trouble explaining to his oldest son, why his mother was always unavailable to talk on the phone. They both asked about her every day, but the oldest wanted to hear his mother's voice.

Akil had made up every excuse in the book. He said that she was sick, she was asleep, her phone was messed up, everything.

"Sleeping at the bottom of the Potomac," the man replied nonchalantly.

Akil's anger bubbled again. He wanted to pound that motherfucker's face in, but he had to keep his composure. He remembered his prayers and the promises he'd made to Allah. He had turned his life around. He knew that vengeance belonged to the Most High. He formed his hands into two fists beneath the table. His sons were completely oblivious. They sat quietly, like the disciplined young men he'd raised them to be.

"Now, I need you to take care of something. Once you complete this assignment, this blood sacrifice, then your family will be passed over."

Akil knew that the man was talking about the three people who meant the world to him, Solomon, Rahmeek, and his mother. He couldn't save Ebony or Deidre, but he'd be damned if he couldn't spare his blood; the fruit of his loins. He'd go down guns blazing before he ever let that happen.

He knew these people were shrewd and calculating. Their hearts were filled with bloodlust for power and consumed by greed for more and more money. Rich and aristocratic, they despised him for his blackness, from his humble impoverished beginnings and they had the ability to off him at any moment. He wondered why they had even spared him.

SIXTY-ONE

AKIL KNEW THAT these people perceived themselves to be supra-governmental. They were the ones who ultimately decided which countries waged war on each other. They manipulated global finances and established rigid and binding monetary rates around the world. They selected political figures who they decreed would become rulers, and targeted those whom they wanted removed from power. It was nothing for them to pick him off, like a gnat.

"What might that assignment be?" Akil asked reluctantly, clearing his throat.

The man gave Akil a picture of Detective Patricia Garbutt's two children and the address to where her mother, Mrs. Ortiz lived. "Take care of everyone at this address. *Everyone.* If it breathes or has a heartbeat, then take care of it."

"And if I don't?" Akil began to sweat. A waitress approached the booth and asked if they were ready for her to take their order. She had soft skin and split ends and a tattoo of an owl on her forearm.

The slightly overweight man, clearly irritated, removed his cigar and waved her off, saying that they would let her know when they were ready to order food.

"But daddy, I'm hungry. Can I have pizza?" Rahmeek said.

"Quiet son. I'll get you both something to eat. Daddy's handling business right now."

"If you don't do it, then the whole family will end up sleeping at the bottom of the Potomac, or the Chattahoochee. Don't you just love the Hooch?"

Akil swallowed again. This time he found it more difficult to swallow. The massive lump in his throat felt like a bone in his neck. He choked before reaching for the glass of water which sat in front of him. He knew the man meant serious business and he also knew that he was referring to his two sons who would be found floating in the Hooch, if he didn't make the hit.

"The other part of your assignment is to take care of this," the man said, while sliding him another picture. This time, it was a picture of Detective Jake Billingsley's son, Noah.

After that meeting, the man promised Akil that he would be totally free to move and live without a single worry. They'd framed him in such a way that he no longer knew what to believe. He went forward with the plan and did what he had to do.

He had an entire family's blood on his hands and he had no idea why. That was the way of powerful men. It had been the way of powerful men of old and it would never change. Powerful men either forced or financed weaker men to kill their enemies for them.

He didn't ask any other questions. He just went forward with the plan because he needed these people to get off his back. It was either somebody else's kids or his kids. Blood had to be sacrificed, either way. He didn't make the rules. He just showed up for the challenge and would play to the best of his ability.

It wasn't personal, he was merely doing what he needed to do to make sure that his children had a chance to grow up and carry on his family name; to carry on the legacy. No matter how soiled, corrupted, and foul that legacy may have been. If it meant he had to commit murder to see to it that his kids would live, then so be it.

Here he was with the little boy from the picture, Noah. The little boy with curly blonde hair and eyes as blue as the Atlantic. When he murdered the other family, he'd broke into someone's apartment—the address on the back of the picture.

That came from his days in the streets. If it was one thing he learned, it was how to do dirt and not get caught. He was dressed like a ninja when he did it. All black ninja, cloaked in the darkness. He moved in silence, unnoticed, unrecognizable against the texture of the nocturnal. He was a panic button on the underside of manic expression.

He'd been shown a picture of Detective Patricia Garbull and her family and given the instructions to do the hit. He recalled the woman being very attractive, especially when she and her partner came to his mother's house. She had soft sensual eyes and private school hair. She was exotic and fine beneath the rough exterior.

Gavin Jones brought the little boy to a storage unit. He had planned on simply leaving the boy.

He really didn't want to kill another man's child—especially a child who wasn't much older than his son Rahmeek. In his old days when he was running the streets he wouldn't have thought twice, but today he was a changed man. He was a man who served Allah.

He vacillated between pumping a slug into the boy's brain and choking him out. But then he would hear himself reciting his daily prayers and the spiritual experience he had while he was in prison.

Allah appeared before him in what felt like a realistic dream. Allah told him that he would give him a second chance if he would just do the right thing and become like his prophet, walking in truth and love.

This was a decision that could either result in his ultimate freedom or losing the last reminders of everything that meant anything to him. What didn't kill him would make him wish it did.

While he sat in his car smoking his joint, he turned the music up in hopes that it would drown out his thoughts. He hoped the beats, the baseline, and the chords would slaughter the emotions rising up within him.

Meanwhile, in the storage unit, Noah had stopped crying and began chewing through the gag in his mouth. He'd used the bathroom on himself and was frightened to death. He hoped that his daddy would come rescue him. He wanted his mommy. Needed them both.

Somehow, he managed to free himself from the rope that was tied around his wrists. It had taken two days of constant tinkering, but somehow he freed his hands. He was hungry—no wait, he was *starving*. And he was so afraid of the man who forced him into the suitcase.

SIXTY-TWO

IT WAS SUNDAY night. Jake had been out drinking again. He started at the Vortex on Peachtree. No food passed between his lips, just Sweetwater 420, Negro Modela, mint juleps, bourbon, Pisco sours, and guava margaritas, interspersed between shots of tequila; whatever the pretty young bartender with perpetually pointed nipples placed in front of him.

She smiled like the girl in Johannes Vermeer's masterwork—lips parted with optimistic eyes and soft pretty hands. Fingers perfect for plucking violin strings. Her skin was whiter than driven snow.

He wondered if she wore special makeup to give her that pale *Twilight Saga* look. Maybe she was from a place that never got much sun, like North Dakota or Maine. She was the type of woman who turned her back on society's stereotypes—ignored the space between lines.

Jake was spent. "I'm not a skinny jean type of God...guy," his words slurred clumsily. "I actually have balls that I want to keep fully functioning. I don't understand how any man would want to wear those nutcrackers," he'd told the bartender before a snicker seeped from his throat.

Fuck, she was sexy, he thought. He wanted to take her in the restroom to score. Imagined what her cunt felt like. He would've settled for the back of the bar or either of their backseats.

He closed his eyes and visualized her giving him head on an unmade bed in some cheap motel. But it was hard for his pecker to stay erect with all these crazy thoughts racing through his head.

The Swedish progressive rock band, Anekdoten, blasted loudly from the speakers in the bar. They sang of a sky that was about to rain. Cigarette smoke and the scent of char grilled meat sauntered through the establishment.

Like a submarine submerged in the sea, the alcohol calmed his nerves and relaxed him. It would keep him from sleep later on, but he didn't care. He didn't care about anything anymore. He felt like a used band-aid, the ones you see discarded on the sidewalk. Everything he touched turned to shit. *That* was the ugliest truth.

The metro Atlanta skyline soared above like mythical steel and glass castles in the sky. Jake blamed himself for what happened to Noah. He believed God hated him.

Perhaps he was suffering from the sins his father committed, or those of his father's father. The truth was plain to see. It was lying there in plain sight, typical of all truths.

Jake blamed and hated himself at the same time. He hated so many things about himself. The ghosts from his past still reared their ugly heads every now and again, reminding him that he had permanent blood on his hands. There were so many secrets, so much betrayal, and so much deception. The skeletons were crowding out his peace of mind.

He'd never felt like more of an incredibly unfit parent as he felt lately. Now that he was off the Roth case, he was restless. So many thoughts zoomed through his mind. He was mad at himself, mad at the world, and mad at his situation. There he was, trying to battle an enemy that lived inside of him. It was the worst kind of battle.

It angered Jake that God allowed things like this to happen to innocent children. What kind of God sat back idle allowing the defenseless to fend for themselves while the strong and mighty ran roughshod?

He didn't feel like a Detective. Yes, there were times while he was working, when it seemed like he should be spending more time with his son, but when he spent quality time with Noah, it felt like he should've been working.

Jake took his anger out on his poor innocent liver. Every day his liver blackened as the toxins moved him closer and closer to cirrhosis.

There was an inner voice that sounded much like his old man…it tugged at his conscience; made him feel guilty for throwing so much of his time and energy into his career, only to leave Noah to be raised by his half wit mother Heidi.

If this is where ambition got a man, he questioned ambition. He was the embodiment of Monday morning blues—a walking melancholic note played out of tune. He was collected shrapnel from unspecified periods. Abuse was his bloodline.

As soon as Jake told Heidi what happened, she accused him of maliciously using this as a ploy to get full custody of their son, like he somehow was behind staging this ordeal. She accused him of scuttling away from his child support responsibilities, as though he'd *ever* been late paying.

She accused him of swindling her out of her parental rights. She knew all too well how he felt about her mothering skills. "How could you let this happen?" she screamed and cursed Jake, glad to finally be off the subpar parenting hook.

Who was Heidi to judge Jake though? The only place she'd ever taken Noah was to Wal-Mart and the liquor store.

Jake didn't have time or energy to debate with his son's mother. He was tired of fighting her. It was a never-ending battle with Heidi. And even if he won the battle, it would be a pyrrhic victory. It always left him feeling shitty inside.

He asked himself why he was being punished. Perhaps he was asking God, or the gods; whoever held the job description of architect of human follies and foibles.

Jake promised Heidi and tried to assure her that he was exhausting every resource he had to get Noah back, but in the back of his mind he knew he couldn't even promise himself anything. He had no idea if Noah was still alive or not.

NOW THAT NOAH had freed his hands, he struggled to remove himself from the Samsonite suitcase. Sweat poured from his pores as he marinated and squirmed around in his own urine and excrement.

He'd never been this terrified. He could no longer scream because his energy was running dangerously low. The odor of terror and ammonia was stifling. There wasn't anything but a small crack in the suitcase allowing a faint hole through which he could breathe. This kid was being forced to grow up fast.

One minute he was having a great time with his daddy, chomping down onion rings, cheeseburgers, and sipping strawberry milkshakes, the next moment he was being snatched out of his daddy's warm comfortable bed. He was being snatched from all that was warm and familiar.

Although he was only a child, his mind raced — to cookouts in his grandparents' backyard. The family and all of his cousins would stay outside until the sky darkened. The stars would emerge and the moon would rise. Catching fireflies in mason jars made it all worthwhile.

The smell of summer was enchanting. If he was lucky, he could squeeze his eyes shut and taste his grandpa's spice-rubbed chicken hot from the grill, grandma's honey-butter grilled corn and smoky shrimp tacos. And her homemade vanilla ice cream. The boy licked his lips. His imagination was powerful.

Noah's tender young memory slipped back to those sunny, fun-filled midsummer nights, the air decorated with cricket songs and especially the festivals and carnivals, sweet pink cotton candy, slurping down melting Rocky road ice cream cones while watching fireworks dance across the sky in fanciful reds, yellows, florescent greens, and blooming blues.

Noah thought about his mommy too. He really loved his mommy. Sometimes it felt like he had to take care of his mommy more than she had to take care of him. He worried about her in ways that a seven year old boy should never have to worry.

SIXTY-THREE

MADE PERFECT SENSE to Patricia, once she began to put two and two together. She waited until Jake went out on one of his drinking binges. She knew he wouldn't be back any time soon.

He'd grown gills, became half fish and a shiftless loquacious alcoholic. His newfound garrulous behavior after a drink or two was beginning to wear her patience thin. She searched for the surveillance cameras, but to her surprise, they'd all been removed.

She immediately began dismantling her cellular—removed the plastic protective case, and then frantically dislodged the back piece that covered the tiny battery.

She noticed that the old memory card, with its miniature yellow logo, had been replaced by a new memory card. The new memory card was red with a foreign insignia on the front. She observed it closely while attempting to recall where she'd last seen the foreign logo.

The locations where the surveillance cameras had been previously located were now left empty. Patricia found that odd. Who removed the cameras? Had they truly been removed or were they merely moved to a more surreptitious spot? Also, what happened to her old memory card? When had it been swapped out? She was truly confused by all the clandestine occurrences.

She knew the FBI had the ability to wiretap just about any phone at any time, as long as the device was turned on. She was aware that they could also locate any person with an enabled device by tracing the GPS in the device. But what was the point of this new memory card?

She knew all too well how federal criminal laws had become dangerously disconnected from the English common law tradition and how prosecutors could pin arguable federal crimes on anyone, for even the most seemingly innocuous behavior. Was the FBI behind this or the Fulton County Police Department?

There are things that happen once and then never happen exactly the same again. She hoped this was one of those times. She wondered if any of this was bait and if so, was she taking it? She hated the notion that she might be involved in a larger web of espionage. She regretted the fact that she'd shared what she found with Jake. Now he was onto her. He treated her differently. They could barely stand to be in each other's presence nowadays.

Much was happening fast. Patricia had to admit that fear was running rampant in her mind. She quietly wrestled with her thoughts. Sometimes we created our own demons and sometimes we were our own stumbling blocks — getting in our own way. She realized that we're not all fractured by the same fall. We all rot separately.

Pride wouldn't allow Patricia to own up to her part in all of this. Trying to take it one day at a time, she often got caught up in the past and memories of the past. An angry woman is often angry with herself and the fucked up choices she's made. She naturally fell into the role of victim. It was a role that became more and more comforting, like a well-worn pair of shoes.

She felt so much enmity towards Jake, towards Brody, and especially towards Anthony. This was confirmation that this was the age of ulcers. She kept replaying her brother's words…like darts directed at her chest. Angel was the equivalent of fingernails on a chalkboard.

Patricia felt as blue as the Belizean sea, and those blues garnered an impulse to uncover and investigate until she got to the very bottom of things. Patricia refused to be a woman in peril. She refused.

Patricia immediately began to look through drawers, containers, cabinets, and closets. She turned over the mattress in Jake's bedroom. She instinctively knew that when one went looking for shit, they were sure to find it.

She searched high and low. She even went through Jake's pantry. The surprise came when she plopped down on the sofa, with a container of vanilla ice cream in hand. She was exhausted, not to mention out of shape.

Since things went south with Anthony and the family, she'd begun to let herself go. At least when she was actively working a case, it kept her active and fit. Lately it had been nonstop stuffing her face with Chik Fil'A, butter pecan ice cream, Zesto's, and Dunkin Donuts. What was it about junk food that was so comforting and irresistible? Sometimes junk food could be more enticing than sex; definitely more fulfilling.

When she opened the top of the ice cream container, she was startled when she found paperwork inside; documents from the Kremlin and the Gulag. A list of outed KGB spies. Some foreign jargon with Yeltsin's name popping out like persimmons on a bush.

There were legal documents that mentioned the Free Trade Zone in Nigeria, something about an international agreement between China and Lagos.

There was International Monetary Fund letterhead mentioning who had eighty percent of the world's GDP.

Jacob Stanislaw was a spy, working for the Kremlin, under Vladimir Putin's administration. Patricia felt the weight of her head melt down to something light and wispy, almost like it was shrinking. She was light headed and nauseous. She'd run head first into a conundrum. This was going to be the longest day of the year, like summer solstice.

SIXTY-FOUR

NOAH'S ANGELS WERE watching over him that day. A few minutes before the blond curly haired, blue-eyed, fearful boy freed his hands, the storage unit security guard decided to do his rounds.

Lucky for Noah and Jake, that security guard listened to V-103, the people's station, and he heard the Amber Alert for Noah. The same Amber Alert came through his Metro PCS cellular nearly a dozen times over the course of a week. They say the Lord takes care of fools and children.

Greg Jenkins, while listening to the Frank and Wanda Show, heard about a missing child who was abducted from his Atlanta Homicide Detective father's home. The details were sketchy and he really hadn't paid it much attention, but he believed in the power of the law. He was passionate about protecting and serving the citizens and taxpayers. It was his duty. Although he was merely a flashlight cop, he had big dreams.

Before taking the job at *SureLock: you store it-we secure it*, Greg Jenkins worked at a prominent mini mall in downtown Atlanta. Less mini mall, more Swapmeet. People loved him. He began wearing a camera around his neck to capture and record the daily antics he had to deal with while securing the Downtown Atlanta mini mall.

After uploading videos of criminal shenanigans for the past nine months, he and his YouTube channel went viral. There was an occasion when he had to taser some ghetto turf bug that jumped in his face talking shit like she was a man. If she had balls enough to act like a man, he was damn sure going to handle her like a man. Had he not been filming it, he probably would have Mayweathered her.

He'd effectively branded himself by accident. Originally from Detroit, he grew up understanding the psychology behind hood niggas and ghetto mentality.

He knew that when generations of welfare and Section 8 recipients were bred in poverty and neglect, they only acted out in self-destructive ways. He'd argue that after all, he'd never been robbed at gunpoint by a white man or car jacked by a Chinamen, or shot at by a Gupta. Only niggas did those things.

This was often the subject matter of his YouTube and Vimeo videos, which garnered him followers by the millions. Love him or hate him, he was a YouTube sensation, but that hadn't changed the fact that he was still a W-2 employee for *SureLock*.

He'd hopped into the golf cart which was provided by his employer.

HERE WAS ALL the evidence Detective Patricia Garbutt needed. She felt like a pawn in the game. She had been restless. She could use a hot dog, some macaroni salad and a Budweiser.

Typically, her sleep pattern was dependent upon her state of mind, or whatever she was obsessing over. When she felt uplifted and optimistic, she could function off limited sleep; as little as three hours. When she was unhappy she became very hypersomniac, needing a lot of sleep.

The past month was brutal on both her nerves and her mind. She stayed up all night, attempting to analyze every possible situation. The memories of her children lay on her chest—their voices rippling through her brain like foam coming off waves of the Caribbean Sea.

It was difficult to relax when your back was against hell and you were simultaneously dangling off a cliff of despair. The murders were hard enough to get through, not to mention the separation. She'd evolved into someone who should never hold a loaded gun. Perhaps Brody in his infinite wisdom and eons of experience intuitively knew this. Maybe that was the real reason he took her and Jake off the Roth case mid-stroke.

She was tired of being tested by fate. When she was in grade school all she needed was a number 2 pencil before exams, now it seemed she needed an ocean of Jack Daniels and a bottle of Vicodin. Pain changed people, and she was obviously a changed woman. She was a different woman.

With age, her circle of friends had been shaved down to a dot. She hated her family—she didn't trust anyone, and her patience was nonexistent.

Detective Patricia Garbutt felt like she housed the universe in her chest—heavy with dust, deserts, and glaciers, spinning pulsars, and comets torpedoing through her blood. She felt as though her soul had spanned the course of vast swathes of civilizations and she was weathered by elements of the ages.

Psychologically, she was running on empty. It wasn't long before she was in her Crown Vic, veering up I-85 under starless, orange-tinted urban skies, on her way to Heidi's parents' house in Norcross.

She drove through the cooling city, as the cosmos blanketed the perimeter with fresh late afternoon sun bending the shadows of amorphous trees. She had a distinctive date with destiny. She was ready for whatever came.

There was a purple sunset in the distance. It was like the sun was sending out lavender rays against a backdrop of scarlet clouds: a Willy Wonka-esque delight for the dreamer and sun gazer alike.

The thought of leaving the big, crowded, dirty, noisy city of Atlanta loomed bright on her mind on a regular basis. She was in desperate need of a real getaway.

Over the phone, Heidi was apprehensive. Patricia let her know that this was personal business, that in no way would Jake have to be included.

It would be akin to throwing salt on Jake's ego if he knew those two women were meeting up behind his back. Women, always masters at conspiring. Heidi relaxed her stance.

Since Noah's kidnapping, Heidi had been a nervous wreck. She was beautifully damaged. Her parents, who now lived in a sprawling two-story home, had her stay with them so they could all be together as family.

Outside, a 2014 Chevrolet Impala in a monochromatic silver hue was parked in the driveway. Tufts of magenta bougainvillea and a rainbow of hibiscus blooms flooded the exquisitely landscaped front yard. A blanket of impossibly green manicured lawn. Mature Birch trees barnacled with Ivy were spilling out from the backyard and framed the sides of the home.

Upon entering the home, there was dark plum everywhere, a warm background of sensual amber Tonka bean and Australian Sandalwood permeated the air.

The scent was an energizing and aromatic blend of juicy watermelon, tangerine, and crisp pear with a splash of ginger. Patricia didn't know if it was a Glade plug-in, some type of special seasonal Febreze, or if this was simply the scent of well-to-do. They walked on dark hardwood floors made of wood imported from Australia.

The walls were painted ash grey, but the mood was cucumber cool. There was a plum rug with lavender leaf imprint, upholding an ebonized cherry coffee table with books and a vase full of lush heady peonies.

Heidi's parents, Rusty and Katherine Berry sat on the Barney-colored, suede sofa. There was a round Caesar mirror on the wall, extending the room far beyond its dimensions.

Heidi sat on the beige La-Z-Boy recliner, with her feet tucked beneath her. Her eyes were bloodshot; a pair of bagged parenthesis beneath her gaze. She had been crying all evening. Even the freckles on her face looked as though they'd been weeping. The two women had a thing in common; they'd both lost their pride and joy: their children. It was amazing how despair brought people together, like war and death.

Rusty opened the heavy wooden front door and welcomed Patricia into his home. He offered her a bottle of Fiji water and quietly left the living room. Katherine and Heidi sat on opposite sides of the room.

"Call me Katie. No one calls me Mrs. Berry. No need for formalities. I guess I'll leave you two alone so you can talk in private." She had a deep Southern drawl, crow's feet around her eyes, and the look of a woman who'd lived a hard life. No amount of wealth or marrying into money could erase the effect of life's blows.

Detective Patricia Garbutt hoped to never grow into *that* kind of woman. Patricia learned not to judge people by their relatives. American women all lost their beauty eventually, especially the ones who lived hard lives. They wore their emotionally tormented, tough, calloused, storm-ridden lives on their shoulders for all to see, like they were pearl earrings.

All the pain and heartache congealed upon their brows. Unlike the Maya, American women allowed struggle to creep into them like water through the cracks of a rickety old boat.

Nothing could affect you or change you, unless you allowed it to get inside of you. Once a thing was allowed entry inside of you, you would be forever changed.

At first, Heidi said nothing. The look on her face spoke volumes though. It said "I hurt too". She seemed to be made of thunder storms, cerulean veins, and fibrous secrets that housed their own cavernous compartments.

"It's nice to talk face-to-face, without...Jake," Patricia hesitated.

"Yeah, it's okay."

Heidi was a Georgia girl through and through. She exuded Georgia DAWGS, the Varsity, Taco Mac, the Big Chicken, Spaghetti junction, and Savannah all rolled up under red hair. She'd dyed her hair bright cherry red, like the color of a stop sign.

Detective Garbutt studied Heidi's body language like marine biologists studied the bioluminescence of cuttlefish.

"I don't want anything from you. I only offer my sincere apologies that we haven't found Noah yet. I can assure you we are utilizing all of our resources to find your son. I understand what you must be feeling. I don't know if Jake told you or not, but my children were murdered in our family's home. We have reason to believe the same person or persons may be behind both incidences."

Heidi sucked her bottom lip in and bit down. Her eyes filled with water. Detective Garbutt rubbed her hands together like she was massaging moisturizer into her skin. She glanced around the room, searched for the origin of that delectable scent. It smelled damn good.

"I think Jake's holding back. I have reason to believe that he may know exactly who is behind Noah's kidnapping, that he refuses to let me in on the details," Patricia said.

"Like what?"

"I don't know. That's where I was hoping you could help me. Maybe you could enlighten me. Do *you* have any enemies or do you know anyone who might want to hurt you or Noah?"

"Of course not!" Heidi cried.

Detective Patricia Garbutt took another look around the house. She could tell that sumptuous dinners and lighthearted bacon and egg breakfasts were had here. Ardent voluble conversations still lingered in the walls. The carpet offered residue from times where Rusty and his golf buddies waxed philosophic or exchanged techniques for improving their swing. This home was a sanctuary of peace.

SIXTY- FIVE

THE LOOK ON Heidi's face said it all. She'd become an open book—her pages splayed spread eagle. To her surprise, Detective Patricia Garbutt found a willing and cooperative accomplice in Jake's baby's mother.

"Jake always had this secret aspect about himself, especially when we were dating. Though, I wouldn't really call it dating."

"I'm coming to learn that myself. We never dated, but being partners, I see that Jake holds back large parts of himself." Detective Patricia Garbutt would die if Heidi knew about her indiscretions with Jake.

She would die if *anyone* knew about her indiscretions with Jake. She prided herself on remaining professional at all times. Although *that* in and of itself was a crock of shit. She'd never cheated on Anthony in all the years they'd been married.

It was impossible to be made love to by a man the way Jake had made love to her body and not feel something strong and deep. He made love to her like he needed her, like he was deeply and madly in love with her. She felt it in his stroke. She felt it in his kiss.

"Yeah, he would never fully open up to me," Heidi exclaimed. "When I first met Jake, he reminded me of a cross between Channing Tatum and Gerard Butler, so sexy and rugged, with a little redneck flair. God, I love rednecks. We'd fuck most anywhere and everywhere."

Sensing the direction Heidi was taking the conversation, Detective Garbutt swiftly changed the subject. Not to mention the fact that she felt a tinge of jealousy crawl up her spine.

"Do you know anything about his relationship to Russia?"

Detective Patricia Garbutt's voice hung on the air like lamp light. It floated and mingled with the silence. It danced with the plum hues of the Berry residence.

For a moment, Heidi sat quietly with a blank expression on her lips. Outside, a hefty gust of wind made the sweetgum trees dance and sway. Their deciduous satin leaves glistened in the warm sunlight.

She stared at a speck of lint on the plum rug and then slowly brought her eyes up like they were scaling a California Redwood. When Heidi's eyes met Detective Garbutt's eyes, both women knew they'd tampered with something deliciously taboo.

So Heidi went on to tell Patricia the story that Jake had told her. How he was actually born to a Hungarian mother and Russian father.

His father served as a USSR spy in Moscow during the height of the Soviet years. In fact he reported directly to Stalin. Jake grew up in a well-to-do party family. Because his father was a high ranking official in the communist party, he was reared with an outstanding education, but he saw countless murders, pernicious beatings in the concentration camps, and unimaginable poverty.

For a time his father moved the family to Uzbekistan, but the truth behind their moving there was never really made clear, not to young Jake.

He would go on to tell Heidi that he didn't see Communist Russia as a bad thing at all. He saw it as a time where although no one was truly rich, everyone had something to eat. Family and community were important, not wealth and greed at all costs.

He and his father ended up getting into a bitter disagreement and Jake left home, traveled back to Moscow from Uzbekistan, and joined the military. He was proud to have served for the military.

It was when he joined the Russian military that he was approached about doing espionage work for the mafia there. The truth behind his involvement was still sketchy. In fact, there were Bermuda triangle size holes in his story.

He killed and maimed several people during his involvement with the Red mafia—the power and presence of the Red mafia is one that transcended the daily life of its country. They were rapacious thugs. Jake explained that Moscow was so much more than Vodka and big burly Bolsheviks.

It was during his time in the Russian army, doing undercover espionage for the mafia that he learned to eliminate his accent completely. This was the reason why he had no Midwestern or any traceable native tongue for that matter. He began in cryptography, Heidi told her.

"But what about his parents and him growing up in the west?" Detective Garbutt inquired.

She clearly replayed him telling her: *my dad was a retired Blue Angel, from Dothan Alabama. That's what brought me down south from the West. After my parents went splitsville, I wanted to know more about this place. I fell in love with all the trees and the way stone grey skies blend into those trees when you're out on the open road.*

"Well, between you and me I think it was all made up. Like he has a story that he tells people. Everything he says is a lie. He's a trained assassin. He's trained to lie. He tells everyone that story about his dad taking him fishing and blah-blah-blah..." Heidi trailed off.

Detective Garbutt was beginning to question everything. The fabric of their working relationship had all been a lie. That was the truth. Thoughts brimming over with terror crowded out everything. Was this a reliable source? Heidi? An informant?

Although part of her insisted Heidi was just a scorned baby's mother, the better part of her told her to listen. The truth always lurks in silence. Now she knew why Jake never wanted the two women to meet or to have words. He always badmouthed Heidi and wrote her off.

Heidi went on to tell Detective Garbutt about numbers stations. Several intelligence services had a long record of broadcasting encrypted numbers messages by shortwave radio to communicate with its clandestine agents abroad.

Detective Garbutt's ears perked up. This was all news to her. Every minute more truth poured out. It was true that when Communist Russia fell, it opened up several avenues for free market. In December of 1991, the world watched in amazement as the USSR disintegrated into fifteen separate countries. The United States rejoiced as its formidable enemy collapsed to its knees.

But now, according to the Kremlin, the underworld of the Russian Mafia controlled over forty percent of the Russian economy. The effects and ramifications were numerous. And they didn't just deal in drugs or women; they dealt in nuclear weapons and rockets. In the nineties, the Red mafia even controlled the banks.

The Russian Mafia was more fearless and treacherous than the Sicilian Mafia, Italian Mafia, and Columbian Mafia combined. Unlike lesser criminals, the Redfellas had Master's degrees. They were economists and engineers.

Jake, or Jacob Stanislaw had his hands in smuggling, arms trade, banking fraud, and gun trafficking. Today he was living as a detective. He exploited every opportunity that came his way.

Jake was sent to the states under the orders of Vyacheslav Ivankov. Ivankov was a Russian godfather and leader of the Redfellas. He'd been sent to prison for extortion, but there were agents running wild all over the world. A section of Brighton Beach, Brooklyn called Little Odessa was the home of countless Russian immigrants. This was where Jake had been sent in the mid nineties.

Jake was then ordered to work under Ludwig "Tarzan". Tarzan was a Russian made man who ran a gentlemen's club in Florida, called Porky's. He was the go-to guy for anyone wanting investments or creative enterprises to launder their money. Tarzan was Jake's link to the southeast.

All of this was taking Detective Garbutt's breath away. It was as if she had walked into a new world, the Russian criminal underworld was totally foreign to her. How could she not have seen any clues? Jake had a completely different identity that she knew nothing about.

Like Jake, Tarzan had ties to the Russian Army and the Russian Mafia, so they both were able to broker sweetheart deals among their cash rich friends. The leftover cold war submarines and missiles was a dynamic stockpile of a goldmine.

Heidi knew the truth about Jake—and the truth was that Jake was a Russian spy infiltrating the United States CIA. Maybe this was the whole teacher-student thing and until this moment Detective Patricia Garbutt was unable to deal with the truth. They say we only receive what we're prepared to receive, *when* we're prepared to receive it.

Things were beginning to make more sense now, but nothing was as clear as Patricia would have liked. She kept milling over different scenarios in her mind. She and Jake had been assigned as partners in a spur of the moment willy-nilly way.

No one really knew anything about him; no one except for Brody Maxwell. Patricia wanted the truth. Everything about her life was beginning to grow increasingly complicated and she didn't know why. She wanted to know who Jake Billingsley was and why these things were coming out now.

SIXTY- SIX

DETECTIVE PATRICIA GARBUTT listened intently, although she felt her stomach lurch, spasm, and collapse upon itself. Life was throwing her curveballs. She was asking herself: *What breaks a man? What breaks a woman?* We all have different breaking points.

Surely she'd moved past the normal breaking point. But what happened after breakage? When did rebirth occur? Thoughts traversed her mind. One thing she knew for sure was that she was growing both tender and cold-hearted. Pain had a special way of doing that—of making soft things hard, like malleable things left out in the sun too long.

She thought of Jonestown, WACO, and Sandy Hook. She thought of whistleblowers old and new: Julian Asange and Edward Snowden; people who stood against the sway of popular opinion, people who refused to be sheep and admitted the truth.

There was so much happening in this great big world of ours. Most of the time the detrimental stuff like mercury in your lipstick, fluoride in your public drinking water, and chemtrails over your skies at sunrise were silently swept under the local news rug. But sometimes we saw the truth in flashes and glimpses. Insider trading. Illegal surveillance. Top secret military experiments. Everyone's slip began to show eventually.

The average American never believed the truth until some insider confirmed their darkest fears. Heidi was blowing the whistle. She spoke gilded words, rife with dark innuendo. This was as close to the inside as Detective Garbutt was going to get. Would she be naïve and close-minded or would she dig deeper?

"While we were in bed I would bury my face in his chest hair and get so quiet that I practically blended into the furniture. I would listen while he talked about his days in Moscow," Heidi chortled. "That's how I finally found out the truth. Well, that and one day he'd gotten so stoned that he forgot who I was. Kept calling me Sophie. I still don't know who Sophie is or was, but he kept calling me Sophie. I'm assuming she was some girl he'd been with when he was in Russia."

"Did you ever question the reason why he didn't have an accent or anything?" It occurred to her that Jake sounded too all-American to be Russian. It didn't make any sense.

"Not really. I didn't care. He made me happy. When a man is making you happy you stop caring about the imperfections and the little red flags. It didn't matter. He didn't judge me. He loved me. He loved being with me. He loved making love to me. We had a baby together. I always thought he was so worldly and smart. He was always reading or talking about something interesting. He'd been almost everywhere, even places I never heard of. Moscow, Germany, Toronto, China. Jake is like no other man I've ever encountered."

"So let me get this straight, you knew he had a past in the Russian Mafia and you didn't think to ask any questions or tell anyone, or did you even find it strange that here he was in Georgia as a Detective?" This just didn't make any sense to Patricia. Was Heidi truly this stupid or just retarded?

"He would tell me that one day he was going to help me find my freedom — whatever that means," Heidi snorted. "You want to know a secret? Oh Gosh, he would kill me if he knew I told you this," she said, pulling strands of her passion red hair behind her ear, "This stays right here between us." Guilt emerged in her eyes.

Detective Garbutt was silent. She allowed her eyes to do her talking for her.

"His guilty pleasure used to be gay porn. He was fascinated by some kid who called himself the Black Spark. Jake would say it was more than just fucking, more than porn. He said it was artistic and erotic. Now I found *that* strange. But I didn't question him." A slanted smile danced across her face.

Detective Patricia Garbutt found herself getting dizzy. The room began to spin. Plum streaks circled her head and she felt herself becoming nauseous. Her cellular began to suddenly sing. She looked down to see that it was her sister Selena calling her.

"Would you please excuse me, I have to take this," she politely excused herself.

She walked outside onto the front porch. The sky was darkening and looked like it could possibly rain at any moment. An ominous cloud the color of old dirty cement moved in from the west.

"Is everything okay, Selena?"

"Yes, well no. Are you busy? Did I catch you at a bad time?"

"No, I can talk. What's up? What's wrong?"

"I just need to talk to you."

"About? It's not your health is it?"

"No, not at all. I have been keeping my flare ups down. As long as I keep stress levels down, my doctors say that I should be fine. I've been on bed rest for the past two weeks. And I've gotten enough sleep for this life and the next one."

"It's not Nathan is it? He's not giving you a hard time is he?"

"No, Nathan's Nathan…" Selena trailed off.

What could it be? Patricia wondered. *Why was her sister beating around the bush?* She hated when her sisters called her expecting her to read their minds. Ever since Selena confessed that she'd been diagnosed with Lupus, Patricia worried about her.

She knew her sister had a tendency of running herself into the ground, making Nathan and the kids happy. In many ways Selena took after their Grauma Papoose, an avid homemaker and the backbone of the family structure.

Rain began to drizzle from that menacing dark cloud. On days like this, Atlanta reminded her of a woman with a dirty wet face — tear stained cheeks and yellow eyes.

"Well, I called because I just couldn't get this off my mind, what Angel is doing and all."

"What is Angel doing now?" Patricia said.

"He didn't tell us, but he took out an insurance policy on mamí."

Patricia felt her breath catch in her throat. The thermometer of her temper flared to one hundred. She could see red.

Her despicable brother had committed the ultimate betrayal. He may as well have put mamí in the ground with his own two hands.

What added insult to injury was that she had been on a payment plan with the funeral home that buried Mrs. Ortiz. No one else stepped up to help cover the costs of the funeral. She knew that Angel had the money; he was just being Angel — tight fisted, greedy and selfish.

"Hello, Patty? You there? Did I lose you?"

Patricia didn't realize how quiet she'd grown. Her eyes glossed over as she looked out into the distance. She could not believe her fucking brother. With family like this, who needed enemies?

"I'm here Selena. Do you know how much the policy was for?"

"Six hundred thousand dollars."

At the sound of that, Patricia dropped the phone.

SIXTY- SEVEN

NOT ONLY HAD Angel lied to the family, but he'd been deceptively plotting for mamí's dying day all this time. What made it painful was the fact that he'd done it behind everyone's back and that scene at the funeral? What a spectacular display of acting. He was a regular thespian. Angel was full of shit, always had been, and always would be.

Patricia felt nauseous upon hearing the news that Selena told her. She couldn't believe it, but then again she could believe it. Angel was capable of some pretty fucked up shit, evident in how he'd not only lied and acted like he had no money to go towards the funeral costs, but how he lied and claimed he couldn't help his sister.

Times like this, Patricia wished she could disown her brother. She fantasized that she could somehow turn him into a pillar of salt or a fragile ice sculpture, or a stranger—someone she could walk past on the street and not look twice.

It was amazing how money was able to fragment family so completely. Nothing was able to detonate the family unit like greed and the love of money. She refused to wallow in the dark place she found herself immersed in. When she wallowed too long in darkness it became addictive; almost desirous, until it spiraled down into something ugly.

She tried to make herself puke, but nothing came of it but frustration and a disgusting taste like a dirty rusted penny. She told Heidi that she would be in touch, but she had to take care of a family emergency. She didn't want Heidi to see her fall apart. Somehow she knew that would erode her credibility.

Climbing into her car had become an arduous task. Her legs were heavy—but not heavier than her heart.

GREG JENKINS HAD just rounded the corner in his employer provided golf cart. For the most part the evening had been uneventful and quiet. He was hungry. Once he finished doing his rounds he would sneak away for an early lunch to grab a bite at one of the East Atlanta Village Bar and Grills.

The Earl stayed open late. He could grab a Pabst Blue Ribbon and a basket of wings. Maybe he'd go to the popular gastropub, Argosy. Their burgers tasted like the ones he made at home—fat, juicy, and medium in the middle. He liked his burgers how he liked his women: fat, juicy and perfectly pink down the middle.

He saw a robust black Navigator parked in front of one of the units. There was a head poking up from the passenger seat. Looked like someone was slouched down in the seat—maybe even had gone to sleep. Greg Jenkins zipped over to see who was in the car. It was awfully late in the evening for someone to be in their unit, but that happened sometimes.

There was a culture of people who went dumpster diving in storage units. Sometimes a treasure turned up. There was no way to judge; but there was a science to it. It was a numbers game.

You'd be surprised how many people packed expensive items into a storage space for $88 a month only to fall over and die. One time a man found nearly $700,000 worth of antiques in one of those units. The original owner was deceased or had gone missing.

One truly could never possibly know what they'd find when they went treasure hunting. Like most things, you had to dig deep to find what was valuable.

Greg Jenkins assumed one of those treasure hunters may have went diving in someone's storage unit. It was dark. As he approached the SUV he saw that the man sitting inside had one hand on his forehead, his face in peaceful repose. He looked like a man that was both stressed and at peace. Behind his shuttered eyes was a mind hard at work, deep in thought.

The strong scent of burning marijuana peppered the air. The man's eyes flew open; he could sense a presence nearing him. He was cagey and paranoid and very high. His eyes were so red it made you wonder if peering out of them was anything like wearing a pair of rose-tinted glasses.

Greg Jenkins didn't want to cause alarm, but he did have to do his job. He removed the key from the golf cart ignition and began slowly walking towards the SUV. The closer he got, the stronger the scent grew. The smell of burning herb was undeniable.

"Evening sir; didn't mean to scare you. *SureLock* security, just doing my job," Greg Jenkins said.

Gavin Jones, also known as Akil Allah, immediately straightened up. He opened the door and climbed from the SUV. He peered up at Greg Jenkins—who was tall, wiry, and soaring above a much shorter and stouter Akil Allah.

The two men stared long and hard at one another. They were like chess players, waiting for the other to make his next move. Male ego puffed with pride and hubris.

Greg Jenkins stood his ground. He couldn't understand where the animosity was coming from. He didn't know who this man was, nor the impact or depth of his secrets. It was at that moment that he knew something was awry. Something was not sitting well with him. You could say it was his gut instincts kicking in.

"Am I committing a crime," Akil Allah asked.

"Well, it depends on what you're doing brotha. Are you treasure hunting?"

"Am I what? Whatchu mean?"

"Are you getting your own items out of that there storage unit?" Greg Jenkins asked as he walked near the open door.

It was wide, like a one-car garage. The suitcase that housed young Noah sat square in the middle of the unit. There wasn't much else in the space.

"Why would I be in someone else's storage?" Akil Allah countered. "The last time I checked, it don't matter if I sit here and take a shit! That would be my damn business. I pay my monthly bill on time. I respect all the rules for renting storage space. I don't see what the problem is. So if you don't mind, I'll be getting back to minding my own damn business." Akil Allah was visibly disturbed yet he didn't climb back into the Navigator.

"I understand what you're saying brotha. I didn't mean any harm. I was just checking...doing my job. You understand?"

Akil Allah took a step back as if he were going to turn and walk away. Then he approached Greg Jenkins — walked right up to him. Eyeball to eyeball. He knew that if he could keep the man's eyes trained on him, that he could also distract him long enough to direct his attention elsewhere.

Greg Jenkins knew something wasn't right with this situation. The man was being overly aggressive. This was a red flag; it screamed. It got Greg Jenkins to thinking that this guy was probably holding weight — what the young guys called "that loud". Slang term for dope. He definitely was holding marijuana. That much was obvious.

"It's niggas like you...that's the shit I don't like. You come around here fucking with me. Profiling. I'll bet if I was one of those candy-ass white boys you wouldn't have had two words to say to me, now would you, faggot?"

Greg Jenkins was speechless. He actually didn't know how to respond. He took a deep breath and looked to the skies. He searched for the right words to say.

"Sir, there's no need to get indignant, and certainly no need for name calling. I'm paid to insure that these storage units are safe. Certainly you would want the same type of security for your things," he said, glancing in the direction of the suitcase.

What in the hell? Did that suitcase just wobble? Greg Jenkins thought to himself.

"Do I look like a criminal to you, nigga? The best part of you is dripping down your daddy's leg, bitch nigga!" Akil Allah suddenly grew malicious. If he was a German shepherd, he'd be baring his teeth at this point.

SIXTY- EIGHT

GREG JENKINS PUT one hand on his walkie. Akil Allah got into a fighting position—feet planted, arms out held like Mike Tyson in his prime.

Greg Jenkins looked over at the suitcase again. He wasn't crazy. It wobbled vigorously. Then it toppled over. Greg Jenkins' eyes grew to the size of two full moons. He was lubricated in a mystery.

Before he knew it, Akil Allah went Muhammad Ali and dealt Greg Jenkins a ferocious right hook. It felt like he'd been hit by a Boeing 747. Akil Allah was fifteen times stronger than he looked. Plus, he had something to hide and to prove, so he was pumped with pure venom and vengeance.

He was eager to use Greg Jenkins as both his Scapegoat and an example to the world that he was not to be fucked with. He nearly toppled the security guard down in one fell swoop. Greg Jenkins felt his heart skip and his jaw bone shift at the same time.

Greg Jenkins didn't see it coming. As he tried to regain his footing, he felt a fresh new punch to his stomach. It hurt like hell. It felt far worse than it looked in the movies. He was now leaning like the Tower of Pisa.

Suddenly he found himself in a real life toe-to-toe sparring battle and he was getting his ass kicked. The man was giving him an old-fashioned ass-whipping. He was catching a prison yard beat down.

An iron heavy blow was delivered fast and hard right between his eyes. A stealth blow hit his chin. He staggered, before Akil Allah dived directly into him. The two men struggled and fought each other.

Greg Jenkins felt like he was fighting a losing battle. Blood began to cloud his eyesight. With his vision blurred, he swung into the air. He couldn't find the man who attacked him.

Akil Allah ran behind Greg Jenkins while he kneeled down on one knee, attempting to gather strength and process what was happening. As he tried to stand to his feet, in pain and disorientation, Akil Allah roundhouse kicked him. Blindsided him.

Although Greg Jenkins was in impossibly profound pain, he gathered enough inner strength to stand to his feet. He knew that if he stood his ground no matter what blows came his way, eventually the younger stronger man would get tired. Every man eventually got tired. He was now swinging into the air, unable to land a single hit. The only thing he connected with was empty space and potential.

Akil Allah sensed his foe standing in front of him, vamping up to pulverize him, so he ducked and hammered Greg Jenkins with an ugly uppercut. Greg Jenkins, although now in intense discomfort, grabbed Akil Allah around the neck. He held the man and squeezed with all his might.

He was choking the man from an awkward position. Akil Allah attempted to wiggle and escape from his foe's grasp, but he had a clam shell, pincer-like clench on his head and neck.

Akil Allah began to suffocate. He couldn't breathe. His energy was quickly dissipating. He tried to knee his enemy in the groin, but Greg Jenkins was limber and agile.

Greg Jenkins now had the upper hand. His foe was going down slowly. Akil Allah was beginning to turn a luminous shade of purple. It was the craziest thing, Greg Jenkins thought. He'd never seen color leave a black man's face. Until that moment, it was something he would've sworn was an impossibility.

Meanwhile, the Samsonite suitcase began to move once again. First Greg Jenkins thought his mind was playing tricks on him, and then he realized there was something inside that case.

It stood to reason that whatever was inside that case was something the man in the robust black Navigator was attempting to hide from prying eyes.

Suddenly it dawned on him that he'd walked head first into a crime scene waiting to happen. Akil Allah was down on his knees, choking, spitting, and turning various shades. His eyes had become two red stained glass windows to his forsaken soul.

He could barely breathe. Somehow, Greg Jenkins had tapped a vein, nerve, or pressure point of some sort. He was applying intense pressure on the man's spine. Like a caught fly in a spider web, his foe was defenseless.

Greg Jenkins used the butt of his flashlight to bash his attacker in the head. He hit the man repeatedly. He wanted to make sure that he didn't get back up any time soon.

Akil Allah had been relentlessly violent with him, so he knew that if the man managed to regain his energy that he would surely try to take his life.

Greg Jenkins was no killer. He'd never killed a man in his life. He was a peace-loving soul. He'd only taken the job at *SureLock* because they were the only ones hiring.

He'd been out of work for months and was just happy to get offered a position. He hadn't dreamed in a thousand years that anything like this would ever happen. He never thought he would be attacked. Until tonight, he'd never had a reason to be armed. This was reason enough why he deserved to carry a firearm. Reason enough for anyone to carry a firearm. A man had to protect himself. You can't show up to a gun fight, with a knife.

What if his attacker was armed? There was no telling if he was or not. There was no telling what lay hidden in that robust black Navigator. Greg Jenkins didn't want to find out. His mind ran wild thinking about the grisly possibilities. Much of this was being captured on the company's camera, but that wouldn't matter if this man managed to murder him.

He did, however, want to know what was in that suitcase. Raging curiosity cloyed at him.

It felt like fate cloaked the night. Greg Jenkins believed in fate. At his church Bishop Paul Morton always preached about fate and God's will on our lives. He believed God wanted him there that night.

He didn't know why, but at that moment he had a keen sense of clarity. When he stopped hitting Akil Allah, the man's head was bloody and his skull was punctured. He was bleeding profusely. Greg Jenkins had drifted off into the depths of his thoughts, while his fists actively drove into his enemy's skull.

The man's head was slumped over, like a broken bobble-head doll that had lost a spring. There was blood everywhere. Blood was all over Greg Jenkins. He hadn't realized it until he looked down, but he was covered in blood. His hands were soaked and there was spatter in a ten foot circumference from where the two men struggled.

Akil Allah was still alive, but barely. His heart still pumped blood through his veins. Oxygen still moved in and out of his lungs, but he was in bad shape. He'd be out of commission for weeks, perhaps months, depending on his will to live.

Both men were in bad shape. It was never anything to be celebrated when a man shed another man's blood. Greg Jenkins wiped his hands on his shirt. All the blood began to creep him out. He looked like a monster. He felt like a monster.

SIXTY- NINE

SOMETHING TOLD DETECTIVE Garbutt to call Brody. It was beyond her control. She felt compelled—as if something outside of her was calling. Beckoning. Like breathing or sneezing, it was an involuntary impulse.

She may not have had much control over her brother's actions or the comings and goings of her husband, but she damn sure had control of her career. This was something that she'd always prided herself on. She didn't understand women who poured all their energy and time into building their home, only to allow their professional lives to crumble by the wayside.

She would never become that woman. She refused to remain entangled in a situation with no say and no way to have her grievances addressed. She knew that she may not have been able to have her cake and eat it at the same time, but she could *either* have her cake or she could eat it. There was still a shadow of choice. And she would not suffer in silence.

There was always choice, in every situation. And there was always a way. She innately knew that though she may not have had much control over what happened outside of her, she always had control over what happened within her mind and heart—how she felt and more importantly, how she thought. It was all hers to do with it what she chose.

Brody agreed to meet her down at the station. It felt strange walking into that brick and steel building after being released from the Roth case. There was no way to describe the ugliness of that place. It was a gray cement fortress with broken angles. Windows similar to dark, soul-less, peering eyes.

It felt surreal—like she didn't belong there. Upon entering the lobby, she smiled and waved at Chris, the old, white-haired, potbellied black man who secured the building. The smell of freshly brewed Columbian coffee wafted down the hall.

She took a deep breath as she walked down the hallway, the sound of her heels click-clacking against the hardwood floors. It was as though she stood at the edge of a precipice. The end of one chapter and the beginning of another.

Kevin Loggins, a seasoned veteran GBI agent with Scandinavian features, walked past her and nodded. He tried to come onto her years ago. He always seemed so querulous, so petulant, and so desperate—it was unbecoming. There was nothing more unattractive than a peevish, overly emotional man. Even if she wasn't married to Anthony, she still would not have given Kevin Loggins the time of day.

In all her foreboding, she was embarrassed and wanted to avoid as many colleagues as possible. She didn't have the desire or inclination to fence questions, although she knew people had been talking.

It was a golden opportunity for drama. If it was one thing she knew for sure, it was that cops were catty. You would expect decorated men to be more mature, more adult, but no...most of the guys on the force were bigger gossipers than an issue of the *Inquirer*.

Brody was in his office finishing up a call. His face lit up when Detective Garbutt materialized in the doorway. He waved for her to come inside and have a seat.

Brody's office walls were decorated with trophies, medals, and framed awards of all sorts. There was a photo of his wife, Tina. She looked as though she'd had more work done on her face than the Department of Labor.

There were a few photos of their children, who were all adults now. Lieutenant Brody Maxwell had a fine family. After he hung up the phone he stood and walked over to Detective Garbutt. He gave her a warm fatherly embrace. He'd gained a considerable amount of weight. His shirt fit tight around his love handles.

"What a pleasant surprise! How have you been Garbutt? Is life treating you okay?" he asked before picking up a coffee mug and taking a sip of coffee.

"Life has been treating me just fine, all things considered," she lied. Life was dragging her through the mud. She replied with a tinge of sarcasm in her voice.

Brody sat back down in his chair, behind his desk. He folded his hands and sucked in his lips, took a deep breath, and asked her what she wanted to discuss.

"Well, I really need you to be straight up and transparent with me Brody…no bullshit."

"Okay, about what?" he nodded.

"About Billingsley."

Brody looked up at her, his chin cocked to the ceiling. Eyes squinted.

"What's on your mind?" Brody said.

"I need to know more about his past. As my partner, I'm beginning to question his integrity as a Detective. So many things have been happening that just aren't really adding up, if that makes any sense."

"Well, can you explain?" Brody was suddenly inquisitive about Detective Jake Billingsley.

"Well, I just left from talking to Heidi, his son's mother. She told me some pretty disheartening things, things I would never imagine in a million years Jake would be involved in."

Brody cut her off, "Heidi? His son's mother?" he chuckled, "In God's name, you cannot be serious, Garbutt! That woman is scorned and you know what they say about a scorned woman."

Detective Garbutt played dumb, "no, tell me what they say about a scorned woman?" she smirked sarcastically.

"Let's just say I wouldn't take anyone's scorned ex-lover too seriously, woman or not. What did she say and what does this have to do with why you're here? Have you spoken to Jake or did you come straight here? I don't have time for this rigmarole, Garbutt. Why are you here?"

"Will you grant me the right to look at Billingsley's employee file?"

"Not without just cause. What are you getting at? What's this about? If it's something fishy going on, I want to be the first one in the know. Now, cut the crap and spit it out Garbutt."

"Who is Jake Billingsley? I learned recently that he tapped my phone and I'm just trying to get to the bottom of things." Patricia Garbutt reached into her bag and pulled out some of the things she'd uncovered. "I've also found some things during my investigations. I found large sums of money, diamonds, bonds, and this passport with his picture, only it's under an alias. If he's going under cover I want to know why I wasn't included. I want to know who this man is. To be quite honest with you, he's been drinking like a fish lately and he's totally out of control. We stand to get hit with the lawsuit of the century if he doesn't slow down. What was he into before he joined the force? Where did you really find him? If you can't answer any of those questions, then I am requesting a new partner." Detective Garbutt's face flushed crimson. She couldn't believe she was sitting there ratting to Brody, but she felt this was the least she could do to get her life turned in a new direction.

Brody took a long deep breath and exhaled. He looked over at the wall to his right, as though he was avoiding her eyes. "Garbutt, I think you're losing your mind. I mean this all sounds ludicrous. What do you think is going on?"

Detective Garbutt found it ironic that Brody was in total disbelief and denial. He wasn't even interested in seeing or hearing about the evidence of her claims. She was beginning to second guess herself.

Brody's intentions were not immediately clear to her, but hers were not clear to him. She had her doubts that he was unaware of what type of life Jake lead.

"Look Brody, that's the least you can do. First you toss me off the case like an old used empty can, in spite of the fact that you know what's been going on in my personal life."

"Exactly, listen to yourself Garbutt. Maybe you should get with your family and take a trip to Florida or South Carolina. Get some R&R. You've been through a lot of trauma. I just want you to be rational."

"Oh, excuse the hell out of me. Am I being overly emotional? Like a scorned woman?"

Silence descended upon the office. Brody still refused to make eye contact with Detective Garbutt. He spun himself around in his black, high-backed, leather chair and gazed outside the window down at the city.

"Am I? Answer me at least. For crying out loud Brody, please!" Detective Garbutt was growing exasperated.

SEVENTY

GREG JENKINS LIMPED over to the suitcase. He was sore all over his blood-covered body. A muscle made a spasm and pain darted down his thighs and into his bones. Even his toes hurt. He was a tapestry of ouch.

He looked back at the man who had brutally attacked him; the man who grew unnecessarily violent after being interrupted from smoking pot in his robust black Navigator. He was lying in a pile like an ancient Nubian kingdom in ruins. The scene made Greg Jenkins think of Nixon and his so-called war on drugs.

He bent down to pick up the Samsonite suitcase and placed it upright. Breathing heavily and squinting in pain, he began to unbuckle it. His knuckles were cramping and his ears were ringing. Adrenaline had his mind in a vice grip. There was a putrid odor coming from that thing. It smelled like stale dry piss and days-old shit. Like a kitty litter box.

Fear fell out of the suitcase once he'd managed to get it open; fear and a strong acrid ammonia odor. It was the disheartening and despicable scent of misery and broken hope—dashed dreams. Fear scampered out into the fresh open air like spiders, scorpions, and hornets.

Everyone experienced it once in their life, some sooner than others. Everyone was broken and disjointed by something in life. For those, who like young Noah Billingsley, experienced it in their youth, were made all the smarter, wiser, and stronger later in life. Like fractured bones and bent cartilage, it tended to grow back much stronger and able to withstand more. But for now the full weight of the situation was stark and unsettling.

He held his breath, but pressed on. There was a chill in the air; a chill that made him shudder.

Once he got the suitcase open, he couldn't believe his eyes. Noah was squeezed into a fetal position. He appeared to be an overgrown newborn who had overstayed his welcome in the wet womb. He would be forever confronted, challenged, and changed by this situation. Everyone involved would be.

Greg Jenkins would never be able to effectively remove this image from his psyche. It would be indelibly etched in a crevice of his mind, transforming his ideas about kidnap victims and children in general; how defenseless they truly were.

Noah looked up at Greg Jenkins with trembling despair. He was sweaty and his skin ruddy. The boy had fear written on his face, in his sunken eyes, and all over his being. His hair stuck to his temples.

Now he knew what secret the man was trying to hide. It made sense that he would be hostile and fight Greg Jenkins because there was no way that man could explain why there was a little blonde-haired, blue-eyed boy in a suitcase being housed in his storage space.

"Don't worry; everything is going to be okay. I'm not going to hurt you," Greg Jenkins said as he reached out to the small frightened child. He tried to touch the boy's hand, but he snatched it back. Noah gave Greg Jenkins an apprehensive doubt-filled glare.

He knew the boy would be frightened, seeing a towering black man covered in blood. A look of relief came over Noah once he tasted the fresh air and saw the terrible man who snatched him away from his daddy. He quickly climbed out of the suitcase, with Greg Jenkins' help.

"I want my daddy! Where's my daddy?" the boy screamed. Suddenly he grew hysterical. He was shaking. There was a huge, dark, lumpy stain on the seat of his pants. The skin on his arms was sallow and feverish.

Greg Jenkins tried once again to calm the boy. "What's your name? What's your father's name? I'm not going to hurt you, just calm down. Everything is going to be just fine. Did that man hurt you?" he pointed at Akil Allah. He wondered if the boy had been...fondled, abused, if his innocence was still intact.

Noah looked at the man lying stiff and still near the big black Navigator, covered in blood, and he tensed up. Dark scary thoughts of that brutal man spilled into young Noah's mind. He shuddered. He couldn't stop shaking. There was so much blood everywhere. He didn't know who the tall man was who let him out of the suitcase, but he was grateful in his own personal way.

Noah started crying and pissing on himself again. The poor child was frightened beyond belief. At that moment, it registered to Greg Jenkins that this was the kid that all the Amber alerts were about.

He felt around for his phone. Once he located it, he pulled it out and began searching for one of the last text messages that had been sent to his phone. Once he confirmed that the young boy that he'd found in the suitcase was in fact Noah, the missing child who was kidnapped from his father's loft a few days ago, Greg Jenkins called the police.

SEVENTY-ONE

DETECTIVE PATRICIA GARBUTT stormed out of Brody's office. None of her questions had been answered. None of her grievances were addressed. "She's onto Billingsley," he spoke into the phone, minutes after the door slammed shut behind her. Her heels could be heard click-clacking down the hall.

"Garbutt is onto Billingsley!" he repeated, only this time louder. Once he knew that she was out of ear shot. Brody knew that Jake Billingsley, better known as Jacob Stanislaw, was a Russian mole. A mole was a deep cover sleeper agent. A defector. A long term spy. "I didn't confirm anything."

It was a secret that was never meant to be revealed or uncovered. Lieutenant Brody Maxwell had been Stanislaw's safe house. He was the only one on the force who knew Billingsley's true identity.

"I'm telling you she just left my office. She came in here with one of his passports and claims she knows her phone's been tapped," he paused for a moment and blew out frustration. "Yes, she must be alienated, isolated, and neutralized. She's asking way too many questions. Putting her nose where it doesn't belong. I can't afford for things to blow up over this bimbo," Brody said.

By the time Detective Patricia Garbutt slid her key into the ignition of her Crown Vic, she had become a marked woman. Her life had been pinned to a deadly radar. She was a moving target to be eradicated.

Brody couldn't allow anything to happen to Billingsley before he handed a dossier to *his* handler. Although both men were operating under diplomatic immunity and cover, the risk was just too great. Garbutt had no idea that Michael Roth had been one big false flag, and she played no more than an accessory to the real operation at hand. She was an incidental pawn in the game. But the truth was beginning to be revealed.

Now that Garbutt was in the way, asking questions, and growing concerned she would have to be eliminated. Brody didn't know whom else she may have spoken to, but he wasn't going to let her speak to anyone going forward.

He knew Garbutt could sometimes be brash and irrational, which is why he initially wanted her on his squad, but he also knew she was capable of doing anything. It was a blessing and a curse with her.

Meanwhile, Detective Patricia Garbutt climbed in her car heading back to Jake's place. She decided she would gather a few things and get a hotel that night. She didn't feel safe there anymore. What if Brody called Jake to tell him she'd been sniffing around inquiring about him? Her life was spinning into an abyss of turmoil and confusion.

Her once normal life was now a portrait of jaded realism. She felt brittle, like she'd fall over and dismantle into pieces if the wind blew too hard.

She could feel pressure building in her bones, back, and shoulder muscles. There was an imaginary weight sitting on her shoulders. It felt like she'd been carrying the weight of the underworld with her bare hands.

She felt like she was made of ashes. Strength was a distant cousin she'd never be reunited with. Hope was as far away as Siberia...and just as barren. She wrestled with despair and fought the sensation of its clawing tentacles as it engulfed everything around her and calcified her fears.

She wondered about young Noah, prayed he was still alive. She hadn't heard anything. She knew Jake was probably somewhere deadening his sobriety in a bottle of booze. She couldn't blame him for that.

Losing a child was something she wouldn't wish on her worst enemy, let alone Jake. It was an experience born of dark intricacies, vulnerabilities and complex nightmares. It made you feel like one of those glass winged butterflies, native to southern Mexico. Like if you focused long and hard enough, you could be seen through.

It was something that couldn't be defined, yet wholly felt. As the days passed, she knew the likelihood and chances of Noah being found alive grew increasingly dismal.

Jake lived in a world of perpetual personal conflict. He had been living a double life and now the lines were beginning to blur. You can only live a double life for so long before stories and lies begin to intersect. Every city planner could explain it in clear kindergarten terms.

When Patricia got to the loft she felt a strange sensation like someone was there. She walked into the bedroom. No one was there, or so it seemed. She gingerly tapped open the bathroom door with her knuckles.

It was dark, but she thought she heard a rustling sound. Something stirred in the shadows. Made her shudder from the base of her spine up to the nape of her neck. Detective Garbutt couldn't lend meaning to the cold dark hollowness she felt. It was terrifying and amazing at the same time.

While standing in the doorway to the bathroom, Detective Patricia Garbutt could feel a mounting sense that someone was in the loft with her.

She felt the hairs on her arms and the back of her neck bristle. She refused to bow to the gale-force winds of fear. Suddenly she felt someone grab her from behind. She felt them cup her mouth. Curtains.

SEVENTY-TWO

JUST WHEN DETECTIVE Patricia Garbutt thought she'd slip out of the back door in the midst of daunting chaos, she found herself being swept up into a shitstorm of epic proportions.

She wrestled with an attacker who was much larger and stronger than she was. His breath smelled bitter with the scent of chewing tobacco. It was so strong and tart that it pronounced itself even with his mouth closed.

He had large white Marvel Comics knuckles. No gloves. That was bold. And he was unshaven. His prickly stubble grazed the side of her forehead as he forcefully held her captive from behind.

She realized that she'd left her gun in the Crown Vic. That was a habit that had cost her one time too many. It was an expensive habit—owning a gun, but leaving it in the car when she needed it most.

Her attacker had a beer gut which protruded out and slumped over his belt. That wasn't the only thing that was protruding as he attacked her. He had an erection. He was harder than Chinese calculus, and all Patricia Garbutt could do was pray that he wouldn't rape her.

She struggled to catch her breath. Felt like she was running a marathon under water, running out of oxygen, attempting to rise to the surface for fresh air. She struggled to buoy herself to an invisible surface, where she could exhale and inhale. She choked and kicked and fought. She gasped out obscenities. Her arms wind milled, but the attacker was just too strong. Big hands on small, soft flesh of her neck.

Her attacker had a firm grip on her mouth. That's when she realized she was being poisoned. He had placed a handkerchief doused with some type of nauseating chemical over her nose and mouth. The last thing she remembered was a vulgar, acrid, metallic and artificial smelling odor moving through her nose and mouth, singing the hairs in her nostrils.

Before she realized what was happening, she felt herself becoming woozy. The room began to spin slowly, like she was on a merry-go-'round. Then the room started to spin faster and faster and faster. She was dizzy and then she blacked out.

She dreamed she was in the jungle. It appeared to be familiar; she'd been there before. It was lush and cool, punctuated in varying shades of green. A river inlet full of bullfrogs and water that took the color of the skies ahead.

Morning sunlight danced across the river's ripples. A subtle breeze pushed through the trees, rousing a toucan into flight. Its beak was as colorful as a bowl of fruit loops—hot yellow, dark teal, and lime that made your lips pucker.

A flock of bright scarlet Ibis sprinkled out across the sky, in preparation to roost amongst the mangroves. There was a white egret here and a flamingo-like roseate spoonbill there.

A jaguar stalked amongst the trees—its eyes full of power and prowess. She could hear the sounds of all manners of creeping and crawling life. Croaking frogs, iguanas, howler monkeys, and the omnipresent rustle of shrubbery as the wind swept through the jungle.

It was undeniable. She was back in the jungles of Belize. She saw a pair of tortoise beetles, native to Belmopan. There was a lone tapir, a kinkajou here, collared peccaries and red brocket deer there. In the distance, there was even a lesser anteater.

The air even tasted sweet. Like mango and moisture. It felt surreal. She breathed in the wild air and floated over pools of carp, past low bluffs and sloping banks thick with willows that enclosed her in a corridor of teal and cerulean.

There was an armada of spiky plants, such as catmint and phormium. A plant playground full of unexpected foliage. Blue fescue, Coral aloe, and agave in shades of burgundy, orange, and chartreuse.

The sky began to grow cool, like a gray dove. Suddenly, out from among the thicket, she noticed her grandmother Papoose. She was just standing there staring at her. Patricia Garbutt felt herself well up with tears. She hadn't seen Papoose in years, not since she was a small girl living in Belize City with the rest of their family. She was overcome with grief and sadness in the presence of Papoose.

Papoose was standing next to a lusty vine which clambered up an aspen trunk. Behind her was a pair of stairs that ironically lead to nowhere; stairs as tall and wide as a Sequoia. Or perhaps the stairs led to someplace invisible to Patricia. They mounted up into cumulus clouds. A huge black pearl hung over her head. The black pearl was the size of the moon. It looked outlandish and cartoon-like.

She called out to Papoose, but Papoose just continued to stare at her. Papoose was always known for being a storyteller. She beckoned to Patricia after a few moments lingered. The wind began to kick up fallen leaves. An oasis of sweet smelling floral fragrances sprinkled the air in front of her face.

Patricia ran to her grandmother and embraced her. Although she was keenly aware of the fact that she was dreaming, the hug felt real. Papoose's skin was tight like it was when Patricia was a young girl, tight and dune-colored, soft like the skin of an olive.

Papoose smelled like her old self—like the sumptuous scent of cooked Belizean food. Panades, salbutes, garnaches and tacos made-from-scratch tortillas. Her hair always smelled of rosewater, and it was still braided down her back. A statuesque woman, she looked slightly younger, and at peace. There was a calming shade of serenity in her eyes.

She was as stately and majestic as Empress Dowager Cixi. Resounding power radiated from her. There was a subtle halo behind her head. It occurred to Detective Patricia Garbutt that perhaps her attacker had killed her and this was what happened when you died — you met with your loved ones on the other side.

Here was a formidable woman who played a pivotal role in young Patricia's life and upbringing.

Papoose had an unusually attractive personality. She was like a heroine in Belize — being so skilled with her hands and bringing respect and financial wealth to her family name, even after her husband's death.

Her greatness did not die with her. She was also a healer. She worked magic with jungle plants: elixirs of flower waters, oils, and teas. Papoose walked over to the stairway, leading up into the skies. She gathered her thoughts before speaking.

"People don't fear failure. They fear shame," Papoose said. Her perfectly patent leather Kriol still intact.

The statement caught Patricia off guard, but she knew her grandmother only spoke truth. "Every man is like a centaur, part human, part beast," Papoose continued. "Even the most docile priest, has a gargoyle living within him. Nothing is as it seems, mi chile. You are the heir to amend my tarnished image."

Patricia had no idea what her grandmother was talking about. What tarnished image? She wanted to ask Papoose about eighty-three questions. There were so many open ended *questions*.

All she'd ever known Papoose as was a woman who exuded greatness and power. In her mind, she would always be immortalized in her native Belizean village. Even as a young girl, there were stories of her being all bravado and snark, fearless in the face of any adversary, her brothers included.

"But what do you mean, Papoose?" she finally asked after taking a ride on her own train of thought.

Papoose sighed heavily. "Nothing is as it seems. I've been patiently and quietly watching you from above and sometimes from within. I have watched how the fabric of our family has slowly diminished. You and your brother, each of you coming apart as though moths eat away at your love for one another. For what? Material possessions," she paused.

Detective Patricia Garbutt could feel her throat tighten and a lump the size of a brick embedded itself there. Guilt blanketed her like a wet sheet. Cowardly self preservation elbowed her— attempted to get her to respond with a snappy response; nudged her to defend herself. But intuition made her think better. This dream world was a lot like being under the influence of a strong hallucinogenic. Everything looked misty and soft. Blemish-free.

"I'm not here to condemn nor am I here to judge. I am here to reveal who you really are," Papoose continued. "I too made my share of mistakes when I was among the living. I wasn't always the best of mothers."

"Papoose you were a wonderful mother and an amazing abuela. What on earth are you talking about?" Patricia interrupted her.

"You only know what you've been told and what you perceive to be the truth, but truth isn't always as it seems. You ask what on earth I am speaking of? That's the thing...right now, I am not on earth."

It felt good to be back in Papoose's presence, in spite of her newfound modesty. Even her voice sounded like her vocal chords were made of frankincense and myrrh.

"Although I loved my husband, I had a long affair," Papoose said. The statement knocked Patricia Garbutt off kilter. It made her take pause. She shook her head to make sure she'd heard her grandmother correctly. She knew then what she'd learned long ago. Truth, like crème, always rose to the top.

"Not only did I have an affair without my husband's knowledge, but I got pregnant with my lover's child. Back in those days we did not do such things like abort our babies. We lived and went to our graves carrying our secrets with us."

Patricia Garbutt was stunned by what she was hearing. She now had no choice but to question everything she thought she knew for sure. What other family secrets lurked behind that good-natured Roman Catholic façade?

She felt like she was in a second hand store, uncovering all types of treasures. All she knew was that Papoose was born and raised in a village shaped like a gun and could be just as deadly when crossed.

Ripe fruit always fell from her lips. Papoose continued. "I always told myself that whatever showed up in my life, no matter what it was, it was there to teach me something. Sometimes the sins of the father, or in this case, of the mother, re-visit the children and the children's children. You are a living witness and testimony to that cold hard fact.

"When I dwelled among the living, I was a living synagogue and at the same time, a brothel. I was a walking contradiction—an enigma. No one knew my secrets…no man, at least. In those days we had no women's liberation. We had no one to empower us. All we had was ourselves."

Patricia Garbutt wondered what this all meant in the grand scheme of things. She wondered why it was happening. She wondered if she was still alive, dreaming, half-sleeping.

"Truthfully, by the time I was married to my husband, I wasn't deserving of him. He was a kind man with a warm soul. He often heard rumors about what I did in secret, but being the good man that he was, he shielded me," Papoose said.

"Yeah, wish I could say the same for Anthony," Detective Patricia Garbutt replied.

Her husband was supportive, but not in a way that she would define as kind, and he was far from being a warm soul. What Anthony did was more out of obligation than it was out of being warm. He provided for the family out of obligation. It was how he was raised. But she wasn't perfect either.

She'd made her share of mistakes, but she never cheated on Anthony. Not until fairly recently. But then again, their marriage was in the toilet and she reasoned with herself that what she shared with

Jake didn't really count. It was like a defensive foul, not a game-changing play.

"The man that I married wasn't the man that I loved. That's the way life goes though, doesn't it? The man that I loved was your mother's true biological father. His name was Lorenzo Gonzalez. He was born in Belmopan, but his roots were also in Guatemala. I could have been killed for giving my body to a man with Guatemalan blood."

Patricia Garbutt knew then that the reason Papoose was so well-versed in dispersing Belizean folklore was because many of those tales dwarfed her real life. Belizeans, even today, hated their neighbors from the west, who crossed their borders illegally, bringing their trash and filth. The Belizean-Guatemalan territorial dispute had been longstanding, carrying on from generation to generation.

From the outside looking in, one wouldn't understand the complexities that lie at the heart of the matter. It was somewhat like the ethnic cleansing that occurred between the Rwandans—the deep-seated hatred that the Hutus had of their neighboring Tutsis, minus the massive genocide.

Or like the atrocities committed by the Bosnian Serb forces. From the outside, they all looked alike, with similar customs and culture, but on the ground, they hated each other. This was the way of humankind, since the days of Cain and Able, brother was pitted against brother.

"As I said before, people don't fear failure, they fear shame. My greatest fear was the shame that I would potentially face if the truth was ever revealed about what I'd done or what I shared with Lorenzo. For many years I wore my shame like a badge of honor, if only to prevent others from inflicting it 'pon me. I did my thing with pride and grace," she said. "The greatest truths are in the invisible and the mysterious."

Papoose was spilling her secrets out to her granddaughter. One by one, they slithered out like lice, their gossamer skin glistening in the sun. Papoose, normally a woman who held her secrets close to her chest like a good poker hand, was now relinquishing them to the grandchild she loved the most.

"I believe your mother knew the truth, although I never uttered these words to her. For whatever reason, she always managed to cling to the Ortiz blood swelling in her veins."

She knew that she was made up of the same substance as Papoose…the same DNA, the same mitochondria, the same temperament, and the same personality.

"I feel like my life is unraveling into this blob of nothingness," Patricia said to Papoose. "My marriage is in the gutter. The kids have been murdered by one of the psychopath murderers that I've been investigating at work, and even mamí and Lisa have been pulled into this disaster. I feel like I'm the blame for it all."

For a moment, Papoose just stood there. She didn't flinch, nor did she budge. She was at peace, a woman undivided. It was as though she knew things that Patricia could barely fathom. The two women had the same blood and DNA, but Papoose was constellations away in wisdom and understanding. She knew that life had an uncanny way of working itself out in the most unexpected ways.

"There is no such 'ting as the truth," Papoose spoke.

It felt warm and good in Papoose's presence. Her words were liquid liberation, like cool dewdrops or a subtle peaceful breeze. If she had died, she found refuge under Papoose's wing.

It felt like what had been scattered was now being re-collected, remembered. "I just don't know what to do anymore," Patricia said, shaking her head. "I am so lost. Where should I turn?"

"Turn within. Turn to God, mi chile," Papoose said. "You're going to fall down and have disappointment in your life. I should know. Sometimes it feels like life was designed to knock you on your rear-end. It comes with the territory. Sometime failure is a part of the most blissful journeys. You don't have to be lost, just like you don't have to possess all 'de answers."

"Can you tell me if Tony and I are finished?" Patricia asked.

"That depends wholly on you and Tony," she replied. "Value the changes you're experiencing in your life. You have somet'ing very special inside. You have greatness in you, chile. Not'ing ever stays the same. No storm ever lasts forever."

"Yeah, I guess you're right. I know you're right Papoose. I love you so much. I miss you and I miss mamí." Patricia's voice broke and tears began to pour down her face.

"There is somet'ing in you that is demanding that you come up higher. You have to begin to think higher thoughts. Believe 'tings will get better. Pray about it and in the midst of your prayer you'll find the answer. Meditate on the beautiful stuff. The *beautiful* stuff. Meditation is always cleansing and purifying. Me and your mamí are always present, watching, sending you beams of love, and hoping that you make the right choices. Be strong. We're always with you. We love you always."

With that said, Papoose turned and began walking up the stairway. Her long hair braided down her back. She didn't turn back to face Patricia. The farther she walked up the stairs, the brighter and the more luminous the top of the staircase grew. There was warmth emanating from the light, and the deeper Papoose walked into the light, the more the light began to oscillate and appeared baby blue. Before long, Papoose had disappeared.

SEVENTY-THREE

SUDDENLY PATRICIA SAT up and decided not to die. She lived through an out-of-body-experience that housed the power to give her a new lease on life. When she opened her eyes she was laying on a ratty orange sofa. The arms of the sofa were filthy and torn.

Not having any idea where she was, Detective Patricia Garbutt realized that her ankles and wrists were bound. Duct tape sealed her lips. Her badge...gone. Her gun...gone. Her cell phone...gone. The pain was atrocious.

A cold wave of panic and fear suddenly engulfed her. She was still alive, but for how long? Her attacker had tied her up and brought her to this place.

She felt that tingling burn in her eyes that came just before tears. Crying was pointless, but she'd cry anyway. Being jaded didn't suit her. If she could, she would have folded herself into an envelope. Return to sender.

A spectrum of freakish thoughts cascaded down the bandwidth of her mind. Outside she could see dawn's early light breaking through the clouds. It was a sky lit in purple, orange, and glowing yellow.

The sun had just arisen and the sweet scent of a new day punctuated the space between the winds. She could also hear jive water flowing and pulsating—like a Charlie Parker song. Melodic and rhythmic.

Looking around, she realized she had been drugged. She could still feel the pull of some type of downer-depressant surging through her bloodstream. She was being housed in a small white-trimmed burgundy cottage, in the middle of nowhere.

The house was more of a log cabin, in the middle of the woods, deep in South Georgia, or maybe she had been driven to Alabama, Tennessee, or South Carolina. There was no way for her to tell. Pines towered into the sky on the left and right of the house, like forest green obelisks shooting into the atmosphere, flanked by tiny green needles.

Wherever she was, she could hear the sound of a rushing river outside the window. White frothed waves could be heard washing by just outside the front door. Roaring rapids amid an empire of cedars and moss-laminated oak trees.

The house was old. It smelled like old people lived there. Like aged skin, mildew and broken promises. For better or worse. The furniture was ancient, the table, kerosene lamps, pillows, and even the wall-mounted art was all antique.

There was a gilded framed portrait of General Stonewall Jackson hung on the wall to her right. She tried to loosen the binding rope around her wrists. Her attacker had tied a mean knot.

The rooms in the cottage were small, as though it was constructed during a time when men built homes with their own two hands. It was clearly a shotgun house. The furniture was small and marked with the energy only found in old secondhand antique furniture.

Everything was quiet. She doubted anyone was in the house with her. Perhaps he'd taken her there to leave her, hoping she'd suffer and drown in her own pity.

There was no doubt about it; the drug was still potent in her bloodstream, casting a dim gaunt hazy shadow over everything she tried to focus on. She could barely move her legs and although her eyes were open, her arms and legs felt like chewing gum.

Suddenly her heart began to pound. It pounded so loud that she thought she was having a heart attack. It was an irregular pounding — something she'd never experienced before. Fear flooded her body. Dread encompassed her thoughts and clouded her mind.

She struggled with the rope. She was powerless. Every conceivable fear entered her mind. It's amazing how the mind could weave together such fantastic nightmarish visions when drenched in fear.

Her mind was like a hurricane crashing onto shore. She realized her life had become a wreck. Not a garden variety wreck. No, it was a mammoth Mother lode of a wreck. And suddenly she began to question herself.

She doubted her courage. If she allowed herself to be murdered, she could be with the kids again, only in paradise. She'd die and go to heaven, where she'd be warmly embraced by Tyler and Maria, mamí and Lisa. She'd see her old partner Detective King and the many friends and relatives she'd lost to cancer.

Death couldn't be that bad. She began to reason with herself. She felt jazz, blues, gospel and soca all writhing inside of her — complex and equally disruptive. Her mind momentarily thought of her friend Rae — short for Renee Schechter.

Rae was a Jewish woman that Patricia met when she was going to therapy. They both were seeing shrinks in the same building, the same office.

Rae was colorful and complex. She also was dealing with a boatload of emotional baggage, no different than anyone else.

Rae ended up fighting a slow and painful battle with pancreatic cancer. Patricia recalled it being in March. The Ides of March. It rained every day for nearly a month after Rae passed. She went to visit Rae in the hospital, brought her favorite movie, *To Sir, with Love*, sat and watched it with her over and over again.

Rae also liked the sound of vinyl — Ethel Waters, Bob Dylan and Sinatra. Patricia even managed to bring Rae's record player, clunky as it was, to the hospital, just so she could hear the crackling sound of vinyl as it spun around.

She may not have been living with or dying from cancer, but she believed she could relate to the agony that she'd seen in Rae's eyes.

She knew in that moment that God put Rae in her life so she would know how to better handle death when it was her time. Rae languished.

She'd been marked down to her lowest possible low. Back then, Patricia was an alchemy of love letters in her prime, when the love was still authentic between she and Anthony.

There had been nineteen years of Sundays since Rae succumbed to cancer. Nineteen years of sunsets, all bedecked by a phosphorus moon.

Yet, it wasn't until now that Patricia understood death as clearly as she did in this moment. Despite the fact that she was a homicide detective, until now, she hadn't viewed death the way she viewed it in that log cabin with her ankles and wrists bound. Duct tape sealing her lips. Defenseless. Vulnerable.

Maybe God was trying to compose something. Maybe her dogged soul was being dried and fermented. She thought of her baby boy—a young phoenix of a boy, gearing up to take flight. He had such a promising future. Just imagine who he could have become.

Her love for her children never wavered. She smelled the scent of jasmine. There was jasmine growing in the kitchen. Night blooming jasmine. There was also potted wisteria, weeping over its reddish terra cotta bed. Gardenia was there too— lamenting for water and sunlight. Patricia wondered how long she'd gone nightie-night.

Outside the mist was heavy and beautiful, even though inside that space, Patricia felt her approaching demise. Then it occurred to her that hitting rock bottom was perhaps necessary for her renewal. Perhaps.

Dawn was breaking her heart through the moss draped oak canopies outside. Voluptuous trees embraced that log cabin, but there was no love there.

She had become a moth in a profession abundant with fireflies, bumblebees, and wasps even. She was snoozing. Snoozing could get you caught up. She cradled the constellations of the dead.

If her pain and frustration could be transformed into electricity, she could power the world. It was uncertainty that upset her the most.

She could feel uncertainty inching through her spinal column, out into her bone marrow, and surging through her blood. She could feel it like it was traveling between her synapses and tying knots in the center of her stomach.

Suddenly, she heard the sound of someone entering the house. Keys jangled. It was a tall, burly, hulking figure that eclipsed the porch like a celestial amoeba.

SEVENTY-FOUR

HE WAS ALL brawn and muscle. Built like a linebacker, he wore a dark overcoat and heavy boots. Another wave of fear blanketed Patricia like a galaxy of demons, monsters, and horrors from every dimension.

Her limbs were still weak and now so too was her breathing. She didn't know what was going on with her lungs, or her mind. Fear had thrown a monkey wrench into the normal working order of her cardiovascular system. Then she saw the shadow of a figure, and another behind him. It was a train of moving shadows on that country rustic porch.

Three men were on the porch and the door opened slowly bringing in a drafty sweet scent of jacarandas.

One of the men had eyes as green as malachite. The other man had one of the bushiest red beards Patricia had ever seen. They were all white. Pale and hairy.

They all were rotund, with guts that housed ample meals. Each of them was corn-fed. They were silent. Not one of them uttered a word.

It was as though they'd all made a pact before entering the house. That pact, Patricia would learn, would be the stuff that her worst nightmare was made of. The first man, the one who unlocked the door, the one with the key, walked towards the kitchen and turned on the faucet. He grabbed a glass from the cabinet and filled it with tap water.

The other two men gathered around Patricia, as she lay tied and gagged, all five senses fully engaged. They just stared at her like she was some type of museum exhibit. She'd never felt that objectified. It was a terrible feeling that brought on another wave of panic and nausea.

As hard as she tried to hide her fear, that only seemed to make it that much more obvious. The man with the bushy red beard smiled as he began to unbuckle his belt and unzip his jeans.

She prayed under her breath. Prayed that if she was still and lifeless that maybe they'd think she was dead and leave her alone. It was her idea of *Batesian* mimicry, what small animals and insects did in nature to spare their lives from predators.

Red beard wiggled out of his jeans and tossed them over the arm of the ratty, old, orange sofa. He began to violently claw at her clothes, shredding buttons away and scraping at her blouse.

It didn't take long for him to disrobe her. His breathing was loud and carnal. She was shaking involuntarily. Not from cold, but from sheer fear of the unknown; from what she thought he might do.

"Please don't do this," she pleaded. But the duct tape covering her lips made it sound distorted and jumbled.

"Don't you worry about a thing, pretty lady. This gon' feel real good." He had an obnoxious, ostentatious, booming voice, with a Welsh lilt. It sounded unnatural and partially farcical.

He was shaped like Mr. Potato Head. His breath smelled of Marlboros and Pabst. Lots of Pabst. He had a beer gut and beer breath. The smell of unfiltered wheat, yeast, and fermented Bavarian bananas splashed her face.

It was the birth and death of an era. That moment brought unthought-of torment. She felt like Christ in the garden of Gethsemane. My God, my God, why hast thou forsaken me?

Red Beard had no trouble sliding inside of Patricia. He was small. Thank goodness. What was painful was the fact that she was being raped. She was being raped with impunity, yet no rhyme or reason.

Detective Patricia Garbutt shut her eyes and imagined she was somewhere else. She conjured up those precious moments she shared with Papoose. The warmth of her grandmother's embrace. The safety of those knowing arms and that voice always encouraging her to be a seeker of the meaning of life. It was like being beneath strawberry skies. Sweet and nostalgic.

When Red Beard was finished, she opened her eyes. His touch scalded her like hot water. He was sweating. His perspiration clung to her breasts.

She thought she would vomit, but nothing came up. She thought that if she could force herself to defecate on herself that maybe that would make them stop. If only she could make herself as disgusting as possible to touch or smell. Maybe, just maybe the foul stench of her excrement would act as a defense mechanism, but nothing came out.

The first man, the husky linebacker, came over and set his glass of tap water down onto the table and pulled his shirt over his head, revealing a ghastly set of man boobs and a mountain of pale pink stomach. It was a wall of pig Latin and tattoos. Prison tattoos. He had the hands of a carpenter. Large, ashen, chunky knuckles.

He tossed her onto her stomach and entered her from behind. He was as big as a mammoth, but deep down he was a coward.

He remained in the shadows for the most part. He didn't have it in him to face her while he raped her. He spoke no words. Only guttural grunts that peaked with a lamenting sound as he ejaculated. After which he fell over on top of her, out of breath, and sweating. His laughter like a hyena.

There was nothing existential about that moment. Everything about it was barbaric and inhumane. Cold and sterile, yet filthy at the same time. She wondered what she could have possibly done to deserve this. She was no longer herself. The men had stolen something from her that could never be regained. Her body was an empty shell — an apparition.

Like a serpent, she had shed that dead husk. This was both her death and her phoenix rebirth. Her body was a vast desert which had once been an enormous expanse of ocean. Perhaps this was her fate. Perhaps this was written somewhere. Inscribed in some tiny corner of her DNA.

After the three men were finished having their way with her body, another person came knocking on the door. She had somehow managed to disengage.

Her body was there, but her mind was somewhere else. Her mind was somewhere off in the distance. Dried tears stained her face. She was like a bird with broken wings. Tainted.

She thought back to the prayer she sent up to God the night she found out Maria had lost her virginity to an older boy. She prayed that God would fix her family and bring her husband back into the fold.

She prayed beneath a freeway overpass, in the parking lot of a Waffle House. She prayed for change. Either God did not exist or he was ignoring her pleas for help.

SEVENTY-FIVE

NOTHING AND NO one could have prepared Detective Patricia Garbutt for who walked through the door of that God-forsaken cabin.

She blinked her eyes several times, just to be sure that she wasn't going crazy; just to be sure that she was seeing things clearly. She may not have lost all her marbles, but it felt like there was definitely a hole in the bag. She was going in and out of consciousness.

It was Jake. Jake, her partner from the force, Detective Jacob Billingsley walked through the door. He wore a pair of faded denim jeans and a long sleeved white thermal shirt with dark and lumpy stains down the front. What was that about? It didn't make any sense. It wasn't consistent with his character to be so slovenly.

There were bags the size of North and South Dakota under his eyes. He looked as though he hadn't shaved in six years. He looked weathered by life.

God, she thought, what had Jake gone through since the last time she'd seen him? He hadn't been responding to any phone calls and he'd been missing in action for days. Had he been drugged too? Who was behind this? Who were these men working for? Questions bounced off the walls of her mind.

Stubble was staging an uprising on his chin. He'd even grown sideburns, like the ones John Lennon once wore. He looked like a modern day hippie—a fan of Grateful Dead. He was out of sorts. Jake didn't look like himself.

There was a deranged glimmer in his eyes, but she couldn't tell if it was her own drugged mind playing games on her or if she was really seeing what she thought she was seeing.

Jake was walking freely. Unlike Detective Garbutt had been throughout this devastating ordeal, Jake wasn't handcuffed, tied, or gagged.

After he entered the cabin, Jake walked into the room where everyone else stood. Even his swagger was slovenly. He appeared to be in his right mind, though he looked spit-bubble crazy. He stood over her and gazed down on her with impunity, contempt and pity.

Although she felt drowsy and weak below the waist, she thought back to everything Heidi had told her about Jake, or Jacob Stanislaw. She thought of all the things she'd uncovered in the past month. She replayed the conversation she had with Brody.

Red Beard slapped Jake on the back, as though he were a member of their sick, sadistic, redneck, good 'ol boys club. Like he was one of them.

Maybe he *was* one of them. Once that thought occurred to Patricia she knew they'd taken her there to murder her. The other two animals sat by silently, like peons.

"Hey Stanislaw, why don't you get a piece of this," Red Beard said to Jake. Now she knew for sure that Jake was on their side.

He was one of them. It was at that moment that she realized she never should have trusted him. Everything Heidi confessed to her was accurate. He was not to be trusted. Jake wasn't who she believed he was. Nearly everything he told her had been a bold-face lie.

Here he was siding with her kidnappers, the same men who had just gang-raped and humiliated her. Their combined scents were all over her. She wept uncontrollably. How could she have been so stupid—so naïve?

All this time here she was under the illusion that their bond was one that eclipsed the responsibilities of the force. Here she was thinking they were beginning to fall in love. Here was the contradiction behind the lie. All the while she had her mind solely focused on caseload after caseload, when she should have been watching her partner from the periphery.

"Nah, I'll just watch you guys have all the fun," Jake replied.

"Oh, don't tell me you've grown soft, Stanislaw. Did you grow tits too?" One of the other men said. They all laughed out loud.

"Yeah, that's not like you to turn down good pussy," Red Beard said. "She's good and tight, just like a good piece of pussy should be. It takes a real man to put a bitch in her place—where a bitch should be, on her back, not toting no damn badge and a gun." Little had any of them known, the two detectives had been intimate on more than one occasion.

"Well, maybe a sniff won't hurt." Jake said, sniffing for dramatic effect.

Patricia couldn't believe what she was hearing. She had to be having a sinister nightmare, the kind that appears to be so real, that you mistakenly believe the dream is reality. Jake pulled his shirt over his head and began to unzip his jeans. At the same time, he attempted to kick off the boots he was wearing.

As Jake struggled to remove his boots, she noticed that they were caked with Georgia red clay. Caked on the bottom and sides of his boots, it was an unmistakable rusty shade. Once you'd experienced that dusky Georgia red clay, you instinctively knew it when you saw it again. It stuck to everything and stained everything else. She knew that she was still somewhere in Georgia, but where?

Even a thick skin still had nerves and nerve endings beneath it. Strong people had chinks in their armor if you poked around in search of them. Clearly, this betrayal was killing Detective Patricia Garbutt. She wondered what was going through Jake's mind; wondered what he was thinking.

How could one man house so many implacably different identities in one mind? There was this stringent unapologetic smirk on his face which belied a callous nonchalance. How and when had he become this contaminated skid mark of a man?

She tasted the bitter taste of betrayal on the back of her tongue. It disgusted her. After he'd gotten his boots kicked off, Jake walked over to where Patricia was laying.

He rubbed her left nipple gently, as if he was priming a pump, igniting the switch, or preheating an oven. By now, he'd emerged from his boxers. He was still flaccid.

He looked around at the other men and rubbed himself. The situation grew more and more glum by the minute.

He'd allowed his lower animal nature to completely overtake him. Had this been the result of Noah being kidnapped? Or was he a part of this disgusting ploy all along? Animal indulgence deluded all four men in that room.

Jake began to climb atop Patricia. It felt wrong. It *was* wrong. She began to squirm. The other men in the room continued to look on quietly. Red Beard began to hoot and holler, and egg Jake on, like he was at a football game.

"Please don't do this. Please, I'm begging you not to do this," she attempted to speak. But it came out like mumbled confusion. She spoke Babel.

Jake carried on. He lay on top of her breathing heavily. She could smell beer on him. Beer was on his breath and oozing from his pores. Just like the others, he smelled like a distillery.

Apparently they'd all went out and got shitfaced before or perhaps during the hatching of their plot to kidnap and rape her. Though Jake didn't appear to be drunk, he did seem to be under some type of influence, like he was being remotely programmed.

As he pressed his heavy drunken body against hers, Patricia felt like Jake wasn't all the way there either. He was there in body, but not in mind. Then something strange happened.

SEVENTY-SIX

TIME STOOD STILL for five minutes. Jake suddenly had a change of heart. Suddenly completely sober, he stood straight up and flung the nearby coffee table at one of the men.

The other two men froze. Red Beard dove for cover, but as he turned on his heels, Jake lurched out and attacked him. He was the leader of the pack.

Both men fell to the floor with a loud heavy thud — sheer testosterone sprinkled the room in gusts and waves of pheromones.

Patricia attempted to move her body to an upright position by throwing herself down onto the floor so that she could at least be below the line of fire just in case bullets started flying. She was already vulnerable and her body totally exposed. Suddenly, the energy in the room became electric.

Jake charged at Red Beard like he was a Spanish bull and Red Beard's facial hair was his Matador red cape. The two men began sparring.

Red Beard tried to get Jake into a choke hold, but Jake was too quick on his toes. He turned around, and in the small space of that tiny antique-laced living room, Jake gave the man a spinning reverse Roundhouse kick. Though he stumbled, the impact from the kick knocked Red Beard off his feet, but his knees were strong and he did not fall.

Red Beard was growing too tired, too fast. He wasn't as energetic as his partner had once known him to be. Alcohol, long sleepless nights, and stress dulled his edge.

Though both men were terribly out of shape, Red Beard was older, heavier, and less agile than Jake was. Whatever had been surging through Jake's bloodstream must have dissipated because he began fighting with provocative fury.

He moved like a man with a Ferrari engine for a heart—fast and furious. He even cried out with each swing he threw, as though that would somehow give it extra juice. He had somehow summoned Joe DiMaggio.

The other two men ducked out of the house. Patricia could hear the sound of an ignition cranking up and then tires skidding off into the distance. The two men kept fighting in the center of that dark and sullen antique-laced living room.

Detective Garbutt wondered if either man was armed—if so, she didn't want to catch a bullet. She knew all too well that bullets were equal opportunists.

Red Beard caught Jake with a mean left hook and then a rapid succession of jabs. A look of pain came over Jake. He was growing exhausted.

Patricia squirmed around on the floor, like a snake. No matter how hard she tried, she couldn't get herself freed from the binding ropes. Resigned to desperation and defeat, Detective Garbutt slumped down to the floor. She witnessed Jake and the man with the red beard fist-fighting like they wanted to kill each other. Adrenaline occupied the cabin.

Suddenly Jake grew frustrated that it was taking so much to get Red Beard to fall. He reached over and picked up a lamp. He used the lamp to hammer into the man's skull. The man blacked out instantly and fell to the floor like a tree.

Jake turned to his partner and began tearing away at her ropes. Once he'd gotten the tape ripped away from Patricia's mouth, she cried out.

"Are you okay? Are you all right?" Jake said frantically.

"I'm okay. My God, who is he? What was that about?"

Jake didn't answer her questions. He grabbed her and embraced her like he truly missed her. They hugged each other for a lingering minute once her hands were totally free from the ropes. This was more like the Jake she knew and had grown to love.

"It's a long story, but I promise I can explain everything to you," he said, giving her direct eye contact. All he wanted to do was lay down and catch his breath.

"Well, you had better start talking. Do you have *any* idea what I've just gone through?" she said tearfully. Although they sat face to face, she still didn't trust him. She hated him for knowingly allowing her to be raped. He hurriedly threw his clothes back on.

"Answer me. Answer me now. Who is that?"

"Look, we have to get out of here. We have to get out of here before he comes to."

Red Beard was on the floor laying on his side. His breathing was subtle enough to see his stomach rise and fall.

He had been knocked out cold, but he wasn't dead. His skin was red and drenched in ample perspiration. Lying on the floor, with his shirt open and unbuttoned, Red Beard looked like a wounded wild animal. He was an edifice that had just experienced a power outage.

Jake was sweating too. For a moment he sat back against the ratty old orange sofa and caught the breath he had been desperately chasing.

He hadn't had hand-to-hand combat against such a formidable opponent in a long time. Patricia didn't know what to think. Everything was happening so fast that she couldn't put two and two together. She couldn't understand Jake's behavior. She didn't know any of the men who desecrated her temple—couldn't recall ever seeing their faces in her life.

"I'm not going anywhere with you until I have answers."

Although she wanted to escape that cabin as fast as possible, she no longer trusted Jake. How deep was his betrayal? She didn't know nor did she want to find out.

Everything about the situation at hand went against his character. Sure it was true that no man or woman was ever exactly how they presented themselves, but this was over the top. Her paradigm had been dropped on its head.

She struggled to sit upright and attempted to gather her articles of clothing. Jake helped her to her feet. She gave him a side eye glare. She was sore between her legs and she wanted nothing more than to take a long hot bath to wash the filth of the experience from her flesh.

SEVENTY-SEVEN

ONCE THE TWO detectives were outside, Jake lead Patricia down a gravel driveway. It felt good to be outside, beneath the light of day. She took a deep breath and felt gratitude that she'd made it out alive. All anyone could ever hope for was to make it out alive.

He instructed her to hop into a car she wasn't familiar with. It was an older model Bronco with a primer black paint job and a dented driver's side door. "Whose hootpy?" she asked.

"It belongs to Liam. He's the one I just floored in there. Listen, I'm an FBI operative; a special agent." Jake took no pains in getting straight to the point. "This operation, Operation Plymouth Rock has been a living hell. Lieutenant Brody is an operations agent with a covert branch of the CIA, but he's gone rogue. It wasn't supposed to happen like this. It wasn't supposed to explode in our face like this. I was investigating Brody all this time, and apparently he was on a mission to investigate me. You were incidental. Roth was incidental, although we believe that he's working for someone."

"What the fuck is Operation Plymouth Rock?"

"If you'd just stay quiet I can tell you." Jake cranked the car's ignition and backed out of the driveway like a bat out of hell. He talked quickly as he sped down a winding country back road, blanketed in a thick canopy of shrubbery and trees. The shocks on the Bronco were shot, so it was a bumpy uncomfortable ride.

"I sort of got the idea that something was bizarre with you, but I don't understand what's going on and why I'm in the middle of it," she said.

"That's just it; you were never supposed to get so intertwined in the middle of this. It's just an unfortunate set of circumstances," he looked into her eyes. "It's a long story but I'll try my best to get to the bottom of everything."

"Where are we going? Where are you taking me?" She felt a carnal instinct that something was very wrong.

"We've got to get back up to Atlanta, but I want you to know that what we shared was real. It wasn't a part of the operation or the investigation. Somehow, in the middle of the investigation, Brody found out that he was under the scope. Someone outed me as an operative and he's been trying to kill us both ever since. I was set to abort the mission when I found myself falling in love with you. Hell, I was supposed to be on a plane to the People's Republic of China when I learned that Brody made the hit to have your family murdered."

"What are you saying?" Detective Garbutt found all of this to be more overwhelming than she could handle. "What is this about you being Russian? Are you Russian or American? Whose side are you on anyway?" she screamed hysterically.

"I'm American," he said slowly. She felt that he was lying to her. The way he responded just sounded and felt like a lie. Plus, it didn't match what Heidi had told her. "You don't understand. You have no idea how deep this rabbit hole goes."

"You didn't answer my question. What is Operation Plymouth Rock?"

"Plymouth Rock, it's the homeland. It's D.C.; it's the Pentagon, Wall Street, and Capitol Hill. Well, the North Koreans, under the direction of supreme leader Kim Jong-un, a group of radical Iranian rebels, under the direction of Mahmoud Ahmadinejad, and a mercenary group under the leadership of President Vladimir Putin they've all joined forces and are staging a cyber attack on this country unlike anything you've ever seen or imagined. If successful, this alliance plans to completely shut down the financial backbone of this country and trigger a Fire Sale. A Fire Sale would render the electricity grid useless. It's a strategic, staged assault on the United States transportation, banking, economy and government through cyber attack. After three to five days of utter darkness, no internet, and Americans unable to utilize their ATM and debit cards, sheer Bedlam will break out. There will be blood in the streets. Fathers will turn against sons, and neighbor against neighbor, as everyone just tries to find food to eat. They're planning on simultaneously launching a nuclear attack on the heart of this country...Plymouth Rock."

Detective Garbutt really couldn't believe what she was hearing. It didn't make any sense. Why hideout in a small, rinky-dink, insignificant police force in Atlanta, Georgia?

"So how does Brody fit into all of this?"

"Brody isn't who you think he is. He's a mercenary. A stone cold killer and a mastermind. This alliance has cells strategically deposited into various segments of the United States government, from the lowest levels, to the very highest levels. I was partnered with you in order to get closer to Brody, so that I could observe him—to gain his trust. Trust is the Holy Grail of betrayal and espionage."

"But how could this happen? With all the surveillance and counter-terrorist agencies formed since nine-eleven, how? This country has the finest scientists and spies in the Bureau to prevent anything like this from ever happening."

"That's what you've been made to believe. That's what you and the rest of America is conditioned to believe, from cradle to the grave, but it's the farthest thing from the truth. This country's security and this country's surveillance are fragile, at best. It's been penetrated. The biggest coup you've ever seen is being hatched. I'm a double agent, trained as a spy. I should know. I know things that I could be killed for repeating. Suffice it to say that we have to get out of here. We have to get on the next plane out of here as fast as possible."

"Jake, Jacob, whoever you are, what exactly are you saying?" Suddenly she felt her heart rate speed up. She felt her blood pressure increase. She could no longer determine between truth and fiction.

"Are you listening to anything I'm saying to you? There has been a planned systematic attack on the government's infrastructure by an alliance of this country's greatest enemies. First the airports and traffic lights will go, and then the banks and all financial systems will be shutdown. No one will be able to access their bank accounts, fly anywhere, or drive anywhere. The buses and subways will be shut down. Last, all satellites, GPS, electricity, and phones will be rendered useless. This has been planned, rehearsed, and is set in action. This is bigger than nine-eleven, bigger than the Taliban, and more complicated than I'm able to explain. The final aspect of the operation will include a nuclear attack, which will totally obliterate the West coast."

Detective Patricia Garbutt knew that at the heart of every lie was truth and although she was devastated to hear what Jake told her, she began to believe him. She felt like an ostrich that had stuck her head in the sand to avoid the truth that had been in her face all this time.

"Diplomats: those in high positions in both the North American and Iranian governments have been pushing for supremacy in the arms race. My focus and specialty has been on missile defense. We've kept a close eye on the leaders itching to pull nuclear triggers on the U.S., but we didn't realize that momentum was building in the International cyber terrorist movement. We didn't realize the scale, or how large they'd grown. Iran and North Korea were working together on laser-based missile defense systems that would fry satellites and shoot down ballistic missiles. For years I worked in the Kremlin, while passing information to the U.S., but they murdered my father and since then, I've worked as a double-agent. Since then, I've helped to smuggle nukes into this country through underground trade networks on the black market. Atlanta is a huge hub for the network and a very prominent home for the alliance and their cells."

"But why Noah? Why *my* family? Why *me*?"

"Because my cover was blown and Brody learned that I was an informant, working for the enemy. He figured you were in on it. Either way, these people are cold-blooded killers who will stop at nothing, and kill anyone who stands in their way. They mainly deal in the black market weapons trade, military secrets, industrial intelligence, medical technology, computer advances, and political agendas. Their clients are international governments, corporations, and wealthy families. Their aim is eventual world domination through control over organized crime and the trade of intelligence. Politics and personal agendas aside, you're in the thick of it now and I don't want to see you get hurt."

As he continued speeding along the highway, Detective Garbutt sat slumped in the passenger seat. She was weary and confused. Suddenly she noticed a black car with tinted black windows behind them. It was racing up quickly; almost rear-ending the Bronco Jake was driving. Soon, Jake also noticed the car behind them.

"Buckle your seat belt. We've got company," he said. "Looks like we're being followed. I knew this would happen. That's why I told you to hurry."

As she snapped her seat belt into locking position, she asked, "Is that the guy from back at the cabin? Liam?"

Taking a closer look in the rearview mirror, Jake said, "No, that's Brody."

SEVENTY-EIGHT

AS JAKE SPED along the highway, it became obvious that what he was saying was real. Detective Garbutt felt an intense wave of fear flood her veins.

"While you were knocked out, they inserted a tracking microchip into your arm," he said. "That's how they were able to locate us so quickly. When we get somewhere safe, I'll help you to remove it."

"What? Microchip?" she said, incredulously. Everything on her body hurt after what she'd just experienced. She began to scan her body with her fingertips, attempting to twist her elbow frontward. Still, she couldn't discern where any microchip had been implanted into her flesh.

The black car with tinted black windows was swiftly gaining on them. It seemed to have materialized from out of nowhere. It rammed into the Bronco twice. The first time was like a warning and the second knocked them off the road. Both detectives watched as their lives flashed before their eyes.

The Bronco veered into the other lane, just barely missing oncoming traffic, and then it toppled and rolled over a few times before coming to a grinding halt on the right shoulder of the highway. Smoke, exhaust, and a rancid oily smell of fumes emerged from under the hood. The truck would go nowhere. Black smoke coughed from the muffler.

"Are you okay, Jake…Jake, are you all right?" she said. He had obviously bumped his head and lost consciousness during the collision. A small river of blood snaked down the side of his face.

Detective Garbutt managed to unbuckle her seat belt, before opening the passenger side door and falling onto the ground. When she looked up, she saw Brody standing above her, peering down on her with an angry glare. The strong smell of gasoline lingered in the air.

"Jake! Jake! Jake! Wake up!" she shouted. She had no way to protect herself.

Then a strange thing happened. Brody reached out his hand like an olive branch to help her to her feet.

"Detective Garbutt. Are you okay?"

"Get your fucking hands off of me." She snapped.

"Aye, hostile, are we? I don't mean you any harm. He's the one I want," he said, pulling out a pistol and pointing it at Jake.

"Jake told me the truth. He told me everything," she said. She darted around to the front of the Bronco, using it as a shield. She crouched down and made her voice carry.

Brody began laughing out loud. "Did he tell you how he's a double-agent? Did he tell you how he double crossed this country? How he even made the hit on your family?"

"You're lying, Brody! You're the one who made the hit on my family. I don't want anything to do with this. I want to walk away from this unscathed.

This has nothing to do with me. This is between you and your handlers. Why involve me, Brody?"

"Is that what he told you, Detective Garbutt? You can't believe everything you hear. If I wanted you dead, you'd be dead. This man is a callous traitor to this country. He manipulated you."

He fired a shot into the Bronco. Within seconds the back of the car went up in flames. There was black smoke, and strong acrid gasoline fumes everywhere.

Jake regained consciousness and began to weakly climb from the Bronco. "Oh thank God, you're alive," Patricia Garbutt said to him. He coughed uncontrollably and fell to the ground. Just as she attempted to help him up by grabbing and pulling his arm, the truck became engulfed in flames.

That was when she noticed that his foot was stuck in the Bronco. Flames threatened to scorch Jake's leg. He reached out his arm to Detective Garbutt. She pulled and tugged, but she couldn't get him out of the Bronco.

"Why are you helping him? He tried to get you killed!" Brody said, standing a few feet away from the flaming Bronco. The heat was intense, like standing in front of fifty-two fireplaces.

Detective Garbutt was truly confused. She no longer knew who to trust or believe. Part of her believed everything Jake told her, but then she kept replaying what Heidi had told her in the middle of her parents' living room. Nothing made any sense. She couldn't believe her own line of reasoning.

"Please, Patricia, don't let me die like this. Please help me. Don't listen to a word that comes from his mouth," Jake said with a weak voice. He coughed and struggled and tried to kick, but his foot had become impossibly stuck between the car seat of the Bronco.

Suddenly the flames, which began in the rear of the truck, near the gas tank, had finally reached the front of the truck. Hot flames of fire roared and licked at his leg. He screamed out in agony as the slow burn set in.

Just then, two shots rang out. One clipped past her face so fast that she felt the sting of the buckshot. The second shot penetrated Jake's shoulder and his body went limp. Brody had shot him. It was the kill shot.

EPILOGUE

THE NEXT DAY Detective Garbutt found herself in a hospital bed at Grady. She was being treated for minor burns and exhaustion. Her brother Maurice sat quietly near her bedside, tinkering with his iPad.

When she opened her eyes, she looked up to see Noah's face on Fox Five News. It was a heart-wrenching story of how he'd been kidnapped and subsequently rescued by a courageous citizen who took justice into his own hands.

She saw him being reunited with his mother Heidi. There was mention of his homicide detective father, Jake Billingsley, who the report said, had lost his life in an automobile accident in Macon, Georgia.

She dropped her head back down onto the pillow. Maurice looked over and smiled. "You all right, sis?" he said.

She let out a deep breath and nodded her head. "What happened? Where's Brody?"

"Who?" her brother said.

"Lieutenant Brody, my boss?"

Her brother shrugged. "I don't know. All I know is I got a call that you had been dropped off here yesterday. Someone found you dazed and unconscious out in the sticks somewhere. You know I don't know all the counties and cities down here, but I do know that someone drove you here to the hospital and found a way to contact me, Selena, Angel, and Jenny. Oh, and I have a surprise for you."

Maurice Garbutt stood up. He walked to the door and looked out to the left, then to the right. He signaled to someone and smiled. She blinked and then saw her husband Tony materialize in the door way. He looked like his old self. He was cleaned up, shaved, and smiling from ear to ear. During his time in jail, he'd been forced into a rigorous rehabilitation program.

"Baby, are you okay?" he said, while walking to join his wife at her bedside.

All Patricia Garbutt could do was well up with tears. Her husband leaned down to kiss his wife gently on her forehead. He even smelled like his old cologne. She smiled, but beneath her smile was a bittersweet longing for their children.

"Can anyone tell me who brought me to the hospital?" she said out loud.

"Baby, it was Brody." Her husband replied.

"That can't be," she said, slightly beneath her breath.

"Yeah, that old fart even gave you a six month leave of absence with pay and for some reason he kept apologizing. Babe, just relax and get some rest. You've been through a lot and now you need to rest. Everything is going to be okay. I even found a new job—a place in Midtown gave me a shot. I got us a small studio apartment off Northside Drive.

It's not much, but it's a start. We can try to put us back together again."

THE END

ABOUT BRANDI

Brandi L. Bates is an international best-selling, American novelist, screenwriter, and philosopher-poet. Pushcart Prize Nominee. Hurston-Wright Legacy Award Nominee.

Author of *SOLEDAD*, *Remains to Be Seen*, *Amid the Cacophony of Cries*, *Mood Swings* and many other titles, Bates is known for her sexy, fast-paced, edgy style of writing.

She gracefully spices up intimacy and mood with juicy blow by blow details, while weaving a thrilling whodunit filled with brevity, taut atmosphere, and strong psychological suspense.

She's been described as a master of suspense, plotting, and vivid characterization by her contemporaries. Her stories have glowing reviews in most literary circles. Best known for her novels that could broadly be described as suspense thrillers, Bates also frequently incorporates poetic elements of erotica, horror, mystery, science fiction, and satire.

COMING SUMMER 2014